Storm Tide

Storm Tide
by Elisabeth Ogilvie

DOWN EAST BOOKS / CAMDEN, MAINE

Copyright 1945, 1972 by Elisabeth Ogilvie
Reprinted by arrangement with the author
ISBN 0-89272-217-7
Cover design by Michael McCurdy
Composition by The Sant Bani Press, Tilton, N.H.
Printed in the United States of America

5   4

Down East Books / Camden, Maine

To my brothers, my friends, and all the other boys in the armed forces who read and liked High Tide at Noon.

The setting of this book is authentic. The
story and the characters are entirely fictitious.

Other novels by Elisabeth Ogilvie
reprinted by Down East books:

High Tide at Noon
The Ebbing Tide

1

THE LAND ASTERN WAS A FADING DARK LINE; the land over the bow gleamed in the end of sunset. Above the bright rocks the spruces had a curious rich green, massed thickly against the paling east. The wake of the boat fanned and foamed creamily back toward the mainland. But for the woman who stood in the bow, there was no mainland. There was only the Island which grew steadily nearer, out of the darkening sea.

The forty-foot seiner, trim and rakish in spite of her sturdiness, beat her swift way out of the west. The competent pulse of her engine throbbed through the woman's feet and was confused with the racing tempo of her blood. Outwardly she was a still, calm figure, standing in the bow with her back to the two men aft by the wheel; her head lifted high on the slim tanned strength of her neck, her dark eyes forever watching the Island, her mouth composed above the firm chin. But in her topcoat pockets her palms were wet. Her throat kept drying, so she must swallow.

She was going home. She said it to herself, her lips moving: "I'm going home. I'm going home. Where's Joanna these days? they'll ask down at the sardine factory. Oh, didn't you know? Joanna's gone home. *For good.*"

She laughed aloud and turned around. The two men at the wheel were deep in conversation, and Joanna studied them for a moment before they noticed her. Her oldest brother, Charles, the captain of *The Four Brothers,* was laughing at something, and the sound of his laughter carried to her. He shoved his cap back on his black head, and against the glowing western sky his profile was strong and hawklike.

She remembered how he had spoken to her just before the wedding in the afternoon—just a few hours ago, but it seemed as if it must have been at least a week ago.

"I never thought I'd be giving my sister away in marriage," he'd told her, as they waited in the dining room of his house in Pruitt's Harbor. "But I want to tell you, Jo, I never felt so good, and so proud, about anything, as seeing you marrying Nils Sorensen."

They'd all felt like that, the whole family. Her mother and all the brothers . . . *It's what they always wanted me to do,* Joanna thought without rancor. *They love Nils and trust him.* . . . Her dark gaze moved to the other man by the wheel.

Not so tall as Charles, but compactly and neatly built, Nils Sorensen stood with his hand on the wheel. He wore gray tweed trousers and a blue pullover sweater, his shirt collar was very white against his sunburnt neck. Joanna tried to look impersonally at this man who had been her friend all her life, who was now her husband.

His hair is the color of wheat, she thought. *His eyes are as blue as the wild flag in the marsh. Nothing ever bothers him, and he's so clean it's refreshing just to look at him.*

Then, abruptly, she couldn't be impersonal. It was when Nils caught her glance, and smiled down the length of the boat at her. She lifted her hand in greeting, and then turned back. The Island had come much closer. It seemed as if she could smell the warm resinous breath of spruce which all day had dreamed in peaceful loneliness under a September sun.

The Four Brothers slipped past the wooded western end of the nearer, larger island, Brigport; the rocky shore flung back the engine's echo, and a late-flying gull drifted past the masthead on strongly beating wings. The sun had dropped quite suddenly into the sea, and in the shadow of the islands the water was dark, the buoys bobbing in the evening chop were restless black dots; in daylight they would have been red and white and orange and yellow and blue.

Joanna thought she could feel her heart speed up as the boat passed the red spar buoy that marked the Outer Breaker, and headed for the southwest point of Bennett's Island. They were avoiding the harbor; Charles would go directly around to Goose Cove, and unload on the small wharf Nils had built out over the rocks during the preceding months when he had lived alone on the Island.

In the shadow of the high rocky shore, and the woods rising above it, the boat passed coves where Joanna had once played, following her brothers on their long expeditions after wood, and in their involved games of pirates and Indians where they'd boiled periwinkles in a can over a driftwood fire, and stormed the walls of rock to capture Arabs, early settlers, and hostile natives of the unnamed South Sea islands on which they were always being washed up as castaways.

"Excited?" said Nils' low voice beside her.

"Why wouldn't I be?" She slipped her arm through his. "Look, as soon as we get around to Schooner Head, we'll see the house. Nils —"

He looked at her, waiting.

"I wish Father could know the Island wasn't going to be alone any more." She felt to her horror an unsteadiness in her chin.

"He knows," said Nils. She accepted the assurance in his voice, and began once more to watch for the house.

It came at last. High on its place between two coves, its western windows fired with the sunset, it stood waiting. The boat headed into the shadowed tranquillity of Goose Cove, darkened now by the long high rocky point on one side, and the wall of spruce woods on the other; a massive defense that stretched to the very south-west tip of the Island, around which *The Four Brothers* had just come. The curve of beach glimmered lavender-white.

The engine stopped abruptly, and there was only the swift rushing of water away from the sides of the boat, as she cut toward the wharf, to break the hush. Joanna's arm tightened in Nils'. She was grateful that he said no word.

She walked alone up to the house. Behind her Nils and Charles unloaded supplies and new trap stuff from the boat, their normal voices sounding crisp and clear in the stillness.

In the little sloping field between the house and Goose Cove, the grass was cool and damp around her ankles; she stepped carefully to avoid the ripening cranberries in the boggy spots. Great drifts of wild asters, chalky-pale in the evening light from which all color had been drawn, brushed her skirt. Her happiness was no wild, exultant thing, but rather it was so deeply rooted in her that it could hardly be called happiness. The word was too ephemeral, and this was something that would never end; she knew it with a certainty that had not been hers for a long time.

She drew long breaths of the cool air, and the last sleepy twitterings from the woods held a peculiar enchantment for her ears. The birds had never sounded like that on the mainland, nor had there been woods like these. She was glad she could walk up to the house alone.

In the kitchen she lit a lamp, and looked around at the room. The last time she had seen it, it had been an empty room full of ghosts; and now, miraculously, it was a room where people lived. Nils had done it all. He had painted the walls the exact tender aquamarine she wanted, he had painted and polished the stove, set an array of lamps with shining chimneys on the lamp shelf, and laid on the floor the braided rugs Donna had sent out; their muted, faded colors glowed softly in the lamplight. The woodbox was full, the stovelengths stacked with Nils' mathematical precision. On an impulse Joanna lifted a stove lid, and then smiled; the kindling was ready to be lighted.

That was Nils. Did he ever forget *anything?* Joanna doubted it. She touched a match to the fine kindling, adjusted the dampers, and took the clean new water pails from the dresser.

Down in the field the well curb had been rebuilt, and the well-pole was firm smooth yellow wood in her hands. The water came up from darkness, icy clear. There was never such water in mainland wells, she thought. There was never such air, so clean-washed, so fragrant with the tall ripe grass and the spruces, the sea, and the cool wind that had sprung up at sunset. Nor such blessed and perfect silence.

There was no one on the Island but themselves. They would be as solitary as Grandpa and Grandma Bennett had been, when they first came. When she awoke in the morning, when she cooked Nils' breakfast before he went out to haul, she would know how Grandma Bennett had felt when she was young Sara Bennett, coming without fear or question to this strange, wild, distant island her husband—her very new husband—had bought from the State of Maine. No one else had ever lived there but Indians. Sara and Grandpa—it seemed disrespectful to call him Charles—had lived in a log cabin the first year. From the well curb Joanna couldn't see over the slope, down into the sheltered place where the woods met

Goose Cove beach, but it had been there that Grandpa had built the cabin. During the long winter he had cut down the trees that would later build the homestead where he had raised his sons; the house that stood now on the breast of the slope, its windows fired with the afterglow.

Joanna walked up the path, half in a dream, and met Nils at the door. He took the pails from her. "What are you thinking, Joanna?" he asked her.

"About Grandpa Bennett. And us." They went into the kitchen and Nils set the pails on the dresser without slopping. He went to the stove and began to fix the fire, his face absorbed, his blond head silvery in the lamplight.

"Nils, we stand almost where they stood," Joanna said.

"I know," Nils answered. He put the covers back on the stove, fixed the dampers, and looked at her quietly, the tall young woman he had loved with such silent intensity for so long. He saw her lifted black head and her rapt, brilliant dark eyes, her cheekbones burned red with wind under the smooth brown, her mouth curved and tender with whatever dream possessed her now, and her shoulders, squared and unafraid under the white blouse; shoulders that asked for no hands to touch and strengthen them. He knew that look of hers, and he waited quietly until she should see him again.

"We'll do what they did," Joanna said. "Only we'll build so strong that nothing can hurt it again." Her voice deepened. "Father died of a broken heart—pneumonia couldn't have killed him if he hadn't been ready to die—because he couldn't live away from the Island. But he had to leave it. I don't intend to let it break *my* heart, Nils."

She lifted her strong hands in a curiously vivid gesture, as if she held the world between them. "It's whether I can keep it in my hand, Nils. Or whether its hand will be over me." Then all at once her expression, her whole body, changed, and she was *seeing* Nils again. She crossed the room swiftly, and put her hands on his shoulders.

"What do you think, Nils?" she demanded. "What do you think when you look like that? We can do it, can't we? We can make the Island what it was meant to be. We can do anything, can't we?"

She wasn't asking for reassurance. It was a chant of triumph. Nils nodded. "But we've got to creep before we can walk," he said.

She stared back at him, her dark eyes narrowing and searching his blue ones, almost as if she hated his caution, and then they heard Charles' gay whistle outside.

"Oh, Nils," she said suddenly, shaking her head. She kissed him lightly on the mouth.

Charles came in, scaled his cap toward the row of hooks on the entry wall. "What the hell, haven't you cooked that beefsteak *yet?*" he demanded. "I know this is a honeymoon, but it's not mine. And I'm due back at the Harbor tonight. I want some grub!"

Then there was laughter, and unbounded cheerful confusion in the Bennett kitchen, until in the lavender afterglow Charles started back across the glassy, opalescent sea toward Pruitt's Harbor.

Joanna and Nils walked back to the house from the wharf, and stood on the rise to watch *The Four Brothers* cut a long, curling wake at the feet of the black-silhouetted ledges; but before she rounded the point of Chip Cove, Charles turned to wave his cap, and they knew they must not watch him out of sight, for that meant bad luck for the boat.

When they came into the kitchen, where the fire snapped in the stove, and the lamplight's warm radiance pushed the dusk back, they knew that they were alone on the Island. Except for the birds who slept in the thick dark forest, they were alone. By the kitchen table with its bright plaid cover they stood looking at each other. Joanna smiled at Nils and rubbed her bare forearms.

"It was cold out there," she said. "Wonderful Bennett's-Island-September cold."

"Wonderful Joanna," said Nils quietly and unexpectedly, and took her in his arms. She felt in his kiss the long-restrained passion of the man, as deep and powerful and boundless as the sea. She felt it in his tightening arms, and the strong quick thudding of his heart against her breast. As she put her arms around his neck, she knew a swift wonder and pain at all the years he had waited for this. How patient he had been, how strong. Eleven years ago, when she was nineteen, she'd married Alec Douglass; and Nils had seen her look at that whimsical and beloved stranger with her heart in her eyes, he had seen her stand by Alec's grave with her whole body frozen in incredulous despair; he had heard her tell him, across Alec's child's crib, that beyond Alec there was nothing else.

But he had been patient. And now she stood in his arms, they were like lovers standing there, and their arms were tight around each other, and his mouth was on hers. It was the first sip to satisfy the terrible thirst and hunger of those years in between; and because of this drought and famine that he had known, he would be thirsty and hungry for her all the rest of his life.

She knew it with a terrible clarity, and she wondered, even as her mouth burned under his, how she could have been so blind about Nils until this instant. Perhaps it was because he had always been so quiet and unhurried and understanding. That day they had agreed to get married, and work together for the Island — was that all she'd thought about? The Island? Oh, she had been ready for marriage. But not for this drive of passionate urgency that made Nils a stranger to her, that called no response except dismay from her body. *I love him,* she thought. *But I'm not in love with him.*

Her face burned with shame at her stupidity. Unconsciously her arms tightened, as if to protect him, and he lifted his head. His eyes blazed into hers, and she thought of blue fire. In a swift involuntary gesture she pulled his fair head down against her shoulder, before he could see her face, and she felt his famished lips against her throat.

I mustn't let him know, she thought. *But it was the Island I thought of, first, last, and always. I thought we could work together and we can. We'll do everything we planned. But he shan't ever know about this.*

This was the dismay and weariness and pity that spread, achingly, through every muscle and sinew of her body. From a dry throat, her voice came, and she pressed close to him as if she too were famished.

"Nils," she whispered against his cheek. "We're home. And together, Nils."

2

THEY WERE UP AT DAYLIGHT in the morning, moving around in a calm breathless hush that meant wind to come. The curious opalescent luster of the sea, and the clear unclouded breadth of sky, the way no faintest breeze stirred the tall grass, and the unnatural loudness of the crows' voices—it all added up to one thing. A weatherbreeder. Let it come, Joanna thought with exultation. She was safe at home, and Nils had plenty of pots stacked on the beach in case he should lose any. The woodpile in the shed was dry, and there was food enough for a siege.

She almost welcomed the thought of it. To feel the force of the gale striking at the house, to see the white water flying high above the rocks wherever she looked, to hear the steady thunder all day and all night, and know it was echoing in her blood as it had always done—she knew she would love it fiercely, not as she loved this silent, unreal morning when she wanted to make no sound to crack the hush.

Nils was quiet too. He brought in fresh water and more wood while she fixed their breakfast, and filled his dinner box. He stood by the stove, immaculate even in faded dungarees and blue shirt, and watched her.

"That's a lot of grub," he observed mildly.

"It's enough for two. I'm going with you, Nils."

"Good," said Nils, and she knew he meant it. When he had gone down to Goose Cove to put his bait aboard the peapod, she changed her dress for slacks, stacked the few dishes in the sink, and went through the house to fling all the windows wide. While she was gone the mellow September sunshine could fill the house, and be held there when the rain came. It seemed to her that she couldn't get enough of the Island's fragrant breath.

From every window of the Bennett house there was something to see; things that had been of the very substance of her being since earliest babyhood. From the north windows she looked down across the meadow and the marsh to the harbor. Its sunlit emptiness didn't make her lonely as it had done, when she watched the boats grow few; already in her mind she saw the other boats that would lie at their moorings, the strong clean boats of the fishermen who, like Nils, would be good fishermen because they felt a deep satisfaction in their work and their way of living.

Beyond the harbor and its two high points of red-brown rock, Brigport stretched its long lean length upon the sea; in the early morning sunlight, pasture and dark spruce forest and white houses, with great barns, looked across the sound at Bennett's. Most of the men on the larger island were farmers as well as fishermen. . . . Twenty miles beyond Brigport the Camden hills billowed out of Penobscot Bay, they were gentle curves of amethyst and plum-color. Below Brigport, to the west, there was Metinic. To the north-east, the cliffs of Vinalhaven, and then the blue, cloudlike mountain of Isle au Haut, like some foreign land, with Mount Cadillac peering past it.

From the east windows Joanna looked across the unruffled azure of Schoolhouse Cove to her Uncle Nate's fields — where the cranberries would be ripening in the mossy spots — and the locked white buildings and barn against the Eastern End woods. Schoolhouse Cove bounded Nate's land on one side, and Long Cove on the opposite side. Beyond Long Cove there was the minute island called Tenpound. In this air which made the land loom, Joanna could see the sheep grazing. So Whit Robey of Brigport still kept his sheep there, she thought, and that little instant bridged the seven years more completely than anything else had done.

She looked back to Schoolhouse Cove and beyond, at the long harsh points of land jutting out into the sea, with the gulls perched on them in white rows. The sun was rising steadily higher, and the water was so bright she couldn't look at it for long, but she gazed long enough to pick out Pirate Island, five miles to the east . . . a barren length of yellow ledge, where no one lived. Yet she knew of a tiny secret meadow, where in May the strawberry blossoms spangled the grass with white stars, and song sparrows caroled from the hummocks of tall grass where they had their nests.

The memory of that hidden meadow brought her from her knees. She could think of it quietly now, not with intolerable longing. The Joanna who had found it there, with Alec to drop beside her in the warm blossoming grass, had lived in another life.

Joanna walked through the rooms and stopped at a window that looked south. The polished glass in the tower at Matinicus Rock caught the sunlight like fire. It looked steadfastly out over the sea toward Spain, as it flashed its light over it at night. When she was little she had thought the light shone all the way to Spain and swung its beam through some little Spanish girl's home as it did through the homestead.

On the ledges between Bennett's and the Rock, there was no play of surf this morning. Close to the Island, on Goose Cove Ledge and Green Ledge, the gulls were at peace with the world. Her gaze dropped to the shimmer of Goose Cove, so still the woods were mirrored darkly in it. Three gulls paddled lazily on the surface, nothing whiter than their breasts above their shimmering white reflections. Two seals dived and tumbled in the water close to the shore, unabashed by Nils. They popped their sleek dripping heads out and looked at him, and then went back to their game, catching a glisten of sunlight on their wet hides. Over in the shadow of the point, among the rockweed-covered boulders, black ducks were feeding. They too were unafraid. It was strange how quickly an island went back to the wild things when it was left alone, she thought.

And then there was Nils. He stood patiently by the double-ender, pipe in mouth and long-visored cap pushed back on his head, looking out across the cove. He was waiting for her; she shook her dreams off, as the seals shook water from their heads, and ran downstairs and out-of-doors.

They went along the south side of the Island, hauling traps set close to the tumbled rocks in the rich kelp growths where the lobsters liked to spend the warmer months. In a little while now it wouldn't be so easy; he would have to start shifting his traps outward, away from the Island. And he couldn't fish from a double-ender then. But the *Donna,* in her cradle in the marsh, was Nils' boat now, to re-fit and paint up as he pleased, and put overboard again. She had once belonged to Joanna's father, Stephen Bennett; his widow, Donna Bennett, had given the lovely and gallant boat to her new son-in-law as a wedding present.

"Remember how you used to take me hauling?" Joanna asked Nils now. "Out of the kindness of your heart, because I was crazy for a peapod of my own?"

"You never thought I'd still be fishing from a peapod, fifteen years later, did you?" Nils balanced the wet trap on the gunwale, reached into it for its lobsters. "You never thought life would turn out like this."

Chin in her hands, she watched him measure, tossing two into the stern of the peapod and a little one overboard. "I wonder if I'd have done differently, if I'd known."

"I guess not," Nils said. "I figure you have to live through a certain kind of life to come out where you're supposed to. No short cuts." He smiled at her somber face. "Look at me — six times around the world and getting to be first mate on that old tub of a freighter — and I never thought that when I was thirty-two I'd be back here a pod fisherman, same as when I was seventeen."

"You never thought Bennett's was going to reach right out and take hold of you so you'd *have* to come back." The peapod rocked only slightly as Nils slid a fresh bait bag onto the baitline, buttoned the trap door, and let the trap slip overboard, its warp trailing after it, to sink down into the oblivion of deep green water. Nils began to row toward the next yellow and black buoy that scarcely moved on the sea. As they approached the high rock cliffs of Sou-West Point, a few gulls rose upward, lazily, and then settled down again.

The luminous blue peace of the day brooded over the man and woman in the rowboat. It laid its hush on Joanna's mind and heart. She watched Nils rowing, standing up to push forward on the oars; his eyes, calm and remote with his own thoughts, looked past her toward the distant horizon, and the rhythm of his stroke was irrevocably steady, as if nothing could ever break it. Like Nils himself. Nothing in all the years had broken Nils' stroke.

He rowed fast, so the red and black buoy seemed to swim past Joanna and bob in the wake of the peapod. She straightened up at once alert.

"Whose buoy is that?"

"Toby Merrill," he said idly.

"But he's set inside yours!" She scanned the water. "There's another one — there's a lot of them. Nils, what's the idea? Brigport fishermen aren't supposed to be fishing around here."

"Plenty of lobsters to catch around here," said Nils. "Guess they figured the grounds were going to waste with everybody gone from here. You can't blame them." He nodded at an orange buoy. "There's one of Ted Robey's. And there's one of the Fowlers'. Winslow's or Randy's."

They had rounded Sou-West Point now, and as they came between the point itself and the black reef beyond, she saw that the whole west side was dotted with buoys of every conceivable color combination.

All the tranquillity she had felt fled abruptly. Her cheeks grew hot. "Nils, *all* of Brigport's over here!"

"Sure. And there's Winslow Fowler's boat up there outside Grant's point — he's working down this way."

She was amazed at his good temper. "Nils, you're peppered with them. Why didn't you say something when you sold your lobsters over there?"

"Why should I, Jo? I couldn't catch all the lobsters over here. It's been a damn' good season — more'n enough for everybody."

Joanna watched the dark green boat with its white-painted hunting cabin move along toward them at a leisurely pace. The drone of its hauling gear was unnaturally loud in the still air. Everywhere she looked, even as far out as Bantam Ledge — barely breaking this morning — she could see boats at work. But Winslow Fowler's boat was the nearest to Bennett's. She became aware of the instant hostility which the sight caused in her, and tried to shunt it off. Nils was right. Had she expected no one to come near the Island during the five long years of its solitude? But she had been conditioned years ago for this instant defense of her own.

She met Nils' glance, and flushed like a girl. "I'm not really steamed up. But never in my life have I seen a Brigport boat hauling so close to Bennett's. Why, the line was settled way back when Grandpa Bennett was a young blade!" She laughed. "I guess seeing Winslow Fowler's boat like that makes it sharper than ever — what's happened to the Island."

"Guess Brigport fishing around the Island didn't make any dent in the lobsters," Nils said.

"But they'll move out, won't they? Now that the Island isn't empty any more?"

"You mean with one fisherman?"

Her mouth twitched at Nils' dry tone, but she realized suddenly that she was as serious as she had ever been in her life. That conditioning, she thought wryly . . . "In six months," she began, "by the time the spring crawl begins — there'll be more than one fisherman here. And it's up to us to get them out now."

"Winter's coming on," said Nils. He braced his feet to haul another trap; the warp fell in wet coils over the toes of his rubber boots. "They'll shift their traps out to deep water anyway. Come spring they won't bother to put 'em back here."

"Maybe. But you can't tell."

"Calamity Jane," said Nils. They smiled at each other, and Joanna knew it was borrowing trouble to start imagining things on this gem of a morning, when for the first time in many years she saw her way clearly and confidently before her. She turned her head and looked up at the steep west side, the rocks tawny and massive in the morning shadow of the woods. Her island. Who could harm it now?

The *Janet F.*, throttle open, roared head-on at the peapod, veered to one side apparently in the nick of time, and circled it, setting it to rolling wildly. "Still the same sweet children that I used to feel like strangling," Joanna said acidly, thinking of the traps resting on the forbidden bottom. Why, it had always been forbidden to Brigport. Let Nils try setting a trap in *their* waters . . . The *Janet F.* circled the peapod once more, leaving a curved silver wake on the pastel water. Then, engine cut to a whisper, she slid close to Nils and Joanna.

Nils' oars held the small boat steady. Joanna said, "They always were brats. Remember when their father used to bring them down to the Island when they were little?"

The green side of the *Janet F.* loomed above them, and the young man at the wheel grinned down at them. "Hi, Nils. How goes the battle? Hi, Joanna. Heard you was comin' back."

"Hello, Randy." Joanna was cool and aloof, but Randy didn't seem to notice. After five years, in which he had grown from his early teens to young manhood, his grin was the same. He stood erect and tense by the wheel, giving the impression of limitless nervous energy, harnessed with difficulty in his slight body.

He wore a black peaked cap tipped back on a close-clipped brown head, and in his thin brown face his eyes had a continual sparkle and motion, like the sea with the sun shining on it, and the wind forever skimming it and making it restless; like the sea except for their color. They were a light sunlit brown.

He leaned toward Joanna now, unaware of her remoteness. "Swell to see you, Jo! By God, it's been a hell of a while since you grabbed me by the collar that time." His thin cheeks were slashed with dimples. "Remember? That time I set off them giant salutes at the 4th of July dance."

First the traps, and then rocking the peapod. Show-off. He needed to be cuffed, Joanna thought, and she looked at him distantly. He and Nils laughed at the memory of the giant salutes, and Nils was stripping off his wet canvas gloves to take a cigarette from Randy's package.

She looked past Randy at Winslow. He lounged against the cuddy, smoking, and taking no part in the conversation. He was older than Randy, and heavier in build; his jaw was fleshier, his eyes sullen and shadowed. He looked at Randy and Nils as if their banter disgusted him.

As if, Joanna thought with a sudden rush of anger, *Nils and I had no right here. As if we were the ones who'd gone over the line.*

At least Randy was civil. And if it annoyed Winslow to have Randy stop to talk with them, then Winslow should be annoyed. "Hello, Winslow," she said deliberately. He took the cigarette out of his mouth and looked at it.

"Hi." He kicked Randy's boot. "Look, you intend to sit here and gas all day?"

"Don't mind him, he was out girlin' last night, and she warn't just what you'd call accommodatin'," said Randy. He twinkled at Joanna. "I told him there's some girls don't go for that strong-arm stuff. But he's got to learn the hard way, that boy."

"Oh, for Christ's sake!" Winslow growled. He ground out his cigarette viciously.

"I suppose," Joanna suggested lightly to Randy, "that you know all the answers." She hoped perversely that it would infuriate Winslow if she prolonged the conversation.

Randy was still twinkling. "Well, almost all of 'em . . . I'm glad there's goin' to be people on Bennett's again. Some place to go."

"Yes, come over," Joanna invited. "Nils would probably like to talk to another man once in a while, instead of just me."

"Is he *crazy?*" said Randy.

"Get that engine goin', can't ye?" Winslow exploded. "Anybody'd think you was out on a yachtin' trip, and we got over a hundred pots to haul this mornin'."

Joanna smiled at Randy, and Nils pulled on his gloves again and took up the oars.

"Nice to have seen you," she said.

Winslow moved bait boxes around noisily, his broad back turned. Randy's fingers touched his visor; his grin flashed out, touching Nils, sliding over to her, and staying.

It was noon when Nils rowed up through the long Gut into Brigport Harbor. There was no slackening of his stroke as he rowed among the moorings in the long narrow harbor, though he had been rowing steadily all morning.

There was warmth and peace in the bay this September noon. The rounding white sides of the boats were mirrored in the still waters below them, the gulls dreamed on the sunlit saffron and red ledges, somewhere on shore there was the sound of whistling. The immense and untroubled autumn sky arched over it all, the sea, the islands dreaming in the sun, the boats that seemed also to dream at their moorings, like the islands and the gulls.

In a little while, Joanna thought — by September next year — the boats would lie in the harbor of Bennett's Island, and there would be women in the houses that looked down across it, lavender smoke rising straight in the crystal motionless air, and men going home to dinner, and a young boy whistling as he hauled a dory up on the beach.

When they came into the big part of the harbor, where the stone wharves were, the fish houses built over the rocks, the store, and Cap'n Merrill's boat shop, there was an amazing bustle of activity around Ralph Fowler's lobster car, moored close to the sheltering wall of the breakwater. Ralph was uncle to Randy and Winslow.

"Who does that big boat belong to?" Joanna asked Nils. "The *Elsie R.* They're getting bait from her, aren't they?"

"They sure are. That's Tom Robey's new boat. Named for his mother. . . . Tom must have got some herring last night. Remember Tom?"

"I remember when the clubhouse kitchen got shacked," said Joanna with dignity. "It was a great disgrace. That Bennett girl resisted Tom Robey's advances, and everybody got into the fight. If she'd had more tact . . . But then, those Bennetts always did look down their long noses at people. . . . Tom's come up in the world, hasn't he?"

"The Robey boys are doing all right for themselves. If a war doesn't come along and break up the seining crew, Tom'll be a rich guy before long."

"I hope they can keep that mess over in Europe," said Joanna. "But when I think of those Nazis, and the things they're doing . . . the way they're bombing London—"

"Well, don't think about 'em right now," said Nils. "Time enough to get mad when we get into it. Look, I'll drop you off at the wharf, and go sell my lobsters and get some bait. I can't lug much, but I can hire somebody to bring it down for me."

"Nils, we ought to get the *Donna* into the water again, so you won't have to be dependent on anybody."

Nils held the peapod close to the foot of the ladder for her to step up. "We can't do everything in a day, Jo. And we've got plenty of time."

"That's what you always say." She smiled down at him from the ladder, and walked up the wharf with her quick light stride. It seemed queer to be getting the mail at Brigport, but it wouldn't be long before there'd be a store and postoffice at Bennett's again. Her eyes were luminous, seeing the Island as she wanted it to be, as she had dreamed of it for years. And now she and Nils stood on the very threshold of reality, and the dreams were no longer dreams. Almost, she could touch them.

She walked up the slope from the wharf to the store. Seeing the sign *R. Fowler* over the door, she remembered how her father used to say he couldn't get accustomed to seeing that name over the door instead of *T. Merrill.* He'd always said that the old-timers of Brigport still called Fowler a foreigner after he and his clan had been there ten years. She smiled; she wondered if now, after thirty years, the Fowlers were still foreigners.

The store was dim and cool after the radiance of the day, spacious and well-stocked as it always had been, with miraculous and fascinating things that Pete Grant had refused to buy for the store at Bennett's. He'd called them pure foolishness . . . Randolph Fowler came out of the postoffice to meet her.

"It's Joanna, isn't it?" he said in the deep pleasant voice she remembered, with its faint trace of mainland accent. She put out her hand and he shook it warmly. "I guess Nils is to be congratulated, from what I hear."

"That's right," she said. "I'm Mrs. Sorensen now." He looked almost the same after five years; thin-faced and short, like Randy, only broader, he still wore an immaculate white shirt, quiet-figured tie, a starched gray cotton-twill coat. There was some gray in his neatly groomed dark hair, but his mustache was the same. She remembered how that mustache used to awe her when she was small, and had been brought to church services on Brigport. Randolph Fowler was always called upon to sing "Shall We Gather at the River," or "The Old Rugged Cross," and while all the grown-ups listened with reverent pleasure to his baritone, Joanna had watched in fascination the way his mustache moved up and down.

Now, while he was getting her mail and packing her few groceries in a small carton, he asked her suddenly, "You think you and Nils can make out all right, living over there alone?"

"Why not? We've both lived out winters there before. Plenty of them."

Fowler smoothed his narrow chin. "It's all right, as long as nobody gets sick."

"At least we can try," Joanna said. *And we won't be alone over there,* she thought, but she didn't want to say it aloud. She didn't know why. She told herself it was because she wasn't certain about the others' coming, except in her heart.

When she came outside again, a big Jersey cow grazed peacefully at the corner of the store, her sleek hide golden under the sun.

The tall old spruces were very green and very sharp, puncturing the sky. Joanna rubbed the cow's nose and went back down to the wharf to wait for Nils.

From the pile of laths where she sat, she could see the peapod tied up at Ralph Fowler's lobster car; powerboats and dories and peapods were clustered around the big, broad-beamed seiner like gulls hungry and impatient for their share of the herring. Through the pellucid stillness of noon she heard Tom's bull-like roar, and it made her smile. The same old Tom.

She looked at each boat in the harbor. Brigport always prided itself on its fine-looking boats, and they were a trim fleet, she had to admit. But she could imagine the *Donna* coming up through the Gut and putting them all to shame.

How humble it made her feel that now it could be true; that it *would* be true. . . . The sound of rowlocks came to her and she saw Nils' peapod crossing the harbor. She was ready at the head of the ladder when he came. As she watched the steady, contained serenity of his face, and saw the long even sweep of the oars, the dismay of the night before seemed like a dream.

It was stupid, even wrong, to feel dismay, for that was a weakening thing, and she had work to do. She and Nils had a lifetime job before them, and they needed each other. Only Nils could help her plans to blossom and bear fruit. And if her heart didn't pound at his touch, if color didn't surge up hotly through her throat and face at his touch, she knew why. That went with being twenty, and meeting Alec Douglass at the door in a sweet flare of passionate welcome. Alec had been a romantic husband. The first year of their marriage had been something a woman could not hope to find twice in one lifetime. When he had been drowned, she knew no other man would ever stir her as Alec had done.

She didn't feel like a traitor, thinking these things as Nils rowed toward her, and seeing the way his face changed at his perception of her up there on the wharf. Rather it made her answering smile more radiant for him. He need never know these things she knew; and now that she understood herself, she would not be dismayed by his passion again.

3

JOANNA TOOK A TURN AT THE OARS now. They rowed out through the Gut and past Tenpound, where a black ram stood on a high red rock cliff and looked down at them through a cloud of circling gulls. Heading straight for the Head, at the Eastern End of Bennett's, they passed in the cool shadow of Shag Ledge and startled a family of fat little sea-pigeons, who took off in a whir of black and white and tiny red feet. Above the beach in Eastern End Cove the houses looked bleak and alone, the grassy field rose high around the doorsteps and touched the window sills. But the Head looked the same, gigantic bare rock towering against the sky, tawny and brilliant in the sunshine.

Then around on the south-eastern side of the Island, where the woods were thick and the shoreline a jumbled mass of the same tawny rock. Today the water murmured with deceptive mildness over the rockweed that turned the shallows to jade-green and amethyst. Loons paddled in the coves, and old-squaws and tousle-headed sheldrakes moved complacently above their own images.

The house was in sight against the Western End woods from the time they rounded the Head. Captain Bennett had built the homestead in a high place, to command a fine view of his lands and waters and the doings of his fishermen. Joanna, rowing in silence while Nils smoked his pipe, tried to imagine the Island without the house, without the Indians who had been there long before the Bennetts. On a day like this it was so wild and alone, with the sea birds playing fearlessly around the shores, the seals venturing close enough to sun themselves on the flat shelving rocks in Goose Cove.

One side of her loved this wild solitude, wishing to be alone and complete with the birds and seals, to be friends with them in this world of unbroken quiet. But the other side of her saw smoke rising from Island chimneys again, and the harbor dotted with moorings, the water spangled with Island buoys, and thousands of pounds of Island lobsters leaving the cars to reach every corner of the United States; her eyes must return again to the homestead and the visions that had driven Grandpa Bennett when he built it in its high place.

They passed the mouth of Schoolhouse Cove, came between Goose Ledge and the long arm of the point, where the wild-rose haws glowed red among lichened granite, and rowed into Goose Cove.

There was a boat lying beside the little wharf, a strange boat, and instantly the sense of remoteness was gone. For the first time in a half-hour Joanna spoke.

"Did you ever see that boat before, Nils?"

Nils narrowed his eyes against the sunglare and studied the boat as the peapod moved steadily toward it. 'I don't think so. She's a line trawler, by the looks of those trawl tubs along the washboards. Been out quite a long spell, too. . . . She needs paint."

"They probably stopped for water," Joanna said. "I hope they found the well all right." The peapod's white paint was bright beside the shabby hull of the line-trawler. Joanna took her bundles ashore, and Nils rowed out toward his mooring, where his skiff waited.

Joanna, feeling starved, thought whole-heartedly about dinner as she left the sturdy, sun-heated planks of the wharf and walked up the slope to the house. This noon it was hot and windless there, perfumed with the bay that grew in glossy-leaved clumps almost as tall as herself. The ripening cranberries turned red cheeks to the sun; they were like tiny apples, lying there in the moss.

Fishermen had always stopped at the Island for water as long as Joanna could remember. So she was not startled when she saw the two men and the boy come around the corner of the house; but they were startled. She knew it by the way they stopped and stared. A tall lank man in a long-visored cap, faded plaid shirt, rubber boots and nondescript work pants riding low on his lean hips; a short, rounding man with a battered felt hat shading his face, except for the stubble of beard and the pipe as short and stubby as himself. His overalls curved over a stoutening girth. He took his pipe out of his mouth and gazed at Joanna.

But it was to the boy she spoke, for he was ahead, a skinny

youngster in dungarees and boots too big for him, the yachting cap jaunty on the back of his close-cut sandy head. He was no more than twelve, she thought, and said, "Hello."

He stared back at her, his eyes round in his pointed face. They were the same odd golden color as the freckles scattered liberally over his sharp cheekbones and brief nose.

"H-h-hello," he said, sounding out of breath.

Joanna looked past him at the men, and smiled. "Hello. Did you find the well all right?"

"We warn't exactly lookin' for the well," said the short man, and pushed back his hat. "We was lookin' for you and Nils. You still chasin' around on his coattails, Jo?" He began to laugh, and at the sound of that chuckle, Joanna knew him beyond a doubt.

She had never dreamed, in the days when Jud Gray was a familiar stubby figure around the shore, always ready to tease her, that she would ever be so glad to see him. She dropped her bundles on the grass to take a firm hold on his hard leathery hand.

"Jud, you devil, what are you doing out here? How are you, anyway? Oh, golly — Nils will be ashore in a minute, and he'll be so darned glad to see you —"

"You sure?" Jud asked her quizzically. "This bein' a honeymoon, I didn't know how you fellers would take to callers so sudden-like . . . This is Caleb Caldwell — and that's his boat down there, we been trawlin' together for quite a spell — and that long-legged gandygut is his boy Joey."

Joey blushed, but he possessed a shy endearing grin. His father had a long face, somberly carved, lantern-jawed; but he smiled in his eyes, and his deep voice held a slow warmth and courtesy that Joanna liked at once.

She felt excited and happy as she led the way into the kitchen. She listened to Jud's news of his family with her eyes shining and her mouth ready to exclaim. As she listened she planned how to make a dinner for two stretch for five. Of course they would stay; they must stay. She could not possibly explain why seeing Jud meant so much to her, except that he too belonged to the Island's past. And because he belonged to it, he had come back, if only for an hour.

She put more corned hake on to freshen, sliced more salt pork, peeled extra potatoes. There were beets from her sister-in-law Mateel's garden, and new piccalilli she and her mother and Mateel had put up just the week before. For dessert she could stir up a molasses cake.

The boy Joey sat on the woodbox, with his knees under his chin, watching her. He was starved, probably. Boys always were. His eyes were almost too big for his sharp solemn face. With one side of her mind she listened to Jud, and the other thought this boy was a world different from her oldest nephew, young Charles, who was sturdy, handsome, and almost too self-assured.

The older Caldwell sat in comfortable silence, smoking his pipe, watching Jud from under shaggy brows. His thick gray hair was in sharp contrast to his seamed, darkly-burnt skin.

Jud's round face shone with sunburn and excitement. "By Golly, Jo, if I'd knowed I was goin' to be seein' you, I'd of brought my razor along this trip."

"Never mind," she told him fondly. "You look just as good to me, beard or no beard."

"Who's that you're handing out that sweet talk to?" said Nils from the doorway. "Hello, Jud, you old coot."

"Toughest old coot afloat," said Jud. "Unsinkable. Like one of them newfangled Coast Guard boats." He pumped Nils' arm fervently. "So you done it, my boy! Congratulations!"

"Thanks," said Nils, imperturbable except for the faint stain of color along his cheekbones. "Well, how'd you happen to stop in today? Did you know we were here?"

Jud winked. "You ain't mad, are you, boy? Us bustin' in like this on a honeymoon?"

"Sit down and behave yourself, Jud. And tell us how come."

"Well, we met Charles last night. He was just comin' from here—hailed us over to the west'ard of Bantam. We was layin' out there for the night." Jud looked from Nils to Joanna with his familiar gnomish grin. " 'Course we didn't figure to come visitin' right off, soon as we found out. We waited till today."

"You'd all better get washed up," said Joanna. "Then we can eat and talk. Nils, this is Mr. Caldwell, and Joey."

"I kinda fell down on my etti-kett," Jud said, beaming. "But now that you two fellers is acquainted, I hope you size each other up right. It's important." He broke off to wash with complete and noisy enjoyment.

"How's the line-trawling these days?" Nils asked.

"All right," Caldwell said in his deep voice. "Could be better. Could be worse."

Jud emerged rosily from the towel. "Ruther be lobsterin', wouldn't ye, Caleb? Me too." He was abruptly serious. "Nils, I been up lookin' my place over. The bushes is kind of wild, and the grass is growed high, but the place looks good to me. Damn' good. There's space around it, and trees with birds in 'em — damned if I ain't missed the little devils all these years."

Joanna, putting food on the table and motioning Joey to his place, was conscious of her deepening heartbeat. She felt as though she knew what Jud was going to say next; as if she had always known it.

"We're due ashore tonight — the boy has to start school in a few days — and I'm goin' to talk to Marion. Our baby graduated from high school last June and got her a job in Portland. Livin' with a cousin of her mother's. They ain't nothin' to keep us over there now. Marion, she's kind of stuffy and tired most of the time, and me, I been ailin' ever since I left the Island. Now I know why. I been suffocated. That air ain't fit to breathe. And I got that somethin'-o-phobia you get in closets."

His faded eyes, set in their crinkled network, were shiny. "All this means I'm movin' back here just as soon as I can get the old lady and our stuff aboard the mailboat. We may be gettin' along, but we got as much courage as we ever had. We'll make out." He put his hand on Caleb's shoulder. "And Caleb here — he never lived on an island, but he's an island man just the same. 'Cause he's been hankerin' after somethin' all his life, and he never knowed what it was till today."

Nils' impassive blue glance moved toward Caleb Caldwell, whose deep-set eyes looked back at him. At the table Joey sat unmoving. Joanna had the impression he was holding his breath.

"I know," Jud went on doggedly, "that most people've held onto their places here, like I have. But you fellers have the say of some of 'em, like that place where Marcus Yetton lived, fr instance. And the Binnacle. What I want to know is — have you got a place for

Caleb, or am I goin' to have him move in with me? 'Cause I'm willin' and glad to have him."

Nils said in his slow pleasant voice, "Let's sit down and eat,
and talk this over."

" What is there to talk over?" Joanna's excitement kindled the
warm color in her face. "Jud, if you vouch for him, we're willing
and glad to have him. After dinner, we'll show him the Binnacle
and the Yetton place, and let him choose. How soon can you move?"
she demanded of Caldwell.

"Why, I'll have to talk to my wife a little, I guess. Then there's
the boy's schoolin'—he goes into the seventh grade this year."

"There's a good school at Brigport,' Joanna said eagerly. "It's
small, but it's good. I want to send my little girl there. Joey could
go, couldn't he, Nils?" She pulled chairs out from the table. "Everything's getting cold. Let's sit down."

This was beyond her wildest dreams, to have people coming
so soon. Why, the Island would be peopled again, long before the
year was up! Over the scraping of chairs and clink of china, she
said to Caldwell, "The Binnacle's big, but it's right in the face and
eyes of everything. Your wife might not like that. Have you any
other children?" She smiled at Joey, who blushed and smiled back.

"Just the boy." Caleb accepted the bowl of pork scraps from
Nils, and looked across the table at him as he spoke. "You understand, I've only lobstered in a small way. Never any deep-sea lobsterin', same as Jud tells me about. Haven't any gear, but I had an
offer of thirty pots the other day. That's kind of small potatoes for
startin' in out here, isn't it?"

"Around here you can do fine with just thirty pots!" said Joanna
enthusiastically. "This time of year, in the fall spurt, you can make
enough to build any number of new ones. That is," she added in
a more practical tone, "if you get them overboard soon enough."

Caldwell must come; her mind was made up to it. She knew
with an instinct deeper than mere thought that the Island could do
with a man like Caldwell. Nils would want to investigate him. But
she *knew*.

Nils said, "There's a lot of things a man ought to understand
before he moves out here. It's home for Jud, so maybe he doesn't
think of 'em as drawbacks." He smiled at Jud, then moved the salt

and pepper shakers contemplatively. "The winters, with the mail-boat only running down as far as Brigport, might be kind of tough for somebody who's never lived through a Bennett's Island winter."

"Anybody would think you were trying to discourage him, Nils!" Joanna exclaimed, laughing. "What is there to be afraid of? You heard Jud say he was an island man at heart, didn't you?" She smiled at Caldwell and, without her conscious knowledge of it, all the vivid heart-warming Bennett charm was in that smile.

" There's always plenty of bait, and you can go hauling all win-ter long, because it never freezes up. Now I'll tell you the draw-backs, Mr. Caldwell. Sometimes the wind blows for a week or two at a time, and you can't go out to haul. But when a good day comes you get more than enough to make up for the windy ones. If you want to get off on the mailboat, you have to go to Brigport in a small boat, and get your groceries over there, too. But as soon as we get some people out here, we'll have a store, and our postoffice back, and then Link will *have* to deliver the mail down here, even if he doesn't like putting the *Aurora B.* into this harbor in winter time."

Caldwell glanced at Nils. "What's the matter with the harbor?"

"The harbor's all right," said Nils. "For lobster boats—"

"It's just that it's small, and the *Aurora's* sixty-five feet long," Joanna said quickly. "It's hard to swing her around when the wind's a certain way." She smiled to see the faint shadow leave Caldwell's face.

"Then there's the school. While it's still good weather the chil-dren can be set ashore on the sand beach over there—it's just a mile from the harbor—and picked up in the afternoon. Later on, they'll have to be boarded during the week. I have to find a place for Ellen, and I can find a nice place for Joey." A new thought struck her. "Nils," she said excitedly, "Cap'n Merrill and his wife—I'll bet they'd like to have a boy staying with them, especially if I vouched for him."

The boy colored and glowed under her luminous gaze.

"You're convincin' me, but remember, there's my wife to be convinced, too," said Caldwell dryly. "And your man there—it's a big risk, lettin' strangers into a place like this."

"Oh, Nils is convinced," said Joanna gayly. "Nils, you show him the houses after dinner. The Yetton place is my favorite, with the harbor right at its feet, and a nice fish house, and a little spruce grove behind it to cut off those north-east winds. Of course it's shabby, but if you think your wife will like it, I imagine we could do something about paint and paper, don't you, Nils? . . . Does your wife like the radio, and reading?"

Caldwell nodded. His eyes seemed amused under the heavy brows. "She does a lot of knittin' and patchwork, too."

"She'll get along fine," said Joanna decisively, and arose to take the gingerbread from the oven.

"My God," said Jud, "she's quite a salesman, ain't she?"

Joanna's cheeks were blazing, not with the steam from the gingerbread, but with triumph. She had done it; she had made sure Caleb Caldwell would come. He had all but said so. And with him and Jud, there would be three families on the island. If she could only find others to talk to as she had talked to Caldwell, others who would come . . .

When at last the gingerbread was gone, and the coffee drunk, Jud was eager to get down to the harbor again.

"You start along," Nils told them. "I'll fill up the woodbox and water pails first."

Joanna stood at the window that looked harborward, and watched them going down the slope, past the chunks of granite rock that overlooked Schoolhouse Cove, toward the alder swamp at the foot of the meadow. The marsh that stretched to the harbor beach was streaked russet and burnt gold, and lavender asters foamed along the road. Beyond the marsh's edge and the old boats on their sides in the tall grass, and the camps huddled on the shore, the harbor shone, blue and brimming and empty.

Nils was coming back from the well. Winged sunlight flashed and danced on the brimming pails, so that they seemed to hold living light instead of water.

She ran to hold the door open for him, and followed him across the kitchen to the dresser. "Nils, didn't you like that man? And Jud coming back, too—if we'd ever *dreamed,* when we left Brigport this noon, that they'd be here!"

Nils took out his pipe and filled it with deliberate fingers. Smiling faintly, he looked past her at the brilliant sea outside the south-east windows, at a gull flashing by close to the pane, and she was reminded with sudden poignance of her father, standing like this in the midst of a swirling maelstrom of young Bennetts.

She put her hand on his arm and looked into his face. "Nils, you hardly said a word the whole time."

He looked down at her, still that faint quirk to his mouth. "You did all right."

"You think I persuaded him?" she demanded radiantly. "Now if only his wife is willing—"

"I'd better get down to the shore and unlock the houses," Nils said.

When he had gone she began to clear up the dishes. To the comfortable humming of the teakettle, the voices of the gulls coming through the screen door, and the nearer sweet chatter of the sparrows, she reviewed the whole morning from the rising at dawn. The meeting with the Fowler boys—her mind quickened to a fresh realization; with more fishermen on the Island the Brigport men *must* move their pots. And soon.

She thought of Nils then, of the way he had stood looking out to sea, like her father; the way he had smiled at her elation. What was it he had said when she reminded him of his silence at dinner? *You did all right.*

Inexplicably her stomach seemed sickeningly empty. She felt as if she had been slapped. Slapped by the realization that she had done all the talking, even when Caldwell seemed to glance toward Nils. It had been Nils they had questioned first, but she had taken over.

She remembered now the openly amused glint in Jud's eye, and felt a rush of fury. Jud and his kind thought a woman didn't have a right to be heard. But she, Joanna, certainly had a right to be heard when it was Bennett business under discussion. She was the Bennett, not Nils.

Only . . . the way Nils had said that . . . Almost as if he thought she'd talked too much, that she might have given him a chance. Her hands slowed on the dishes she was washing, and she felt hot and irritable. She looked up then and saw her reflection in the mirror over the sink; she saw the level dark eyes, the black brows knitted above them; the flush under her brown skin, the strong, straight Bennett nose, the firm cleft Bennett chin.

It was when she met those mirrored eyes that she felt her discomfort vanish and lightness flood through her. What foolishness she had been thinking! It was as if the sight of herself had reminded her of the eternal truth. She was first and foremost what she had always been: Joanna Bennett, who belonged to the Island.

The Island must be peopled again. If Caldwell came, if other men followed, why this silly concern about anything else? As long as they *came*.

You did all right, Nils had said. Perhaps she ought to tell him when he came in that she hadn't meant to do all the talking. But even as she thought of it the impossibility was so strong she knew she would never mention it at all.

4

THE ALDER LEAVES HAD TURNED YELLOW, and the line storm had blown most of them away by the first of October. The spruces remained unchanging, looking black in the dawn and at sunset; but the alders were almost bare, and the birches stood slim and white at the foot of the meadow. But still, when Joanna walked down to the harbor on her way to the Yetton house, the birds played among the branches and fed on the seeds; the fearless chickadees and their cousins, the nuthatches, the juncoes, and the warblers who stopped to rest and feed on their trip south.

Myrtle, Magnolia, Chestnut-sided, Bay-breasted — the warblers darted and chirped among the branches and were not abashed by Joanna. Ever since she was small and going to school, she had stopped here to watch the birds in the spring and fall. One day soon they would be gone, except for the juncoes and chickadees. It was hard to believe, when the sun lay so warm along her bare arms, and the sea stretched far over the horizon in its gentle and infinite blue.

From the time Caleb Caldwell's letter had come, saying he was moving out when Jud did, early in October, she had worked daily in the Yetton house, washing windows and woodwork, sweeping, dusting down cobwebs. She tried to do a room a day. When the days were cold and windy, with rain battering at the panes, Nils came down and worked with her. Days he went to haul, he gave her a few hours in the afternoon.

New paper came from Montgomery Ward, the ceilings were whitewashed, the woodwork and floors repainted. It hardly seemed the same house where Marcus Yetton had grown old and harassed before his time, but still able to produce a baby a year until Susie's worn-out and under-nourished body refused to deliver living children. . . . Hardly the same house where young Julian had grown to the age of twelve, and where he should have been having his supper one September night instead of smoking stolen cigarettes in Stephen Bennett's boat shop.

Scrubbing, painting, papering with the energy of a dozen women, Joanna felt as if she were eradicating for all time any trace of the Yettons. She was surprised at the bitterness that tinged her memories of them. After five years there should have been no bitterness, she thought. But why not? For years her father had kept them, literally fed them from his own pocket, because Marcus was so shiftless a fisherman; and then, when everybody else, even the Bennett boys, had left the Island, and Stephen was hanging on by sheer will power — to have Julian's dropped cigarette send the boatshop and two hundred and fifty traps, with warps and buoys, up in flames!

When Nils was there working with her, Joanna said nothing of what she felt. It was better to keep it silent, and hope it would be washed away, as the dust and cobwebs were being washed away by her brooms and cloths, by the Caldwells.

She wanted to paint the outside of the house too.

"I don't know," Nils said. "I've got to haul every good day and do what I can about fixing up the old wharf, and the *Donna*. I don't see how I can do it, Joanna."

"I can do it myself. I've always wanted to paint a house, and it's only one story high, anyway." She laughed. "Every time I look at that faded-out weather-beaten green, I think of Marcus. Just like his complexion."

Nils got white paint for her at Brigport, and told her to go to it. After that, when he was out in the peapod, she painted through the long warm mornings, glorying in the smell of the paint, the blue sky overhead, the solitude all around her; yet not dreading the fact that the solitude was soon to be broken.

When she had finished, the low-roofed house looked tidy and pleasant, snuggled into the shelter of Eastern Harbor Point. It didn't look as if it had been flung there by a giant hand, and remained huddled fearfully against the spruce-dotted rise. She made Nils walk out on Pete Grant's wharf, and they looked across the harbor at the house.

"Now, how will that look to Mrs. Caldwell when she comes into the harbor on the mailboat?" she demanded.

"Good," said Nils. "But what about the fish house? It looks pretty drab, now." They looked across the expanse of harbor at the weathered building built out over the rocks. It was low tide, and the little wharf looked high and spindle-shanked.

"The fish house is solid, and so is the wharf," Joanna said firmly. "You know it, and so does Caleb. And Mrs. Caldwell will be interested in the house, not the shop. Besides," she added eagerly, "you can cover it with that pretty green tarpaper that Charles put on his shop over at Pruitt's Harbor."

"You want me to do it right now?" inquired Nils. "Or can I have my dinner first?"

She laughed, and then her dark eyes went intensely serious. "Nils, do I sound like Aunt Mary teaming Uncle Nate around?"

"You sound like Joanna. The way you always sounded." His hand gave her shoulder a quick squeeze. "Full of ideas for yourself and everybody else. Let's go home and eat."

"But I did a good job on the house, inside and out, didn't I?" Young Joanna had learned to row, to fish for cod, to waltz, as Nils had taught her, not her brothers. It had always been for Nils' approval that she looked.

"You did fine on the house. Now let's see how well you did on the fish hash."

They walked back, lightly and carefully, over the wharf to firm land. It had been a long time since anything had been done to Pete Grant's wharf. Pete, who had kept the store and bought lobsters at

Bennett's Island since long before Joanna was born, lived on the mainland now. But he still owned the western harbor point, and the wharf and buildings.

Joanna stopped by the store, and looked through the dust-filmed windows. "You think Pete will let us have the postoffice in here?" she asked. "We ought to be able to have one, if we start working on it right away."

"Not today, Lady," said Nils firmly, and took her by the elbow.

It was a sunny day, with a fresh little north-west breeze ruffling the water into a frothy edge of white around the rocks, when the *Aurora B.* was due to steam down between the islands and land Mrs. Jud Gray and Mrs. Caleb Caldwell on the wharf with their assorted household goods. The men and Joey would come in Caleb's boat.

When the day had been set for the migration, Joanna had made arrangements for Ellen to be brought up from Pruitt's Harbor and put on the mailboat. Now, as Joanna walked down to the wharf, she knew three kinds of pleasant anticipation. She was to see Marion Gray again, after all these years; she was to meet Mrs. Caldwell, who, like it or not, would be bound together with Joanna and Marion in the enforced camaraderie of the only women on the Island; and she would see Ellen. It had been a month she and Nils were married, a month since she'd brushed out Ellen's Alice-in-Wonderland mane and braided it, and saw the saucy starched bow of her gingham pinafore bounce around the corner on the way to the second grade.

Now Ellen was to sleep in the little room that had been Joanna's, she was to begin her Island childhood, to wake to the same sounds and scents and colors Joanna had known. It was, to Joanna, a thing too wonderful for ordinary contemplation. And there would be something else for Ellen to see with her solemn gray-blue eyes. She would grow with the Island, see it reach its full stature, become what her great-grandfather had intended it to be. The young Joanna had been born into a time of richness and plenty for the Island; and she had seen it die. Now it was beginning to live again. And Ellen would see it, she would be a part of it.

Nils had gone out to haul, intending to be home before the boat came, but he wasn't in yet, and Joanna waited alone on the wharf.

The freshening wind whipped at her wine-red corduroy skirt and jacket, tugged at her crisp black hair. She loved the wind. Anyone who had grown up in a houseful of Bennett boys was afraid of nothing that was strong and vigorous and noisy.

She thought of her brothers now; of Charles, comfortably settled at Pruitt's Harbor with his Mateel and his five youngsters and his mother; of Philip, the next oldest, still unmarried, still quiet-spoken, partner with Charles on *The Four Brothers*. Mark and Stevie, younger than Joanna, had gone with Charles in the beginning, that was how the big seiner had got her name. Now they were partners by themselves, line-trawling like Jud and Caleb.

And there was Owen . . . Her mind slipped quickly past the thought of him. She was afraid to think of Owen too much. He was the next older than herself. He had outgrown the Island — or thought he had — and had left it without a backward glance. He had left his boat too, the *White Lady,* the boat he'd designed and built himself, and loved more than any woman. No one in the family had heard a word about or from him for six years now. For all they knew, he might be dead, and she didn't want to dwell on that. Or there were things harder to think about than death. Owen had always been so violent; he liked his liquor, he made conquests of women who should have been forbidden to him. He had been the strange, wild one in the Bennett clan. And he had been a law unto himself.

The boys had not wanted to come back. All except Owen, they had seen her married to Nils, had kissed her and hugged her, and told her they were glad to see her and Nils together at last, and watched them set off for the Island. But not one had wanted to come back. To come home.

Thinking of it, Joanna's shoulders straightened, her mouth hardened. *Let them stay over there,* she thought. *We'll do all right.*

A boat's whistle sounded outside Eastern Harbor Point, and then she saw the *Aurora B.* plunging through the tide rip with a bone in her teeth. She forgot all resentment. *Those poor women,* she thought. *They'll be frozen almost to death.*

Marion Gray, moving briskly around Joanna's kitchen helping to set the table, was the same as ever, plump and sturdy like her husband, rosy from the wind, no speck of gray in her neat brown hair.

Mrs. Caldwell—Vinnie, Marion called her—was a trim, birdlike little woman. It was from her Joey took his big golden eyes, freckles, and short nose. She was young, not thirty-five yet, Joanna guessed, but there was a timeless quality about her, as if Joanna had always known her, tiny and dependable, and full of energy and ambition that seemed too big for such a slight creature. She had been woefully seasick, but she was undaunted. She sat by the window, sipping hot coffee, and looked down at her house.

"There's room between it and the trees in back for a vegetable garden, isn't there?" she asked. "And space for a nice little lawn in front, between the house and the shore. I brought some dahlia bulbs. They'll look handsome, dahlias will, against that white paint next fall."

"I hope you won't be lonely on that side of the harbor," Joanna said, delighted with her.

"Lonely? When all my life I've wanted space to throw out my arms without hittin' somebody on the nose?" She laughed. "And when my work's done, you'll see me climbin' up on that point to watch for Caleb to come in from haulin'."

Marion went over to look out at the harbor. "Those menfolks ought to be showin' up soon, hadn't they? They left before the mailboat did."

"Sakes, I don't worry about Caleb." Vinnie Caldwell rocked comfortably, then stopped. "I better not do that, or I'll be topsy-turvy again, and this coffee's too good to lose. . . . Marion, you know that old engine of his just chugs along. Nothin' flashy about her, but she gets where she's goin'—sooner or later."

"Looks like it's later, in this case," said Marion tartly. "Jud bought a case of beer yesterday. They get thirsty on the way, there won't be anything to move on."

"Caleb never drinks in front of the boy, not even beer." Mrs. Caldwell leaned back in her chair and sighed. It was a sigh of pure contentment. There had never been a sweeter sound to Joanna's ears. *I was right from the start,* she thought, *about the Caldwells. . . .*

Ellen was coming down the stairs, hopping from one step to the next and humming under her breath. That was how Joanna used to come downstairs, wrapped in her private imaginings. She remembered ruefully that half the time *her* deepest contemplation had to do with the best way to get even with Owen. . . . Hearing her daughter now, Joanna half-wished she could see into Ellen's head and know what she was thinking, what stayed in her mind of the view she had just now seen, from the window of the little room with the faded red sailboats on the walls.

But on the whole, she was glad she couldn't see. For it was what Ellen thought and considered and dreamed that made of her seven-year-old self a real, inviolable, personality.

She had been very mysterious when she came into the house. Her slender face solemn, her blue-gray eyes wide, she had refused to let Joanna stay with her while she changed her clothes.

"That Mrs. Caldwell was awful seasick. You better go tend to her." she had admonished Joanna. "You wait till I come downstairs. You'll be surprised."

And now she was coming into the kitchen. She was slim and tall in a pair of her cousin Charles' outgrown and faded overalls. Except for her fair coloring, it might have been Joanna herself standing in the doorway, watching the grown-ups unsmilingly. Joanna didn't speak. She hadn't expected the overalls. Ellen looked back at her, waiting, and then Marion Gray said heartily,

"Well! Who's this boy? A little girl came over with us, but I don't know where this boy came from!"

Suddenly the somberness was gone, Ellen's smile flashed into being, her eyes crinkled up into sparkles, a deep dimple pricked her cheek, her front-teeth-missing grin was delicious.

"Mother, are you surprised? Aunt Mateel let me have them. She said you *always* used to wear overalls when you were little!"

"And so I did," said Joanna. She wanted to put down the soup ladle and hug Ellen as she hugged her at night, at bedtime; she wanted to take her daughter's hand and lead her outdoors into the great sun-drenched world of sea and sky and tawny field, to sit with her on the red-brown rocks that sloped from the soil of the Island into the sea and then went down and down and were still the Island. . . . She wanted to show her the grassy places between the coves and the woods where the Indians' supper fires had pricked the lilac dusk with flame; and the treeless, rolling ground at the Western End where the wild strawberries carpeted the slopes in July, and the ripe raspberries trembled on the bushes in August, and where the gulls nested on the sheer naked cliffs at the very tip of the Island, and where the surf rolled even on calm days over long black reefs that the men must know as they knew the lines in the palms of their hands,

All these things flashed through her mind as she stood there, ladling hot lobster chowder. The women talked to Ellen, and she answered them, neither shyly nor boldly. But Joanna, smiling a little, her brown hands steady and certain, thought of the million things she would show her daughter.

Marion Gray said to her in a hushed tone, "If you don't mind my sayin it, Joanna . . . She may have your mother's colorin', and your build, but when she smiles she's her father all over again."

Joanna nodded. "Everyone notices that resemblance to Alec."

Relieved that she spoke so casually, Marion added, "I always said there never was a sweeter smile than Alec's. . . . But there, I have to say there's no better man than Nils. How's Ellen like him?"

Marion's frank curiosity didn't anger Joanna. "Ellen loves him," she said. "She calls him Nils, because she's always been interested in her own father. But she thinks Nils is wonderful."

"That's lovely," said Marion, her eyes moist.

"I'm going to have a playhouse," said Ellen to Mrs. Caldwell, "out on the rocks. My mother had a playhouse. I want mine the same place hers was."

"I'll show you where, this afternoon," Joanna said.

No one happened to see Caldwell's boat come into the harbor, with Nils' peapod in tow—they had picked him up between the islands. They came unexpectedly into the kitchen, with Joey trailing hungrily behind them.

There was another man with them. Jud introduced him as Matthew Fennell; he lobstered out of the little fishing port where the Grays and Caldwells had lived. He was in his early thirties, like Nils. He had not much to say, and a slow, pleasant smile. Burnt brown like the others, he was shaved and neat, his reddish-brown hair recently clipped. Joanna liked his ruddy face and clear, friendly gray eyes. You could tell a lot about a man by his friends, her father used to say, and if this was a friend of Caleb Caldwell's it was a good sign.

Mrs. Caldwell, helping Joanna with the second table while

Marion washed up the first lot of dishes, spoke about him while she and Joanna were at the stove.

"He's a real nice young fellow, Matthew is. A nice wife, too — about ten years younger than him, but a good girl. They have their hands full looking out for Gram — that's his grandmother, who brought him up. Old battle-ax," said Mrs. Caldwell without viciousness. "Matthew'd give his eye-teeth to be on his own — he's been lobsterin' on shares for Clyde Sparrow. You know him, he owns Sparrow Island, to the west'ard of here. What Caleb says, lobsterin's a good life for a man who knows he owns his own gear."

Joanna nodded. "It's nice he could come along and help. That'll be two men to each house. It's no fun, wheeling stuff up that slope to Jud's, or around the shore to your house."

Mrs. Caldwell took two plates of chowder to the table, and Joanna wondered if Matthew Fennell were goweled by the fact that the other three men eating with him were their own masters. She knew it would gowel her! But Matthew Fennell looked easy-going enough.

They ate heartily, for they planned to have everything moved and the stoves set up by late afternoon, when the warmth of the day would be gone. Joanna intended to help each of the women set things to rights.

But before she did anything else, she was going to do what she had promised; find for Ellen the place among the rocks where her own playhouse had been. Already she had collected, in her walks along the beach, bits of blunt-edged colored glass and china for dishes. And a battered teakettle from out in the shop, and a rusty pan or two. Oh, she would set Ellen up in great style, and leave her there with her dolls, with Goose Cove shimmering on one side of the point and Schoolhouse Cove on the other side, a great rise of rock for her housewall, a small square one for her stove, and a floor of wonderful flatness, with hardly any slant to it at all.

By sunset it was all done, and smoke lifted from the chimneys as triumphantly as any banners. Joanna came out of the Caldwell house, leaving a weary but profoundly happy Vinnie starting supper in the kitchen, and collected Ellen, who with Joey was exploring the tidewater pools among the rocks by the fish house.

She was not a talkative child, and she said nothing as she walked around the shore with her mother, but her very silence had the essence of contentment in it. She had played in her playhouse until it was in shadow from the high rock, and then she had come down to the Caldwells' to wait for Joanna. *Perhaps when she goes to bed,* Joanna thought, *she'll tell me something.* It would be some little thing she had seen — a fish hawk held motionless against the sky by his beating wings before he swooped, seals playing in the cove, the funny way a loon laughed. . . . It would be some one thing, out of the hundreds of treasures her mind had gathered during the long afternoon.

The south-eastern sky was flushed rosy-lavender, and the house looked white against it, its windows catching the fire of the western sky. As they went through the gate, Ellen cried out and pointed. "Look, Nils is home!"

Joanna looked up, and saw smoke rising in a thin blue plume from the chimney of her own house. She felt a vast, quiet warmth flow through her; her very weariness was a part of it, and Ellen's hand so firm and confident in hers, and Nils coming down to the well with the water pails.

She and Ellen walked up toward him. Ellen leaned over the curb to look down into the cold liquid darkness and watch the pails come up. Joanna looked down at the harbor.

"Three families getting supper right now, Nils," she said to him. "There's smoke going up past Eastern Harbor Point. And over there we can see Jud's roof and chimney among the trees — and there's a fire there, too."

"And in our house," added Ellen. She giggled as cold water splashed on her shoe.

Nils set down the pail and stood beside Joanna; together they looked at the Island, their shadows long behind them.

"It looks good," Nils said. "Tonight after dark there'll be other lights besides ours. . . . Joanna, Fennell wants to come here."

She turned to him quickly. "Is he sure?"

"Well, he has to talk to his wife and grandmother first." Nils grinned his unexpected youthful grin. "And I have to talk to my wife. He wants a place by himself, you see; wants to get away from people."

She knew what he meant. The Whitcomb house, the house where she and Alec had lived, and from which he had gone out to be drowned, was the sort of a place a man would want, to be by himself. And Nils wanted her to let these strangers have it, though he would not suggest it.

She said nothing for a long moment as they stood there by the well, with Ellen picking the asters that grew around their knees. Four families on the Island; four families to face the winter, to drive the Brigport men back, to love the Island and cherish it and help it grow. . . . She looked at Nils with no shadow in her eyes, no misgivings deep within her.

"Let's go home and talk it over while we have supper," she said.

5

NILS, JUD, AND CALEB HAD THEIR PLAN of work all laid out within a week of the moving-in. They talked it out around the *Donna*'s hull, beautiful even after she had lain in the marsh for five years.

Joanna, who had come down to the shore to tell Nils there was a mug-up of coffee and fresh coffee cake waiting for him, found them standing there at the edge of the beach and marsh, looking the *Donna* over.

"Always wisht I was the feller built that boat," Jud said, shaking his head. "Feller built her, he's got one good monument to himself, anyhow."

Caldwell said nothing. He prowled around the hull in the bent-over marsh grass, drenched from the recent high tide, and looked at her lines. Joey imitated him, narrowing his amber eyes the way his father narrowed his deep-set ones. Nils smoked his pipe and looked impassive.

Joanna stood listening, by the old anchor that had been sunk in the beach ever since the storm that sank the *Portland*. She wondered if Nils was as impassive as he looked. She had known him too long not to catch the faint tightening of his jawline, as if his teeth were gripping the pipestem hard. When he glanced sidewise at the *Donna*, his eyelids dropped even more. *He loves her,* Joanna thought, and blinked her own eyes hastily, because they were suddenly moist. Nils had looked up to her father as he had never looked up to his own; and he had always loved the *Donna*. He and Owen had been fourteen when Stephen had brought her home from the boat-yard at Thomaston. . . . Joanna, watching Nils now, remembered that day, Owen's wild, vivid enthusiasm, Nils' silence. Like his silence of this present moment. But a twelve-year-old Joanna in dungarees had seen for one fiery instant the blaze in his eyes when he first saw the *Donna*.

Later, years later, Jud had built a boat for Nils, and she had been fine and strong. But though he had been quietly confident of her ability, Joanna had never seen him look at his own boat as he had looked for the first time at Stephen Bennett's boat.

So she watched him now, and wondered what he was thinking. She ached to have him get the *Donna* overboard as soon as was humanly possible. The *Donna* had been the last boat to be put on the beach, and Stephen had put his hand on the lovely sheer of her bow and promised her he would be back. . . . But it had been Nils who had come; and now the *Donna* must go down to the water again and be the first Bennett's Island boat to ride at her mooring in her own harbor.

Jud's eyes had taken on a watery sheen, and Caleb was still prowling silently about the boat like the Indian who had certainly got into the Caldwell bloodstream some generations back. Nils said suddenly, "How many traps you two plan to build with that trap stuff you brought down?"

"A hundred apiece — we hope," said Jud. "And quick."

"Can't get 'em overboard too quick, the way lobsters crawl around this place," Caldwell said, coming to a stop beside them with the boy Joey at his heels. "Before God, I never see such lobsters."

"Didn't I tell ye, for God's sake?" demanded Jud. "Look, Nils, we brought fifty-odd pots with us, set 'em where I said, and we've hauled together from Caleb's boat. We been here a week, hauled four times, and averaged eighty bucks apiece."

"The price of lobsters right now helps some," Caldwell said moderately.

"Hell, it's goin' even higher," Jud snorted. "Ralph Fowler's payin' two cents less than they're payin' inshore, as 'tis now—and we're still doin' all right." He added darkly, "Ralph pays you out money like he had fish hooks in his pockets, and when you go ashore brother Randolph tries to take it all off'n you. But I can't say his prices are any worse'n Pete Grant's used to be."

"I'm pretty good at building traps," Nils said. "You any good at overhauling a boat?"

"I get it," said Jud. "We give you two hours, you give us two. Same as it always was, huh, Nils?" He turned to Caldwell and clapped him heartily on the shoulder. "You like that idea, Caleb? With this Swede on the job we can get a hell of a lot of pots built in a week, and he gets his boat overboard."

"Sure," said Caleb, "Why not?" His slow smile creased his leathery cheeks, and he put out his hand. Nils' hand met it.

"Now let's go up and have a cup of coffee to bind the bargain," he said. He caught the boy's anxious eagerness. "Joey too, Joanna?"

"Joey of course," she said promptly. "He's an Island man, isn't he?"

When they came into the kitchen, warm and bright with the fire and the flood of afternoon sunshine, Nils glanced around the room. "Where's Ellen? Doesn't she want a mug-up too?"

"She's too busy keeping house," Joanna said. It always filled her with a deep serenity, the fact that Nils was so fond of Ellen. It was as if they had always been together, all three of them, and that was the right of it, as far as Nils was concerned. Ellen's fair hair was like his, and that seemed natural, just as the weight of her slim, strong little body leaning against his shoulder as he read seemed natural.

Tall, smiling, not intruding on their male conversation of boats, engines, and fishing, Joanna moved about the room, getting the mug-up ready on the table for them.

"The boy's new riggin' came today," Caleb said to her. "I guess he's all set."

Joanna met his twinkle with one of her own, nodded, and went into the sitting room to resume her sewing. She knew what he meant.

Vinnie had ordered some new school clothes for Joey, and had refused to let him go among strangers until he was what she called
"decently clad." So he and Ellen had both had a week of pure holiday before starting school.

The idea of taking them to the sand beach in the morning and
picking them up in the afternoon had been abandoned. The trip
would take too much out of the working day, and the men had all
they could handle before the fall weather really shut down. Old Captain Merrill and his wife, whose boys had grown up and started families of their own, were anxious to have Joey come as soon as possible.
Mrs. Whit Robey, who had been one of Donna's few close friends,
was to take Ellen. Whit Robey was an uncle to Tom and Milt. He
roared, like all the Robeys, but he was a truly pleasant man, and
Mrs. Whit had a gentle humor that reminded Joanna much of her
mother. She knew Ellen would like and obey her.

There was no reason why the children couldn't start school at
once now that Joey's "new riggin' " had come. Joanna was finishing
the buttonholes in a new blouse for Ellen. It was Saturday now.
On Monday, if it was good, the children could go.

She smoothed out the little white blouse, and looked down across
the meadow to the harbor. The bushes at the edge of the alder swamp
were crimson; the berries on the rowan tree were red-orange, tiny
clustered globes of pure brilliant color. Crows were feeding on something in the marsh. They were rich and startling blackness against
the dying yellow-brown grass.

October on Bennett's Island, and children getting ready for
school. How many would there be by next October, she wondered.
If she moved a little, she could see the schoolhouse, with the narrow
field behind it and then the dark brilliance of the blue sound between the islands. She knew that when she heard the bell ringing
from the white belfry, and saw the everlasting game of catch going
on in the sandy yard between the steps and the tumble-down sea
wall, she would be almost satisfied.

She heard chairs being pushed back in the kitchen, and knew
the men were getting ready to go. Jud came to the doorway of the
sitting room.

"Damn' good mug-up, Jo." He beamed at her. Caleb called in
past him, 'Thanks, Mrs. Sorensen."

"Thanks, Mrs. Sorensen," Joey's young voice echoed him.

"I'm glad you liked it," she said. "That's the way Nils' grandmother makes coffee cake. Nils taught me." In a few moments she heard the back door close, and thought they had all gone back to the shore. But Nils crossed the kitchen with his soundless step, and came into the sitting room.

He said nothing, but leaned over, putting a hand on either arm of her chair, and looked long and searchingly into her face. It was warm and very still in the room. The sunlight fell in squarish patterns on the dark-blue painted floor, and the braided rug under their feet. They were motionless, so near to each other, so quiet. It was one of those moments when she wished he would tell her in words what he was thinking, what lay behind his intent gaze.

His face was so close to hers that she knew he could count every black lash, every fine black hair that made her brows like peaked wings across her forehead; he could swing forward only a little and touch her mouth with his own, yet still he said nothing. She thought of Alec. Tender phrases were never imprisoned behind Alec's eyes, compliments and loving words had always come easily to his tongue. . . .

Nils looked somberly at her and she looked back, seeing her face mirrored in miniature in his blue eyes, and the tiny white semi-circular scar on the bridge of his nose.

"What is it, Nils?" she teased him softly. "Did you come to tell me it was a good coffee cake — as good as your grandmother's?" She put her hands on either side of his face, feeling its bones and taut spare flesh warm under her palms, and kissed his mouth.

Whatever he came to tell me, she thought, knowing well that he was not thinking of the coffee cake, *I can answer him as he wants to be answered.* She knew that from her kiss and the touch of her hands he could never guess that the same voiceless current which impelled him didn't swirl through her blood too.

On Monday morning a brisk wind sent the sea racing up the sound between the two islands, and whipped each blue-green wavelet into a tiny crest of white. Great snowy billows of clouds, under-shadowed with faint purple, blew across the sky, turning the water from bright blue to lavender-gray, thence to cold green, thence to blue again. Nothing stayed still, and the gulls dived and soared crazily; the sound of their shrieking went on eternally against the wash of the sea and the wind.

Icy spray flashed again and again over the bows of Caldwell's boat as she rounded Tenpound and headed for the Gut. Caleb and Nils stood by the wheel, their brown faces streaming with the salt water that made their yellow oilclothes glitter, Joey was close behind them, valiantly braving the wet. He had oilclothes too. Ellen and Joanna were in the cabin. Except for Ellen, Joanna would have been outside too, but she didn't want Ellen to start her new school career with the sniffles.

Vinnie Caldwell had refused to come along. "It'll be a long day before anybody gets me on a boat again," she'd stated firmly. "Caleb wanted me to come, and here I am. And here I stay. I haven't forgot yet how I suffered comin' out on that mailboat!"

Joanna couldn't blame her. But Joey, standing behind his father, was rigid with excitement, and Ellen, sitting on the locker in the cabin, watched everything shining-eyed; no threat of seasickness here.

The boat lunged wildly, and rolled as she hit the backwash of the surf on the big yellow rocks that guarded the Gut. It was only for a moment; then all at once she was in smooth water, and Ellen and Joanna came out of the cabin into the drenched cockpit to watch their progress among the moorings. It wasn't too choppy for some to go out to haul. The *Janet F.* was out, Joanna noticed.

Now it was warm and windless, and the men took off their oilskins. " 'Magine it blows some out there in winter," Caldwell said mildly.

"Some," Nils agreed gravely. Joanna touched his arm.

"There's Tom Robey over there, and he must have some bait." She motioned toward the big boat anchored near the breakwater. Smaller boats and dories were clustered around, and in the sudden hush as Caleb shut off the engine, they could hear the men's voices.

"It's Tom all right, and he's loaded down with herring, by the looks of him. Saw him seining down around Pirate Island last night." Nils turned to Caldwell. "There's our bait, and I guess it's just in time. We sure need it. . . . We'll drop this crew off, and go over."

"This is what I call mighty convenient," said Caldwell. "Over home, bait come down in a truck, and didn't come, half the time. Feller used to get drunk."

"How many bushels can you lug in this boat?" Nils asked. "We can get some fresh bait and some to corn."

"Let's fill 'er up and see," Caldwell suggested, "Jud and me are figgerin' to go haul this afternoon, if it dies away. Some fresh bait would go good. And I almost like herrin' better'n bream."

Nils set the suitcases ashore and helped Ellen get started on the ladder. Joanna was already at the top to meet her. Joey followed.

"You behave now, young feller," said Caleb. "Be a credit to the family. After all, we're furriners around here, and we don't want 'em to think we're Hottentots, or some such."

Joey grinned. Ellen said, "A Hottentot is *black.*"

"Well, so's Joey, 'bout the time his mother gets after his neck and ears," said Caleb without smiling, Ellen's eyes danced with her suppressed mirth, while Joey turned pink under the freckles.

"So long till Friday, Ellen," Nils said. "Jo, we'll pick you up on the wharf here in about an hour."

She left Joey first, at the Merrills'. Mrs. Merrill opened the door to them with a welcome that was heartening to a boy starting a new school in strange country. The Captain was down at the shore, she said, working on the new boat; he'd most likely want Joey to come down and help him after school. That was, if Joey wanted to.

Joey's amber eyes were very big. *"Gosh,"* he breathed reverently. "Sure I want to. Boats—I mean—I—" His words strangled in his throat. He turned very red, and Mrs. Merrill and Joanna, knowing what he meant, mercifully forgot he was there.

They talked for a few minutes, and then it was time to take Ellen to Mrs. Robey. It was still early enough so the children could present themselves at morning recess and not lose the whole session.

"Joey," Joanna said to him, "Ellen will be just around the bend in the road, in the little white house nestled against the hill. Be sure to fasten the gate behind you, or somebody's cows will be into Whit's dahlias. Would you mind calling for Ellen and walking to school with her just this first day?"

"Gosh no," said Joey earnestly, if vaguely. He was still in a dream of boat-building.

"He'll be along, soon as he's fortified with a glass of milk and a couple of doughnuts," said Mrs. Merrill. "My, Joanna, with that build and that fair hair, he puts me in mind of my Bob, when he was that age."

This is going to work out all right, Joanna thought as she left him. It was a responsibility, finding a boarding place for another woman's child. But she should have known it would work out all right. Boats were Joey's passion. So were they Cap'n Merrill's. And Mrs. Merrill loved boys. Good or bad, it made no difference to her; besides, they were usually all good after a concentrated dose of her grandmothering.

It's a pretty house," said Ellen, walking backward. "Is mine as nice as that?"

"Oh yes, you'll like it."

"I hope so." Ellen sounded dubious. "Can I come down and call on Mrs Merrill?" She could hardly take her eyes from the spotless white house with its ell kitchen, and red vines climbing over the sprawling porch, the heavily fruited apple trees around it and the wall of spruces around it. The fieldstone well curb had a special fascination for her.

Joanna hoped prayerfully that the Robeys' white picket fence, with dahlias, would make up for the well curb. And it did. Other things helped. For instance, the way the rambling, low-posted house fitted against the hillside, and the ice-pond on the other side of the twisty road through the spruces. . . . Oh, this was almost better than apple trees, Ellen's eyes said.

Mrs. Robey was not a plump white-haired grandmother like Mrs. Merrill, but a slender, quiet-voiced one, who showed Ellen a little low-ceilinged room with a flowery quilt on the bed. There was a rocker just Ellen's size with an old-fashioned doll sitting in it; she looked at Ellen with bright blue eyes painted in her china face. She wore full rose-sprigged skirts, and it was clear from Ellen's first enchanted glimpse of her that they were going to be friends.

"Her name is Phoebe," said Mrs. Robey.

"Phoebe," repeated Ellen in a soft, careful voice. She kissed Joanna good-bye very serenely.

"I thought I was going to miss you," she said, her arms around her mother's neck. "But now I don't think so."

"I don't think so either," Joanna agreed. "And after all, if you walk up to the top of the hill, you can look down across Brigport to Bennett's and see the house over there."

"Good-bye," Ellen said. "I want to count Phoebe's petticoats before Joey comes. One of them has ruffles on it."

"I'm dismissed," Joanna said to Mrs. Whit. She felt proud of Ellen's poise. All in all she felt satisfied with the morning. She knew in her bones that all would go well with Joey and Ellen as far as their boarding-places were concerned. For school, that was another matter. But it would be the same in any new school, and Joey would look out for Ellen until she had made her own friends.

She met no one on the road back to the harbor. The birds darted and twittered in the spruces, and in the places where the sun had not yet struck, there was still the glitter of dew. The coolness was giving way to the delicious warmth of an October day.

Soon she saw the blue harbor shining through the trees, and the roofs of the fish houses below her, black against the sun glare on the water, and she heard the impotent clatter of the gulls who sat on the breakwater and watched the transfer of herring which they couldn't touch.

She didn't mind the prospect of having to ride home with a boat-load of fish. From her earliest childhood she had understood the importance of bait. Why, the smell of the baitsheds had been sweet to her, and to get her hands into rich corned herring, and help Charles or Philip bait up, had been heaven. Seeing the hogsheads full was like opening your cupboard doors and seeing the laden shelves, or going down into the cellar where the jars of canned stuff—your own canning—were stored. It gave you a safe warm feeling; a knowledge that there was something put by against the long winter days ahead.

Caldwell's boat wasn't back at the wharf yet, and she went into the store. Randolph Fowler was behind the counter. A big hulk of a man whose clothes glittered with herring scales was lounging against the apple barrel, drinking a bottle of pop. After the brilliance outside he was a black bulk which she didn't recognize as she shut the screen door quietly behind her.

Fowler was talking. "You did just right," he said. "You want to do that every time, Tom. They'll soon catch on."

The big man's laughter rumbled in his chest, and he put the pop bottle down with a flourish. It was Tom Robey. "They better," he said. "And the sooner they catch on, the healthier for the bastards."

Joanna had to smile. In the old days Tom had always been calling somebody a bastard, too. ' Hello, Tom," she said, and put out her hand to him. "How are you?"

Fowler nodded at her and began to arrange canned fruit on the shelves Tom looked down at her hand, his heavy brows drawn; he seemed confused. "My hands is filthy, Jo," he said.

She wondered if he was embarrassed by the memory of the time when he'd tried to kiss her against her will, at a dance in the club-house; it had been years ago, when they were in their teens. Her brother Owen had knocked Tom down, and the ensuing row between the boys of Brigport and Bennett's had made island history. "Tom, you don't think I hold *that* against you, do you?" She smiled at him. "We were all kids together. Let bygones be bygones."

After all, he was letting the men have bait — it didn't hurt to put him at his ease. But he still looked as if he wanted to get away in a hurry. "Well, thanks, Jo," he mumbled, and strode past her, pulling his cap down over his eyes.

Fowler came back to the counter. "Something I can do for you?"

Joanna laughed. "What ails Tom, anyway? . . . Let's see, I've got three lists here. I'm a regular shopping service this morning." Pleasantly, she met Fowler's eyes. But his usual genial manner was absent; he was looking past her at nothing, with an air of remote patience.

I feel so happy, she thought, *and everybody else has something on his mind.* She began to read the first list aloud. Silently Fowler moved to collect the groceries.

She borrowed the wheelbarrow outside the store to take the box of provisions down to the wharf, and met Nils coming up. Without a word he took the box under his arm.

"It's not very heavy," she said. "He didn't have half the things I wanted. Or else he'd mislaid them. Either he's running on a shoe string or it's time for him to reorder. How's the herring, Nils? Big enough for us to have some fried for dinner?"

"See for yourself," said Nils. It was then that she noticed the immobility of his face was tighter, harder than usual. It started a little pulse of warning in her brain. The brilliant day was suddenly shadowed, though the sun burned as bright. There was no warmth in it.

They came to the end of the wharf and looked down at the boat. Caleb sat on a firkin, smoking his pipe. In the bait and lobster boxes near his feet, there was herring. Possibly two bushels. There was no brimming cockpit-load of blue and silver fish.

"Is that all you could get?" she asked. "Is that all there was left?"

"There was plenty left," said Caleb, looking up from under his shaggy brows. Joanna turned to Nils.

"But it wasn't Tom who turned you down, was it? It couldn't have been. Tom was up in the store just now. . . . There he goes along the beach. He'd let you have all you wanted. He gives the orders, doesn't he?"

"He gives the orders, yes," said Nils. "And he gave them, before he went ashore. I don't know why, or how, or anything about it. . . . Let's get started back."

His lips came together hard on the last word, and he said nothing more. But that he was furious Joanna knew from the faint whitening around his mouth.

6

THAT NIGHT THEY TORCHED HERRING in Goose Cove, where the fish were schooling. By dusk you could hear the tiny, fast, whispering sound they made in the water; you could smell them, Joanna insisted.

With three men there could only be one team, and they took the biggest dory; Caleb and Jud rowing and Nils dipping. Joanna collected the rags for the torches while Nils made the torch basket and fastened it to the side of the dory. Then, as darkness shut down, they began to work. Marion Gray and Vinnie Caldwell came up to watch with Joanna from behind the house. Out of the wind there, they could see the whole cove. The torch made a mockery of the darkness, it threw its great ruddy flickering light far and wide.

Joanna loved to watch torching. The men's yellow oilclothes glistened like some burnished stuff in the firelight, and the oars gleamed strangely; the light shot its radiance down through the water so that the dory flew forward over a sea of translucent jade green. The movements of the men who rowed and the man who stood in the bow and swung the big net down, and brought it up full of living, squirming silver, held for her the charm of accomplished dancers, or the effortless flight of gulls.

But tonight the scene was robbed of some of its poetry by the knowledge that they shouldn't be out there working like this for a handful of bait. They had no big boats to fill with their catch, so even if the sea were alive with herring, at best they could only get enough for the next few days; none to salt down for the winter. Tom Robey should have supplied them, and he didn't. This sudden inexplicable refusal was like a stone wall forever hemming her in, whichever way she turned. *Why, why, why,* her mind kept saying, even while she laughed and talked with the women.

The herring were thick in the cove that night, and they worked until their shoulders ached from rowing and dipping. Then they came ashore, hauled the full dory up and covered it with a tarpaulin to keep the early-rising gulls away. Nils' peapod was full too. They had plenty for a few days.

Joanna had coffee ready, but Caleb and Jud said they preferred to wash the soot off their faces in their own kitchens, and then have their mug-up. Joanna was not sorry to be alone with Nils. He had been out working all day, and she hadn't had a chance to talk to him about Tom Robey.

She said nothing while he washed the smut from his face and ears, but poured his coffee for him, and set out man-sized sandwiches. As he came to the table she thought he masked his weariness and anger well. It was another way in which he reminded her of her father.

She poured out coffee for herself and sat down opposite him. "What do you think of it?" she asked him at last. "Of Tom, I mean."

"I don't know." Nils watched his coffee as he stirred it. "If he'd been on a drunk, I'd think he was ugly from a hangover, and took it out on us. But he's been seining right along."

"Did anyone over there say anything to you about it? Ralph Fowler, or anybody?"

"They'd already cleared away. Ralph had gone home from the car to dinner, and Tom was just going over the side to go ashore when our turn came. He kept on going, and I tried to argue Milt into giving us some. But he was under Tom's orders." Nils stopped stirring. His blue eyes looked reflectively into space, as if he were seeing the scene again. "Finally I told him to take his bait and go to hell with it."

"Nils, you didn't." Her eyes danced. "You don't talk like that!"

His mouth twitched. "I did this morning. Well, here we are. Caldwell's been here a week, and this hits us in the face. If he thinks it'll be like this all the time, he'll be going back to the feller that comes in a truck, drunk or not."

Joanna said fiercely, "To think I was nice to that ape in the store this morning!"

"Especially when he's seining out by Goose Cove Ledge, right now," said Nils dryly. Joanna jumped up and ran to the window that looked seaward. There, beyond the black loom of the point, were the swaying lights of the *Elsie R.*

"Right in our own backyard!" she exclaimed. "That's adding insult to injury! Why doesn't Brigport just move onto the Island and be done with it?"

Nils drank his coffee calmly. "Now, don't connect the traps up with this bait business. They'll move their pots out, now that they see we're getting populated again. But the seining's always been different. I could go torching in Brigport harbor, if I had a mind to."

"Yes, and if you could spare a few bushels of herring and somebody wanted to buy them, you'd sell 'em, wouldn't you? That's always been the way."

"Tom," said Nils, with the flicker of a smile, "is different."

"*Different!*" She came back to the table. "Nils, what can we do when anybody gets in our way like this? You three can't torch enough herring to put in your winter's supply—"

"I think," said Nils slowly, "that I'm going ashore on the mailboat tomorrow. I'll go down to Pruitt's Harbor and see what your brother Charles is doing. Might be he'd come out and catch us some — then we can have plenty of bait, fresh and to salt down for the winter, right here. No sense thinking about Tom any more."

Her eyes lit up at once. "Nils, that's wonderful. I know Charles will come!"

"Charles might have too much on his hands, or be out somewhere," Nils warned her. "So don't look for him. But I'll get somebody." He got up and carried his dishes to the sink. "I'm about ready for bed, I guess."

"Go ahead," said Joanna, "I'll be right along." He took a lamp from the shelf, lighted it, and went through the sitting room to the big room that had been Stephen's and Donna's. He walked silently in his moccasins. Joanna, alone in the kitchen, did the last tasks of the day; filled the teakettle, adjusted the dampers on the stove, washed the cups and saucers they had just used. She would have left them till morning but Nils, who got up first and made the coffee, hated to see dishes left over.

A strange man she was married to, she thought. A mild man, in appearance and speech. He had been mild, almost gentle, when he had said, "I'll get somebody." But she knew what lay behind those quiet words. Somebody would come twenty-five miles from the mainland to do what he had planned; he would not come home until he had made sure of it.

Bennett's Island would have its bait.

The morning was gray and still. A pearly light lay over the Island and in it nothing seemed to move. Caleb took Nils over to Brigport to board the mailboat, and when the sound of the engine had died away outside Eastern Harbor Point, Joanna walked home in a stillness so perfect she hated to break it with the slight sound of her feet. The water was motionless, the pale lovely gray of silk. The fading asters gleamed along the road, the birches at the edge of the alder swamp were very white; but their bare branches were a cloudy network of soft amethyst. The woods of both the Eastern End and the Western End looked black and impenetrable, somehow forbidding.

By the time she reached the house the dampness was striking through her shoes. But she paused on the doorstep to look across the pale mirror of Schoolhouse Cove toward her Uncle Nate's big house and barn. Perhaps one of her cousins, Jeff or Hugo, would come back some time and live there. But she doubted it. The Island had always been too small for them.

It gave her a lonely feeling, to think how long it had been since smoke drifted from those chimneys, and she went inside quickly, to her own companionable wood fire. A delicious sense of holiday came to her. She was all alone. She could do as she pleased all day, unless Vinnie or Marion came up to keep her company. Perhaps by afternoon she would welcome them. But now . . .

She went into the sitting room and took a book from the shelves. It was an old favorite; to read it as she drank a leisurely cup of coffee was like having an old friend drop in. Sometimes she wished she had an old friend, with whom she had shared her childhood on the Island. There had been Kristi Sorensen, Nils' sister, but she was married to one of Jud's boys and living in Massachusetts. They had five children and a car, and Kristi was fat now, and liked to go to the movies.

No, her book would have to do for company this morning. She drank her mid-morning coffee, had some coffee cake, and then moved to the rocking chair by the stove and went on reading. Her dinner would be warmed-up fish chowder. No work to that. Nils was on his way to the mainland to do something about the bait, Ellen was all right . . . Joanna read on, unconsciously relaxing after the tension of the last few days.

She was abruptly alert when she heard someone try the back door. She got up to open it. But it was not Vinnie or Marion. It was Randy Fowler.

"Hi," he said, and grinned at her. "Can I have a drink of water?"

Automatically she motioned him in. "Where did you come from?"

"From your wharf in the cove," he said easily. "Win stayed home this morning—toothache—and I was haulin' alone, so there was nobody to growl at me if I got thirsty and wanted to come ashore for a drink."

"There's the water pails," said Joanna.

"You wouldn't offer a guy coffee, would ye?"

"I wouldn't," said Joanna, "unless he was in distress, and you're not. What's the idea, Randy?"

His sparkling glance traveled around the kitchen while he thought up his answer. But she sensed what the idea was. Of course he knew

Nils was out; perhaps he'd been late starting to haul, and had seen Nils board the mailboat. It was something one of her own brothers might try. Smart-alec stuff.

"Well, I was haulin' a few off the point here, and just dropped in. Anything wrong with that?" He put his booted foot on the stove hearth and took out a cigarette. Over the match flame his eyes stayed on her, watching for her reaction.

"Nothing's wrong," she said casually. "Nothing at all. . . . Your traps must be pretty handy to shore, for you to drop in here without going out of your way."

"You ain't splittin' hairs, are ye?" He grinned audaciously into her eyes. "Not with all the lobsters there is to catch, and prices gettin' higher by the minute. Come this war the Democrats are headin' us for, prices'll shoot sky-high for any kind of sea food, and we'll all be in the gravy."

"In the trenches, in your case," she suggested.

"Sure, they'll haul me in by the neck," he agreed. "So why begrudge me a few lobsters? There's plenty to go 'round."

"Are you just as willing to share Brigport waters with us, Randy?"

Randy looked hurt. "Hell, Jo, I never came to get into no arguments! Chew, chew, chew — that's all I hear to home. You the chewin' kind, too?"

"I'm a woman of few words," Joanna said. "It won't do you any good to try to get me into a conversation. So you might as well run along."

"You mean that, Jo?" He was not smiling now. He had, oddly, the surprised look of a child who has stubbed his toe and fallen hard.

"I mean it," she said.

"Jo, you mad at me for comin' in like this?" he demanded.

"No, not mad. A little annoyed, maybe."

Randy's face had been flushed and excited when he came in. It was rather pale now. He looked at once miserably embarrassed and meek. But only for an instant. He took off a stove cover, dropped his cigarette into it, and with that gesture recovered his flippant poise.

"O.K., I'll go. As the old feller said, 'I been kicked out of better places.' " At the door he turned back and looked at her, the familiar twinkle in his bright brown eyes. "All right if I drop in when the old man's home?"

He shut the door before she could answer, and she was left alone to remember his impudence, and the peculiar unhappiness that had flashed over him for an instant.

I believe he's smitten, she thought suddenly, and laughed aloud. But it might not be so laughable after all. Boys like Randy didn't often take the first hint; they were persistent, if nothing else. They considered themselves invincible, and the more remote a woman was, the more determined they became. She didn't look forward to snubbing Randy, but if this morning's snub didn't work — she shrugged, and went into the sitting room to watch the *Janet F.* pull away from the wharf, her engine shattering the gray quiet of noon.

He'd turned the subject neatly when she had tried to speak about the pots, with his talk of high prices in sea food. He knew very well what she meant, and he hadn't intended to give her a satisfactory answer, admit his pots and the others from Brigport shouldn't be set so close to Bennett's. Maybe he'd take it better from Nils. It seemed to her that the Brigport men should be starting to shift their traps by now, if they intended to abide by the unwritten law. . . .

That nagged at her, like a hidden thorn in her finger. That, and the bait business. In her mind she reviewed that bright morning, and the indefinable smell of the store as she came into it, and Tom lounging against the counter, drinking pop . . . *I wish I'd turned up my nose at him,* she thought now.

She remembered Fowler's smooth baritone voice. "You want to do that every time, Tom. They'll soon catch on." And then Tom's answer. The fragment of conversation came back to her with a vividness that was disturbing.

They could have been talking about the bait, she thought now, her mind dashing at each possibility like a terrier after a rat. Suppose Tom had given his orders to Milt, and had come ashore, and told Fowler about it. . . . Suppose Fowler, with his suave, strong personality, had given the orders to Tom in the first place —

But why? Her fingers drummed on the window pane. The *Janet F.* was out of sight around the point by now. Why should they want to discourage the men from Bennett's like that? Both Fowlers — Ralph with his lobster-buying, Randolph with his store — profited by the trade from Bennett's. She couldn't understand it; she couldn't find any sensible angle from which to survey the problem.

She walked into the kitchen, and all her peace was gone for the day. Perhaps it was just her imagination; perhaps Fowler's remark and Tom's answer had no concern with bait, was about feeding cows, or settling arguments among the seining crew.

But there was one thing she did know; something was wrong. Some hostile force was working against the Island. Against her. She drove one clenched fist into the other palm and walked the length of the house and back again. She wanted Nils to come home. It seemed a year since he had left, and it was scarcely three hours.

But if he came home, if he should walk through the door this instant, what could she say to him? All the things that had been swirling through her head since Randy's visit? She saw with a too-sharp clarity the way his blue eyes would begin to crinkle at the corners, she almost heard his unhurried voice telling her not to be impatient and suspicious, she couldn't have everything come to perfection in the first month.

She wouldn't tell him, then. She would wait until she had something to tell him; something he must recognize as fact, and not her imaginings. So she must watch, and listen, and weigh everything carefully—

But if they're trying to go against me—if anybody is, she thought, *I'll know. And I'll stop them.*

7

Nils came home late the next afternoon. Charles didn't bring him, but Joanna recognized the boat that dropped anchor outside Goose Cove as a Pruitt's Harbor craft. She was the *Marianne,* belonging to two cousins who had been in friendly competition with Charles for a long time.

They set Nils ashore, and he came up to the house, quietly satisfied with his accomplishment. He held Joanna as if he had been gone a month.

"Charles was going down to Portland with a load of mackerel," he said, still keeping her in his arms when she would have got coffee for him. "He talked the Kimballs into coming out. Promised 'em all kinds of herring. Well, they'll get their fish, and we'll get our bait."

"Are there any in Goose Cove now?"

"I don't know. We may have to chase around some, but we'll do all right." He kissed her deeply and let her go. "How about some supper? We want to get started."

But they didn't have to go away from Goose Cove for their night's work. Caleb Caldwell brought his boat around from the harbor, with his and Jud's dories in tow, to be filled with herring. The women sat in the kitchen with Joanna, busy with patchwork and mending. Occasionally they went out beyond the dooryard to watch the seining operations; the boat was brightly lighted.

To Joanna the sound of the hoisting gear was a goodly one. She thought of the riches they were bailing out of the big net, and she liked to think of it. She went out once alone and stood on the back doorstep, listening. The men's voices were clear. She heard Harry Kimball yelling, "You down-east chowderhead!" It made her laugh. Harry was always calling his cousin that.

She turned to go back into the kitchen, when she heard another engine. She stood listening, her hand on the knob, trying to place the sound. It seemed to come from Schoolhouse Cove. She stepped off the doorstep and walked across the dooryard, feeling the wild growth of asters and goldenrod brush her knees as she passed the barn. Now she was on the point, an arm of blackness stretching out on the sea, under the stars. Matinicus Rock Light threw its beam toward her; between flashes she saw the shadow world of night. A few more steps and she reached a big granite rock, familiar to her even when she had to feel her way. She scrambled through a growth of bay and wild roses and stood up on the rock, and looked down into Schoolhouse Cove.

Another boat beat her steady way past the opposite point, running straight for Goose Cove Ledge. She knew beyond a doubt that it would be Tom Robey's boat, out for another evening's seining around the mouth of the cove. She chuckled. He'd be surprised to find another boat there; to see that Bennett's Island didn't need *his* herring. She wondered how he'd take it. She'd seen boats seining within fifty yards of each other, the men shouting back and forth in great good will. But Tom was jealous and bull-headed, he always had been.

He'll swear, she thought happily. *How he'll swear.* . . . She went back into the house, and Vinnie Caldwell said, "I declare, you look as if you'd been talkin' to a young man, your cheeks are that red."

"It's cold out!" Laughing, Joanna held her hands over the stove. "I've been watching them. Wasn't it good they could come!"

Marion rocked placidly. "Jud says them Robeys was always notional."

Notional was no word for it, Joanna thought. Around the Islands you weren't notional about selling your bait to one man and not to another unless you were ready to cause a lot of criticism and hard feeling. Hard feeling on the part of those whom you refused, criticism on the part of the others. At least, that was the way it always had been. . . . She wondered with dismay if the island ways had changed so much in five years; if Brigport had changed so much that Tom wouldn't be criticized for turning down the Bennett's Island men.

She didn't like the thought. Again the conviction rose strongly within her that there was something else behind Tom's behavior, something more powerful than a notional whim. She wanted to talk about it to someone; but how could she put it into words? It was like seeing something from the corner of your eye, only to have it disappear completely when you turned both eyes upon it. Yet, when you looked away, there it was, dancing like a shadow on the edge of vision. . . .

She rose automatically as someone knocked at the door. "I sh'd think those men would know better than to knock, by this time," Marion said.

Vinnie laughed. "Caleb's got one of his old-fashioned streaks on, I guess. Wonder what they've come ashore for."

Joanna opened the entry door to see Tom Robey standing there, massive in the lamplight that shone on his black rubber clothes. His jaw shot out and his brows drew down thickly over his eyes as he saw Joanna.

"Where's Nils?" he rumbled.

"Nils is out aboard the *Marianne,*" she said politely. "Any message for him?"

Beyond his shoulder, dimly lighted in the shadows, she saw Winslow Fowler's face, and spoke to him. His greeting was unintelligible, and then Tom's voice was rumbling out of his barrel chest again.

"Maybe *you* can tell me," he said, and his surliness brought the familiar fire of anger to her cheeks. Behind her Marion had stopped rocking. "Maybe *you* can tell me what's the idea of outsiders comin' here and seinin'. We've always kept the islands to ourselves, ain't we? Christ, with all the ocean they be, what's them Pruitt's Harbor bastards doin' in Goose Cove?"

"Seining herring, I hope," Joanna said serenely. "The waters are free, Tom. I know we always *have* kept the islands to ourselves, but we need bait over here. And when you don't have enough to sell us," — she smiled at him — "you can't blame us for getting it any way we can."

"By God," Tom said loudly, "we don't want strangers runnin' around here, cuttin' our pot-buoys off with their propellers! We ain't got our pots out jest for some seiner from inshore to snag off!"

Joanna said steadily, "The *Marianne's* got just as much right to go seining here as you have. And she's no more likely to cut off a pot buoy than your own boat."

"Come on back aboard, Tom," Winslow said suddenly. "You're jest wastin' time tryin' to argue with a woman."

Feet planted wide apart, impervious to Winslow's hand on his arm, Tom looked down at Joanna from under his sou-wester brim. But when he spoke it was not in his usual bullying roar. His voice was so quiet it startled her.

"Jest tell me one thing, Joanna. Did Nils go to Pruitt's Harbor and bring them sons o' bitches out here?"

"I don't see," said Joanna, her own voice as quiet, "that it's any of your business. You'd better go back aboard. Think of all the herring they're getting while you're standing here making a fool of yourself."

She shut the door in his face, gently and decisively, and walked back into the kitchen. Marion looked at her anxiously, and Vinnie's amber-colored eyes were wide.

"What an awful man!" she said. "Wasn't you scared?"

Joanna laughed. "Scared of Tom? I think he was more scared of me." Inwardly she was trembling with rage. That she should be bullied and sworn at in her own house, because there were none of her own men-folk there—and the insolence of him, declaring who should seine in *her* cove!

Marion said, "Tom always did roar. All them Robeys do. Make up in lungs what they ain't got in brains, I guess."

"You think he'll go alongside the *Marianne* and make trouble?" Vinnie asked.

Their eyes followed Joanna as she crossed the kitchen and went to stand at the window looking seaward. She heard their voices, but not their words, for her own words went on endlessly in her brain.

Her own words, and Tom's loud-mouthed, offensive ones. It didn't do to get so mad with him, because he didn't know any better. But she couldn't help it. She'd been furious about the bait, she was more than furious now. He'd come ashore to bluster and bully. He thought he had a right to swear at her and Nils—had he expected they'd go meekly without bait because he wouldn't give them any?

But he hadn't blustered and bullied the whole time. She remembered, with a renewal of the odd feeling she'd known at the time, the sudden quieting of his voice on the last question. There'd been something strange and unnatural about it; like the sudden flat hush that comes sometimes in the middle of a storm and is dreaded, rather than appreciated, because it means the wind will crash down with new strength.

That didn't sound like Tom, she thought now, staring out at the darkness beyond the window. *It wasn't Tom.* She was as positive at that instant as she'd ever been about anything in her whole life. Tom's voice, but not his words; for the space of a few minutes, Tom had been an actor speaking some other man's lines. *But whose lines?*

She didn't hear the women's voices behind her, she felt her nerves tightening up into a knot of almost unbearable suspense. In a moment now she would have it . . . here was the shadow dancing on the edge of her consciousness again—

"Who was that with him?" Marion Gray asked suddenly, and Joanna answered her silently. *Winslow Fowler.* He had stood behind Tom's shoulder, not speaking. Winslow Fowler. The shadow was a shadow no longer, and again the tiny scene, the brief exchange of dialogue she had heard in the store was there in her mind. Not Winslow, but his father, Randolph; and Tom Robey.

Now she knew. Now she did not tell herself it was a discussion about feeding cows, or stopping arguments among the seining crew. She knew the truth of that instant, and she would never believe any other explanation of it. It all fitted together so perfectly that she could not doubt her own logic. Only the *why* remained; why Randolph didn't want Tom to let the Bennett's men have bait; why Randolph had put it in Tom's mind to come ashore tonight and ask that question. . . . She was sure the bullying was Tom's own idea. Harmless, profane noise. But not his last question. . . .

She felt cold suddenly. What if Nils *did* ask the *Marianne* to come out? What did they expect to make of it? She wished that Nils would come ashore soon so she could talk it over with him.

They talked it over, late that night, long after the others had gone home and the seiner was heading back to Pruitt's Harbor. At least they talked over Tom's visit. When Joanna tried to form the words to tell him about Randolph and Tom in the store, they all sounded weak and futile, and she realized again that she had so painfully little to tell, to convince Nils as she was convinced, heart and soul.

Nils chuckled about Tom. "So he swore, did he? Well, let him swear. If he doesn't want the *Marianne* here, let him give us some bait."

"He wanted to know if you brought the *Marianne* out here," she pointed out. They were in bed, and Nils' arm tightened around her.

"I'm dog-tired, but I feel good," he said. "What did you tell Tom?"

"That it was none of his business. But Nils, you know he sounded funny when he asked me . . . not like Tom, I mean. Too quiet."

"He'd probably run out of wind about that time." Nils laid his cheek against her hair. "He'd been drinking today, I guess. Sounds like it."

Nils was tired, his body was heavy with contented weariness, but Joanna felt strung-up and alert. "But what could he *do* if he wanted to keep you from bringing another seiner here?" she insisted.

"Do? Oh, make a hell of a lot more noise and wave his arms around. . . . What did you think he could do? Poor old Tom."

But it's not Tom alone, she thought with something very like agony. *Not Tom alone. And how am I going to make you see it?*

8

WITH THE BAIT IN, the men could put their minds to other things, and by the first of November the *Donna* was overboard. In her new white paint, her name in dazzling black on either side of her lovely bow, her engine installed, she rode at her mooring in the harbor. Joanna could see her from the house. When the wind was from the west'ard, and swung her around so that her stern-lettering showed, Joanna could read it with the field glasses, and the sight of those crisp black letters was like a defiant banner unfurled to the wind:

DONNA

BENNETT'S ISLAND

Yes, there was her name, and her home port's name; the first boat in five years to carry the Island's name. As Nils went about his business, hauling his traps or slipping into Brigport Harbor to sell his lobsters and get his mail and groceries, the name was there for all the world to see, and let Brigport know that Bennett's Island was alive again. That was how Joanna thought about it; for her conviction was growing that Brigport didn't *want* to see Bennett's alive again.

It was a secret conviction, because there was nothing tangible to base it on, and Nils was like Joanna's father, Stephen. He didn't hold with wildcat suspicions, he asked for proof, he didn't look for evil until it confronted him.

He implied that the bait episode was just another display of the Robey "queer streak." Like Marion Gray, he thought the Robeys were notional. Moreover, the Brigport fishermen were shifting their traps outward. Nils came home almost daily with an account of seeing them hauling up pots and taking a boatload out toward Bantam, or in the other direction, toward Pirate Island, or out around the Island toward the Rock. The Fowler boys, the Merrills, the other Robeys — Tom's cousins — and a scattering of men who didn't belong to any· one of the three principal families on Brigport — they were all moving into deeper water. There were all in all some fifteen fishermen from Brigport, not counting the old men who puttered around with their handful of pots and two-cycle engines, who didn't need to work but couldn't give it up because it was their lifeblood.

There were tranquil and lovely days in November, but there were gray and blustery ones too. On such a day, when it was too rough to haul, Nils took the *Donna* to Brigport, with Caleb and Jud aboard, to meet the mailboat, put in groceries, and bring Ellen and Joey home for the weekend.

Joanna stood at the window to watch the *Donna* plunge through the tide rip at the harbor mouth. The water was slate gray under a dark sky, the wave crests very white. The trees on the harbor point looked black, and Joanna was grateful for the smoke blowing from the Caldwells' chimney, and the white paint she'd put on the house. It looked snug and friendly on the bleak day.

She turned from the window, so as not to watch the *Donna* out of sight. If she hadn't been doing some special baking in Ellen's honor, she would have wanted to go with them this morning. Spray would be flying over the bow and the gulls would be swooping low into the glistening dark valleys between the waves, and Tenpound would be lashed with exploding white water this morning.

She had a special sympathy for anyone who'd come out to Brigport on the *Aurora B.* today. The *Aurora* rolled and pitched frightfully, and two hours could stretch to two years if you were down in the after cabin with the slide pulled over to keep out the water that constantly washed the narrow decks. It was cold and miserable even for a good sailor.

But the *Donna* . . . She smiled absently at the devil's food cake cooling on its rack, inspected the beans in the oven. *There* was a boat. She'd never loved any other boat so well, unless it was the *White Lady*. Her brother Owen had designed and built the *White Lady* himself in the boatshop long since burned down. She wondered about the *White Lady* now. Somebody over in Pleasant Point had her. Owen had dreamed of her for all his life, until he could bring her into being; and then he had walked away from her without a backward glance.

Joanna could understand how one could part with people as Owen had parted from his family; she could almost understand how he could leave the Island. It had mocked him and suffocated him. But a boat . . .

She shook her head, and her brown hands were strong and swift, kneading yeast dough. Maybe it had been dreams Owen had lived for; and when the dream came true, was solid timber and paint under his touch, it was not in his system any more, and he felt an emptiness, because he had lived with the dream for so long.

Maybe he had used up all the dreams the Island could offer him, so he had gone looking for more. She hoped with all her heart that he had found them. She would never know; for it was in her blood, the conviction that she would never see him again.

The morning went swiftly and she was busy with dinner when she saw the *Donna* come into the harbor again, as unflurried and serene as the real Donna for whom the boat had been named. Mother of Joanna and the five boys, wife of Stephen, in the days of her family's youth she had been like a slender tree beset by tumultuous winds; yet a deep-rooted tree, who knew how to stand through the storms without giving way. She was the same today, keeping house for her bachelor son Philip, in Pruitt's Harbor, living close to her eldest son Charles and the robust, strong-willed brood that swirled around their grandmother like a whirlpool. They could never tarnish her shining peace, but sometimes they caught and carried a little of it away with them.

Time to stop dreaming. Ellen and Nils would be ready for fish and potatoes and pork scraps, and she'd fixed enough so they could have fish hash for breakfast Sunday morning. . . .

Ellen liked school, she liked Mrs. Robey and Whit, she was learning how to sew for Phoebe, and none of the big children in the school teased her or pulled her pigtails; if they did, Joey would fix them, she assured her mother. Meanwhile Joey spent every possible hour in Cap'n Merrill's boatshop, and talked Vinnie and Caleb deaf every weekend. He was quite definite that he was going to be a boat builder.

So everything was going all right, at least for the present. She began to set the table.

Ellen came in first. Her plaid raincoat flying open, her scarlet hood slipping back on her smooth fair head, blue eyes aglisten and cheeks almost as scarlet as her hood, she burst in and ran across the kitchen to Joanna.

"Hi, Mother!" Her laughter pealed out. She hugged Joanna tightly and Joanna hugged her back, at the same time wondering at her daughter's exuberance. Usually she came in so quietly, with all her happiness contained in her gravely delighted smile.

"Did you have a rough trip, darling?"

Ellen was pulling off her hood. Her pigtails fairly bounced. "Yes, and I stayed out all the way, and was it fun!" Off came the raincoat. Ellen seemed possessed of an excitement bigger than her body, it burst out of her in little chuckles, in the blue blaze of her eyes, in her dancing feet and flying fingers. "Mother, I brought you a surprise."

"You're the surprise girl, aren't you? Always something new. Shall I guess?"

"You can't ever guess!" said Ellen triumphantly. Her merry brown oxfords carried her toward the entry door. "And anyway, I can't wait for you to guess, because it'd take you 'bout all day, and then you wouldn't hit it! . . . Close your eyes."

Obediently Joanna set down the plates she was carrying, shut her eyes, and stood quite still in the middle of the kitchen. She heard Ellen's breathless chuckles, and the opening of the entry door; a faint creaking of the board that always creaked, and then a presence near her; the mingled fragrances of soft leather and tobacco smoke and the cold November air. An unbearable excitement possessed her; it was all she could do to wait for Ellen's ecstatic shriek. "*Now* you can look!"

Joanna looked, and saw her brother Stevie standing before her, smiling. It had been only a little while since he had kissed her at her wedding; yet the sight of his thin brown face and warm black eyes smiling from behind the thick lashes, in the kitchen of the house where he had grown up, was enough to send a rush of tears into her eyes.

She caught him by his broad Bennett shoulders and hugged him hard, and he hugged her back. "Gosh, Jo, how are you?" he said in the identical way he had always said it.

"Stevie, I'm fine. . . . You look fine, too, only thin. . . ." She shook him a little, tenderly. "I don't want to ask you how long you're staying, but I want to know how long I can count on."

"Well—" Stevie's mouth tucked up at the corner in the funny mischievous way it had. "You may get damn' sick of me before I leave, Jo. You see, Mark and I don't go line-trawlin' any more."

"Stevie, are you going to *stay?*" She sobered quickly. "What's Mark doing? You two haven't had a fight, have you?"

"Mark's here," said Stevie. He nodded toward the window. "There he comes now. With his wife. And Nils."

"Isn't this a *good* surprise?" Ellen was demanding, and Joanna, with Stevie's words echoing in her head, smiled at her and said, "The best in the world, darling. . . . Let's get the table set for them all."

Stevie hung up his jacket and washed at the sink, combed his black hair before the old mirror, as if time had gone backward and he had never been away. "Stevie, tell me about Mark's wife," she commanded. "Quick. Before they get here. When did they get married? Mother's last letter didn't mention it."

"It was only last week," Stevie said. "Kind of sudden. Mark didn't know her for long. She's a good kid, about twenty. Worked in the library at Port George. She's a Finn. Her name's Helmi."

There was no time for anything more, and no time for Joanna to contemplate the facts, because the others were coming in by then. Mark, twenty-eight, older and handsomer and noisier than Stevie, hugged Joanna fiercely. He was laughing and excited, his brown cheeks reddened by the cold wind, his black hair tumbling over his forehead, his voice vibrant and strong.

"Darlin' mine, I want you to meet my other darlin'!" he proclaimed, and with one arm still tightly around Joanna, he reached out the other to grip the shoulder of the tall girl who stood quietly beside Nils. She came forward slowly at his command, without a word or a smile. She was very blonde, blonder even than Nils; the thick hair that fell to the shoulders of her trench coat was silvery, with a glint of pale gold in the shadows of its faint wave. It was the most beautiful hair Joanna had ever seen.

"Hello, Helmi," she said, and put out her hand.

The girl looked at her. Her apple green scarf and beret turned her eyes green too, and they saw Joanna with a cool and measuring glance. She was pale—her skin had an almost translucent pallor beside the healthy bronze of the others; in it her strange eyes and the clear, brilliant lipstick on her mouth were startling.

Joanna felt the girl's hand touch hers. "Hello," Helmi murmured. Joanna thought, *She doesn't trust anybody. Even Mark.* She stood beside Mark as if she didn't feel his hand on her shoulder. Her tall slim body was straight and as rigid as stone.

The room seemed suddenly chilly. Nils, standing beside the bags, was lighting his pipe. Stevie stood with one foot up on the stove hearth, watching her and Helmi and Mark. She couldn't read his face. Mark was still proudly smiling.

"We've come to stay," Mark said. "I've seen Charles. We can move into his place."

"Way down there?" said Joanna. "That's lonely." She smiled at Helmi, whose mouth curved only a little in response.

"We want to be lonely," said Mark, and laughed. He was very happy.

The rest of the day went by somehow. It was a very odd day for Joanna. The wind threw itself hard against the house, and keened at the corners of the eaves like a lost soul, and the gulls were forever circling against the scudding masses of blue-black cloud. Ellen busied herself at the kitchen table with her paper dolls, and crayons and paper to make new dresses for them. The men talked, sitting around the kitchen stove; Nils told them about the Island, what had been done since Jud and Caleb came, and they added their plans to his. Stevie was quietly happy at being home again. Mark was loudly happy. Not only had he come home, but he'd brought a wife to show to the family, and they'd never seen hair like that before!

Joanna saw his eyes follow Helmi, whenever the girl was in the room. He didn't seem to mind her immobility; perhaps it was the thing that had attracted him to her. . . . At first, Joanna tried to penetrate it, to make Helmi feel welcome and at home. They made the beds together, and since time immemorial women have always exchanged confidences on opposite sides of quilts. But Helmi said nothing at all, and for once the charm which Joanna could use so well had come up against a stone wall. After a while she stopped trying. Perhaps it was just as well that Mark was going to live way down at the other end of the Island, she thought dryly, and went into the kitchen to listen to the men's conversation.

"We're goin' to be in this war," Mark was saying, through the tobacco smoke. "In it up to our necks. I'll be fightin' in it. We all will. But in the meantime, God and the draft board willin', I figure on catchin' a hell of a lot of lobsters and makin a hell of a lot of money."

"You think the price is going up, too?" asked Nils.

"Of course it's goin' up! Sky-high. You fellers came back to old Bennett's just in time, and you started somethin'." He leaned back in his chair, blew out a beautiful smoke ring, and laughed. "I'll bet Brigport was some goweled to have men start fishin' out of here right now, when both Randolph and Ralph Fowler stood to make a heap of money out of our waters!"

"Why?" demanded Stevie. "We have to do our buyin' and our sellin' over there, don't we? Maybe the fishermen don't think much of havin' to move out, but the Fowlers stand to make more money, with a good crowd out here."

Mark roared. "How long do you think we're goin' to cart our lobsters over there and sell 'em to that goddamned Ralph? In another year we'll have our own buyer, right here. And a store, too. And won't that physic the Fowlers?" He chuckled. "Goddam foreigners!"

Nils was smiling, and Joanna caught his eye and winked to show her appreciation of the way he was taking Mark's proprietary air. *We Bennetts do move in,* she thought ruefully. *Move in and take over. . . .* And then she was sitting up straight in her chair, with feathers of cold astonishment brushing her backbone, and her hands gripped tight in her lap lest they show her excitement.

But that was it! That was the whole reason, the thing she'd been trying to catch and put her finger on, and couldn't. Oh, how could she be so stupid? Mark had been here less than four hours, and he had put it into words for her. Of course he didn't know that was what he had done. He had just been wondering aloud, and laughing. To Mark and the others it was practically an accomplished fact—the store, the gasoline, the buyer, the money from Bennett's Island lobsters going into Bennett's Island pockets.

But to Joanna, there was something else to be reckoned with. Didn't they realize that if Brigport didn't want that to happen, Brigport could fight? Perhaps not all of Brigport — not the old-timers, the ground-keepers like Cap'n Merrill and Whit Robey and the others. But what about the Fowlers? Surely they remembered what their father had told them of the way the Fowler brothers had come to Brigport thirty-five years ago; and without the Brigport people quite knowing how it happened, except for those immediately concerned, it seemed that Randolph Fowler was running the store there instead of Tim Merrill; and Ralph Fowler had a car out in the harbor, across from Gil Marsh's, and was buying lobsters. Little by little Gil stopped buying. Those who were loyal to him were too few. Then Randolph received the postmaster's appointment — still without anyone's realizing quite how he managed it.

Ralph was a good-hearted chap who was not above handing out a stiff drink when a man came in to the car on a cold wet day, and Randolph was always willing to sing a solo in church, and he contributed lavishly to buying the new organ. So all at once the Fowlers were solid citizens.

But there were a few who still called them foreigners. . . . who had things to remember about the Fowlers that everybody didn't know.

I still call them foreigners, Joanna said in her mind. *But foreigners or natives, they'll keep their hands off Bennett's Island.*

She wanted to tell Nils when they went to bed that night. It burned on her lips, the thing she wanted to say. Yet, when at last everyone had settled down for the night and she and Nils were alone in their downstairs bedroom, close together for warmth and because Nils liked to go to sleep with her in his arms, she couldn't tell him. *Not yet.* There was not enough to go on for Nils' logical Swedish mind.

Everything looked all right now. Peaceful. She would wait till the Fowlers showed their hand and made even Nils suspicious. Resolutely she put the matter out of her mind and said, "What do you think of Mark's wife?"

"I don't know," said Nils truthfully. "Now you've got two Scandinavians in the family. How about it ?"

"I don't know either," murmured Joanna. "I like my Scandinavian, but I can't make up my mind about Helmi. Either she's very deep—"

"Or dumb," finished Nils. His arm tightened around Joanna. His breathing was strong and peaceful, and his cheek lay against her hair. "Be a family disgrace if Mark married a moron, huh?"

Joanna chuckled against Nils' chest. "She's got beautiful hair, anyway. No, I guess she's not a moron. Just reserved. Tomorrow I'll get Stevie to tell me more about her."

Nils' breathing sounded as if he was almost asleep. She lay there in silence, listening to it, and the wind trying to shake the house, the muted thunder of surf on the ledges. The voice of the Island. It was all around her. *Forever and ever, Amen,* she thought, like a prayer, and began to fall asleep.

9

MARK WANTED TO MOVE DOWN to the Eastern End right away. Joanna had her doubts about putting a young girl down there for her first winter on the Island. The wind blew constantly across the narrow ridges of meadowland, even in summer; in November it howled. But apparently they had made up their minds, so she did the best she could to help them make the small gray house homelike with their limited amount of furniture. Helmi was a good housekeeper, like most of the Finnish girls Joanna had known, and Finns weren't afraid of work or loneliness.

Stevie had his old room back, in the Bennett homestead. He'd planned to live by himself in one of the old camps on the beach, but Joanna and Nils wouldn't hear of it. He went down to the Eastern End in the daytime to help Mark build pots; they would work together this winter, like Jud and Caleb, until a boat for sale turned up somewhere and Stevie could be independent.

"That's goin' to be a funny feelin'," he told Joanna. "We worked together for so long. But I guess it's time we split up. Mark's a family man now."

He had come in at dusk from his work at the Eastern End, and Nils hadn't yet come back from Brigport. Joanna welcomed the chance to be alone with Stevie for a few minutes. She had always been close to her youngest brother, and there were things she wanted to ask him.

"Tell me about Helmi," she said now. "Is she always like that? Stony-faced? Or is she one of these fire and ice people you read about?"

Stevie grinned. "You'd have to ask Mark that. How should I know? . . . I figure it's just as well she doesn't pay much attention to other folks."

Joanna gave him a curious look. He was slouched deep in the old rocker, his long legs thrust out before him, his eyes smiling absently at the ceiling.

"What do you mean by that?" she asked him.

"Well, you ought to know how some of these Bennetts are. God help their wives. Mark's wife is his woman, and that's all there is to it. . . . What do you suppose he had to whisk her out here for, and then down to the Eastern End where he hopes to God nobody will even come and call?"

"Sounds like jealousy to me," said Joanna, sounding less perturbed than she felt. What new tangle was now being dropped into her lap?

"He's so jealous he isn't hardly fit to live with," said Stevie. "Wonder to me he doesn't start makin' her lock all the doors when he goes out to haul, so no one'll stop in for a drink of water. That poor girl's got one hell of a life ahead of her, married to our sweet brother!"

He sounded unusually vehement—for Stevie—and Joanna gave him a quick sidewise glance. He caught it and grinned. "Well, you know him as well as I do. Maybe by the time he's Charles' age, he'll quiet down. . . . But at that I guess she figures it's a better prospect than livin' at home with a yellow million relatives."

"She's in love with Mark, isn't she? You sound as if she married him to get away from home."

Stevie blew a cloud of pale blue smoke toward the ceiling. "Oh, I guess she's in love with him all right. If she isn't, it's not Mark's fault. He set out to do it, first time we met her."

Joanna imagined the meeting, the two tall dark boys who took every girl's eye, the tall blonde girl listening so impassively to their patter. . . . Or had she been impassive? It was hard to imagine her being anything else but remote. "What sort of people does she have?" she demanded.

"Decent, respectable, hard-working Finns. *And* Lutherans." He grinned at her. "Remember Nils' grandfather — old Gunnar? Well that's it. Let me tell you, sis, Mark hasn't taken a drink since he met Helmi. Or played poker."

"Is he suffering?" asked Joanna dryly.

"He's too much in love. But wait till the new wears off and Mark starts bein' himself again. She'll tell him."

"I'm glad somebody can tell a Bennett something," said Joanna.

Stevie grinned. "Hell, can't Nils tell you anything? No, I'll bet he can't. Nobody ever could."

Joanna was angry with herself for flushing. No, she'd never been meek, but why be embarrassed because her baby brother wanted to twit her about it? She got up and began to work busily around the kitchen, lighting another lamp to send away the shadows and shine down across the meadow when Nils came into the harbor. Stevie lit a fresh cigarette and began to talk about lobstering.

To begin all over again, with winter so near, held no fears for him and Mark. The long hours on the water, the coming home after dark, the flying spray, so icy it burned the skin before it numbed it, the vapor storms that froze the flesh, the sliding hills of cold green water — they took it in their stride, they were like gulls, born to it, bred in it.

Joanna hoped Helmi wasn't the anxious sort. Mrs. Caldwell, in spite of her quick, nervous movements, didn't seem to be a worrier. Marion had faith in Jud's sea-sense, as Joanna had faith in Nils and the *Donna*. The young man Matthew Fennell had written that he would be there definitely in the spring. He would like to come now, and his wife was game, but his grandmother was very old, and the Island was a long way from a doctor.

Joanna wondered about young Mrs. Fennell, who was game. Game was what you had to be, if you were an Island woman; you had to learn not to worry, even while fear nagged at you like chronic pain, and you had to gird yourself at every waking to the possibility that something might happen *today;* some boat not come in at dusk, some man not walk up the path to his home with his empty dinner bucket. And that man might be yours.

Placed as it was, the Bennett house heard the slightest whisper of wind, but you couldn't hear the engines in the harbor when the night breeze was rising from the sea. Nils kept the *Donna* in the harbor now, and Joanna wouldn't know he was back until he walked into the house.

So suddenly there he was, unzipping his heavy leather jacket, hanging up his blue plaid cap, warming his hands over the stove, hardly speaking; yet in his eyes, very blue in his ruddy face, there was his appreciation of his home and of Joanna greeting him from the dresser. When he came in and Stevie was already there, he never touched Joanna, for to Nils his love for her was an intensely private thing. But his eyes and his smile signaled her across the room, and then he began to talk to Stevie.

"When are you going to get those pots out? Lobsters went up three cents today, and they'll be up more tomorrow."

"God Almighty, man, we've built seventy in three days. If we can get some bait, we can set those before long — soon as we get them headed. Think we'll get much in 'em, or — "

"Well, no new trap fishes like an old one," said Nils mildly, "but you can make a living, I guess. That same seventy'll serve you better come spring, though."

"If we don't have a couple of willie-waws to knock 'em all to hell," said Stevie cheerfully. "Oh well, we'll have plenty more built. We've got to order some laths from Ralph Fowler pretty soon, I guess."

"Ralph was a little sticky today," Nils said.

"Why?" Joanna asked quickly, pausing at the stove.

Nils shrugged. "I don't know. Just ugly. . . . Time to wash up, isn't it?" He went to the sink and washed, then ran his pocket comb through his hair before he came to the table. Even at the end of a long day, which had begun before daylight, he looked freshly scrubbed and at peace with the world.

Joanna halted to glance over the box of groceries before she joined the men at the table. "How was Brother Randolph? Did he have anything more in the store this time than he did the other day?"

"Not much more. He said the meat was all gone an hour after the mailboat had brought it."

"Next year we'd better have a pig and a lamb," Joanna said.

"Though it'll break Ellen's heart when we slaughter them. Mine too, probably. . . . Anyone else around the store?"

"Randy and Winslow were hanging around. Randy said he'd be over some night soon."

"He'd better wait for an invitation, hadn't he?"

"Randy's not a bad kid," Nils said.

"You'd say the devil himself wasn't bad, just a mite difficult," said Joanna tartly. "Randy's a spoiled brat. Winslow's worse. Nils, I don't like any of the Fowlers." She wanted badly to tell him what she thought about the Fowlers, and as he stirred his coffee serenely, she felt a painful surge of irritation. If he were like any other man, he'd have been annoyed by Ralph's ugliness at the car, and by Randolph's never having half the things on the list, or being just out of them. Then she could make good use of his annoyance. But no, as far as he was concerned all was right with the world.

"You never liked anybody on Brigport much, Jo," Stevie said. "What's the matter with the Fowlers? You ought to be sorry for 'em. Look at all the money they've been makin' off these grounds, and now *we're* goin' to make it instead. . . . Nils, when are you goin' to start buyin' lobsters?"

"Why me?" said Nils.

"Why not you? You're the one to do it."

"Nils isn't any kind of a business man," said Joanna, laughing. "Now, that's a job I'd like to have."

"Sure," said Stevie. "Anything to keep you away from the dishpan and the stove all day. You haven't changed a mite, Jo."

"That's the second poke you've taken at me tonight, Stephen Bennett," she accused him. She was laughing, but under the laughter she thought in amazement, *What's the matter with me?* For she was slightly cross with Stevie. It was almost as if he were implying that she took too much on herself. As if she could ever take too much on herself where the Island was concerned!

Jud came in just as they were finishing. While Joanna cleared the table, he had a cup of coffee with the men and discussed the day's haul. He was doing all right on the Western Ground, he said. How was it with Nils at the Ripper?

"Mark and I, we're plannin' on droppin' a few at the Coombs Spot, if nobody's lugged it off," said Stevie.

"I wouldn't be surprised if it warn't there when you went to look for it," said Jud darkly. "Some of them Brigport bastards'd tow Ten-pound home if they was to find it adrift."

"Well, that would save Whit Robey a trip when it came time to shear his sheep," said Nils. "What's the matter, Jud? You found some Brigport buoys mixed up with yours?"

Jud snorted, and set his stubbled jaw. "Huh! You think they're goin' to take any chance o' gettin' fouled in my warps and losin' their own? Not them! They'd rather hand out a lot of cheap talk, so a man don't even feel like goin' over there to sell his lobsters."

"Somebody on the prod?" said Stevie. "Who's been ridin' you, Jud?"

Jud turned to Nils. "How was Ralph when you was over there, late this afternoon?"

"Sticky. Why?"

"*Why?* I'll tell ye." Jud's round face turned deep red, as if his memories were bringing his rage to the boiling point. "Caleb and me, we was over there just after Ralph comes out to the car—he'd been home for his dinner. A nice hot dinner by the kitchen stove, and then he comes out to the car, and he's got a good fire goin', and a bottle of whiskey on the shelf to keep his stomach clear of germs, and warm besides—" Jud took a deep breath. "Well, Caleb and me, we been out since daylight, and we was pretty cold and hungry and it was beginnin' to air up some, so we knew how that boat of Caleb's would slat around when we came out of the Gut. So we come alongside the car, and there's a crowd hangin' around—them smart-alec nephews of his, and a couple of Robeys, and some fellers old enough to know better."

Jud was alarmingly red. Joanna watched him in worried fascination. Stevie looked sympathetic, with only a dark twinkle in his eyes. Nils listened meditatively, as if he were seeing the scene Jud painted.

"Well, d'ye think Ralph would offer *us* a drink? D'ye think he'd hold out that bottle and say, 'Here, boys, it's goddamned cold and wet out today, and here's something to revive your droopin' spirits. Go on, have another drink, you can't fly on one wing.' *No!* He was laughin' and jokin' one minute and then he comes out and looks at us like we was so much guts an' gurry. Caleb swings the boxes over the side, and Ralph—" Here Jud took a long breath and a gulp of coffee. "And Ralph, he waits till some of 'em come out of the shed, and nobody's talkin' for a minute, and then he gets that mean sly look on him and says, 'Jud, I hope you been careful about not gettin' any short lobsters in these boxes. I'm used to honest fishermen,' he says, 'and I got more to do than cull every haul that comes to this car.' He says that to *me*, that never had a short lobster in all the hauls I ever made since I started lobsterin'!'"

Joanna could sense his shock and indignation. "And with everybody standing around," she prompted. "What happened then?"

"One of them Brigport loud-mouths has to laugh, of course. I said, 'Listen here, Ralph Fowler, how many shorts you ever weighed back out of any hauls I ever brought in?' Well, he was just as smooth and mealy-mouthed as a man could be and live. 'No call for you to get mad, Jud, if you ain't got nothin' to hide. I'm just remindin' ye.' "

Jud dragged out his red and white bandanna and wiped his glistening face. "I was jest liftin' a tub to the washboards, and I like to threw the whole business straight in his face. I'm tellin' ye, right then and there I didn't care if I never sold a lobster to Ralph Fowler. But half the haul was Caleb's, so I never said nothin' more." On the edge of the table his thick knotted brown hand, curved as a fisherman's hand is always curved, made a fist. "Ralph Fowler wants to be careful—goddamned careful—what he says to me in the future. Or else he's likely to feel some day like he's in hell with no claws."

When he finished there was a silence in the kitchen, except for his quick harsh breathing. Stevie said softly, "He's a son of a bitch." Joanna, her hands clenched under the table, glanced at Nils. His face said nothing at all as he pushed back his chair and went over to the window looking out at the dark sea and the frosty burning of the stars above it. He sat down, picked up a filled traphead needle from the window sill, and began to work on a half-finished head which dangled from the hook. Jud's eyes followed him, fastened on the back of Nils' fair head, his strong clean-cut neck and square shoulders, as if there were no one else in the room.

"What do you think about it, Nils?" he asked.

"Looks like Ralph picked you out to take over because you've got a quick temper, and he knew he could gowel you," said Nils without turning around. "How was it in the store?"

"And that's somethin' else!" said Jud with renewed vigor. "I didn't want much in the store, but Caleb, he wanted some fresh meat, and I told him the mailboat most always brings some. So he asked Randolph for it, and Randolph, lookin' like a gentleman with his white shirt and his necktie, he smiles, and says he's sorry, but it's all gone already. Caleb, he's got no reason to doubt him, so we went across to look at the candy counter, in case they was somethin' Marion and Vinnie'd like, and some old hen floats in there — Sophie Dyer, I think 'twas — and wants some meat. . . ." Jud's faded eyes were suffused redly with his wrath. "Does he tell *her* he's all out of it? No, he starts namin' off all the different kinds he's got! I tried to make Caleb go over and show Randolph up, but Caleb, he's too proud. 'If my money ain't good enough for him,' he says, 'he don't need to take it.' "

"Caleb must have a funny idea of Islanders," said Nils. "Brigport Islanders. First Tom with the bait, and then this. . . ."

"What do ye think makes 'em act like this?" said Jud insistently.

"They've got a mad to get over. They will. Give 'em time." Nils left off his knitting and came back to the table. He put his hand on Jud's shoulder.

"Jud, you going to lose any sleep over it tonight?"

Jud shook his head slowly. "I figure not to. But God A'mighty, I never knew anybody'd get mad just because some of us came home!"

Joanna, looking at his stocky, dejected shoulders, and grizzled head, the creases of angry bewilderment across his forehead, opened her mouth to speak, and then shut it again. What she had to say to Nils she could say when they were alone.

10

AFTER JUD HAD GONE, Stevie went to the woodshed to split some kindling for the morning. Nils came over to the sink where Joanna was wiping the last of the dishes, and she felt his fingers close gently on her elbow.

"What are you thinking?" he said.

"You ought to know," she answered. She felt the familiar crusading excitement rising in her. It was a good feeling. She liked it. It was time for action, to do battle, to come out of it untouched and victorious. Nils' glance moved over her vivid face, his fingers tightened on her arm.

They heard Stevie whistling as he came through the woodshed. Nils' fingers moved away; he smiled faintly, and went back to his trapheads.

"Time to crawl under the kelp," Stevie said. "If Mark had his way, we'd be buildin' pots at three in the morning, instead of five." He stood in the middle of the kitchen, very tall, and narrower in build than most of the Bennetts, and stretched with slow delight. "Dunno why I sleep so good here. Unless it's because I'm home."

"That's it," said Joanna, and Stevie dropped his arm around her shoulders. "For the last ten years," she said, "I've been surprised because you're taller than I am. Once I could spank you."

"With a kind of a struggle," said Stevie. He squeezed her shoulders briefly. "But I wouldn't put it past you to try it again, if you thought I needed it."

"I'm going to take a lath to a lot of people around here," said Joanna. "And very soon, too."

"You mean the Fowlers?" He released her shoulders and went

over to sit on the window sill where Nils was knitting trapheads. His thin dark face was alert and eager. "Hey, that was a funny way for them to act over there, Nils. What do you make of it? Why pick on Jud?"

Joanna stood behind Nils' chair, her hands tense on the back of it. "Because Jud would get mad," she said. "If he'd said that to Nils, Nils wouldn't even bother to repeat it. They'll find a different way to bother Nils."

"Hey, what are you driving at?" demanded Stevie. He knew that look of hers: lifted chin, the particular deepening intensity of her dark Bennett eyes. Nils didn't look around. He kept on knitting; the flat wooden needle slipped in and out of the green marlin meshes, pulled the twine taut with a faint sibilant sound, wove and made fast the next knot. The resinous oily scent was pleasantly mingled with the smell of the wood fire.

Joanna looked down at his fair head, and waited. . . . "You mean they'll start bothering the traps?" insisted Stevie.

"Nothing as simple as that," said Joanna. "But they'll think of something. If Nils doesn't think of it first."

Stevie grinned at his brother-in-law. "Seems like old times, Joanna teamin' us around again."

Joanna wished she could see Nils' face. It would be easier to talk if she could see his face and not the back of his head, its hair very fair against the warm tan of his neck, and his strong shoulders under his clean chambray shirt. She wished Stevie would go to bed, and then she could sit where he was sitting now, on the wide window sill, so she could face Nils.

But she couldn't stop now, and wait until Stevie had gone. Besides, he had a right to know what she thought, and what she knew she must say. Her fingers tightened imperceptibly on the back of Nils' chair.

"It's the Fowlers," she said quietly. "The Fowlers, and I don't know who else on Brigport is in it. Tom Robey is, because I think he's letting Randolph Fowler tell him what to do. But they want to get rid of us over here. It's more than a mad that they'll get over. . . . Randolph's just as determined to drive us out of here as he was to drive Tim Merrill out of the store over there, and to get rid of Gil Marsh as a lobster buyer."

She had the satisfaction of seeing the traphead needle stop. Stevie was watching her, his thin brown face absorbed as he followed her words. Nils said evenly, "Go on. I'm listening."

It was to him she spoke now; he was the one who must believe her, and not think she was dreaming up things. "Nils, at first they thought we were just playing around over here, you and me. But the trouble started when Jud and Caleb came. It's been getting worse. Can't you see it?" She flicked her tongue over lips that kept drying. "If Bennett's keeps building up again, they know what'll happen. Our own store, our own lobster buyer. . . . And there's a war coming in which the Fowlers can make a fortune from the lobster business — especially if they have free run of these waters. I don't think it's all of Brigport . . . I hope it isn't. Just the Fowlers, and their boys, and the young crowd that don't go by any laws and never did."

Nils swung around in his chair and looked up at her, his blue eyes steady on hers. "You think they're going to make things uncomfortable for us? Try to make it so hard for us to get a living that we'll leave?"

She nodded, and at once her voice escaped its level calm. "That's it! Make things disagreeable and inconvenient, and even go farther than that, till they wear us down. They don't want us to have a buyer here, buying thousands of pounds of lobsters and making a lot of money that could go into Fowler pockets. And the more people come here, the sooner the buyer will come —"

"Makes sense to me," Stevie said. "Just like somethin' those bastards would think up. Well, if they think they're goin' to get me off Bennett's Island, they're in for a hell of a surprise!"

"What Stevie says is right,' said Nils. "Nobody can budge us. We've been through something like this before, haven't we? And when they know they can't budge us, they'll get tired of it. They don't dare go outside the law, and they'll run out of ideas pretty soon."

"Oh, sure!" said Joanna bitterly. "They can't budge us, because we're home. We know them, and we can hang on through everything! But what about the others? Caleb and Vinnie? The Fennells? What if Mark's wife doesn't feel like going without, and fighting and worrying all the time? What about Jud? You saw how he was tonight. He's getting old, and he can't fight back!"

"Joanna, we don't need to fight," Nils said patiently. "Let Randolph wear himself down to a nub—he can't hurt us. In the long run he can't do us any harm. None of 'em—Fowlers or the young gang—can go openly outside the law without a warden coming down on their necks. Don't you think they know it?"

"We've got to fight for anything we want in this world!" Joanna said. "Nils, I know what you think. You've got things by sitting and waiting—" The instant she said it she saw his eyes darken, she saw the infinitesimal lift at the corner of his mouth, and she felt her whole tense body grow hot, as if her pounding blood was suffusing every inch of her skin. Oh, yes, he had waited for her, without fighting, unless you could call his stubborn, passive patience a battle, and now she was his. . . . At least she had his name, and he had a right to her body.

She was shocked suddenly by the way she felt; for she was fighting Nils now, and the thought appalled her. *Nils.* They were facing each other like duelists, and Stevie, listening, didn't realize it. To him, Jo was just teaming her men around, the way she'd always done. . . .

Her pause was only momentary. She gathered her defenses together and said calmly, "Maybe we *can* wear them down. But when they start insulting the others, that's different. *They* don't have any call to accept somebody's cheap talk as if they couldn't do anything but take it."

"What's your idea?" said Nils.

"Yep, what is it?" demanded Stevie. "You've probably got somethin' up your sleeve. I hope it's good," he added frankly. "Not just one of those woman-ideas."

"I want us to stop selling lobsters at Brigport altogether," said Joanna. "I know we haven't got the capital to start buying, and we'd have a job to find a company to back us. But what's to prevent all the Bennett's men from carring their lobsters and taking them ashore once a week? One man could take the whole business, turn about." This was it; this was her stride, never a fight without a plan. She felt calm and easy and sure of herself; she smiled at her men.

"How about gas and oil? Trap stuff? Rope?" Nils questioned her. "You don't think Ralph will supply us if we don't take him our lobsters."

"Whoever buys the lobsters inshore can look out for that," she assured him. "And they will, too. You know it as well as I do. Gas and oil —" she paused. "Well, what about those tanks of Pete Grant's, up on the hill behind the wharf?"

"They're rusted all to hell, Jo," Stevie said. "I looked 'em over yesterday when I was around the point looking for ducks."

"Nils, you ought to be able to think of something," she appealed to him. He hadn't said yet that her plan was good, but that would come, because it *was* good.

"We could have it come out in drums right from the oil company," he said slowly. "Come out as freight on the mailboat. That'd mean picking it up at Brigport, though. And our mail would still come there. . . . You see, we'd still be dependent, Jo."

"Just till we got one of the wharves fixed, and the postoffice back, so the mailboat came down here again!" She hadn't felt so happy for a long time, she thought exultantly. What did it matter if they had to mail and freight at Brigport — that wasn't real dependence; you weren't put in a position that could turn your food to gall and wormwood in your mouth. She thought suddenly of groceries, but she put it hastily out of her mind. That would take care of itself. Tomorrow she would figure it out.

"You think the others will like the idea?" Nils said. "Maybe they won't. But I'll tell you the truth, Jo. It's a good plan." She felt herself relax imperceptibly. She knew it was a good plan, she knew she could put it through, but if Nils agreed, that made things so much easier. After all, she didn't want to be a driving woman.

Stevie said, "I like it all right. Mark will, too. He can't stomach those Fowlers anyway — you ought to hear him cuss when the *Janet F.* goes up by the cove."

"Nils, let me talk to the others," she said confidently. "Why wouldn't they like it, anyway? They'll get all their money in one lump instead of thirty here and forty there — that's all the difference."

"Convince 'em, if you can,' said Nils. "If you work on them the way you work on me, they won't stand a show."

Stevie stood up, stretching. "Holy cow, I'm tired, but my mind isn't. What a woman . . . huh, Nils?"

"She's all right," said Nils, and smiled at Joanna with his eyes. And she felt a quick stab of wonder at what he must be thinking behind that glance. Sometimes it seemed to her, in strange, swift, and somehow lonesome instants like this one, that she had never known Nils at all.

The instant passed. Stevie was taking his lamp from the shelf and lighting it. He said "Goodnight," and left them. Nils filled his needles methodically, so they'd be ready for the next time, he hung the finished trapheads in the entry. Joanna did her last small tasks in the kitchen, and they were ready for bed.

He took the lamp from the table and walked ahead of her to their room, holding the lamp high to light her way. They walked through the quiet house; quiet inside, a sleeping quiet, and quiet outside tonight. There was hardly a murmur of wind, and the sea's rote was a faint, far-off sound.

"Fog tomorrow," Nils said, as they reached their room, and he set the lamp on the dresser. He walked to the window and stood looking out. Joanna joined him there and they watched, without speaking. The fog was creeping in from the east already, but overhead the stars still burned, and Orion climbed the sky. Joanna put her arm through Nils'.

"Nils, is it really a good idea?" she asked him.

"Sure it is," he said. "What's the matter? Don't you believe me?" He slipped his arm free of hers and put it around her, tightening it.

"I only wanted to be sure," she said, and the feeling of Nils' strangeness was quite gone, and it was the way it had always been with Nils, ever since she could first remember.

11

WHENEVER JOANNA AWOKE DURING THE NIGHT, she saw the ghostly pallor of the fog against the windows, and heard the muffled sound of the fog horn at the Rock blowing at its brief intervals. She would come awake slowly, first conscious of the comfortable warmth and perfect relaxation of her strong, healthy body under the covers, and the fresh-smelling cold in the room, and of Nils beside her in his sound sleep. Then she would remember how they had talked in the kitchen, and what she was to do in the morning. She would look then at the fog outside the windows, creeping quietly across the sea to fill all the darkness with its pale, wreathing breath, and she would listen to the foghorn and think, *Tomorrow nobody will go out, and I can see them all.*

Then she would fall asleep again, lying separately in the bed, independent of Nils. At the first of the night, when she lay in his arms with her head against his shoulder, she lay awake until she knew he was asleep, and then slipped gently free from him. He was usually tired enough, after a long day on the water, to sleep so deeply that he never moved when she left his arms, no matter how tightly they had held her.

Sometimes in spite of herself she thought of her brief marriage with Alec Douglass, and how closely they had slept together, like healthy young animals. It seemed almost impossible that she had ever been so free and unselfconscious with anyone.

But tonight she didn't think about it. She thought of tomorrow . . .

In the morning her inner excitement woke her before Nils, and that was exceptional. Usually he was up and moving around quietly in the kitchen, building the fire, making the coffee. She lay there and watched him sleeping, her eyes tracing the familiar moulding of his forehead, cheekbones and nose; the controlled yet generous lines of his mouth; the whole strong impassivity of his sleeping face. The early light caught the glint of his blond beard, very faint on his tanned jaw.

If I loved him—her thought began, and then she corrected herself, for she did love him; *If I were in love with him, it would be all the way, with nothing left out,* she thought. And that was what he deserved. She felt her regret stirring again, and then, suddenly, Nils was awake; his sea-blue eyes looked calmly into hers, and he smiled.

"Hello, Nils," she said softly.

"Hello," he answered. He pulled her gently to him and kissed her cheek, still flushed and moist with sleep, her throat, and finally her mouth. She smiled at him drowsily as he looked down into her face. Then he lowered himself from his elbow and rolled out from under the covers.

The day was about to begin. Already Nils had turned his mind from her to the day's work. . . . She followed him out to the kitchen in a few minutes and found the fire already burning briskly.

They didn't have much to say during breakfast. Joanna was used to Nils' spells of silence, and they suited her, because then she could think her own thoughts, and this morning she had a great deal to think about. She would start with Jud, she thought. Probably Caleb would follow Jud's lead. But there wasn't any reason to think they wouldn't all agree; after all, her plan was to their advantage.

She looked across the table at Nils and said directly, "Do you know why anybody mightn't think it was a good idea, carring the lobsters and taking them in?"

"Well, no. Except that folks think more about dictators than they used to. Might be they'd think they were being bossed." He saw the quick lifting of her chin and added, "People get funny ideas. So don't be surprised if somebody feels like fighting this Brigport mess out in their own way."

"I don't see why they should," Joanna said stiffly. "Everyone of us here on Bennett's has been slapped in the face." She watched him pour out a second cup of coffee and thought of something else. "Nils, you don't mean that you've got a better idea than mine, do you? Because I wish you'd tell it to me, if you have." Her grin across the table at him was comic, nose-wrinkling. "Or maybe, way down underneath, you don't think there's anything to worry about — that it's all my imagination."

He shook his head at her. "Nope. It's real enough. Somebody's acting up. And I *haven't* got a better plan."

They heard Stevie coming downstairs. Nils pushed back his chair and took out his pipe, Joanna got up to put more bacon in the iron spider.

When at last the men had gone, Nils to the shore, Stevie to the Eastern End, she put on her boots and raincoat and went down across the sodden, yellow-brown meadow to the woods. She walked in a small, circular clearing in the fog that moved with her; it made the way through the meadow seem over-long, and she could almost imagine that this sloping, uneven ground with its dead wind-matted grasses and spiny skeletons of raspberry and rose bushes, its occasional granite outcroppings, went on forever, with no high wall of green-black spruces to end it.

The fog eddied thickly around her, brushing her face and deepening her color, clinging to her thick black hair in little beads of moisture. Her raincoat was beaded too, and her boots were wet and shiny. She liked the fog, as she had always loved every face of the Island. A little fog didn't hurt. It was when there was a long fog mull that she, like the others, hated it; yet it was not quite hate on Joanna's part, for she walked in the fog every day, as long as it lasted, and took a guilty pleasure in it when she knew the men were cursing it.

When she came to the woods she didn't follow the path through the narrow part between the meadow and the Whitcomb place. Some day, she thought, she would stop avoiding it, but not today, when the old white house would look so cold and deserted against the dark hillside. She turned into the little grove of birch and spruce and alder swamp that belonged to the Sorensen property. When she came out of that dripping, silent place, where even the chickadees were voiceless this morning, there was Gunnar Sorensen's barn with its hip roof, and the many-gabled house that had once been half-hidden in Anna Sorensen's flowers.

This was the house where Nils had grown up. Gunnar and Anna were his grandparents, his mother had died when he was small. She skirted the buildings, following the overgrown path, and reached the windbreak of spruces which Gunnar had planted when he was a young man. The water dripped from the thick boughs. It was a wet, gray, dripping world, and through it the harbor gulls made their ceaseless thin crying.

But it was not a depressing world. Not for Joanna, at least. Her eyes caught with delight at a handful of rose haws still left on their naked bush, glowing like tiny circles of orange flame against the wet grass. The contrast deepened the grass color to a rich tawniness; and the gray of the granite chunks was a cool, clear, uncomplicated thing.

More spruces made a thick shelter over the path up to Jud Gray's house. Joanna's feet quickened. She went around to the back door.

Jud was home, and that was what she had counted on. In the small, cosy kitchen, lamplit against the shade of the trees outside, Marion was making pies and Jud was knitting trapheads. The radio was playing. Joanna came in to the accompaniment of organ music and a soothing male voice pleading that the listener should tune in tomorrow and hear how Susan conquered her predicament.

Marion's rosy face was absorbed; she nodded with an absent-minded smile at Joanna. Jud pushed back his chair.

"Come in, come in, Jo!" he roared above the radio. "Get off them wet things and set down by the stove. God A'mighty, Marion, turn off that guts-'n'-gurry. I can't stomach no more of it!"

Marion snapped the switch. "Don't act like you was such a brute, Jud Gray," she said placidly. "You know you been just as much worried 'bout Susan as I've been."

"Susan," said Jud, "is a goddam fool. Anybody that says I'm interested in her doin's, or any other o' them idiots, I'm goin' to have up for libel. Set, Joanna. What's Nils doin'?"

"Something or other down at the shore." Joanna grinned at them both. "You didn't have to stop listening to your program just for me, Jud."

"You ain't got past the age when you need a trimmin', Jo," he warned her.

"And I haven't got past the age when I've got some ideas," she retorted. "I'm not going to beat around the bush. I've got something on my mind this morning."

"Is it what Jud come up and told you last night?" Marion asked. "Those Fowlers! I never did like them, even when they first come to Brigport." Her mouth tightened. "And that Randolph singin' solos in church, and cheatin' everybody out of their eyeteeth—"

"Now, old lady, you remember your blood pressure," Jud said. "And give the girl a chance. Might be she's collectin' a fund, or somethin'."

"To feed the starving Fowlers," said Joanna. "Well, that's what it's about, anyway. Jud, would you like it if you didn't have to sell your lobsters to Ralph?"

Jud's round face was alight. "You mean *Nils* is goin' to buy?"

"No, not now. Maybe later. But this is the idea. Everybody can car their lobsters, either in separate cars, or in a big one like that old one of Pete Grant's down on the beach—keeping count of what they put in, of course—and then it'll be turn about, taking the lobsters ashore and selling them direct to the company."

Marion arranged apples in the pieplate, sprinkled them liberally with sugar and nutmeg, laid on the upper crust with care and delicacy. But she was listening. Her eyes fairly snapped.

"Now that's the first sensible remark I've heard in this kitchen for a long time," she said. "It's a lot more practical than a string of curses that's goin' to make it mighty hard for Jud to look his Maker straight in the eye."

Jud puffed violently on his pipe. "You be quiet, woman. Jo, what about oil 'n' gas?"

"Nils says we can have it come out as freight on the mailboat."

"Well . . ." Jud squinted judicially. "That's all right. It's even better'n all right. It's fine. The only thing is . . ." He took out his pipe and scowled at it. "I haven't got a boat. Only way I can take my turn is to borry Caleb's boat."

"You can work that out with the men—*if* they all agree." She grinned at Jud. "Well, I didn't have to argue with you, did I?"

"No, and you won't have to argue with Caleb, I'm thinkin'. He's an independent feller, Caleb is. He ain't takin' no—"

"*Jud,*" said Marion, looking over her glasses.

"Hell, I wasn't goin' to say anythin', and if I was, I think Jo's heard that word before." He twinkled at Joanna like an elderly cherub. "As I was sayin', Caleb don't want much more truck with the Fowlers. Gettin' the mail over there is about all we can stomach."

"And we won't have to be doing that for long, I hope." Joanna stood up and reached for her raincoat. "When we get a few more families here, I'm going to write about the postoffice."

"You don't need to hurry about goin'," said Marion. "Sit down again."

"I'll be in again one of these days. Only today I've got a couple more calls to make." She stood by the door, laughing and at ease; a tall and vibrant presence in the small room. The elderly people looked at her with a shiny mist in their eyes.

"She's her father's girl, Jud," Marion said. " 'Member how he used to come in here?"

Jud cleared his throat and was busy with his pipe. "Yep. . . . Well, Joanny, you won't have any trouble with Caleb, and you was always able to twist your brothers 'round your little finger."

"Oh, everything's going to turn out all right," said Joanna. She was still smiling and assured. And as she went down the white clam-shell path under the dripping dark spruces, she too was remembering her father. When they said she was her father's girl, she was always secretly warmed, and proud. . . . If Stephen had been so minded, there would have been almost nothing that he couldn't have done with his smile and his voice.

But there was another way in which she was not like Stephen, nor like Donna either. Jud and Marion didn't know it, yet. Perhaps nobody would ever realize it. All they would realize was that there were no Marcus Yettons on Bennett's Island any more.

She walked past the other empty houses at the harbor and past the remains of the boatshop, and the old wharf where a few gulls sat on the wet rocks, fluting absently into the fog. The tide was down and the pebbled beach gleamed gray and black and steel-blue; the rock-weed strewn by the sea was tinged with bronze. The fog had lifted a little, so the space around her had widened somewhat. As she went along the boardwalk over the beach stones, she could see, and enjoy afresh, the white paint on the Caldwell house and the starched, flow-ered curtains in the sitting room windows.

Vinnie was a tireless housekeeper. She washed the outside of the windows several times a week, to clean them of the continual salt film, and took as much pride in her shining glass as some women take in their flower arrangements. Remembering Susan Yetton,

Joanna always felt a burst of affection for the lightning-swift and indefatigable Vinnie.

The Caldwells were listening to the radio too. They turned it off when Joanna came in. News . . . Vinnie looked at Joanna, her small sharp face drawn in compassion, and said, "Them poor Londoners, gettin' bombed out and burned out in this weather. . . . When are we goin' to help 'em? That's what I want to know!"

"Now, Vinnie, you keep calm," Caleb said in his slow, deep voice. He took Joanna's raincoat and beckoned her to the deep chair where he'd been sitting and whittling lobster plugs.

"I don't know when we'll get started," said Joanna. "But we will. We always do. . . . And meantime we're having a little persecution trouble of our own."

They both looked at her questioningly. She looked steadily back at them. Vinnie's amber eyes were wide, like Joey's. Caleb's, set in their bony hollows, met Joanna's in a long glance of comprehension.

"Brigport," he said.

"You feel that, then," Joanna said.

"A man can't help but put two and two together," Caleb answered. His slow voice fell into the silence of the room like the heavy striking of a clock. "There's been enough, since I come here, for me to go on."

"Does Joey say anything?" Joanna asked.

Vinnie said eagerly, "The Merrills are real nice people. He thinks Cap'n Merrill is about all there is. . . . He seems real contented over there, and his rank card was awful good last week."

"I guess nothin's spread as far as the schoolyard," Caleb said. "Seems to me, from what Jud says, it's kind of local . . . centered right around the harbor."

"Ellen hasn't said anything either." Joanna recognized her relief for what it was. Before, she hadn't quite dared bring her worry about the children out into the open, even in her own mind. But it had been there, just the same. Ellen was such an absorbed child, going about wrapped in her own thoughts, that she wouldn't have noticed too much what might be hurled at her in the pure, primitive cruelty of childhood. But Joey was older, he was a sensitive adolescent, he would have noticed. . . .

It was surprising how much lighter she felt. She smiled at

Vinnie and Caleb, liking them very much, and told them about the new idea. Vinnie, her knitting needles flying, was excited about it. Caleb sat leaning forward, his elbows on his knees, his hands loosely clasped between them, and looked at the tiger kitten who dreamed under the stove with her white paws tucked in.

His long, weathered face was unreadable, and for an instant Joanna recalled Nils' warning. Then Caleb said, "You mean you think we ought to back down?"

"*Back down?*" With an effort she kept her voice as calm as his. "No. Backing down would mean to give up to them all around. We're not backing down if we sell direct to the company who'd buy them from Ralph anyway."

"Supposin' Ralph fixes it with the company so they don't want our lobsters unless they come by way of him?"

"There's more than one lobster company in Limerock," Joanna retorted. "And I don't think Ralph can do anything. . . . Island men have always taken their own lobsters in when they felt like it. Besides, you get about three cents a pound extra if you're carring."

"Well . . ." said Caleb. He took the slender stick of soft pine from which he'd been whittling pegs, and poked the cat gently. His deep-set eyes began to smile as one white paw darted out to catch the stick. It was odd how his craggy face softened.

"It sounds all right to me."

"Then we're dependent on Brigport only when we get our mail and freight," Joanna said happily.

Vinnie said unexpectedly, "What about food?"

In one swift instant of shock, Joanna realized she'd been so pre-occupied with the lobsters, she'd forgotten food. And Marion and Jud hadn't mentioned it, either. . . . She blushed at her own thoughtlessness, vexed to be tripped up like this. And then, because Vinnie was looking at her with Joey's gentle, anxious, questioning look, she forgot her vexation.

"I didn't remember food," she confessed. "I guess I thought we could live on lobsters."

"Fowler's don't give us Bennett's Island stump-jumpers much in the way of service," Caleb observed without rancor.

"He never has half what I put on my list." Vinnie knitted fast, her mouth tightening. "If you can figure us out some way to buy our groceries that'd be fine."

Joanna was thinking hard. It was a point of honor with her, never to be at a loss. She said recklessly, "I know. We'll each have a list of everything we'll be needing for ten days or two weeks, and whoever goes in can take them up to Marston's Market in Limerock the first thing, and have the orders put up and ready for him when he's ready to leave. I think they'll even deliver them down to the Public Landing or wherever he ties up."

Shining-eyed, now that she had caught up all the loose ends, she looked for their approval and found it.

"Marston's is a good place," Caleb said. "Don't know why we couldn't do as well there as at Fowler's."

"Better!" Vinnie chirped. "That Fowler over-charges somethin' awful!"

It was a successful visit, and Joanna arose to go, feeling deeply satisfied with herself and with everybody else.

"Who's goin' to make the first trip in?" Caleb said.

"Nils," said Joanna serenely. She hadn't asked him, but it was only right that he should lead off, and thus back her up. Besides, there was no reason why he shouldn't be willing to go first.

The Caldwells didn't want her to leave so soon, but she couldn't bear to sit still and make idle conversation when her brain was teeming with ideas and excitement. She told them she must be thinking of starting dinner, with a pang of guilt at the fib, because dinner was ready except for warming up.

She walked briskly around the boardwalk and turned at the anchor into the sandy road through the marsh. The freshening wind eddied the fog thickly around her again; it was wet on her lips and smelled fresh and cold in her nostrils, mingled with the damp, decadent fragrance of the marsh. From Matinicus Rock the fog horn sounded, loud and mournful on the wind, with its little grunt on the end.

No, she couldn't go home now, there was nothing to do in the empty house, and she wanted to keep moving, to talk. When she reached the turning, where the gravelly sand wanted to sift into her shoes, she turned resolutely along the road that followed the seawall around Schoolhouse Cove. She hadn't been down to see Helmi since

Mark had moved to the Eastern End. Mark might notice it, though she was sure the girl wouldn't care if no one came near her. . . .

Dreams crowded around her when she walked up between the over grownfields where almost everybody on the Island had had a garden spot back in the old days. In the long, sunny hour after supper, husbands and wives walked up there together to weed and to cultivate; there was calling back and forth, and a communal sharing of tools, and of the vegetables when they were harvested. . . . It would take a long time to get the fields, with the sea on either side, into condition for gardens again. That would be the next thing to tackle, after life settled into an uncomplicated rhythm.

Uncle Nate's barn loomed through the fog. There were some shingles off the roof; Nils would have to look out for that. The white paint of the house was scabby. She would get in touch with Uncle Nate—he was living in Thomaston now, where Aunt Mary had quite a field in which to make her presence felt—and see about painting the house in the spring.

The woods were silent and dripping, wreathed in fog. Far below the path the sea's lazy swell curled itself over shaggy black rocks that looked ugly and sharp in the half-tide. Joanna loved them. She loved the harshness of them, she loved the bristly, austere angles of the spruces, the gnarled unevenness of the wind-tortured ones, the leafless, tangled tracery of blackberry bushes on either side of the path.

She prolonged her walk; but the moment came when she let herself through the gate and walked down over the open land to the houses of the Eastern End. It was fantastic how life repeated itself. She had come down through this gate to see the girl her brother Charles had married; and she had been reluctant then, as now. Only then, her reluctance had been sick and resentful.

The boys would be in the barn, working on their new traps, and she walked past without stopping.

Smoke blew gently down from the chimney, but otherwise there was no motion from the house as she knocked at the door. After a little while, Helmi came. The first glimpse of her was always a shock. She stood silently in the doorway, with her silver hair brushing her shoulders. Then, with a little tilt of her head on its long, slim neck, she said, "Oh . . . hello, Joanna. Come in."

Joanna said, "Am I interrupting you at anything? Cake-baking, or radio programs?" She followed Helmi's willowy, yet strong, figure through the entry into the warm, immaculate kitchen.

"No, I was just sitting down," Helmi said. She gestured vaguely toward a chair by the window that looked out across the rolling yellow-brown field into the fog, beyond which lay the stretch of tumbled rocks and then the open sea. In that instant Joanna noticed there was no sign of knitting, sewing, book, or paper, near the chair. Did Helmi just *sit,* she wondered, and met the girl's coolly translucent blue-green gaze.

It made her faintly uncomfortable. She sat down and said at once, "Haven't you scrubbed the floor up nice and white? I haven't seen such a floor for a long time."

Helmi shrugged. "Something to do," she said.

"Helmi, when you get lonesome, why don't you come up to the harbor? Bring your mending and we'll have a kaffeeklatsch." She laughed. "Isn't that what they call it?"

"Would you drink some coffee now?" Helmi demanded. She had been standing by the dresser. Now she moved, measuring coffee into a brightly polished pot with her strong, broad hands.

"I can always drink coffee," said Joanna, determined to be at ease, wishing she could fathom what lay behind the high-cheekboned face with the slightly tilted eyes, and its frame of palely shining hair. "Nils has turned me into a real coffee-drinker. He's Swedish, you probably knew that the minute you looked at him."

"I didn't notice," Helmi said indifferently.

"I wish you'd come up and get acquainted with us," Joanna said, catching Helmi's eyes and smiling straight into them. Her reaching out to the girl was almost a tangible thing; but she couldn't touch her, and she heard her own voice going on when she would have liked to get out and shake off the spell of the silent, shining kitchen, and the silent, shining girl.

"Of course anybody's husband's family is a poor substitute for your own, but we can try to be company for you, if you're lonesome for them."

"I am not lonesome," said Helmi, and began to pour the coffee.

It's no use, I can't talk to her, Joanna thought. Her mind sought frantically for conversation.

"The boys will be setting their traps soon."

"Yes." Helmi set a coffee cup before her, milk and sugar in a squat blue pitcher and bowl. "There is no coffee cake. I'm sorry."

"I'd rather have just coffee, anyway." Joanna smiled, but Helmi, beginning to stir her own coffee, looked past her as if she were not there.

On an incontrollable impulse Joanna turned her own head, and looked through the long, low window over the sink. She saw what Helmi must be seeing—Mark and Stevie coming out of the barn. The fog had cleared again; and in the shadowless gray light they showed up with wonderful clarity, like figures on a movie screen. They were talking seriously, as Mark slid the heavy door shut behind them. Joanna saw him run his hand through his black hair, shake his head, and then begin to laugh. The laughter spread to Stevie, his dark face crinkled, and then was alight. It was one of their private jokes. When they were children no two persons enjoyed life and each other more than Mark and Stevie. And now that they were grown up it was the same.

Still caught up in their mirth, they started down the slope toward the house with their similar long-legged strides, as if the heavy rubber boots were no more than moccasins.

Joanna turned back to Helmi, opening her lips to speak, but she remained silent. She was astonished by the expression in Helmi's face as she watched the two brothers through the window. There was a faint stain of color along her high cheekbones, and such an intensity in her eyes that Joanna felt the tightening of shock in her throat. She saw the girl's teeth catch her under lip and whiten it.

And then, as if it had not happened at all, the expression was gone. Helmi met Joanna's glance and her eyes were cool and noncommittal, color ebbed from her cheeks and flowed redly into the bitten lip.

"Will you have some more coffee?" she asked.

"It's lovely coffee, but it's so near dinner time I'd better not have any more," Joanna said evenly. But she felt as though her heart were beating over-hard. If she could fathom that look on Helmi's face, she would know the secret that *was* Helmi.

But what was it? In a moment now the boys would come in, and she knew she couldn't endure their noise and horseplay, she must be by herself and think this out.

"I'll be going," she said lightly. "Here come your men, and I've got one at home who'll be looking for his dinner. Come up, won't you, Helmi?"

"I will," said Helmi. "Some time."

Outside the boys stopped her but she fended off their humor, laughing at them all the time. "Go get your dinner," she told them. "I smelled it cooking. It was wonderful."

Mark made a noise like an ape and sprinted for the house with Stevie behind him, and Joanna, going through the gate, was alone again.

On the way back, she didn't look at the rocks, or notice the angles of the trees and the sparkle of moisture on the blackberry vines. She saw only Helmi's face. Odd, that when the girl's face had been so immobile, the first definite expression Joanna had seen had been so *intense* . . . Love? she wondered. A passion for Mark so great and fiery that the sight of him must change her like that? But it could have been another sort of passion . . . Hate, for instance.

Hate. *Or jealousy.* Joanna felt slightly sick and empty in the pit of her stomach. Of course. Why, she'd hardly been alone with Mark since their marriage. Stevie was there from half-past-five in the morning until dark. Perhaps she saw before her a whole lifetime of sharing Mark with Stevie, of never feeling that Mark was completely her own.

Suddenly she felt that she understood the tides of possessive love that rose and fell in Helmi. The secret was clear now. She knew a quick wave of sympathy for the girl, who in other circumstances would probably have liked Stevie for his pleasant, sunny self. But now she hated him. It made Joanna feel cold to think of anyone hating Stevie.

She wished she could take him out of the partnership with Mark now, instead of waiting till he got his own boat. But she knew there was no way to do it without telling him, and that would set a cloud between him and his brother.

No, she would have to wait until he saw the boat he wanted. She would wait, and pray that the banked fires in Mark's wife would not leap beyond the surface too soon.

12

THE FOG WENT AS QUICKLY as it had come, and a strong gale from the north-west chased it out to sea. And the sea that had washed lazily around the rocks, pearly gray in the fog, was a wilderness of brilliant water as far as the horizon. Under the sun it looked like crumpled metal foil. Along the shores of the Island, where it rolled up on the slanting red-brown rocks, it was a dark, pure blue; but the heart of each comber that crashed toward the land was shining and translucent green. The combers rose out of the sea, fled shorewards to crash in an explosion of smoky white foam, and rainbow-catching prisms that flew up to the wood and soaked the sere brown grass. Then the prisms were flung sea-water; but in the air, against the sun, they were diamonds.

All day and all night the thunder hung around the Island, like the mist from the spray. The men worried about their traps, but not too much; they had moved most of them to the south-east of the Island where they were in the lee.

It lasted until noon of the second day, and then began to die out. The radio weather reports promised good weather for a while, and in the afternoon the men went down to the shore to bait up. They would go out early to haul in the morning.

They had enough crates between them, including several Mark found at the Eastern End—left behind by Jake Trudeau—to keep their lobsters until they had a big car ready. And that would be soon. Listening to the whole-hearted interest everybody had in the idea, Joanna felt proud and happy. Nils hadn't objected to making the first trip in, either. She hadn't expected that he would; but she'd felt a twinge—just a tiny one—of embarrassment when she'd said, "I told

Jud and Caleb you were going in first. Is that all right?"

"Well, somebody has to be first," Nils had said reasonably.

So that was all right. . . . The day the wind died down they had an early supper, and in a still, frosty sunset they had walked around Schoolhouse Cove to Nathan Bennett's place. They had the keys to the buildings, and Nils thought there might be some lumber in the barn he could use for making a car. The old cars in the marsh were rotten, after five years of idleness. Jud, who was a carpenter of sorts, having built many a boat in his day, would take charge of the building.

He came over to walk up to the barn with them and look over the lumber. Their three shadows were before them, Joanna's and Nils' grotesquely tall, Jud's short and very wide. Between puffs on his pipe he told Nils how he intended to build the car. Joanna listened to their voices, and was content to be silent.

In the dusty, chilly gloom of the barn the men at once fell into an absorbed study of the lumber. Joanna prowled around by herself. The dust lay thick on the work bench and on the farm machinery that had been Uncle Nate's pride and joy. He had run the only farm on Bennett's Island. . . . The stalls where Hugo and Jeff had milked the cows, while a sometimes roistering game of hide-and-seek went on in the hayloft overhead, looked sadly empty. She thought about going up into the silo, but changed her mind. She wasn't fifteen any more, skinny and tense in dungarees, shinnying up to the hayloft on a rope and swinging out of it in the same way. She remembered Tim Gray, Jud's oldest boy, catching her once and kissing her. That had been her first kiss from a boy, and it hadn't been a very expert one, and Tim had turned so red afterwards she'd been too surprised to be mad. . . .

Now she was twice as old as that, and had a daughter all of seven years old, going on eight; she was mistress of the Bennett homestead, and the years seemed to go by so fast that she would be forty before she knew it. What was she doing, standing in a cold, empty barn and seeing it peopled with ghosts? The ghosts of stripling boys in rubber boots, and girls—one girl in particular, with Indian-black braids swinging forward as she jumped.

There was no memory of Nils in the barn, for the Sorensens had their own cows, and Nils wasn't one of the crowd who met here every night. She watched him now as he talked with Jud, and they made arrangements for getting the lumber down to the shore. She wondered what Jud thought about her and Nils.

We're a settled-down married couple, she thought. *Both old enough to behave, and I should stop thinking foolishness. . . .*

She walked over to them and slipped her arm through Nils'. She saw, from the almost imperceptible change in his face, what her touch meant to him, and her heart contracted. Then she said lightly, "Got it all figured out, boys?"

"Yep," said Jud. "We can get it down the bank into Schoolhouse Cove — on the old wharf down there — and load it on the *Donna,* and take it around to the harbor."

Nils' arm pressed her hand against her side. "In another week we'll have us a good big car," he said.

"Sooner'n that," Jud maintained stoutly. "I may be old, but I ain't lost my steam yet, b'God!"

When they walked back again, Jud left them at the turning in the road. The dusk was falling swiftly, scented with the sea and frost and dead grass, as Joanna and Nils walked up to the house. Stevie had lighted a lamp in the kitchen, and the warm yellow windows, set in the dark bulk of the house against the southern sky's graying lavender, looked down at Joanna as they had always looked in the winter dusk. Except for the intimacy of her arm linked with Nils', she could almost imagine that they would all be in the kitchen — her parents and the boys; that when the door opened and the warmth and light streamed out, the familiar, beloved voices would stream out too.

On the granite doorstep, Nils stopped her, and took her into his arms. His mouth was cool and firm on hers, he smelled of his own cleanliness and the cold, sweet air. It was pleasant to be kissed by Nils, and she gave herself to the moment with a completeness that to Nils seemed perfection. For outwardly she *had* given herself; only she knew of her innermost reserves. Only she knew how she wished with all her heart that his kiss could be more than pleasant to her.

"Is this what I get for taking your arm?" she murmured.

"That's what you get," he told her. "You ought to know by now."

She laughed and took his kiss again—a longer one than the first—and then went ahead of him into the house.

She heard Stevie's voice as she opened the inner door, and when she came in he was sprawled in the rocker by the stove, his long leg over the arm. Beyond him she saw Randy Fowler.

She stiffened in amazement and anger. He sat in her kitchen, perfectly at ease, talking with her brother, while his family schemed against her. She walked into the room, and Randy stood up, his bright eyes on her face.

"Hi, Jo. Surprised? It was such a pretty evenin' after the wind died out, I thought—Hi, Nils."

His smile showed up the slashes of dimples in his thin cheeks. She was irritated to see Nils smiling too. He said, "Hello, Randy. Good to see you."

She took a long time hanging up her coat, rearranging the jackets and sweaters on the hooks. His soft-voiced impudence echoed in her mind *All right for me to come over when the old man's home?* he'd said as he'd walked out that morning. And here he was. The pure gall of him. She wanted to take him by the shoulders and shake him hard and throw him out right now. But how could she, with Nils already talking to him in a friendly manner?

She got her darning from the sitting room and sat down to work. As long as the men talked, she could be silent. Of course Nils would be nice to Randy. He didn't have any call to be rude to the boy—as far as she knew—and besides, it was policy to show that there wasn't anything in the wind. There was no mention of a lobster car. The conversation went from the lobster's winter habits into its breeding habits, and stayed right there; every fisherman seemed to have a different theory on the subject.

She knew that Randy was watching her. At last, she deliberately met his gaze. Her own was remote, uncommunicative. It should have chilled his sparkle, but it didn't. He talked on with Stevie and Nils, and as she listened to his soft, quick voice she had to admit that he had a certain odd charm that didn't seem pure Fowler. Perhaps he got it from his mother. . . .

After a while she remembered a radio program she wanted to hear, and went into the sitting room to listen. She doubted that Randy

would ever come again, when he saw that it got him nowhere. . . .
She stayed on in the sitting room after her program was over, and
didn't go into the kitchen until she heard Nils say, "It's airing up again.
I'll walk down with you, Randy, and take a look at the punts."

She went into the kitchen and found them putting on outdoor
clothes. Randy twinkled at her. "I had a real pleasant evenin', Jo,"
he said.

"You're not goin' without some coffee, are you?" Stevie said
sociably.

"Hell, I guess I stayed long enough." Randy looked bland. "Don't
want to wear out my welcome."

"That bein' the case, guess I'll speed the parting guest," said Stevie
and unfolded his long legs. "Might's well walk down to the shore with
you boys and keep you out of mischief. Where you tied up, Randy?"

"The old wharf. Or what's left of it." Nils was busy with his boots
and Stevie was getting his jacket from the hook; Randy tried to catch
Joanna's eye again, and missed. She waited patiently for them to get
out. Really, she couldn't have Nils and Stevie encouraging him, telling her he wasn't to blame for what his father was. Perhaps tonight
she'd tell Nils about Randy coming when he was gone.

They went out, finally. And just as the outer door closed behind
them, she saw Randy's gloves lying on the dresser. Her lips hardened. Randy was a brat, and she felt like telling him so. She wasn't
surprised, after a few minutes, when the door opened, and he came
through the entry and into the room.

She was putting a stick of wood into the stove, and spoke without turning toward him. "Your gloves are on the dresser, Randy.
You should take better care of them."

"You know, that's what my old lady's always sayin'."

He was motionless in the room behind her. He wasn't picking
up the gloves, then. The others were probably halfway to the gate
by now. She said, "You'd better hurry."

"No need to hurry,' his soft voice replied easily.

She swung around and faced him. "But that's just it, Randy,"
she said, her words as soft and easy as his. Only a little cooler. "There
is need to hurry. Will you take your gloves and get out of this house
just as fast as you can? *And stay out?*"

A flush ran over his thin face, and his eyes darkened.

"You're speakin' kind of sharp, ain't you, Jo?"

"I don't like to be sharp to anyone," she said, "unless I'm forced to be. I don't want to have to carry this to Nils."

"Oh, I'll get out!" he said, and picked up his gloves. He sounded surprisingly good-natured, not at all sulky. He grinned at her, and again the long dimples showed. The brightness, the myriad sparkles and twinkles, came back to his eyes. He didn't appear to have been caught up very short. "So long, Jo. Sweet dreams!" He touched the gloves to the peak of his cap in an impudent salute, and went out whistling.

Joanna smiled in spite of herself. He'd taken it well, and that took care of *that*. But he seemed like a straightforward sort. She wondered if he knew what plans his father and uncle were surely laying for Bennett's Island. It passed through her mind that a boy whom most people liked could pick up a lot of casual information to pass on to others and let them know how the wind was blowing. Then she dismissed the idea from her mind. Randy wouldn't be back again. She'd nipped his romantic urge in the bud, and had actually forbidden him the house.

So — she shrugged, and decided to make a pot of coffee for Nils and Stevie when they came back from the shore.

They were a long time coming. She thought of going down to meet them. Maybe a punt had been caught down under the wharf when the tide came, and they had to get it out. . . . She looked around the kitchen, feeling wonderfully lighthearted. So many problems had been wound up successfully in the past month. Now for the next one. Which should it be? She had a whole list of problems to choose from, each one offering her a stiff and exhilarating battle.

She heard voices outside, and she began taking cups from the cupboard. She had some filled cookies to go with the coffee, Vinnie Caldwell had brought them up in the afternoon.

Stevie came in first, his dark face bright with his laughter. "My God, of all the landlubbers! I told him he was more farmer than fisherman."

"Who?" said Joanna.

"Randy. Skidded on the deck when he was casting off, and went hellety larrup right overboard! Went down clip and clean — talk about your fancy diving!" His brown face sobered. "Of course it wasn't any joke when it happened. That water's cold as hell, and it was pounding in against the old wharf. He floundered some, but we fished him up."

She wondered if Randy had kept his twinkle through that. "Where is he now? Gone home?"

"Not on your life. It's getting colder all the time, and besides, he was kind of shaky. Nils went out to put the *Janet F.* on that empty mooring, and Randy, he was set on going with him to see he got the lady settled all right. But they'll be here in a minute." He held his hands over the stove. "My God, if my hands are cold, Randy must feel like an icicle. . . . What did you say, Jo?"

"Nothing," said Joanna, looking perfectly composed. "I'll have to collect up some hot water bottles. And make up a bed."

"I'll help you." Stevie followed her as she went toward the back stairs, lamp in hand. "This is a nuisance for you, huh?"

"Accidents," said Joanna, still serenely, "will happen." She thought, *This is my judgment for thinking I'd got rid of him. He probably fell overboard on purpose.* And suddenly she was sure she was right. Of course they'd bring him back to the house, and he knew it.

The bed was made in the room that had been Mark's, and the hot water bottles were warming it; dry clothes and hot coffee were waiting when Nils came in with Randy. She was ready for him. Of course he would gloat. . . .

She was unprepared for the white and shaky Randy whose hands could hardly hold a mug of coffee, they shivered so, and whose cheek was streaked with blood where he'd scraped it. If he'd fallen overboard on purpose, he'd got more than he bargained for.

"You didn't guess you were goin' to see me again right off," he told her between chattering teeth. "I'm sorry if I'm makin' a lot of mess."

"You'd better go right to bed," said Joanna. She felt almost sorry for him. He looked wobbly as he stood up, and very slight and youthful between Nils and Stevie. They went upstairs with him and Joanna began to fix a tall glass of hot lemonade. When Nils called to her, she took it up to Mark's room.

Randy was sitting up in the bed. The lamplight threw his shadow on the slanting ceiling. In flannel pajamas, and with one of Donna's warmest quilts throwing its glowing, prismatic colors across the bed, he had managed to comb his soaked brown hair, and the mingled blood and sea water had been wiped away. He still looked white, however, and this, along with his thinness and his hair's tendency to curl when wet, added to his youthfulness.

Nils and Stevie had gone on separate errands to bring other things calculated to add to the invalid's comfort during the night. Randy took the hot lemonade meekly from Joanna's hands.

"Is there anythin' in it?" he inquired. "Besides lemon and hot water and sugar, I mean?"

"Not a thing," said Joanna. She watched him drink. "You should have come right up to the house instead of going to the mooring."

"I was scared to come rushin' right in again," he said vaguely "You know what they say, somethin' about where angels fear to tread . . . or whatever it is. . . ."

Joanna said, "You can put the glass on the stand when you're through." She started for the door.

"Only I figgered," the meek voice went on, "you'd be real hospitable to somethin' your husband lugged home to ye."

She turned once; and before the certain and brilliant triumph in his eyes, she knew so great a rush of pure rage that she almost ran the last few steps to the door, lest she give in and slap his face.

13

AT FIVE O'CLOCK IN THE MORNING, the Sorensens and Stevie ate breakfast by lamplight. The house was like a lighted island in the windless December morning which lay around it, still pricked by stars and the pale unreality of moonlight. Breakfast was warmed-up baked beans — that was when they were best — fresh johnnycake, and strong coffee. Upstairs, in the room over the kitchen, Randy still slept.

"He'll be going home today," Nils said. "Wonder if his father is worried about him being down here with us south-island cannibals."

"Fowler's as bad as Squire Merrill used to be. Father used to tell about him," Joanna said. "The Squire thought Bennett's was really a hunk of Brigport that seceded, like the Confederacy. But he didn't want to start any Civil War and hang all the rebels."

Stevie pushed back his chair and patted a non-existent stomach. "I'm so full my riggin's about to part, Jo. How's a man to set traps when he's so groggy?"

"By the time you get yourself down to the Eastern End you'll be ready for another breakfast," Joanna said. She got up to mix the coffee for the thermos bottles. The dinner-boxes were all packed, husky sandwiches and Vinnie's thick, filled cookies. Homemade mince meat was the filling; and it was made from the meat of the deer Caleb had shot last autumn.

Stevie puttered around the kitchen, collecting his thick wool socks and rubber boots and outdoor clothes, whistling under his breath. Nils stood by the seaward window, looking out to where the light at the Rock still swung its beam through the dark. There was no lightening along the horizon yet. By the time it came, Joanna thought, glancing past his shoulder at the outside world, both he and Stevie would be out there, Nils on his way to his traps, Stevie with Mark and a load of the spanking-new traps they'd been building. It was going to be a clear, calmly beautiful day, with the colors of midsummer intensified to an almost poignant degree, and all the more exquisite because it was a winter day and not a summer day.

Joanna knew those days and loved them. She wished suddenly that she could go with Nils, and breathe all day the pure cold air of the sea, build up a fire in the cuddy stove and drop jewel-bubbling lobsters into boiling salt water; eat them hot, along with the coffee from the thermos bottle, and then begin the afternoon's hauling.

But she couldn't leave the house because of Randy sleeping so peacefully and smugly upstairs. Her longing to go out on the water suffered a quick change and became anger. Trust Nils to bring Randy right back to the house again, as Randy had intended him to do. . . . Oh, Nils couldn't know the young devil had slipped overboard on purpose. He probably wouldn't believe it if she told him. . . . She clamped Nils' dinner-box shut with an eloquent snap, and he looked around at her.

"All ready?" he said. "I'd better be starting along, then. Don't look for me early. I'll probably have to chase around some, if that gale threw my gear out of line the way I think it did."

He pulled on his sheepskin vest and then his mackinaw. Stevie, still looking absent-minded, began to dress too.

Joanna said thoughtfully, "Then you probably won't be able to do anything about shingling today."

"Shingling?"

"The barn over at Uncle Nate's," she explained. "I noticed last night some more shingles had blown off. It ought to be fixed before the next storm." Nils stopped putting on his boots and looked at her quietly.

"Isn't that your uncle's worry?" he asked.

She felt a quick surprise. "Nils, if we see something to be done, we ought to do it."

"If there wasn't somebody to do it, that would be different." Nils pulled on the other boot. "Only Hugo's working over in the shipyard with nothing much to do on his weekends—"

"But raise hell," Stevie said, grinning. "So I hear."

"And he could come out and nail shingles just as well as I can. And better. I've got all I can handle now, Joanna."

Her astonishment had the effect of setting her back on her heels, hard. She could only stare at him, and he looked back, his blue eyes very calm. With just as much simple, unadorned conviction as he had ever said he *would* do a thing, he had now said he wouldn't. She wished suddenly that Stevie hadn't been there.

"You can write to your uncle," Nils said, "and tell him about the shingles."

"He'll wonder why we can't do it," she objected. She smiled at Nils, gathering her forces. "It would only take an hour or so."

Nils stood up. He took his cap from its hook. His voice came quietly, but it was the quiet of gray granite.

"Joanna, maybe you don't know what an hour means to me right now. But we've the old wharf to fix, and the boatshop; the long fish house needs to be straightened up and tar-papered. We've got to do something about Pete Grant's wharf before it gets any worse—"

"That's not your worry any more than Uncle Nate's place, then," she flashed out at him. "That isn't even in the family." Her cheeks were fiery. Nils had never been like this before.

"The whole Island uses Pete's wharf when they need it, and they don't use Nate's barn."

Stevie said eagerly from the door, "Look here, if Hugo can't do it, Mark and I'd be the ones to fix the barn, anyway. It's a Bennett barn, isn't it?"

Joanna didn't look at him. Neither did Nils. Their eyes stayed on each other's faces. Joanna felt a desperation stir within her. This was something more important than a few shingles on a barn. It was something that threatened her scheme of days, her whole life.

She said in a low voice, "Maybe you don't call it any of your affair to fix that saddleboard on the — the Whitcomb place. Or ploughing up the field for the gardens. Or any of the other things our family always looked out for."

"Joanna, I know what I've got to do," said Nils. He pulled the blue plaid cap on over his fair head; beneath the long visor his eyes regarded her bright dark ones, her flushed cheeks, her mouth held so straight and firm that there were tiny dents at either corner. "I get my work done. First things first. . . . Maybe you've forgotten that besides everything else I've got two hundred traps to tend. And I've got to take off at least two good days to take the lobsters ashore next week."

"You said you'd go," she reminded him passionately. "You said you didn't mind."

"I knew somebody had to go first, and I'd back you up in your plan, anyway. But — " His hand on the knob, he looked back at her. "But don't plan out anything more for me to do for a while yet, Joanna."

He went out. Joanna didn't move from where she was standing, neither did Stevie. He didn't look at her, and she was furious with him. Pitying her, was he, because she'd come off second best?

She began swiftly to clear the table and stack the dishes, determined not to watch Nils go down to the harbor through the paling light, wishing Stevie would take his dinner-box and get out of the house.

"Jo," he said hesitantly behind her. She slid the silver into the dishpan and reached for the teakettle.

"What is it?" she said, her voice even and pleasant.

"Maybe I shouldn't have hung around. I know that. But I want to tell you something before I go out."

She swung around and looked at him, and he smiled at her, a little shyly. "Maybe you think it's none of my business. Well, it isn't, except that you're my sister, and you've always been swell to me, and Nils is the finest kind. But sometimes a woman can't see so good as a man what gets under another man's skin."

"You'd better hurry up and get it said, Stevie. I've got a lot to do, and so have you."

Stevie fidgeted. "Well, look, Jo—maybe you've kind of forgot that most of his life Nils had somebody following him around and asking him when he was going to get this or that done—"

"You mean *Gunnar?*" Her hands behind her clenched hard at the edge of the dresser. "You mean I'm like Nils' grandfather, Stevie?" She smiled as if it was very amusing. Inwardly she was sickened with her rage and humiliation.

"No, I don't mean you're like Gunnar, but it's just the idea, see? At least that's the way I figure it. I think Nils used to get so damn' mad at that old bastard that the minute he thinks somebody's checking up on him—no matter who it is—he gets those feelings all over again." Stevie waved his hands vaguely, and knotted his brow. "See what I mean? And if anybody keeps it up, without reading the storm warnings, well, someday they're likely to see him rise up like hell coming sideways on a pair of wheels."

Joanna laughed aloud. "Stevie, you don't change. You're still that bird of ill-omen. Every good day was a weather-breeder, remember? You always believed in looking for the worst."

"And preparing for it," said Stevie. He grinned back at her. "Of course, you're married to the guy. You ought to know him better than I do, I suppose. Probably he'd never lose his temper with you—you're a lot more sightly than his grandpap was."

He grabbed up his dinner-box, took his cap and went out whistling. Joanna sat down. She didn't feel the rush of vigor and energy that usually came with her anger. She felt suddenly drained of all vitality. Again in her mind she saw Nils' blue eyes, and heard his voice; she wondered almost feverishly how long he had been thinking these things, if all the time when he had listened and agreed so calmly he had been preparing to say what he had said this morning. Or whether it had come on him all at once. Perhaps she would know sometime.

She began to do her morning tasks. She'd planned on a few hours work on her Christmas gifts, but now she had no heart for them. She told herself it was silly to feel so disturbed. What had happened this morning had no importance, really. When Nils came home that night everything would be as it always was.

But she couldn't keep from thinking about it. She washed and dried the dishes, shook the braided rugs from the back doorstep, the first apricot glow of morning over the black trees of the Eastern End hill lighting her face, and the quiet cold, sweet with frost, prickling her nostrils. She wiped off the stove and the teakettle, swept the floor and laid the rugs back in place. Her strong hands were quick and automatic. All the time her brain wondered, struggling toward a solution that would give her peace of mind. As soon as she arrived at some conclusion that turned the situation to her own advantage — as soon as she knew how to keep it from occurring again — she would be all right.

She started violently as she heard a knocking overhead. Then she remembered Randy. He was awake, and pounding on the floor for attention. Well, he'd get it. . . . She took his clothes from the drying rack over the stove. Except for his heavy trousers, she had washed the salt water out of everything last night, before she went to bed, taking no chances on his having an excuse to hang around. Stevie had contributed a pair of pants and some woolen socks. She had pressed Randy's shirt this morning while the beans were warming and the johnnycake was baking. With the clothing on her arm, she went upstairs. The morning light had flushed the walls of Mark's room a delicate warm tint; as she paused in the doorway she had a glimpse of the pale silvery unreal blue of the quiet sea beneath the blackness of the forest; and of the sky above it, pure glowing gold, flushed with rose, shading through clear yellow to apple green and thence to an unclouded transparent blue like that of the sea below.

Randy looked very comfortable in the four-poster, under Donna's quilts. He smiled at her, as if he didn't notice the line of her mouth and the set of her Bennett jaw.

"Mornin', Jo. What kind of a day is it?"

"If you'd lift your head an inch or so, you'd see. It's a perfect day for a trip to Brigport." She laid his clothes on the chair beside the bed. "Your breakfast will be ready when you come down."

Randy stopped smiling. A look of indefinable distress crossed his narrow brown face. He seemed to sink lower among the pillows.

"Honest, Jo, I don't see how I'm goin' to do it. Get up and dress, and then make that trip home. . . . Golly, I couldn't even set up, the way I feel now."

He stared unflinchingly into Joanna's unsympathetic dark eyes. The small dressing on his temple was very white against his skin. Skeptically she put her hand on his wrinkled forehead and felt the furrows dissolve; also, she felt the faint moist warmth of normal, healthy, young flesh.

"Where do you feel the worst?" she asked.

"All over. Achey. Like I was havin' the grippe." He shut his eyes and his smile was beatific. "Golly, your hand's cool, Jo."

She took her hand away. "Let me feel your pulse," she said briskly.

"If I pull my arm out from under the covers, I'll freeze." He shuddered. "You don't think I'm lyin', do ye? Honest, ever since I was a little tike, it don't take no more'n gettin' my feet wet to give me a good chill."

He turned his tumbled brown head languidly on the pillow. "They always been afraid of pneumonia."

Joanna went downstairs. *I'll ignore him,* she thought. *Nils brought him here, Nils can handle him.*

At another time she could have laughed at her predicament, appreciated its irony, and decided on a strategy to rout Randy. But not today. She was too taut and restless. If he managed to make her lose her temper, that would be his victory.

Downstairs she tidied her room and the sitting room, turned on the radio and turned it off again, paced through the kitchen like a caged animal. . . . Someone knocked at the back door. Eagerly she went to open it, and found Vinnie there. She had never been so glad to see the bright-eyed, birdlike little woman.

"Ain't this an ungodly hour to come callin'?" Vinnie said apologetically. "But I jest took a chance on it — seemed like I felt like talkin' to somebody this mornin'. Caleb's an awful silent soul."

"I've been up for hours," said Joanna. "I was just thinking of another cup of coffee. Will you have one too?"

"I guess I will!" Vinnie sat down in the rocker by the harbor window. Her bright amber gaze flew around the kitchen. "Look, Joanna, ain't that the Fowler boys' boat in the harbor? Caleb said it was. Now what do you suppose —?"

"I don't suppose, I know," said Joanna grimly. "Randy fell overboard last night, and Nils brought him up here."

"Oh, my!" Vinnie dropped her voice. "Imagine that! Randy's the pleasant-looking one, ain't he?"

"Yes." Joanna poured boiling water into the drip coffeepot. "He's going home today, if he ever gets up."

They both looked toward the ceiling as Randy pounded hard on the floor. "There he is!" Vinnie said brightly. "Jest wakin' up. And hungry too, I'll bet!"

Joanna had welcomed Vinnie, but now she wished she hadn't come. She couldn't very well ignore Randy's pounding now. Making pleasant conversation to cover up her inner grimness, she fixed a tray for Randy.

When she came into his room, he smiled at her with a reasonable facsimile of meekness and said, "Gosh, thanks, Jo."

"Don't mention it." She set the tray on the chair beside the bed, and turned to leave. Randy's voice followed her hungrily.

"My God, Jo, I can eat more'n that!"

"Sick as you are, toast and coffee are enough." She paused in the doorway, a secret glint in her eyes. "I'll bring up your medicine in a little while."

Randy pulled the covers around his neck. His thin pointed eyebrows lifted apprehensively. "What kind of medicine?"

"Castor oil," said Joanna serenely, and went downstairs. When she rejoined Vinnie she felt in a much better mood. The sun was high now, above a sea so blue as to hurt the eyes. On the horizon, the ledge and towers of the Rock rode like some great bronze ship. On the Island itself every rooftop glittered, every tree was haloed with light. The melting frost sparkled on the fields. All the boats were gone from the harbor now, and Joanna, while she talked children, husbands, and Christmas with Vinnie, thought of Nils out there, guiding the *Donna* from trap to trap, across a sea no bluer than his eyes.

Those eyes would be scanning the water. But what lay behind them?

Anyway, when he came in tonight, she'd tell him about Randy and the castor oil, and they would laugh together, and this morning would vanish as if it had never happened. As if Stevie had never reminded her about Gunnar. As if . . .

She said, with a sort of angry desperation, "Vinnie, are you having goose or turkey for Christmas dinner?"

"Whatever Marston's has." Vinnie giggled. "You know, I got a list already as long as my arm for Nils. You sure he don't mind?"

"Of course he doesn't mind!" said Joanna heartily. But she was glad when Vinnie left.

She waited a little while for Randy to show up, but all was silence from above. She took the castor oil bottle from the cupboard where the medicines were kept, and looked at it reflectively. She'd brought it from Pruitt's Harbor under protest, but Donna had insisted on it. There were other things easier to take that would serve the same purpose, but Donna said no one could live on an island without a bottle of castor oil on the shelf, and that the time might come when Joanna would be grateful to have it.

She patted the bottle now, and her mouth twitched. She could imagine how her mother's gentle blue-gray gaze would suddenly break into sparkles of welling mirth, when she heard how her prophecy had come true. Joanna took a dessert spoon from the drawer and went upstairs. Now that the duel had reached its climax, she was sure of victory.

Randy, reading a western story magazine, looked at the bottle without alarm. "I can't take that stuff," he told her glibly. "Makes me sick. You mix me up some hot buttered rum and I'll be fine." He smiled at her with all his charm. In the sunlit room his eyes were full of sunlight too.

Joanna uncorked the bottle. "I'm sorry, there's no rum in the house. This shouldn't make you sick. It's only your imagination."

Now he was vanquished. She was sure of it, as she poured the thick, viscous liquid into the spoon, conscious that Randy's gaze was on the thick glugging stream too. Now he would say he was ready to get out of bed and go home.

"Well," he said in a resolute voice, and sat up, "if you say I should take it, Jo, all right."

He shut his eyes and opened his mouth. Mutely, with a definite conviction that she herself was the vanquished, she put the spoon in his mouth. He swallowed convulsively, his thin face was agonized, and then he opened his eyes and stared straight into hers. He smiled.

"By Jesus," he murmured thickly, "you was right, Jo. Guess it *was* my imagination."

She turned to leave him again, and he caught at her arm.

"Stay and talk to me, Jo," he said wheedlingly. "I'm lonesome as hell."

"There are a lot of people on Brigport," she said, "who would probably be glad to talk to you, if you were over there." She left him.

After an interminable morning, she got herself some lunch. Then she put on her outdoor things and went out. It was the warmest part of the day. All color was at its highest peak, and as she felt on her face the mingled warmth and sharpness, and breathed the clean, coldly fragrant air, she felt her tenseness relax and float away. She walked around Schoolhouse Cove, past the schoolhouse and along the ruined seawall built of boulders smoothed and rounded by the seas that had tumbled over them into the very schoolyard and flooded the marsh. In the sunshine the boulders were pale blue, silvery gray, warm pinkish-brown, and lavender; they were picked out with the diamond sparkle of quartz. Over the wall, in summer, the wild roses bloomed, and the morning glories entangled their vines; beyond the wall the beach peas and evening primrose grew, and the beach, white in the noonday, slipped gently to an un-urgent, lazy-edged sea. And between the wall and the sandy road, where it was always sunny and sheltered in July, there would be wild strawberries, the first ones of the year.

Now, the places where the wild roses, the morning glories, the beach peas and vetch and evening primroses, and the strawberries, grew, were tangles of brown and yellow. In the cove there were loons swimming, and the winter sharpness of detail was in the air; the spruces marching over the hill to the Eastern End stood out in the sunshine, each one green and sharp among its fellows, and Uncle Nate's buildings looked as white and dazzling against them as if they didn't need paint. And over all mounted the sky, palely luminous along the horizon as if there were a hidden light behind it, deepening, as the eye climbed, to azure.

It was a day to wear forever on your heart like a diamond, Joanna thought, and indeed the world might have been sprayed with diamond dust.

She walked up through the Eastern End gate, but it was cold in the shadows of the trees, and she turned to go back again, into the sunshine. Caleb's boat was working her way home past Green Ledge, a throng of gulls fluttering down in her wake like blown scraps of paper. She wondered where Nils was.

She came out of the shade of the trees into the cleared rocky ground by the gate, and saw a man standing there. At first the sun was in her eyes. Then, as she kept walking, she recognized Randy. He came through the gate to meet her, a slight wiry figure in his boots and pea jacket and Stevie's trousers. He walked with a quick, conscious, self-assurance that was almost a strut. She thought that now he had decided to give up his annoying behavior and go home, and had come to tell her.

"Hello, Randy," she said. "Feeling better?"

He shoved his cap back, and she thought he looked a little drawn. Perhaps the castor oil *had* made him sick.

"Joanna," he said in a strained, husky voice. "I saw you goin' up this way. . . . Look, you know why I been hangin' around, bein' a nuisance. You know, don't ye?"

"No, I don't know," Joanna said evenly. But something in the steady darkening of his eyes and the whiteness at each corner of his mouth warned her. She felt the familiar signals, the quickening heartbeat, the flush along her throat. *Trouble.* She said, "Let's talk about it as we walk along."

Randy barred her way to the gate. "We'll talk about it here," he said.

"I'm going home, Randy," she answered him as if he were a child. But it was no child's hand that came out and seized her wrist.

"Not till you listen to me, by God!"

This was no laughing, clowning Randy. She was not afraid of him, almost she felt pity for him. But even in that instant of tolerance, he caught her off guard and pushed her back against a lichened wall of rock under the spruces, and his mouth was on hers.

She was as tall as he was, but her strength didn't equal his. His muscles were rock-hard; his mouth was fiery hot against her chilled lips, and it clung. She couldn't rid herself of it. One of his hands circled her left wrist in a fantastically unbreakable grip, the other held her right arm at the elbow. His slim, tough body held hers immobile. She swung her head from side to side to escape his mouth, but his lips were everywhere, voracious on her cheeks, her eyelids, on her throat.

After the first shock of pure astonishment, she was furious. She said between her teeth, "You *fool!* You *damn* fool!" To open her mouth was a mistake—he kissed it with a violence that left it smarting.

He pressed her back against the rock; a low branch caught in her hair and pulled it with every motion of her head. She heard the peacefully industrious sound of Caleb's engine chugging home, and the crows calling in the woods, and she was conscious of her thudding heart, her incredulous rage, the hard rock against her back, and of Randy's body against hers. She looked straight into his thin strained face, pale under the tan, and eyes from which all sunlight and laughter had gone. They were tormented eyes.

"Randy," she said gently. "Let me go. I'll give you a head start and you can be out of the harbor by the time I reach the house."

"You called me a damn' fool," he said. "Well, that's what I am. Damn' fool about you. I'm like to go crazy every time I see you. The way you walk, the way you hold your head, like you don't give a damn—I'm crazy about you, Jo." He took a breath and moistened his dry lips. "You could be nice to me, Jo. You gotta be. It won't hurt you none. You're a married woman, you—" He swallowed. "Jo, if you knew how I feel about you, you'd be nice to me! Please, Jo—"

It was as if his plea took all his strength. Joanna freed herself, and he made no move to hold her. He stood watching her, no strut left to him now, his eyes on her face.

"You'd better go home, Randy," she said. "And don't ever come back." Her voice was very quiet. "You stay on your own island. You don't belong on mine."

She walked quickly through the gate without looking back. She became aware, by the time she reached the schoolhouse, that her legs were shaky, her wrists and arm hurt, and that she felt like sitting down. But there would be no sitting down until she reached her own kitchen—a sanctuary where she could wash her face and comb her hair, and drink some strong coffee before Nils or Stevie came home.

Still she didn't look back. It wasn't until she had reached the doorstep that she paused, and looked down toward the harbor. She saw Randy then, following the path through the marsh. He walked as he had always walked, with a quick wiry arrogance.

She went into the house, feeling the homely, familiar peace of it drop like a mantle on her shoulders.

I've had a horrible day, she thought. *But its all over now.*

14

CRYSTAL DAY SLIPPED INTO AMETHYST TWILIGHT, and the men came home tired and cold and hungry, preoccupied by thoughts of warmth and a hearty supper; corned hake, boiled potatoes, pork scraps, mashed squash and piccalilli. And there was apple pie, still warm; Joanna had made it from the last of the Gravensteins that had grown on the twisted little tree close to the cemetery gate. They were Nils' favorite apples for pie, and this pie Joanna had made as his grandmother always made apple pie; in her biggest biscuit pan, with a thick snowfall of sugar and cinnamon and nutmeg over the tart apple slices, and the whole dotted with tiny bits of pork before the top crust was laid deftly upon it.

It was really a beautiful pie. "A real John Rogers pie!" Stevie said when it came out of the oven, sending its fragrant steam into the room. But it was at Nils that Joanna looked, and when she saw him smile, she felt a sudden loosening of muscles that had been oddly tense ever since he came into the house.

When they asked about Randy, Joanna merely said that he had taken his own time about getting up, but had gone home eventually. Already the incident under the spruces beyond the gate had become as remote as a dream. She could exclude it from her daily scheme of thought, for Randy was a person of no importance. Far more im-

portant was what Nils had said at breakfast time, and it had upset
her more than she would have believed it could do. For in her heart
she knew it was no slight thing. Without Nils and his unquestioning
support, there was so much she couldn't do; and one fact of which
she had been certain, when she married him, was that she would work
and dream and plan for the Island to the utmost, and what she couldn't
do with her own two hands, Nils could do. But if he was to be unexpectedly stubborn and strange, Nils, whose very dependability had
been one of the certainties in her life—it was incredible. And it mustn't
happen.

That had been a small thing this morning. But there would be
bigger things. And Stevie had sided with him. Stevie, of all people.
But he was only behaving as her other brothers had acted, she reflected
with a fatalistic bitterness that didn't show on her calm, firm-lipped
face. Not one of them could really know what the Island meant to
her; it was as if the mystic heritage of *oneness* with the Island had been
passed down to only one of the Bennetts, and that was herself.

She didn't suppose, as she darned Ellen's socks while the men
listened to the weather reports, that a few shingles on Uncle Nate's
roof meant all the difference between the rich growth or stagnation
of the Island. But she was certain of one thing; that Nils had never
said *no* to her before. And she wanted, more than anything in the
world, to be certain that he would not say it again.

She went to bed before Nils and Stevie did. From the unheated
room beyond the sitting room, she heard faintly the sounds from the
kitchen; the rattle of water pails and the shutting of the back door
as someone went down to the well. The wood dropping in the woodbox —that was Stevie—and the muted blows of the axe as he split
kindling in the shed. Then there was the return of Nils with the water pails—in the starbright silence of the night she had heard the cover
of the well drop back into place—and the men's goodnights, and Stevie
whistling as he ran upstairs, three steps at a time.

When Nils came into the bedroom, Joanna was sitting up in the
big pineapple-topped four-poster that had been Grandma Bennett's;
the room was lit by lamplight and in spite of its coldness it looked
warm, with the pastel-flowered paper, the old hooked rugs on the wide,
painted floor boards, and Grandma Bennett's Rose-of-Sharon quilt
on the bed. Joanna, in her flannel nightdress, was brushing her hair.

Nils got into bed and lay beside her, watching her, his arms folded behind his head. She gave him a quick smile and went on brushing her hair, her head bent over. His quietness seemed strange to her sometimes; Alec could never have lain so still, merely watching her. In another moment he would have pulled her down against his chest, laughing into her eyes, pulling at her nightdress till he could kiss her bare shoulders. But not Nils. Though she couldn't see his face she felt his blue eyes, and their look was as tangible as a touch.

"Your hair shines like a crow's wing," he said quietly. He took the brush from her hand and laid it on the stand beside the lamp. He turned down the lamp and blew it out. Then, with neither hesitation nor urgency, he pulled Joanna down beside him and put his arms around her. The stars came into the room; she saw Orion, frost-brilliant, against the upper panes.

For a long time they lay close and warm. The cold in the room was scented faintly with the lavender she liked to keep among the clean sheets. But near to her she smelled Nils' cleanliness, and the new flannel of her nightdress. Nils' breathing was deep and contented. Now was the time for her to speak.

She murmured his name into the darkness. "I'm sorry about this morning," she said, her voice warm with her sincere penitence. "I shouldn't have jumped on you like that. So early in the morning, too." She chuckled ruefully. "After you'd gone out I realized . . . but it was too late to call you back." She lifted her face so that she felt the warmth of his cheek near her mouth when she spoke. "I hated to have you go out like that and be mad all day because of my foolishness. Stevie looked at me as if I was a moron, and I guess I acted like one."

"I wasn't mad," Nils said. "You didn't have to worry."

"If you weren't mad, you gave a good imitation of it. Your eyes looked like blue ice." She chuckled again. "Anyway, I'll know better than to nag any more. You're right, Nils—Uncle Nate's roof isn't your affair."

She felt she had made a generous apology, and the matter had been taken care of. She felt wonderfully light and free. She was happy and even more generous. In the darkness she kissed his cheek and murmured, "Do you mind about taking the lobsters in, and going to the market? Because we could get Mark and Stevie to go—"

"I'll go," Nils said. "I've told you that already. But from here on you'd better let us men decide who'll make the trips, Joanna. Caleb and Jud, Mark and Stevie and myself." She stiffened instinctively, and he tightened his arm around her. His voice was easy and friendly. "I wasn't mad this morning, Joanna, but I thought I'd better make things clear. . . . I'd already figured out what to do about the saddle-board on the Whitcomb house, and the gardens. I've always got my work done, and kept all the loose-ends tied up, but I've never figured that I had to talk about it. Seemed as if doing it was enough. . . ."

She was rigid now. In the cold darkness she was not cold, and her skin burned. "I've already apologized," she warned him. "I guess I've got it through my head what you wanted me to know, Nils."

"I don't know if you have or not, Jo," he said. "No, don't move away from me. It's cold on the other side of the bed. . . . I think we ought to get this settled between us. We haven't been married very long, and we've got a long life ahead of us, and I want to tell you this. I'm not speaking ill of the dead, because I liked Alec, though God knows there were times when I wanted to cut his throat for what he was doing to you—"

She said in a desperate, smothered voice, " Nils, you'd better stop—" It was the first time he had mentioned Alec's name since they'd been married.

"I'll not stop," said Nils, and he wouldn't let her move away from him. "I know what kind of a woman you had to be, Jo—what kind of a wife. You were his backbone, and you'd have made a man of him if he hadn't drowned when he did. But it was a damned hard fight, wasn't it, Jo? Every step of the way you had to watch him and pick up the pieces each time, and a lot of the time you had to tell him what to do—didn't you, Joanna?"

"Why do you have to *talk* about it! What difference does it make to you what Alec did? Oh, Nils, I never thought you were so smug and self-righteous, and—"

She felt his hand come firmly over her mouth. "Be quiet, Jo. God in heaven, I'm not being smug. But maybe you think I wasn't supposed to notice the hollows under your eyes and the times you were sick with worrying because he was gone every night. . . . And here's what you don't know, and what I'm getting at. I made up my mind then that if I ever had you, you'd know what it was to take life easy and not be anxious and shamed every day of your life. Not driven. I wanted you to know what peace was, and I wanted to work for you, Jo. I guess that's what I wanted most. To wait on you and give you things, and give you a chance to laugh a lot, and keep your chin up the way you always did when you were a kid."

She said quietly, "Well?"

"I guess I've been taking the long way around, Jo. But what I meant to say was — you can take it easy now. You don't have to drive anybody — me or yourself. We've got a lot of time, and nothing's going to wash away the Island before we get it the way we want it to be. And I'll do my job without being told how, and you — you be easy, Joanna. And happy. That's all I want."

The silence came into the room, with the stars. Orion had moved. . . . Nils' arms tightened even more, and she lay against him rigidly, feeling the deep steady thud of his heart, and her own heart's swiftness. She sorted out his words in her mind, and what did they amount to? That he loved her, she had already known; that he had despised Alec's way of life, she had already known; and now she knew, beyond a doubt, what he expected of her beyond her body.

But it's my Island! her soul cried out in outraged protest. *I wasn't trying to drive him. I was only suggesting—* Words flooded to her lips in an angry torrent, but she held them back.

"We've always been honest with each other," he reminded her.

"Yes," she said in a tight, aching voice.

"That's why I told you those things." He searched for her mouth and found it, and kissed it. "If I wasn't so crazy about you, I wouldn't give a damn. But I've wanted you too long to let things go wrong now."

He kissed her throat gently, yet she sensed the passion behind the simple gesture. But tonight she could neither meet it nor pretend to meet it, and turned away from him with a gasping sound, as if she were suffocating. She actually felt stifled. He let her go. Quietly he said, "You thought I was smug about Alec. Well, I never was. Because no matter what he did, he could make you forget it when he touched you. I knew it, by the way you looked at him." His low voice stopped for a moment. "Know something, Joanna? You've never looked at me like that. Not once."

She turned back to him. She found herself crying and put out her hand to touch him. But it touched only sheets, still warm from his body; and Nils was shutting the bedroom door quietly behind him.

She waited for a time that seemed like an hour, though it couldn't have been more than fifteen minutes. The silence of the night deepened, and in it she could hear her heart beating. There was no other sound in the house. She wiped away her tears; they had come as an outlet for her almost unbearable nervous tension, and now she felt tired in every bone, as if with no effort at all she could sink into sleep.

But not with Nils gone. As she felt for her slippers in the dark, and pulled on her robe, she was faced with bewilderment. It was a new sensation for her. She didn't know what to do. She must tell Nils to come back to bed. He'd had a long day, and he needed his rest. After that — well, after that she would see. She put the thought resolutely from her and went out to the kitchen.

He was not there. The room was still warm from the dying fire, and the clock ticked placidly on the shelf. Amazing that this was the same kitchen into which she had come, also in darkness, at five o'clock this morning, to start breakfast; then the chief problem of her existence had been Randy Fowler. . . .

She halted in the middle of the room and listened. The light from the dock swept through the kitchen and caught her for a brief instant, tall in her robe, her eyes big and dark. The barn was connected with the house by the shed; and it was from the barn that the sounds came. Faint, yet distinct, the clean-cut rhythms of a hammer.

She went through the shed, past the orderly woodpile on one side and the oilskins hanging on the other — when she brushed against them their coldness sent chills over her; past the washtubs, the brooms and mops, and the other miscellany that had its place in the shed, and opened the door into the barn. Years ago, her father had fitted the barn up for a work shop, saying he was no farmer. And it was here that she found Nils.

He was patching pots. A lantern on the workbench gave him a yellow light by which to work, and he had kindled a sputtering driftwood fire in the old-fashioned stove.

Standing in the shadows around the doorway, watching him, she remembered how many times Nils had worked like this, with the same unflagging concentration, as if work were his one cure for everything that beset him. Going far back into her childhood, as far back as she could remember Nils, he had been like this. She remembered when he had first asked her to marry him — she had been nineteen then, and Nils twenty-one — and when she had shaken her head, he had turned back to his bench and his trapbuilding.

And now, past midnight, with the whole world sleeping around him, he was patching pots. Joanna walked forward into the yellow circle of lantern light and said, "Nils, I'm going to make some coffee. Do you want some?"

"I'll be in," he said. Another nail went home; tap, tap, *tap*. She went back through the shed and to her dismay found she wanted to cry again. She didn't know why. She realized all at once that she was living under an intense strain. At the moment it seemed unbearable. How had she ever dreamed she could live like this?

She stood by the stove waiting for the water to boil for the coffee, her head bent and her eyes closed. They ached. Her whole body ached. It didn't seem as if day would ever come again, and she dreaded it while she wanted it. The water boiled and she poured it over the coffee. At the same time she heard Nils' step in the shed. In a moment now she must meet his blue gaze, and here she stood, shamed and uncertain and tear-streaked as if she were ten again, and in disgrace. . . .

She lifted her head. *He wanted me,* she thought very clearly, her mind saying each word. *He wanted me under any conditions. We'd work together for the Island. And that's what it will be.*

He came into the kitchen and she turned her head toward him and smiled. *He had no right to reproach me for anything,* she thought. She said aloud, "Let's have some coffee and start all over again." Her eyes sought his and held them. "And I'm glad you were honest with me, Nils."

She saw how his strong, clean-boned face held its immobility for the fraction of a moment more; and then his slow smile broke through, lighting his eyes and lifting the somberness from his mouth. It was Nils' own smile; not dazzling, but as open and warming as sunshine itself.

He took out his pipe and began to fill it. "It's a good idea," he said.

"Coffee or honesty?" said Joanna quizzically. Her knotted nerves were beginning to loosen up.

"Both," said Nils. He smiled into her eyes, but he did not offer to touch her.

15

JANUARY BEGAN ODDLY; there would be two or three days of clear, almost mild weather, and then two or three days of high winds, sometimes with snow, sometimes dry and bright. But snow or not, the thunder of seas around the Island and the white water pouring over the harbor ledges were the same. As yet there had been no bad vapor storms, and for that they were all thankful. For the misty wreaths that rose like white smoke from the bright water, and shimmered in the winter sunshine, froze the flesh unmercifully.

The lobster car was finished now, and moored near the old wharf, in the most sheltered part of the harbor. Mark and Stevie had made the second trip ashore with the lobsters, and Caleb the third; it was working out, the men agreed, and so did the women.

It was something not to have to run into Brigport after their day's work to sell to a sardonic Ralph, who was either uncivil or who had just shut up the car and gone ashore. It was something for the wives to unpack a grocery order with everything in it they'd asked for. It was a much easier proposition to go across to Brigport only once or twice a week, when the tides and weather suited, to pick up the mail and the freight. Oil and gasoline constituted the largest items of freight. Sometimes there was trap stuff, or lumber, but more often that came out with the men who had taken the lobsters ashore.

With Christmas over and done with, Joey and Ellen went back to school. Lobsters were coming thickly on the days when the men could get out to haul and the Island was ready to draw a long breath. . . . It was Mark who first complained about his engine, and then Nils' engine stopped one day, out near the Rock. Then Caleb had trouble. It was too much of a coincidence.

Joanna heard them talking about it when she walked down to the shore one mild afternoon, and her heart sank. She was on her way to spend the afternoon with Marion Gray, and the men were clustered around the engine box in Caleb's boat, tied up beside the old wharf. Their voices were clear in the Island's quiet.

"I've just about decided," Caleb said, "that it ain't the engine that's at fault."

"You're damn' right it ain't the engine," said Mark bluntly. "It's water in the gas. And them Brigport bastards are doin' it."

It seemed to Joanna as if she had known all along what he was going to say. Brigport would think of something; water in the gasoline. Not Randolph or Ralph, or Tom Robey, had actually done it, probably, but it all belonged together. And if Randolph knew of it, he wouldn't protest. . . . She walked on up through the deserted village, toward Marion Gray's. She felt churned-up and uneasy. How could she endure it to sit still for an interminable afternoon and make casual conversation when this sickening anger made her want to fight?

But fight *what?* There it was, back again. . . . It was a mild gray afternoon, with a smell of snow in the air; Gunnar Sorensen's dark line of spruces seemed to pierce a soft pearly sky. The sea was gray too, and calm. By dusk the snow would be falling; as Joanna reached the clamshell path under the spruces, one flake drifted against her cheek with a light, cold touch.

Somehow the afternoon passed, and then she was walking homeward. It had been a pleasant enough two hours, talking and sewing and drinking tea with Marion and Vinnie. Helmi had been asked too, but she hadn't come, and already she had slipped into her allotted niche in Island life as "an odd girl." Joanna thought seriously about Helmi and Mark sometimes, but her own life seemed too complicated for her to concern herself with her brother's affairs.

Now as she walked home her footsteps on the frozen ground were the loudest sound in the tranquil dusk. The snow fell like a soft veil dropping from heaven, the touch of the flakes on her face was lighter than a breath. She thought how excited Ellen would be; she had taken her new sled back to Brigport with her.

The Caldwells' light shone across the harbor through the snow, and when she passed between the beach and the long fish house, and turned by the anchor and the tilted hulls in the marsh, she saw the lights of her own house, far at the top of the meadow. The marsh was powdered with snow, and the spruces were lightly coated. It was a still and beautiful evening. She felt as if she could walk forever. But there was supper to get for the men, and besides, she must know what they'd decided to do about the water in the gasoline.

Nils was reviving the fire. He looked up as she came in, her cheeks red from the cold, snow crystals melting on her uncovered dark hair, and the dampness making it wave.

"You look like the Snow Maiden my grandmother used to tell about," he said.

"Only I won't melt." She held her hands over the stove. "Nils, what are you going to do? About the gas, I mean?"

"Has that got around already?" he said good-naturedly. He took out his pipe and began to fill it. "Well, there's only one thing we can do. It's a sure bet one of the young gang over there is raising hell with our freight, loosening the vent in the tops of the barrels and putting water in." He stopped to draw and puff his pipe into life, his face absorbed. "Well, the idea that we sort of pulled out of the hat this afternoon is for somebody to go over there and wait for the boat on the days when the oil is due, and mount guard over it till we can get it off the wharf."

"That's all we *can* do," Joanna said.

"We'll have the stuff come out when the tide's high in the morning, so it won't have to hang around too long. And on real good days, we'll hire Link to come all the way down here with our freight. He'll do it when he's sure of getting in and out of the harbor all right."

"Well, you've covered all the loopholes," Joanna said. "Let's see what Brigport can do about *that* plan. But won't life be simple when we get the postoffice back, so Link'll have to come down here every mailday, whether he feels like it or not?" She sighed. "I never really appreciated Link and the *Aurora B.* till they disinherited us."

Nils grinned and went into the sitting room to get the news. Joanna began to prepare supper. Lobster hash tonight. And Stevie would be home in a little while, famished as usual.

A new supply of oil was due at the end of the week, and Mark, spoiling for a fight, had volunteered to look out for it. If it was a good day, Stevie could leave him at Brigport, and then go to haul. Captain Merrill's boatshop was handy to the wharf, and the Cap'n had a soft spot for Stephen Bennett's boys; Mark could warm himself at the Cap'n's fire until the *Aurora B.* steamed in past the breakwater.

The day was as mild and tranquil as the glass had said it would be. Nils, who had hauled his complete string of two hundred pots in the last few days, intended to work on the Island till mid-morning, when the mailboat would have arrived, and then go over to Brigport. He and Mark would lash the oil drums on the *Donna* and bring them home.

He was out of the house at sunrise, to put new tarpaper on the roof of the long fish house. In the late morning Joanna saw him coming up through the meadow that glittered with a new snowfall, and she had fresh coffee and mince turnovers waiting for him. Behind him the sparkling marsh reached to the harbor that shone doubly blue against the whitened shores. Nils' plaid mackinaw and bare blond head were spots of pure color against the clean brightness of the blue and white world.

She knew how he would be when he came in; in his voice and manner and expression he would be exactly the same Nils. *Almost* exactly. . . . Sometimes she could hardly believe there had been a night when he went out to the shop at midnight to patch pots. Neither of them ever mentioned it, and it might never have happened at all; except that he rarely touched her. And that was not very strange, she told herself, because he was working so hard. On days when he hauled he was gone for ten hours at a stretch. When he didn't haul he was busy around the Island from daylight till dusk, and no day was too cold for him. He was becoming a byword with the others. He had enough energy and industry for ten men.

Sometimes Joanna had a queer, unsettled feeling about the whole thing, a self-reproach that she couldn't understand. After all, she reminded herself now as she watched him come toward the house, she had done nothing wrong.

Today he told her the coffee was good, and the turnovers. Then he added unexpectedly, "It's a good day. You want to take a sail over to Brigport?"

"Oh, *yes!*" She felt fifteen again, with Nils asking her to go to haul with him, as she changed into flannel slacks and a warm plaid shirt. When they left the harbor, the *Donna* riding effortlessly across the pale blue swells, he told her to take the wheel, and it felt good under her hands, just as the floor boards felt good under her feet, with the steady purring beat of the engine going up through her legs. She turned her head to look at Nils.

"Thanks, Nils."

"She feels good, doesn't she?" he said. "Acts like a lady." He went forward into the cuddy and began to set things in order. Joanna smiled at him. Nils and his housekeeping. She doubted if even her father had kept the *Donna*'s cuddy so immaculate. . . . She felt curiously light-hearted and confident when she was on the water, with the boat's sturdy timbers under her feet and the wheel obeying her fingers, and the clean high bow obeying the wheel. Even with a January breeze stinging her face and tightening her skin, it was glorious. It would be more glorious if she and Nils could always be like this, as they had been when they were young; friends — no, comrades who liked the same things and to be together. If they could forget the interlude in between — a shadow of her spasmodic heavy-heartedness came over her and she brushed it impatiently away. Now it was time to concentrate on getting around Tenpound. There was a tricky surge here, even on the finest days. The gulls flew between the shining swells, and Whit Robey's sheep looked down from the peaks of rock.

The *Aurora B.* was at the big wharf in Brigport's harbor when the *Donna* came up through the Gut. There weren't many power boats at their moorings, it was a good day to haul. Nils shut off the engine, and in the sudden silence they heard the breathy puffing of the hoisting gear aboard the *Aurora* as she got rid of her freight.

"No time for Mark to have a fight today," Nils said.

"I'm glad," Joanna said. "Helmi wouldn't like it if he came home with a black eye and a split lip. She probably thinks he's beautiful."

"Nice for Mark," Nils said dryly. He slipped the *Donna* safely by the *Aurora*'s broad stern and tied up beside Cap'n Merrill's float. Joanna looked for Mark among the group on the wharf, but she didn't see him. As she went ashore, Nils was already climbing over the side of the mailboat, and thence to the wharf.

Cap'n Merrill wasn't in his boatshop — at mail time the store was the center of attraction. She glanced in at the half-finished boat, remembering with a smile how Joey had talked about it when he was home for Christmas vacation — he had forgotten to be shy, then. She picked her way around the rocky path, icy in places, behind the fish houses, and went up the slope to the store.

The mail had already been handed out, and the store looked more like a clubroom at the moment. On most winter boat-days, the women who lived far up on the island didn't come down to the harbor, but today's mildness had brought out quite a crowd. Joanna, walking among them, greeted them and was greeted; she didn't notice any restraint. Most of these people she had known since babyhood. . . . Because it was a good day, and almost windless, there weren't many men in the store, except a scattering of older ones like Cap'n Merrill, who was hearty in his welcome, and Whit Robey, who boomed at her.

"I'm thinkin' of keepin' that girl of yours, Joanna! By gorry, she's a hummin' star!"

And so, smiling, Joanna came to the postoffice window, and Randolph Fowler.

"Good morning," she said. "I'll take all the Bennett's Island mail, if you please."

He turned away from the window and began to collect the mail. Joanna looked at his back in the clean gray twill jacket, and listened. She listened for any change in the tempo of conversation around her; for that would tell her how Brigport—the real Brigport—thought about her and about Bennett's. But there was no sudden silence. The talk went on about war news and recipes and grandchildren and husbands. Joanna didn't know exactly why, but she began to relax a little. After all, the Fowlers and their associates weren't the whole of Brigport. And some day they'd be gone—

Randolph Fowler came back to the window, and slid the mail under the grating. "I want to thank you," he said, "for looking out for Randy the night he fell overboard."

"You're welcome," she murmured. Their eyes met. Neither smiled. She thought, *It hurts him to have to thank me. But he'd do it, because he's that kind of a hypocrite.* . . . She was astounded by the depth of her antagonism. She turned away from the window and went out of the store.

The winter sunshine and the clean, cold air were good against her face. She took long breaths, and thought of Randolph Fowler who spent his days in the dimness of the store, moving and speaking quietly, never shouting or swearing; but always weaving his plans, giving his quiet orders to those who must obey him. His brother, his sons, Tom Robey; and they, in turn, had those whom they influenced.

As she reached the wharf she saw Mark lounging against an oil drum, smoking, and Nils was standing a little apart from the others, with Link Hall; probably paying him for the freight. It was such a commonplace scene, the wharf at boat time, that her dark thoughts began to dissolve. The Pierce boy who did odd jobs for everybody was wheeling boxes of bread and crates of oranges up to the store. He grinned at Joanna, who winked at him. His grin expanded even more and he trudged on, whistling.

She reached Nils, and Link grunted his usual salutation in her direction and left. She watched his thick, rolling figure go toward the store, and then Mark approached.

"Well, what next?" he said. His black eyes were brilliant. "My God, if there hasn't been some tongue-wagging around here this morning! Nobody could figure out what I was hanging around for."

"What did the Cap'n say?" asked Joanna.

"He guessed. Told me it was a good thing. Some of the men don't take it too kindly, our taking our trade away from Fuss-face and his brother out yonder." He waved his arm at the lobster car in the harbor. Smoke wreathed from the chimney of the little shack on it, and Ralph's double-ender was tied up alongside. It was too early for any boats to be in from hauling yet.

"As soon as Link gets the *Aurora* out of the way, we'll start rolling the oil aboard," Nils said. "I brought some planks along so we won't have to use any of Brother Randolph's property."

"Except his wharf," said Joanna. "Maybe we ought to pay him wharfage. Just in case."

Link came back with the mailbags, and there was a stir on the wharf. He had two passengers today, the elderly Merrill sisters; Fred Bowers, the engineer who had grown grizzled and mahogany-colored in the *Aurora B.*'s service, helped them down the gangplank with their blankets and suitcases, and then went below to warm up the engine.

"All aboard!" Link growled around his cigar.

With the *Aurora B.* steaming out of the harbor, Nils swung the *Donna* around until she was close to the wharf. The tide was high, and with the planks laid, there was just enough gentle incline for Mark to roll the drums aboard the stern, where Nils lashed them so they couldn't move.

The wharf was deserted now in the flood of sunshine. The two men worked quickly, and Joanna sat on a crate and watched them. If Randolph should be watching from the store, and Ralph from the lobster car, she hoped they were grinding their teeth at the way they'd been circumvented. If Randolph's mustache were longer, she thought, he could twist the ends and say "Curses, foiled again!" She giggled at the thought. Mark said, "What's the matter? You nuts?"

"Slightly!"

Mark grunted, heaved his strong body, and another full drum rolled slowly over the planks. Nils steadied it, pushed and tugged it into position on the *Donna*'s broad stern, and his hands were fast as lightning with the ropes.

Joanna opened a letter from her mother. . . . Footsteps began at the far end of the wharf. She looked back, idly, and saw Winslow Fowler and one of the younger Robeys sauntering toward her. She returned to her letter. A boat came into the harbor, its engine loud in the stillness, and stopped briefly at the lobster car before it went to its mooring.

Winslow and the Robey boy—it was Tom's nephew, Earl—stopped at the edge of the wharf, near the planks, and watched the job. Mark and Nils worked as if they had no audience, and Joanna, glancing up from her letter, noticed how Winslow's face darkened. He didn't like being ignored. . . . Apparently Randy was out hauling alone today; Winslow was limping slightly, and she remembered a snatch of words she'd heard in the store, about Winslow wrenching his knee.

He didn't look toward Joanna, his narrowed gaze was intent, first on Nils, aboard the *Donna,* and then on Mark, on the wharf. Joanna watched his sulky face. Even his shoulders were sullen, under the soft new leather jacket. The other boy, Earl Robey, was a weedy youth, and pimply. He might have been a Robey, Joanna thought, but he had none of the Robeys' breadth of chest. He turned to Winslow with a remark under his breath, and then snickered.

Two men rowed in from the boat they had just put at her mooring. They were middle-aged men; she knew one as the Pierce boy's father, and the other was a Merrill, a distant cousin of the Cap'n's.

They greeted Nils civilly as they tied up their double-ender to a spiling near the *Donna*'s bow, climbed up the ladder and touched their
longvisored caps to Joanna.

They had barely passed Winslow and his chum when it happened. It was quick, yet Joanna saw it in its entirety, by some lucky
fluke; if she had glanced back at her mail, she would have missed
the incident. She saw Mark roll an oil drum toward the gangway of
planks, gather his muscles for a quick heave—and she saw Earl
Robey's boot shoot out. She heard the planks clatter, hesitate, and
then rattle downward—one to fall into the *Donna*'s cockpit with an
astonishingly loud sound, the other to slip endwise into the space of
water between boat and wharf.

With one swift motion Mark's hands flew out and balanced the
drum before it could roll overboard. ""You goddam son of a bitch!"
he said. He rolled the barrel back to safety and walked toward the
other two. Nils climbed up to the wharf; the older men turned back
and waited, a lively curiosity in their faces.

Earl Robey stepped back behind Winslow. Hands in his pockets,
Winslow faced Mark insolently. "Who you callin' a son of a bitch?"
he said.

"Both of you," said Mark, "unless one of you prefers to be called
a bastard." He balanced lightly, his big brown fists swinging at his
sides. "You're kind of free with your feet, Earl. Let's see how good
you are with your hands."

Earl laughed from beyond Winslow's shoulder. Some of his teeth
weren't very good, Joanna noticed. It was odd how you saw such
things in an instant when you were holding your breath, when the
whole world seemed to be standing still, as still as the older men who
were looking on, as still as Nils, at the edge of the wharf.

"Come and get me," Earl said. He was skinny, and Winslow
wasn't very big, but there was no telling what dirty stunt they'd worked
up. Mark took another step forward.

"Looks like I'll have to move Turd-heels out of the way first,"
Mark said, and his hand fell on Winslow's shoulder, took a good hold
on the soft leather, and jerked him to one side. Winslow's knuckles
grazed his cheekbone, and instantly Mark forgot about Earl Robey,
who retreated to a safer distance.

Jonas Pierce said hastily, "Christ, I don't blame you none, Mark, but Win's got a bad leg. You oughtn't to—"

Merrill nodded gravely. Nils, no expression flickering in his face, walked forward and touched Mark's arm. "Better stop before you beat him up," he said easily. "You want a fair fight, don't you?"

"Hell, that bastard don't know the meanin' of a fair fight!" Earl sneered. Winslow, unable to move in Mark's grip, said, "Leave him be. He'd liefer fight a man with a game leg—that's the only way he can lick him."

He was released so suddenly that he staggered. Mark's brown face was savage. "I never tackled a little guy yet, or a lame one."

"But that's what he was trying to get you to do, Mark," Joanna said quietly. "Before witnesses. It's been done before." She ignored Nils' quick warning frown. She was so furious that she could not have kept silent, yet her words came evenly. "It's another one of those dirty Fowler tricks. And he's fixed it so even a couple of decent men would have to swear to it."

Pierce and Merrill seemed suddenly embarrassed. Mark lit a cigarette with a violent gesture. As if nothing at all had happened, and neither Winslow nor Earl Robey existed, Nils said, "Well, let's get the rest of that oil aboard."

"I shouldn't be surprised," said Joanna, surveying Winslow as if he were a particularly repugnant specimen of eel, "if he was responsible for putting the water in the gasoline. Its just the kind of scummy underhanded thing his crowd goes in for."

"And who do you think you are?" said Winslow, his voice thick and dark. "The Queen of the Bennett's Island bastards?"

"You want to be careful, Winslow." Nils spoke gently. But he had been standing apart from the others, and now he was between Winslow and Joanna; and though his hands were in his pockets, his eyes silenced Winslow as thoroughly as a hand across the sullen mouth. "You don't want to say too much," Nils said. "You may have to answer for it some day."

There was a little wake of silence behind his words. Winslow's eyes clung to Nils' face as if they were held there, beyond his will. Then he laughed jerkily. "Why don't you slap me down, if you think I've insulted your wife?"

Nils regarded him for another long moment, then turned toward Mark. "Come on, let's get back to work."

The incident was over. Jonas Pierce and George Merrill murmured awkward good-byes and left the wharf. Earl Robey, who had stopped grinning a while back, started after them. Winslow followed.

16

FEBRUARY BROUGHT THE WORST STORM YET. It was a time of cold and of exceedingly high tides, a time of nervous tension, of worry, of getting up in the night to dress and fight the wind that tried to keep you from reaching the shore, and in the wild moonlight you looked to see if the boats were all right. Joanna would get up whenever the men did, and watch from the house; she couldn't decide whether the surf looked more deadly by sunlight or moonlight. But she was certain that the endless thunder and surge, and the keening of the wind around the house, were not easy to endure. Oddly, it was better if you were out in it, even if the cold burned the skin of your face and the wind knifed through your heaviest clothes. When you were in the house, and looked out at the ceaseless assault of the sea against the rocks, and heard how the wind shook the house with a fury that seemed always to mount instead of to decrease, you felt sometimes the stirring of a primitive alarm. But outside, you felt the solidity of the Island under your feet, and remembered how many years it had remained like this, how many storms had battered its shores and lashed at its trees . . . and then you felt secure.

She wondered how the other women took these things. Marion Gray was used to them, but she was getting along in years; and the Island life was completely new to Vinnie and Helmi.

But Marion complained only of the continual rush of wind

through the trees around her house. "Sounds like we was bein' taken over by a tidal wave," she said. "But I guess I like it just as well as hearin' those banshees howl around your place!"

Vinnie admitted she was nervous, worrying about Caleb's traps, and she missed Joey on the weekends when the children couldn't come home. And it was impossible to keep the windows clean. That was her biggest complaint. Then she laughed.

"But now I've gone and fussed about it, I'll feel all right. It's good to have somebody to complain to," she said. "Caleb's one of them men of few words. Less even than Nils, I think sometimes."

As for Helmi, Joanna couldn't find out. One day she braved the wind and walked down to the Eastern End. It was bad enough across the open field between the schoolhouse and Uncle Nate's place; the woods offered respite for a while, though the ground seemed to tremble under her feet with the undiminished strength of the sea piling up on the rocks below the path. Sometimes she felt flying spray against her face. Five miles out, the Rock was almost hidden in a smother of white; the nearer ledges were buried in surf, showed briefly, black and deadly against the gray-blue, and then disappeared again; spray flew up in great fountains where they had been. The gulls rode the wind.

The instant she came out of the woods, on the rise by the gate, the wind attacked her. She held to the gatepost with one hand and her beret with the other, and narrowed her eyes against the cutting edge of the wind and looked around her. The smoke from the chimneys was whipped away in shreds. At the far end of the brown field, the Head rose, solid rock sown with dead grass and spangled with wind-dwarfed spruces; immutable. On either side of the field, which sloped down from the ridge where the buildings were, the sea rolled in without pause. In Eastern End Cove it was not as fierce. But on the seaward side breaker after breaker reared up and rushed shoreward and tumbled, roaring, into frothing white confusion among the jumbled rocks. When Joanna remembered that for a week there had been a sea and a wind like this, she wondered if her sister-in-law would show any signs of tension.

But when she asked Helmi, later, over the coffee cups, the girl shrugged. "I don't notice it much," she said. Something about her kept Joanna from telling her what Vinnie and Marion had said. Helmi wouldn't be interested in them, or even in Joanna. It wasn't conceit, Joanna thought; it was just that nobody else existed for her except Mark. So she wouldn't notice the wind shrieking around the house at night because she would have Mark to herself then.

The boys came in for a mug-up, and again Joanna saw the clear, brooding, green gaze rest on them. The other look, which Joanna had caught once, didn't come back. Watching Helmi's way with the boys, a silent way of serving them, of nodding at their compliments on her turnovers, of shrugging at their jokes, she thought with a tinge of sadness, *We all have something. She has her jealousy. Nils and I . . .*

It must have been the wind that made her feel like this. She wouldn't stay very long. In her own kitchen she would feel better. And if the wind would stop blowing she wouldn't have these morbid thoughts.

Walking briskly homeward she thought about herself and Nils. *There isn't really anything wrong with us,* she reflected. *We're honest with each other, anyway.*

The next day was boat-day but nobody went over to Brigport. The mouth of the harbor was rough enough; but even if anyone had wanted to get through it, the way back from Brigport would be too dangerous. Nils went down to the shore to work with Caleb and Jud on the old wharf. They were re-planking it, and had cut stout straight spruces for the new spilings. Mark came up, and he and Stevie went down to help out. So Joanna was alone in the kitchen. She paused frequently to look down across the wintry marsh at the harbor and the surf on the rugged point beyond Caldwells'.

It was in one of those pauses, when she was getting dinner on the table, that she saw the boat come into the harbor. She saw it plunge down almost out of sight between the swells, rise up again, wallowing crazily in the tide-rip. Panic tightened her throat. It was a Brigport boat coming. That could mean a telephone call — a telegram — an emergency. She wondered if the men down at the shore saw it. She wanted to put on her things and hurry down there. Watching the boat come into the comparative peace of the harbor, heading straight for the old wharf, she felt as if she couldn't bear to stand here dumbly and wait. She dressed and went out into the bitter wind that tried to blow her down the slope to the marsh.

The boat was almost up to the wharf, and the men had stopped to look. Caleb was lighting his pipe, and the puffs of smoke were blue in the bright air. He glanced up from under his shaggy brows at Joanna.

"Kind of in a pucker, ain't ye?"

She grinned at him, a little anxiously. "It's an occasion, isn't it?"

"The rest of 'em think so." He nodded his head toward the end of the wharf, where Nils, Mark and Stevie stood, with Jud craning his short neck to see past them as the boat slid within hailing distance.

"It's Jonas Pierce," Joanna said. "I wonder what he wants." Her heart was hammering. She told herself it was from her quick walk down from the house.

"Looks like he's got a passenger," Caleb said. They walked down to the others, just as Pierce cut off his engine and the boat reached the wharf. He grinned up at them, his angular Yankee face burned red with cold across cheekbones and nose.

"Mite cold, ain't it?" he called up. "Got company for ye. He come out in the mailboat. Tried to keep him with me till better weather, but he wan't interested." He clambered up on the bow and threw a line to Nils, who made it fast around a spiling. There was someone coming out of the cuddy, a tall man in a leather jacket and brown tweed trousers. He had to bend his head and broad shoulders to get through the small opening. It was Owen Bennett. For six years they'd half-believed him dead; and they'd believed beyond halfway that they'd never see him back on the Island again, big and handsome, with a sort of wild, glowing strength that flashed out from him like too-dazzling sunshine from the sea. He had never written, or looked back in all those years. Now he had come home.

Joanna's first thought was, *I never saw him look like that before,* and her heart felt a great shock. The dark Bennett eyes that swept over the silent group in that instant were the same, but not the gaunt face, with the big bones showing so clearly, and the sallow-tinged pallor instead of the warm, healthy brown.

It was Mark who recovered first from his astonishment. "Jesus Christ!" he exploded, and jumped down into the cockpit. "You old— where the hell have you been?" He was pummeling Owen in the ribs, and Owen was laughing; it brought him back then, the old Owen. No, it was a ghost of Owen. No wonder her throat kept drying.

"My brother," she said swiftly to Caleb. She ran forward over the new planking, conscious suddenly of movement all around her. Stevie was handing up Owen's bag to Nils, Jud was shaking his head and repeating, "I never would of knew him!" The water surged in long swells against the spilings and washed over the rocks beneath the planks, the surf roared and flashed on the harbor points, the gulls swooped down to the sea and rose straight upward again on the wind.

Owen climbed up on the wharf. He shook hands all around, and his voice was the same. "How goes it, Nils?" "Hi, kid," to Stevie. "That you, Jud? I'll be damned!" Yes, his voice was the same. . . . *Almost* the same. *But it's too quiet,* Joanna thought in bewilderment. Everything about him was too quiet. Where was the magnificent noise of him?

His eyes met hers then, and his whole expression sharpened, as if he saw her questioning. It was only for a moment, and then as she smiled at him, she could have sworn she saw his eyes go blank. It was as if she had spoken her question aloud and he was pretending he hadn't heard it. Instead he put his arms around her and kissed her cheek. She hugged him back, and felt his thinness.

"Anything to eat up at the house?" he demanded.

"Pea soup and johnnycake," she said promptly.

"Then what are we waiting for?" He picked up his bag. Nils and Mark and Stevie began to pick up the tools they'd been using on the wharf.

Jud said, "Makes me think—I'm kind of lank. Wait till I tell the old lady who come! . . . Come on up to the house, Jonas, and have a mug-up!"

"Wait a minute, Owen," Joanna said. "Here's a new Bennett's Islander. Caleb Caldwell."

Owen, his eyes appraising, put out his hand to meet Caleb's. "How do you like it?"

"I like it fine," said Caleb, and if Owen's glance was appraising, Caleb's took in every line and plane and indentation of Owen's face in the brief moment when his eyes looked out from their shaggy-browed hollows.

Then Owen smiled, and in that smile and the way it warmed his voice, he was completely Owen. "That's good. It needs men like you." He walked on, toward the road, and Joanna followed him. Behind her came Nils, and the boys.

It seemed to Joanna that she had no time at all that day to be alone with her thoughts; if she could just be alone a half-hour she could figure things out, and adapt herself to Owen's being home again. To this new Owen, rather; for she could not reconcile him with the Owen who had alternately tormented and cajoled her, who had taken her tongue-lashings and sworn good-naturedly at her temper, who had filled the house with storm or a very boisterous sort of sunshine. There was racket enough in the homestead that afternoon, but it was Stevie and Mark who made it, it was Owen who sat still, talking sometimes with Nils, or not talking at all, but merely smoking, and listening.

She would watch him covertly; his profile was the same, decisively cut, with quick, strong strokes as if the sculptor had known exactly where he was going. It was like all Bennett profiles, bold of nose and chin, with eyes deep-set.

But this quietness. . . . That was what baffled her.

Late in the afternoon, when the foot of the meadow was hidden in a faintly purple cloak of shadow, Mark went home. He bade them all a blithe farewell. "Five of us, now," he said exultantly. "Five Bennetts. Jesus, we're doin' all right!"

"Who makes five?" Joanna asked quickly, laughing at his excitement. "You can't even count straight."

"I forgot. Nils isn't a Bennett." Mark grinned at Nils. "But he's the same as one."

Joanna didn't know why she felt uncomfortable. She glanced quickly at Nils, and said, "Maybe that's a doubtful compliment. He'd probably rather be a Sorensen."

Mark laughed and shrugged. "Well, anyway . . . Take a walk down one of these days, Owen. Everybody come down. My God, it isn't the end of the world down there!"

"Pretty damn' near it," Owen observed. He lit another cigarette. "Remember me to your wife."

Stevie picked up the water pails and went out with Mark. Owen stood up and stretched his long, lean body. Too lean for Owen, Joanna thought, remembering how he had always made even the biggest room seem small. He said, "Hey, Jo, where am I supposed to turn in?"

"In your own room, of course," she said. "It's all straightened up for you."

"I'm going up then. Take a soshe before supper." "Take a soshe!" That was what he'd always said for "take a nap." Joanna said suddenly, "Are you glad to be home, Owen?"

"Happy as a clam at high water." He grinned down at her, and then went past her. They heard him going up the stairs. Not running, the way he'd done six years ago. She and Nils stood in the kitchen, listening to the sound of his feet, and their own silence lay immutably between them. Then Nils said, "He forgot his bag." He picked it up, and then Joanna was alone. Distantly she heard their voices, and then the shutting of a door. She turned back to her supper preparations.

While she worked, she tried to remember what Owen had said since his arrival at noon. Not one word of what he'd done in those six years, since the morning he'd said the Island was too small for him, and had walked out of this kitchen. He had kissed Ellen goodbye, she remembered, lifting her out of the high chair and touching his big nose to her diminutive one. He'd been splendidly confident, ready for anything, he'd had money in his pocket and the superb health of a young lion.

And that was all they had known of him. She'd had her own griefs and preoccupations; trying to darn smoothly over the cruel tear in her life's fabric that had been Alec's death; seeking a way to a clear independent future for Ellen and herself; watching the Island life go to pieces. Then, when only her father was left, stubbornly hanging to his boat and his traps, sure the tide was on the turn, there had been the fire that took the traps, and so they had left the Island. But they had not thought it would be for long. They had never dreamed that Stephen, her father, would never see it again, and that it would be five years before she set foot on its red rocks again.

It had been hard, trying to find a new rhythm for life on the mainland. Sometimes it had been torment for her, who had been so passionate and stubborn in her oneness with the Island.

So she had not thought about Owen too much, except to believe he would fall on his feet, whatever happened to him. . . . But now, in her thirties, with Ellen growing fast, she looked back to that time and wondered at the iron courage of Donna and Stephen. What agony of spirit must have been theirs! What torment her mother must have endured, thinking of Owen, for whom she had always feared! She remembered her father's steel-lipped face when Charles, the oldest son, had brought home the girl he'd "got into trouble." So how had he felt about Owen?. . . Some day she could speak about it with her mother, but she would never find out what Stephen had really thought. . . .

Dusk was filtering softly into the corners of the kitchen, and behind the saw-toothed black wall of woods the sky was darkening bronze. Nils hadn't come down from upstairs yet. She felt a pang of jealousy because they were talking; yes, they'd always been chums, but so had she and Owen been comrades of a sort, and sometimes, in rare moments that she had never forgotten, they had come close to each other.

But the pang didn't last for long. She knew she should light a lamp, and dispel the dreamy sadness that surrounded her, but at the same time she wanted to hold on to it. She wondered if her father knew that tonight two of his sons and his daughter were to be sleeping in this house—the boys in their old rooms, and the girl, as mistress of the house, in the room where he and his wife had slept. And that Owen had come home. . . .

She wasn't surprised to feel tears slipping down her cheeks. She stood alone, looking down at the dusk-rimmed harbor, the shadows thickening behind her, and let her sadness possess her. She felt weak and tired, and it was a relief to let go, if only for a moment. She didn't know Nils had come down until he spoke quietly from the darkness behind her.

"You want a light, Joanna?"

"No!" she said swiftly, and then, with a quietness to match his: "I didn't know you were here—you startled me. No, don't light the lamp, Nils. Not yet."

She didn't want him to see the tears. They were a sign of weakness. She stared out toward a harbor that was no longer to be seen. Nils came and stood beside her. He didn't touch her, but she felt his nearness.

"Tired tonight?" he asked her gently.

"Not tired." And then, because of the bewilderment that had pursued her all day, and her sense of weakness, she surrendered to an impulse and said, "I'm worried, Nils."

"About Owen?"

"Yes." She turned to him quickly, straining to see him in the dimness. "What's the matter with him, Nils? He's not himself."

"He's tired, Jo, that's all." She felt Nils' hand brush her cheek, and his finger discovered a tear. He put his arm around her shoulders and she was oddly grateful for it.

"Tired?" she repeated.

"Worn out. He told me a little about it. He's done about everything a man could do and still live, I guess. And it's nearly killed him." Nils spoke calmly and uncritically. "He collapsed after a while. Came home as soon as he could crawl, he said." He paused for a moment. "He didn't say much. Probably will talk more, later. But there was one thing he said—that he never thought he needed the Island, till he found out he *did* need it. So he came home."

"So he came home," Joanna said slowly. She stood in the circle of Nils' arm without moving. "Thanks for telling me, Nils. About what ails him, I mean."

"Don't let it get you down, Joanna." His arm tightened around her shoulders.

"I'm not letting it get me down," she said, and suddenly the moment of weakness was past. She straightened her shoulders imperatively against his arm. "Nils, we'll have to get him back into shape. Plenty of eggs and milk and fresh air, and sleep—he'll be himself in no time." Her eagerness gathered momentum. "Let's see, what can he do around here? He'll need a boat, and he'll probably want the *White Lady* back again. I'll talk to him about it tomorrow. We might as well start working on that right away." Excitedly, her natural energy flowing back into her, she walked away from Nils' arm and reached for a lamp.

"I'd better be getting supper on. I wonder where Stevie is. . . . Nils, where do you think we could get hold of some money to get Owen a boat?" The lamplight flared up and reflected twin radiances in her eyes. "You could let him have a few traps for the spring crawl—"

"Maybe he doesn't want to go lobstering," said Nils.

"Oh, fiddlesticks! Of course he'll go lobstering! That's the best thing for him if he needs fresh air and exercise!" She felt so happy it seemed impossible that she'd been sad and tearful only a few moments ago.

Nils contemplated her steadily across the kitchen. "You can convince him, if anybody can, Jo," he said. "Need the woodbox filled? I'll tend to it." He went out to the shed. Joanna began to peel potatoes, singing under her breath. By spring Owen would have a boat and traps, and there'd be a crowd of Bennetts fishing out of Bennett's Island. Her knife paused, her mouth smiled. Mark was right — you could, after all, consider Nils almost a Bennett, and that strengthened the Island even more.

17

LIFE IN THE HOUSE SEEMED suddenly to be revolving around Owen. It was a way he had. And Joanna was concentrating on him, with a fierce determination to build him up again. He had come back to the Island when he needed it, and the outcome was simple. He would be willing to work for it now, as he had never worked for it before.

He slept late, and went to bed early. The first few days he hardly stirred away from the house; he would sit in the kitchen with Joanna, pipe in his mouth, watching the snow drift down silently across the gunmetal flatness of Goose Cove, or watching her work, his dark head tilted forward, his elbows on his knees. They talked, but not of himself. Joanna wouldn't ask him any questions about where he had been and what he had seen. She was too proud to seek his confidence. To her the years of his absence were a void in his life, as if he had simply dropped out of existence for that time and then had come back into it.

She knew he had lived hard. Owen had always gone to extremes. This was one of them . . . this new uncanny quietude of his, watching the snow fall or, later, watching the blue shadows of the woods lengthen across the white meadow. The other extremes were too many women, too much liquor, too much of the hell-raising he'd always liked to tell about. Only now he didn't tell about it. At thirty-two, there was a frosting of white at his temples, and deep sardonic lines in his face, an odd twist to his mouth sometimes. His eyes looked tired.

It was pneumonia that had slowed him down. That was all he told Joanna. She wondered if he had changed so much that he shrank from telling her the rest; he'd always been frank enough about his affairs when they were kids together, and she'd been one of the gang.

She talked to him as if she could never get caught up on the six years. Of their father and his dying, of Donna, their mother, of Charles, thirty-six, and his newest children, of Philip — thirty-four now and still an old bach, of their Uncle Nate's family and the last she'd heard of their cousins Jeff and Hugo.

She talked to him also of Brigport; more than she'd ever talked to Nils about it. In the old days Owen was always the first to call them "those Brigport bastards." Now he didn't call them anything, but she knew he could understand her far better than Nils, because they were of the same stock. They were Bennetts, and this was Bennett's Island. As good as Nils was, he couldn't feel a *something* that wasn't there. He loved the Island, she knew that; but not with the deep-rooted love the Bennetts bore for it. Else he could never be so calm. . . .

Sometimes Owen walked down to the well and got water for her, and went down to the shore when Nils was due in from hauling. He hadn't yet gone down to the Eastern End to meet Helmi, and he seemed indifferent to the fact that he had a new sister-in-law.

"I might have known Mark would pick a Finn," he said.

"What kind would you pick?" Joanna asked casually. She was mixing batter for pancakes, and as she watched the thick creaminess swirling around the spoon in the yellow bowl she was wondering how many women's lives he had disrupted in that six years, how many women sobbed at night into their pillows and alternately damned and prayed for him.

"I'm not pickin' any," he said with a grin. "A man's an oary-eyed fool if he thinks he can't get along without women." Nils came into the room then, and Owen, sudden deviltry lighting his tired eyes, said, "Look at Nils, there. Been waitin' for you since Adam was a kitten, and now what's he got? Bet he wonders what all the shouting was about!"

He laughed, and Nils laughed too. They went out together. Joanna didn't look up from the pancake batter. Her anger at Owen made the spoon beat till the batter flew over the rim of the yellow bowl. Then she left it abruptly, feeling out of breath. No, Owen wasn't twitting her—he didn't know—he *couldn't* know anything to go on. It had just been his idea of fun. Nils had carried it off—why couldn't *she?*

She crossed the kitchen and looked down at the beach in Goose Cove, and saw them walking along the beach. It was a mild, sunny day, in spite of the snow lying heavy and white along the boughs of the spruces, and there were seabirds swimming and feeding in the Cove. Owen and Nils stopped to watch them. She wondered what they were talking about, her husband and her brother.

In a week Owen showed more color in his face, a new browning of his skin, a quickening in his step. Joanna had written to her mother, knowing how Donna would look when she read the letter and knew he was safe at last. Whatever had happened to him away from the Island, he was secure now that he had come back to it. . . . Joanna told him as the first week came to an end, that she had written. He was standing by the sink, shaving, his eyes intent on the mirror.

"I'd like to see Mother," he said.

"She's only in Pruitt's Harbor, Owen! Two hours away." She came and stood beside him, " She'd be so darned happy to see you," she said eagerly.

"Not the way I look now," he said, and his smile had the sardonic twist that didn't seem like Owen. "I'll wait till I get some of the devil's fingerprints off my face, first."

It was at the end of that week, too, that Ellen came home for the weekend. The storm had kept her and Joey at Brigport the weekend before. Nils hadn't told her about Owen. When she came into the entry in the bright blue snowsuit Donna had sent her for Christmas, her pink-cheeked, narrow-boned face framed in a hood pointed like a brownie's, she stopped short in the doorway to look at the tall stranger standing by the stove.

Joanna waited, Nils, coming into the entry behind Ellen, waited. Owen didn't move while Ellen's eyes moved over his face, comparing his thick black eyebrows and widow's peak, strong nose and cleft chin with her mother's and Stevie's. She looked at them all consideringly, and then back at Owen.

"You must be Owen," she said finally.

"Hello, young Donna," he said, as soberly as she had spoken. She smiled at him then, knowing what he meant.

After dinner Owen said suddenly, "Let's go for a walk, Ellen."

"I'm going to wipe the dishes for Mother," she said.

"You ask Mother if she always wiped the dishes when she was supposed to," Owen suggested, and winked at her. Her wide, humorous mouth, so much like Alec's, quirked. Joanna said hastily, "You can go this time, Ellen. It's better to go for a walk now, while it's warm."

Ellen looked gravely delighted, and began to get into her snow-suit. Stevie had gone down to the shore, and Nils was attending to the wood fire in the sitting room. Over Ellen's absorbed fair head, parted into neat and shining pigtails, Joanna's eyes met Owen's. He grinned at her, and she felt a sudden upsurging of happiness, because then he looked exactly as he used to look. He was on the way back. It might take a long time, but she would get him there, and when he was strong and hard again, with the *White Lady* solid under his feet, he would have his two hundred traps, and Brigport would see then just how dead Bennett's Island was.

When he and Ellen had gone out, she went into the sitting room where Nils was. From the window they could see the tall figure and the diminutive bright blue one making for the flat rocks that reached along the shore from Goose Cove to Chip Cove.

"Do you realize it's the first real walk he's taken?" she murmured.

Nils said, "Does he think he's going to shoot any seabirds with that rifle? He doesn't know Fair Ellen."

"Oh, she made him promise he wouldn't kill anything with it," Joanna laughed. Then, soberly, she turned to Nils.

"Do you mind them being here, Nils? First Stevie, and then Owen?"

"Why should I mind? It's their home."

She felt herself flushing, though there was no slur in his tone. "Your home, Nils," she corrected him.

"Look, Jo, they were raised here. The house belongs to your mother and you and the boys."

She knew she should leave it at that, but for the life of her she couldn't. "But we're running the household—you and I. You're my husband, so that makes you the man of the house."

"Does it? Thanks," said Nils, and, surprisingly, grinned at her. "Well, I'm going back to work. Anything you want done first?"

"No," she said absently. But as he walked out of the room and through the kitchen she had an impulse to run after him and shake him hard and—no, what good would it do? Somewhere along the line Nils had developed this new and annoying habit of making her say things he could pick up; and if he didn't pick them up in words, he had a look. . . .

But there was something to say, after all. She went out into the kitchen where he was pulling on his boots. "Nils, I wanted to tell you while Owen's not around. . . . If he wants to borrow from you, you mustn't let him have too much."

He glanced at her remotely, as if deep in thought. "Why?"

"Well, the other boys can let him have some pots too, and we can find him some sort of boat till he can earn enough to get the *White Lady* back. Unless you want to let him go with you for a while."

"He's your brother, isn't he? And you want him back on his feet as soon as you can get him there."

"Yes, but why should everything be handed to him without any effort on his part?" she argued. "He walked out on the *White Lady*, why should you make it easy for him to get her back? Let him work for her."

"Is that the only reason?" Nils asked her quietly. "Or is it because you don't think I know how to handle my money?"

She stared at him, and then turned quickly and went out of the kitchen. He followed her into the sitting room and came up behind her where she stood at the window, her forehead against the cold glass. She felt his hands grip her shoulders lightly.

"Listen, Jo," he said softly, "why don't you relax? When are you going to stop worrying about me? I'll do my part, and I'll do my job, and I'll do it right, too. You don't have to plague yourself with thinking there'll be nothing in the money box when we need it. . . . You had to plan for the both of you, once, but not any longer. . . ."

"Do you always have to go back to that?" she demanded, shrugging her shoulders out from under his hands. "It's not like you, Nils."

"I have to go back to it, Joanna. I know what makes you fuss, sometimes. And you don't have to fuss now. I'm not —"

"No, you're not Alec," she said. "Why don't you say it, Nils?" She swung her head around and saw how brilliantly, coldly blue his eyes were.

"I wasn't going to say that, Jo. But you've said it yourself, and you know the truth of it, and that ought to be enough for you." He left her abruptly. She was alone in the house again. It seemed to her that she was forever listening to the sharp sound of a door closing, and then knowing she was alone.

By the first of March Owen's Saturday walks with Ellen became a regular feature of her weekends at home. . . . It was a March that came in like a lamb, and it promised an early spring. March was full of promises. The young Fennells would be out by the end of the month, and there was the Whitcomb place to be cleaned and aired for them. And then there was the loveliest promise of all — that of the Island spring.

After the storms of February, it was a heaven-sent boon to the Islanders to have March come in with skies of blown blue and white to be seen through the bare, amethyst-tinged branches of a birch tree, to feel that certain softness in the wind, to see the summery, glistening blue of the sea on a fine morning. It might not last, the Islanders said, but by golly they'd make the most of it. . . . Mark and Stevie took the lobsters ashore that lovely weekend; Caleb and Jud brought the children home from school Friday afternoon, and on Saturday Nils went out early, to get in a good day's work while the weather held. He intended to start shifting his gear, a few pots at a time, so that when the spring crawl began in April, he would be ready.

In honor of the weather, which was affecting Ellen the way such days always affect young puppies, kittens, and children, she asked Owen if Joey could go for a walk with them.

Joanna watched them disappear into the woods; they would come out past the Whitcomb place and go wandering on the West Side this afternoon. She marveled to see how patient Owen was with the children. He'd never noticed children much before. But perhaps he was weary of adults, she thought; and perhaps it was refreshing to his spirit, the candid, unaffected innocence that looked out at him from Ellen's blue-gray eyes and Joey's amber ones. To walk the shores of the Island with a rifle in the crook of your elbow, to speak or not to speak — because the children didn't demand your attention — that would be balm and healing for anyone.

She was left with an afternoon to herself, and what to do with it she didn't know. She was caught up on the washing, ironing, and mending for the household, and she didn't want to go calling. She mixed the dough for the Saturday night yeast rolls, and left it to set; she inspected the beans, browning in the two squat bean pots with the chunks of pork crusty on the tops. Then she put on her boots, and went out to walk by herself.

She walked down through the soggy marsh, and around the shore of the harbor, to climb up past Pete Grant's boarded-up house, high on the rocky point that reared beyond the wharf. Here the jumbled slabs of stone gleamed a warm, rose-shaded saffron in the sunlight; streaked here and there with glinting granite. They slanted down into the sea, so that she walked above the roistering water. There were no big breakers today, but there was a cheerful sloshing and gurgle and slap-slap. The sea was very blue; close to her, where she could see the thick shaggy manes of rockweed, it was dark green and purple, and sometimes a surprising creamy jade. She walked slowly over the springy moss, around the juniper and the boggy places where the frost was coming out of the ground; her boots protected her legs as she walked on slopes that were thick with raspberry bushes and blackberry vines. The wind was as she wanted it, with both a nip and a softness, and a perfume of salt and wet earth. The gulls were crying; they sounded like summer. She wondered what the summer would be like. Perhaps there would be a lobster buyer here then. Herself, maybe. Her heart jumped at the idea. It was no sense for Nils to think of doing it, or one of her brothers. They couldn't haul their traps and buy lobsters too. She could tend the car, and still get her work done.

The mildness in the air, the crying of the gulls, the new brightness that seemed to have settled over the dried, yellow-brown slopes and the dark somberness of the spruces above her — all these things and her own thoughts worked like an intoxication within her. Nils could start her out. He had money in the bank from his seven years on the freighter and his lobstering since he came back. In almost no time she could replace the funds he gave her. It was a perfect job for her. Lobsters were going up in price. There was no reason why she couldn't make a sucess of it. Perhaps some Brigport men would sell their lobsters to her—*everybody* on Brigport didn't like the Fowlers.

She went down over the rocks into the little cove that went with the Whitcomb place; it was called Barque Cove, because long ago when her grandfather was a young man, a barque had run ashore in a blinding snowstorm on one of the cove's points. As she crossed the beach she looked up, and saw the roof and chimneys of the house above the scrub spruces. She thought fleetingly of the nights she had come down here from the house with Alec, and the nights when she'd come alone, to sit on a driftwood log and listen to the soft murmur and rattle of the sea on the pebbles, and try to plan a tomorrow for herself and Alec.

She did not think of it long, for this was her tomorrow, and the plans she'd made for herself and Alec had never flowered. He hadn't even known about Ellen when he died; she'd intended to tell him when he came home to supper, and he had never come home. Instead, he had been drowned. . . .

Now she was on the West Side, and would be catching up with Owen and the children soon. This was the high side of the Island; she was following a narrow path that twisted along the abrupt hillside, and below her the water kept up its cheerful voice. A sparrow sang from a fallen spruce, and an engine made a steady, industrious sound somewhere out on the dancing, glittering sea. She shaded her eyes and tried to make out the boat. It was the *Donna*. She wondered when she would have to chance to tell Nils about her new idea. It was a good thing she'd remembered to tell him about not lending money to Owen.

She went up on the higher ground, almost to the trees, to circle around Old Man's Cove. It was like a deep fissure in the shoreline, a fissure lined with steep walls of rock. She rounded the opposite point, and the whole West Side, down to the very tip of Sou'west Point, lay before her, scalloped with its coves and its long arms of rock, and fringed with its narrow edge of white. Not far from her the crows were calling harshly and circling, big black birds against the delicate sky. A raven—there were a few left on the Island—flew past her on rusty, shaggy-edged wings. Something had disturbed them. It must be that Owen and the children were down there along the shore. There was a dark boat with a few pots on it at some distance outside Marshall Cove, but a boat wouldn't bother the crows.

She walked faster. She would sound Owen out on her idea, when the children were safely behind or ahead—she didn't want Joey to say anything at home yet.

She went over a small headland and came down to Marshall Cove. They were there. They didn't see her at first, as she stopped in the shelter of the trees and watched them. Owen was sitting on a massive log that the tide had rolled up to the very edge of the woods. Ellen was on one side, Joey on the other, and they watched him with an intensity that Joanna could feel. Owen was squinting along the sights of the .22. Joanna leaned against a tree trunk and watched them, smiling. Once she'd thought anyone who could fire a rifle was a species of god, too. It didn't matter if the biggest game was a pot-buoy; just the fact that he could hit it would make the children adore him.

She heard the crack of the rifle, swung her gaze involuntarily toward the sea. Yes, there was a dancing pot-buoy there, a round wetness glistening in the sunshine. Only—she stiffened, and almost cried out. The dark boat—from Brigport—was less than half a mile beyond, and that was too close for Owen to be taking any chances. The boat was right in line with the pot-buoy. . . .

"Owen!" she called down to him, before he lifted the rifle to his shoulder again. She started down across the beach.

"It's Mother!" Ellen shrieked rapturously, and ran to meet her.

"Well, I'll be damned," said Owen pleasantly. He laid the rifle down and took out a cigarette. Joey gave her a bashful grin and wandered down to the high water mark to inspect the fruits of the tide, and Ellen, torn between love and curiosity, finally ran down to see what he had found. Joanna sat down on the log beside Owen and refused a cigarette.

"I don't smoke now. Look, Owen, there's a boat out there. Didn't you see it?"

"Sure I saw it." He grinned. "Brigport bastard. Shifting pots a little close to us, isn't he?"

"Yes, but you don't want to shoot him, do you? Besides, he's not too close," she added, wanting to be fair. "You should have seen them last fall." She squinted her dark eyes against the sunlight. "That's

Theron Pierce. Jonas' brother. . . . You'd better wait till he gets out of range before you fire again."

"Maybe I want him to stay within range," Owen said deliberately. "What in hell do you think I was shooting at?"

"Owen, you're not — you wouldn't —" She said between her teeth, "Just what *were* you shooting at?"

Owen ground out his cigarette under his heel. "Rest yourself, darlin' mine, I wasn't aiming straight at his head, or anything like that. But I figure if we're going to teach them to stay in their own dooryard, it won't hurt none to kick up a little water around them. Only Theron's kind of numb, and he hasn't just figured out what's happened to him. Guess I'd better make it more definite." He lifted the rifle to his shoulder again, and before Joanna could stop him he had fired. They saw the black figure in the cockpit whirl around, and Owen laughed. "Almost dusted him off that time, didn't I?"

Joanna set her teeth and caught the rifle. He let her have it, still laughing. "You want to try it, Jo?" he suggested blandly.

"Oh, you blasted *idiot*," she said. "Do those kids know what you've been up to?"

"They think I'm firing at a pot-buoy. I tell them I hit it each time, and they believe me." He chuckled, and the sound of that chuckle made her look at him sharply. The weariness was gone; and almost gone, the sardonic twist. He looked completely and richly happy. He laughed aloud as the boat made a wide circle and disappeared behind the point, leaving a lusty wake behind it.

"High-tailin' it home at full speed!" Owen said. At the sound of his laughter, Joey and Ellen turned and came back, Ellen running, Joey walking with his twelve-year-old dignity. With a mixture of emotions, Joanna stood up.

"You need your neck wrung," she told Owen under her breath. "Have I got to hide that rifle from you? Can't you be trusted, Owen? God only knows what he'll tell when he gets back to Brigport! And if Tom Robey's gang or the Fowlers get hold of it —"

"You scared of them?"

"No, I'm not!" she said furiously, and then realized that Owen was acting like himself again; very much like himself, when he could make her so angry. In spite of herself, her mouth quirked. "But I'm not going to leave you alone out here with a gun, you're not responsible," she told him, before Ellen reached them. And louder, so the children could hear, she said, "Let's all go back to the house and have some cocoa and lobster sandwiches. How about it?"

She smiled at Owen, and tightened her hands on the rifle. Excited by the prospect of food, the children charged on ahead. Owen, following Joanna along the path, said, "Still too big for your boots, ain't ye? Oh, what the hell, I'll find something else to amuse me."

18

NILS CAME IN AT SUPPER TIME, ruddy-cheeked, hungry, and well satisfied with his day's haul. He'd averaged a lobster to a trap, and that was good for the tail-end of winter.

"Funny thing, though," he said thoughtfully, laying his heavy canvas gloves to dry on the stove shelf. "I met Theron Pierce down between Long Cove and Tenpound. He was speeding right along and never gave me a look. I waved, but—" He shook his head. "I always got along all right with the Pierces. I wonder what ailed him?"

"Maybe he had a toothache come on him," Joanna heard herself saying. Across the kitchen she met Owen's eyes, and turned away from his wink. *Damn him!* she thought. *He knows I won't tell Nils. . . . Well, I will tell him. But not just now. . . .* There was no reason why she shouldn't tell Nils what Owen had done. He had grown up with Owen, he knew what deviltry Owen could carry out. Maybe he'd only laugh. But maybe—and this was stronger to Joanna's mind— he'd be like their father, and take it too seriously. As if Theron would ever know who'd done it! Perhaps he'd taken it as an accident when the bullet came too near. But still he'd snubbed Nils—

She gave up conjecturing, and hurried to get supper on the table. No sense to worry about it now. It would never happen again, probably. . . . Nils was sitting down to have his first good smoke for the day, and he and Owen began to talk about the relative merits of dry-salted bait and pickled; he kept his eye on the clock so he could get the six o'clock news. Ellen played alone in the sitting room, her paper dolls laid out on the rug around the base of the curlicued stove. It was a pleasant family scene, all around, and why worry because of Owen's pranks? At least it showed that he was feeling well again. And who knew but what it might serve as a warning to the lawless faction on Brigport?

And besides, she had more to think about. Her idea of being lobster-buyer, for instance. She moved quickly around the kitchen, between stove and dresser and table, tall, firmly slim, in spite of her big Bennett bones, still youthfully narrow-flanked in her wine wool skirt, her strong smooth throat lifting from the open neck of her white blouse, her mouth curved in a secret excited happiness, her dark eyes smiling under the lashes. Nils' glance followed her sometimes, and pulled away by an almost perceptible effort, but she didn't notice. She was too intent on herself. To be lobster-buyer would mean that at last she could fulfill her desire; she would be doing something real and tangible to help the Island grow.

The beans were on, deep bronzy-brown, steaming and aromatic to blend with the perfume of hot yeast rolls; the chili sauce and the piccalilli glistened in their separate dishes, the apple jelly was a tawny jewel, the grape jelly was the color of garnet, and the cole slaw rested lightly in its blue bowl, gleaming shreds of palest yellow and green, starred with the pinky-orange of grated carrot. Joanna stood off and surveyed her table as an artist surveyed his work, and reached for the coffeepot. Ellen came in and looked hungrily around her.

"My golly, I bet Mark and Stevie wish they didn't have to eat in any restaurant *tonight!*" she said fervently. "Even if they *can* go to the movies afterward!"

Joanna poured the coffee, and its pungence was the crowning touch. How wonderful everything looked and smelled tonight! she thought. And all because she was going to do something she'd always wanted to do. As the premature breath of spring had laid a new sheen over the Island today, so had her plan laid a sheen over her.

"Come and get it!" she sang out happily to the men. "Or I'll throw it out to the gulls!"

*   *   *

Nils went to bed before she did, and was asleep when she went in, and so when she awoke in the morning her plan was still inside her head, warming her like a secret sun. It was Sunday, and a good day to work outside; when the repairs were done and the work caught up, Nils could rest on Sunday as he had been brought up to do by his grandfather, and as Stephen Bennett had always done. But until then, each Sunday must count, either as a good day to haul, or a good day to work ashore. Owen went down to the harbor to help him, and the day slipped by quickly. By bedtime she had not yet told Nils her plan. But she could wait. It was only the first of March yet, and besides, there was always the one, absolutely right, moment for telling those things. . . .

The Fennells were due sometime this month. Already Matthew Fennell had written to say so. On Monday, with Ellen back to school, Joanna began to clean the Whitcomb place. It was a cold day, but a sunny one, and Joanna had never feared the cold anyway. By the time the sun was high she was crossing the meadow in her slacks and jacket, a kerchief holding her dark hair in place, broom and dry mop over one shoulder, dusters in her pockets, dustpan and brush under one arm. This morning she'd limit to a thorough sweeping and dusting. Later the washing of floors and paintwork and windows. . . .

Nils was out to haul again, and Owen was home, reading beside the stove and keeping the fire going under the mammoth kettle of soup. She was alone, and oddly happy. She was not afraid of memories coming to her while she worked in the house where she had lived with Alec. She would think instead of the young couple who were coming here, Matthew Fennell, and his wife Nora. She liked the name Nora, and tried to visualize the girl who carried it. She was "game," Matthew had said, and somehow that made her a likeable, honest, tomboyish girl who wasn't afraid of an adventure. *I think I'll like Nora,* she thought as she unlocked the door of her house, and stepped into its chill, resounding, emptiness.

With all that she had to think about, the memories were like leaves blown in the wind; they drifted by, but she didn't try to catch them. Here was where Alec had sat and played his fiddle while she got supper on the table . . . here by the dresser he had caught and hugged her. It made her smile. He'd been so loving and so lovable.

Ellen was like him in a way—she had his slimness and his height, his wide humorous mouth. But in her reserve she was oddly like Nils. No wonder he loved her as if she were his own. There seemed to be a spiritual kinship between them. But Alec would have loved Ellen too. . . .

Here in the sitting room was the writing desk. Where the money box had been kept; the money box that so rarely had money in it, because when Alec knew there was money in the house he must use it somehow. It might be on a foolish, extravagant gift for her, it might be a gift to someone down on his luck, it might be for gambling. It was the gambling that had put an end to the ecstasy of that first year. You always came back to the gambling when you thought of Alec. It was as if his story had been written from the start, his pattern laid out for him to follow; and when he swerved from it—she remembered when he had burned the pack of cards he'd always carried—he had broken some mystic law and had been wiped out, as must be all who deviate from their pattern.

She went over to the windows and opened them quickly, letting in a rush of pure cold air flavored by the sea. Where did these queer thoughts come from, she asked herself, and, leaning out, saw Helmi coming along the path to the steps.

She ran to open the door for her. "Hello! Isn't this nice!"

"Hello." There was a faint color in the girl's face. "I thought I'd walk up to see you, and then you weren't home. Your brother told me you were here."

"Well, I'm glad you came," Joanna said. "Come in and warm yourself. I've built a little fire to take the chill off." She led the way into the kitchen, astonished and yet pleased that Helmi had sought her out. "Are you nervous about Mark being gone over the weekend?"

"No, I am never nervous about being alone. And what is there on the Island to be nervous about?" She pulled off her flowered kerchief and her silver-blonde hair fell free.

"Nothing," Joanna admitted. "And the boys ought to be back this morning."

"I know. I thought I would come to see you, and be here when they came. Now I'll help you. What do you want me to do?"

"Well—" Joanna laughed. "Gosh, I don't know. I've swept and

dusted nearly the whole house. Next thing is washing the floors. But it's a little cold today—"

"Where is the water? The cold is nothing."

"You're a girl after my own heart," said Joanna, "but the soap and the buckets and the mop are up at the house. Come and have dinner with Owen and me, and we'll wash the floors this afternoon."

As far as Joanna was concerned, Owen's rest-cure was complete. At least his reaction to Helmi was normal, though he showed a little more finesse than he had used in the days gone by. Watching him, and watching Helmi's polite indifference, she was amused, and at the same time certain that he would be wanting to get to work soon. The day down in Marshall Cove with the gun had been the turning point. Whatever had been hanging over him when he came home, it was gone now; or at least he had thrust it into its proper place.

If Helmi seemed unmoved by his charm, Owen wasn't annoyed. Instead he announced that he would help them wash floors. It was rather an amazing offer, coming from Owen. When he went into the sitting room to get the noon war news, Joanna followed him.

"If you think you can break her down, you're mistaken, my boy," she told him, her eyes laughing. "She's unbreakable. There's one girl who's practically immune to us Bennetts. I'll bet you didn't think there was such a critter."

"Hell, she wasn't immune to Mark, was she?" Owen grinned at her, the big, youthful, vivid grin he'd always had.

"She's crazy about Mark." Her laughter faded. As he reached out to turn off the radio, she put her hand on his arm. "Owen, I know you're feeling full of beans and you want some fun. But—"

"Oh, my God!" he said violently. "What do you think I am! Not altogether foolish, I hope!"

"Well, you *have* been, sometimes—haven't you?"

He didn't get mad. Instead he rumpled her hair roughly. "Still the same Jo. Trying to make silk purses out of sows' ears. Golly, when you married a feller as well-behaved as Nils you sort of wasted your talents, didn't you?"

"Nils," said Joanna with dignity, "is restful after a lifetime of my brothers."

Owen really worked that afternoon. He carried water and kept the fire going to heat it; he whistled and mopped, while Helmi and Joanna washed woodwork and windows. In an hour the house was perfumed with soap and water and fresh air. Owen pursued the girls indefatigably from room to room, sloshing suds with abandon, singing ribald songs under his breath. When they got too ribald, Joanna and Helmi moved to another room.

The day moved on. From the upstairs windows Joanna showed Helmi the view over the roofs of the village; they saw the smoke from Jud Gray's chimney come up from among the green-black spruces, to be caught and torn to shreds by the gusty March wind. They saw Gunnar Sorensen's barn and house, and beyond the windbreak of spruces Eric Sorensen's red roof showed. They could look past the other empty houses and see the new, bright, tarpaper roof on the long fish house, and the ruins of the boatshop that Nils wanted to rebuild. Across the harbor Vinnie Caldwell was taking in her wash, white sheets snapping against the rise of Eastern Harbor Point and a brilliant dark blue corner of Long Cove; white sheets no whiter than the surf on the ledges and the whitecaps in the tide rip at the harbor mouth.

The day was washed in sunshine and wind, and the Camden mountains bloomed purple and blueberry colored on the horizon. And a boat was working her steady way down past the western end of Brigport, heading for Bennett's Island.

"There they are," Helmi said. She was smiling; her face looked young and softened. Her lips were parted as she watched the tiny boat. When Grant's point hid it, some of the light went out of her eyes. She began to polish a window pane.

"If you start now you'll get to the shore in time to meet them," Joanna said, taking the cloth out of Helmi's hand. "Go on."

Helmi didn't argue. "Thank you," she said, and went out of the room. Joanna heard her shoes on the stairs, light and fast. She went on polishing the glass, knowing a strangeness about the sound; for it might have been her own feet running on the stairs, running to meet Alec.

Owen's voice from the doorway startled her. "What the hell's she running for? She sounds scared."

"Not to me!" Joanna laughed. "She sounds like a girl in love with her husband. The boys are coming."

Owen lit a cigarette and leaned against the door casing, his eyes thoughtful through the faint blue smoke. "Wouldn't you know," he said as he had said once before, "that Mark would marry a Finn?"

Eventually the excitement was over, the grocery orders parceled out, the money for the lobsters stowed safely away in the billfolds. Mark and Helmi refused an invitation to stay for supper and walked back to the Eastern End; during the winter Mark kept his boat up in the harbor. After supper Owen and Stevie went down to Caleb's, and Nils and Joanna were alone.

It seemed a heaven-sent interval to Joanna. The silence of the house lay about her and Nils. He read and smoked, and at first she read too, but her thoughts and her secret delight wouldn't let her relax enough to follow the story. Now was the time to talk to Nils about buying lobsters. It was almost as if Fate had meant it to be so. She laid her book aside and leaned forward till she could see Nils clearly, where he sat at the other side of the sitting room table. The Aladdin lamp between them poured its yellow radiance over them both, lighting her face and his.

She watched him for a long moment without speaking. Then, as if he felt her gaze, he looked up. As always, the blueness of his eyes gave her a shock; she never quite remembered how blue they were, and how intent.

"Hello," he said, and smiled.

"Nils, I want to tell you something," she said, her hands clasped in her lap. "I had an idea. I think it's one of the best I ever had."

Nils laid aside his paper and began to refill his pipe. Joanna said frankly, "I know you don't like some of my ideas, but I can't see a thing wrong with this one. I've thought of it from all angles."

"Well, why don't you tell me what it is?" he said reasonably.

Her eyes glowing, she began to tell him what she had in her mind. When she had finished she waited, erect with her eagerness and pride, and watched his face. His eyes had not moved from hers. Now he took his pipe from his mouth and looked down at it.

"You've got it all figured out, haven't you?" he said. "Is that why you didn't want me to lend the money to Owen?"

"No," she said truthfully. "I didn't have the idea till afterwards. But now I think the money would do more general good if it was used to start me off than if you lent it to Owen. Nils, I could put it all back in a month, with the lobsters coming in good, and the price so high—" She leaned eagerly toward him. "And Nils, I'd love doing it. It would be something *real* for the Island."

"Yes," he said slowly. "We need a buyer here. No reason why we shouldn't have one. I've been thinking of that. I knew it was no job for me."

"Well, then—"

He looked at her radiant face. "I'm sorry, Jo, that you've got your heart set on it. But it's no job for a woman, tending a lobster car."

Her hands tightened on each other. "What do you mean, no job for a woman?" she asked him quietly. "It's my own Island, my own people. Who else would do it, then?"

"I've been thinking of Jud," Nils said. "His back's bothering him so he's finding it too much of a chore to get out to haul all the time— but Jud would do all right on the car."

Joanna sat very still. Only the whitening of her knuckles showed the feeling that was beginning to possess her. *Jud on the car,* she thought, and wondered, when she replied, how she could speak so quietly.

"Nils, I want to do it. I never wanted so much to do anything in my life. Have you—" Her lips were dry. "Have you said anything to Jud yet?"

Nils shook his head. "No, I was going to talk to you about it, first."

"Thanks," she said, and her bitterness seeped out a little in the word. She couldn't sit quiet now. She got up and walked around the room, and came at last to the window overlooking the darkness of Goose Cove. Beyond the point the Rock light came and went. "Nils, don't you think I'm smart enough to tend car?"

"It's not that, Jo, and you know it." She heard him get up and walk toward her, out of the circle of lamplight. "If there wasn't any man to do the job, it might be different. But you don't need to do it. You've got enough to keep you busy."

She swung around and faced him. "You sound like those Germans—church, children, and kitchen, or whatever it is! Nils, I never thought you'd be like this. I'm a *Bennett*. Isn't it right that a Bennett should run the lobster business here? It's our island, isn't it?"

"Everybody's working for the Island, Joanna," Nils said imperturbably. "Jud as much as any of us. And it's his island too. He owns a chunk of it."

She was baffled and furious. It seemed to her that she almost hated Nils. She wanted to buy lobsters; she needed his help. And he was refusing her. Until now, it had been little things, and she could make her own compromises and adjustments. But there was no compromise or adjustment here. It was an intolerable situation. She walked by him toward the door and he reached out and took her wrist, his fingers gentle but unbreakable in their hold.

"Going out?" he asked quietly.

"Yes" she said. "Don't come with me, please." She spoke as quietly as he.

He let her go, and she went through the kitchen, took her jacket and scarf from the hook and went out. The wind caught at her with rough, wilful hands and cut her to the bone. Without lowering her head she walked into it, out on the long high point behind the house. The smell of the sea was all around her, cold and salty, and the light from the Rock swung its beam across her and away, and then back again. Spiny rosebushes caught at her slacks and once she bumped her shin on a sharp edge of rock. It brought involuntary tears to her eyes but still she kept walking, driven by a fire of furious energy. She knew she couldn't go back to the house and face Nils until she walked off this intensity of anger, which amounted to passion.

We were to work together for the Island, she thought, *and this is what it is. This it what it will be.* . . . She hoped she wouldn't hate Jud. That would be foolish. For Jud hadn't taken anything away from her. It was Nils who had done it. Her husband.

She found a place at the very end of the point, a shelf of rock where she used to read when she was a girl; with sheltering walls of rock behind her, and the sea gurgling and splashing below her, tossing up a salty bead of spray to her sometimes, she sat with her knees drawn up and her chin resting on them. Between the flashes of the Rock light it was very dark, and the darkness was full of sound; she found herself listening. The night-voice of the sea, the wind blowing across the point and rustling in the dry dead leaves and grass; the gulls on the ledges—did they never sleep?

The Island was talking to her. It was all around her. She listened, and forgot her anger and her bitterness in the moment when the Island spoke to her. She found the old certainty again, the sure knowledge that she was the Island's child; and as if the hard rock behind her and under her were sheltering arms, she leaned back, relaxed, and was comforted.

The Island was with her. In spite of Brigport, in spite of Nils and all the others, she would find a way to work for it. Let Jud have the car, even though it was her right. There would be something else for her.

19

WHILE HE WAS ASHORE WITH MARK, Stevie had seen a boat he wanted. And he had discovered something else too—the whereabouts of the *White Lady*. His news was the final spark to set aflame Owen's desire to have his boat back. If he had forsaken her for all these years, he had only to hear that she was fishing out of Pleasant Point, with a canopy top disfiguring her long, lovely lines, and he would not rest until she was back in her own harbor again.

She was his, for all he'd left her for his father to sell. He had designed her himself, sworn and struggled while he built her, fought those who'd tried to hinder him, who'd dared to lay a malicious hand on her hull, and launched her on a shining blue day in June. She was his as much as a child is flesh and blood of its parents.

He said none of these things in words, but Joanna knew they were there. She knew by the way he walked the floor after Stevie had told him, by the way he stood at the window, his dark face brooding, and, finally, by the way he went out of the house into the raw March afternoon and prowled alone in the woods until evening. She was not surprised when he came downstairs the next morning, while

Nils was eating his breakfast by lamplight, and announced that he was going to start building pots that day, if Nils would lend him laths and the nails.

So he had begun to work for the *White Lady*. He spent eight hours a day building pots. Between times he ate a good deal, slept heavily, walked sometimes to the Eastern End to see Mark, but never for long. Now that he had begun to work he was like a dynamo. He was himself again in his impatient drive and energy; in two things only was he not himself. He was getting along without liquor. And he rarely mentioned women. It made Joanna wonder even more intensely about the six years of his life that were lost to his family.

There was something else she wondered, as she watched her menfolk come and go. She knew that when Owen had his pots built, he would have to use another man's boat to work from, and it would still be a long time before he could make a clear profit of a thousand dollars to buy the *White Lady*. And so she wondered if, after her warning, Nils would lend him the money. He probably would, she thought as she mended and washed and cooked for the men; she had been foolish to think anything she said could influence Nils, if his mind was made up. It was odd, how little she had known him after all. . . .

She showed no resentment when it became common knowledge that Jud was going to buy lobsters. She even congratulated him, and the eyes that met Nils' were darkly clear and guileless. It didn't really matter. If she could not have the car, she would have something else. She would know it when she came to it, and even Nils couldn't interfere with destiny.

Stevie brought his boat home less than a week after he had spotted her. He had the money, made in the winter's fishing, and the *Elaine* was ready for use. She was being sold by the widow of a fisherman who had just died, and he had kept his engine in smooth-running condition. Stevie sailed her home proudly; she was a broad-beamed, sturdy, 28-footer, with power in her engine.

"She's not much for looks," he admitted, when almost everybody assembled on the old wharf to view the *Elaine*. "But she can go. Of course, she's a mite wet. She throws a hell of a lot of water, but I figure that'll keep the women from pestering me to go sailing."

"What women do you mean?" Joanna teased him. She winked

at Helmi, who stood beside her, her fair head uncovered in the crisp breeze. "Helmi and me? Can't we pester?"

"Present company always excluded," Stevie said gravely. "You want to go now? I ll take you out around the harbor ledge buoy and back."

"Come on, Helmi," Joanna said eagerly. "It's nice and choppy out, too. There'll be spray flying."

"Too bad you got just the family females to tote around, Stevie boy," Jud said. "But they're good-lookers, anyhow."

Stevie grinned, and jumped down from the wharf to the beach where his punt was tied. "You girls coming or not?" He stood looking up at them, his dark eyes narrowed against the sun, his teeth white in his brown face. Joanna slipped her arm through Helmi's.

"Come on—" She felt the younger girl's arm tighten.

"No," Helmi said. "You go, Joanna. But I don't feel like it." She seemed uneasy. "I think it's too rough—"

"I didn't know you were afraid of a little water," Stevie called to her. "But it will be kind of wet, at that. You nervous, Joanna?"

"Not me!" Some sixth sense told her not to urge Helmi to come. The girl had her reasons. The choppiness was not really one of them, she was sure. Perhaps it was Mark. He took odd spells of temper— perhaps Helmi thought he wouldn't like it if he came in from hauling and found she'd been running around in another boat, even Stevie's.

Joanna released Helmi's arm and said, "Then go up to the house where it's warm, Helmi. And would you start some coffee for us? Nils ought to be in pretty soon, and we'll all have a mug-up."

"I will start the coffee," Helmi said, her sea-green eyes wide and serious on Joanna's face. "But then I think I'd better walk home, and be there when Mark comes in."

Owen, who had been talking boats with Jud at the end of the wharf, came up beside them, and shoved his dark yachting cap back on his head. He grinned down at his sister and sister-in-law, his eyes full of black diamond glints behind thick lashes. There was a ruddy color in his skin. "Stop lallygaggin', Jo. Steve's waiting. I'll walk Helmi up to the house and make her drink a cup of coffee before she starts for home."

"That's right, Owen, you look out for her," Joanna said, and jumped down to the wet, pebbly beach. Jud's wheezy laughter followed her.

"That's mighty like tellin' a rabbit to look out for a head o' lettuce, ain't it?"

She half-turned back toward the round and ribald little man, but Owen and Helmi were already leaving the wharf, and Stevie was saying, "Grab hold there and help me shove this punt down, Jo."

When they were rowing out to the mooring, the water slapping smartly under the punt's bow, Joanna said, "Jud goes too far with his humor, sometimes."

"Oh, nobody minds what Jud says," answered Stevie. He looked over his shoulder toward the *Elaine.* "See the little sweetheart. Maybe she looks kind of stubby alongside the *Donna,* but she looks good to me."

"Me too," said Joanna, and prepared to ask all the questions that were routine when you went aboard a new boat; they were, she thought, equivalent to what you inquired about a new baby. Smiling at this thought, she clambered over the *Elaine's* washboards and forgot about Jud.

March brought the Fennells. It was a March that was beginning to look like April, and the day they came showed buds on the alders, new green grass in the sunny sheltered places around the houses, and a sweet chattering of sparrows and kinglets and nuthatches in the spruces. From the Bennett house one heard the noisy spring crying of the gulls out on the ledges, and in the sunlit blue of Goose Cove the seals were playing. There was a faint nip in the wind, and a splashing of white around the rocks, but in the road through the marsh the mud puddles reflected the skies of spring.

A good day for them to come, Joanna thought. She had a fire going down at the Whitcomb house so it would be warm, and on her own stove their dinner was cooking. It was a Saturday and Ellen was home; but the men were out to haul, after a week of rain and wind. Owen had gone out with Nils, and was setting his first load of pots.

Ellen was so excited about the newcomers that she kept running up from her playhouse on the point to stand on a high rock near the house and peer down across the harbor, toward the western end of Brigport. Joanna, laughing at her daughter's eagerness, was almost as excited. Another family for the Island; it was enough to excite anybody. Nils was pleased too, and he intended to be in early enough to help move the Fennells' furniture.

Another family for the Island. One less empty house. In another year how many empty houses would there be? None, she prayed. If God was good. And He *was* good. He would send others. And plenty of lobsters, so the men wouldn't be discouraged; and not too many storms. She laughed aloud at her specifications. If everybody prayed as she did, God would have a hard time filling the orders. Then she was at the window again, looking down at the harbor. Joey Caldwell was rowing his father's dory—he had five traps of his own, and because the harbor mouth was quiet today, he could go and haul them. Marion Gray was going past the old camps where the hand-to-mouth fishermen used to live, when Joanna was a girl. Maybe in another year even the camps would be occupied. But not with old pod fishermen, but with men who knew how to work, and to get the most from it. The camps could be fixed up; she'd talk to Nils about it.

She'd liked the weatherbeaten old men who'd lived there during her girlhood; everybody had. And if they'd been living in the camps now, she wouldn't want to put them out. But they were gone, and what was the sense of bringing back others like them?

While she was at the window she saw the *Janet F.* hauling out beyond the western end of Brigport. She wondered if Randy and Winslow were together. If Randy was alone, and looking over at Bennett's, what did he think? Probably not of her, unless to wonder how he'd come to act so foolishly about a woman almost ten years older than he. Randy's sort was easily consoled. Was his father as easily consoled? Or did he still plot and dream behind his smooth, expressionless face?

With spring so richly promising in the air and the lobsters coming so well, and the Brigport traps not set so close as they had been, Joanna found it hard to worry.

There was only one thing to consider, and it made a vertical line between her black eyebrows as she turned away from the window and the lusty, flashing day outside. Randolph Fowler hadn't given up in the long, silent fight to put Timothy Merrill out of the business the Merrills had run on Brigport since long before the Civil War. And maybe Timothy had thought himself safe too — safe, and a little smarter than the "foreigners."

There's danger in being safe, Stephen Bennett used to say to his arrogant and cock-sure children. And Joanna, repeating his words now, almost as some mystic incantation to rise with the steam from the boiling lobsters, knew beyond a doubt the truth of them.

She dipped the smoking hot, red-orange lobsters from the kettle into the white-enameled pan and put fresh ones into the bubbling sea water, their noses down so they would die quickly. Ellen burst into the kitchen.

"They're coming, Mother! Two boats, past Brigport." She saw Joanna pick up another live lobster, holding it behind the waving claws, and her vivid face clouded. "Does it hurt them, Mother?" she asked in a small voice. She had asked it many times before, and always Joanna answered her carefully.

"Only for a minute, Ellen. And we're supposed to eat them. God wouldn't have told men how to build boats and make traps if he hadn't meant for them to catch lobsters."

Ellen said doubtfully, "Yes. . . . But how could anybody get a little tiny calf, and love it, and feed it, and know all the time they were going to kill it to eat?" Her blue-gray eyes misted. Joanna said, "I don't know, dear," and mentally crossed a calf off next summer's purchases. She did hope Ellen would let them have a pig, however.

"Did you say they were coming?" she asked. And Ellen's sparkle came back.

"Let's go down and meet them, Mother! Come on!"

The tide was coming and the two boats tied up alongside the old wharf; when the tide was high, it would be easy to unload the furniture. Matthew Fennell's boat was a neat, high-bowed craft with a roomy cuddy, and a jigger mast on the stern. The other, larger, boat carried even more furniture, piled on the deck around the cuddy, on the washboards and stern, and in the cockpit, leaving the owner just enough room to stand at the wheel and move around the engine box. He was a strapping, ruddy man with a loud voice and an infectious laugh.

"This is Clyde Sparrow, Mrs. Sorensen," Matthew Fennell said in the serious, shy manner she remembered. "He owns Sparrow's Island. I used to work for him."

Clyde shook Joanna's hand hard. "I've heard a lot about the Bennetts and the Sorensens, Ma'am. I guess everybody knew what kind of a feller Stephen Bennett was, and I run into your brother, Cap'n Charles, 'bout every time I turn around, seems like." He laughed heartily and still held her hand, smiling down into her eyes. "And then I know a nice feller in Port George—Karl Sorensen—"

"My husband's father," Joanna said, and finally got her hand free. "This is my daughter, Ellen." Ellen bravely put out her hand to be lost in his huge one. He twinkled down at her. "Now I'd know her father was a squarehead—I mean a Swede," he said, unabashed. "She's a real Svenska flicka, ain't she?"

Matthew said quickly, "Hey, Clyde, give me a hand with Gram, will ye?"

"Right you are, my boy. Now, Mrs. Fennell—" With surprising agility for such a big man he was down into the cockpit; and between them the two men lifted the little old lady to the wharf.

She was a very little old lady, bundled up in respectable and well-brushed black. Her hat was moored securely on her white head by several long and imposing hatpins; she held her large bag tightly in both hands, and peered up at Joanna from under the magnificent hat, which was clearly the splendor of another day. Little she was, and shrunken, and thin; but not frail. There was nothing frail in the fiery regard of her sunken but unfaded gray eyes; they took Joanna in from head to toe.

Her nose was imposing. It was arched and big in her seamed face, a strange contrast to the crumpled delicacy of her skin and the faint rose-pink color in her cheeks.

"How do you do, Mrs. Fennell," Joanna said, feeling suddenly no older than Ellen.

"How do you do, my girl!" The voice matched the nose and the eyes. Its vigor was amazing. "Where's the house? Any one of these?" She waved a small black-gloved hand at the houses across the harbor. "My grandson says it's a good house but I won't believe it till I see it. Menfolks don't see half what they should."

"Gram, Gram." The girl's voice was laughing and embarrassed at once. She swung up from the cockpit without any help, looking like a tall slim young boy except for the mop of hair that hung to her shoulders like Helmi's; it was as glossy as a horse chestnut. Her face was wide at the cheekbones, her nose short and powdered with tiny freckles. Her hazel eyes looked candidly into Joanna's.

"I'm Nora Fennell, but you probably know it already."

"I'm glad you've come," said Joanna, and meant it.

"I'm glad I'm here. I thought the winter'd never end." She looked around her, smiling, and took a long breath of the cold bright air that was softened by the sun's warmth. "All this sky—and sea. And woods. I love woods."

"They begin right in your backyard," Joanna said. So this was Nora, who was game. She looked game. She looked sturdy and honest; and she looked like an Island woman.

"Come up to the house, Mrs Fennell and Nora," she said. "Dinner's ready for you."

"That sounds like heaven," said Nora. She called down into the cuddy of her husband's boat. "Clyde, you better save that stuff to move on—Mrs. Sorensen's got dinner for us. Matthew, hand me up the baby, will you?"

"Baby?" said Ellen ecstatically at Joanna's elbow. "Have they got a baby?"

Nora heard her and laughed. "Well, it's all the baby we have for now—till we get us a real one."

She leaned down and took the shaggy black puppy from Matthew's arms. Its oversized feet paddled the air, its nondescript tail beat in a wild circle, its tongue sought vainly to lap Nora's chin, and at Ellen's long "O-o-o!" of delight, the ears perked, the head whirled, and two bright brown eyes gleamed out from under a frowsty black bang. The wrigglings increased in fervor and Nora said, "You can get down in a minute, Bosun, but you're so foolish you'd probably jump overboard first thing. . . . Can I take him to the house, Mrs. Sorensen? He's clean."

Gram snorted violently. "Fiddlesticks! Let the pup stay aboard the boat! And I should have thought if you had to get a dog, you'd at least get one that *looked* like a dog! That's the homeliest critter I ever laid eyes on!"

"I think he's nice," said Ellen's clear, determined voice. "He can come with us, can't he, Mother?"

"Of course he can," Joanna said hastily, pretending not to see the hurt color in Nora's face. The old lady was a Tartar. . . . "He can have some dinner too. Out of old Winnie's dish. We still have it."

The men came up on the wharf then, after seeing that the boats were properly made fast, and the procession started for the house with Joanna leading the way. Ellen walked beside Nora, her eyes on Bosun's beguilingly whiskered face. Old Mrs. Fennell was escorted by the two men, Clyde Sparrow courtly, Matthew Fennell with his usual sober, diffident manner, lighted sometimes with his rare smile.

"Matthew," said Gram in her penetrating voice, "you want to do something about that wife of yours. First thing you know folks'll think she's foolish, luggin' a dog around and fussin' about it. You ought to—"

"Gram." Matthew sounded calm enough. "Look up there. There's the Bennett homestead Cap'n Bennett built. You used to know him once, you said."

"Met him when I was a girl—he come up to Camden with his wife to visit her folks. They didn't have any young ones then. That reminds me, Matthew. About Nora." Joanna walked a little faster, and didn't look at Nora, who was silent. Ellen murmured to Bosun.

"You'd ought to do something, give her a family to take up her time, Matthew. Any normal woman that takes on so about a dog— she needs a whole handful of young ones."

"Gram—" Matthew's calm was strained.

"Nora's built for having babies." Gram rode him down. "Look at her, now." Poor Nora, Joanna thought. Pood kid. She wished she could think of something to say. Clyde Sparrow was whistling.

"I'm telling you for your own good, Matthew Fennell. And Nora's good, too, for all she's making believe she don't hear me. A woman don't know what life is, till she's done her daily toil with one hanging at her skirts and a nursing babe in her arms."

With a swift gesture Nora bent down and released the puppy. "Come on, Bosun! Come on, Ellen!" she called in a clear, defiant voice. "Let's race for the house!" They ran, long-legged girl and child and puppy, up across the wind-blown, tawny slope toward the house built four-square against the sky.

20

A SERIES OF WARM DAYS FOLLOWED the arrival of the Fennells. The Island April was rarely mild, and these days were so unseasonably balmy that it was almost impossible for anyone to stay in the house. A curious unrest possessed everybody, even Caleb, who was seen walking along Long Cove Beach with Vinnie at sunset one night.

Jud and Marion went up to the cemetery one soft, placid, gray afternoon and worked there until supper time. They cleared away the wild, tangled undergrowth of years from Jud's parents' graves and from the little grave where their last baby lay. Joanna, out walking by herself, found them puttering around in the little fenced and sheltered spot among the tall spruces on the hill, across Goose Cove from the Bennett house. She leaned on the gate to talk with them, hearing the soft whistling and chirping of sparrows and chickadees in the avenue of bare apple trees behind her. She knew she must clear Alec's grave soon. But she wanted to be alone when she did that; alone, or with Ellen.

She didn't want Ellen to shun the cemetery. From her earliest memories Joanna had loved it, and it was still beloved, even with Alec there. Oh, there had been a little while when she had stayed away, especially when the apple trees were in bloom; but those days were gone now, and she wanted Ellen to know what a spot it was for dreaming when the apple blossoms filled the orchard with a pink and white cloud of bloom, fairylike against the walls of great dark spruces, and the sheltered sunny air was loud with the sound of bees and of birdsong.

In midsummer it had been even quieter, a haven of blessed silence where all that had moved had been the pools of sunshine on the grass, a swaying birch bough, and the cuckoo's soundless wings; then the scent of the blackberry blossoms, whose vines trailed white-starred through the orchard's tall grass, rose to blend with the aromatic essence of all spruce woods under a hot summer sun.

Yes, Ellen must learn to love it here as she did, and it should be a place of refuge to her, whenever she needed one; and Alec's stone should not make her stay away. "Alexander Charles-Edward Douglass," it said. "Twenty-eight years . . . beloved husband of Joanna Douglass." The Charles-Edward was for Bonnie Prince Charlie. She must tell Ellen that story, soon.

She said good-bye to the Grays and walked down through the bare, twisted apple trees, the ground soggy under her feet. When she reached the other end of the orchard she could look up through the lane to the Whitcomb place; she supposed she should call it the Fennell place now. She wondered if Nora was putting things where she wanted them, or if Gram was in charge. . . . She shook her head and turned down the opposite path, out of the woods and into the Bennett meadow.

The men came home early to supper. Nils had been working all day at the shore, with Owen, pulling down what remained of the boatshop. Stevie had the *Elaine* grounded out and had been painting her. Supper over, both he and Owen went out again, down to the Eastern End.

"I'd almost think Helmi would like to be alone with Mark once in a while," Joanna remarked dryly.

Nils was helping to clear the table. "Well, she won't be alone until Mark gets his gear fixed. He's been bringing in his pots and tying small buoys on his short warps, getting ready for inshore fishing."

"How does he manage to get everybody working for him?" said Joanna. "Owen could always do it. But Mark—"

"Oh, Owen'll get it back." He laughed. "He's probably got Mark to build pots for him for the next six months." He put the bread in the breadbox, covered the butter and took it to the cool cellarway. Then he sat down by the window looking out to sea, with the Rock light just beginning to stab the dusk, and began to whittle plugs from the neat, small sticks of soft pine in a candy box on the window sill.

Joanna came to get the teakettle from the stove. She paused for a moment, watching him, her eyes contemplative under their dark brows. As the dusk deepened outside, the lamps seemed to brighten. The blade of his pocket knife caught the yellow flame of the bracket lamp over the stove; his hair caught it too. He was, as always, completely absorbed in what he was doing. The knife moved in short crisp sweeps, the shavings fell in a tidy little heap on the newspaper he had laid between his moccasins. He didn't look up, and she wondered what he was thinking.

Now was the time to ask him if he intended to lend Owen money for the *White Lady*. Surely it was her business to know. If Owen borrowed money she must be sure he stayed on his good behavior and didn't backslide once the *White Lady* was solid under his feet again.

"Nils," she said, and he looked up, his whole attention focused on her at once.

"What can I do for you? Need water?" He laid down his knife.

"No, don't get up. I won't need anything. It's just —" She closed her lips firmly. She'd be damned if she'd ask him! If he wouldn't tell her, let him keep it to himself. "Well, it's such a nice night," she said easily, "I thought we might walk down to the Eastern End ourselves. Helmi's been up a couple of times lately."

"Sure. . . . Is there anything you want me to do first?"

"No, thanks. I'll wash the dishes and then we can go." She smiled at him and took the teakettle across to the sink. The steam rose up in a cloud of hot fog around her face.

Coming out of the shadowy path at Mark's gate, they saw the moon rising from the sea, a pale and misty moon. Little wreaths of fog floated past it, and the night was neither light nor dark. Joanna and Nils walked in a soft, damp, curiously luminous atmosphere, yet their faces were indistinct, their eyes set in hollows of shadow. Their footprints showed black in the silvery moisture on the path. Toward Brigport and the mainland the world faded away into nothingness; toward the moonrise there was a faint light on the restless sea, and the surf that tumbled on the uneven rocks gleamed with an almost spectral whiteness.

Joanna and Nils had been discussing the Fennells as they came through the woods. Now they were silent, as if speech were forbidden in this ghostly world. Nils moved to open the gate, but Joanna stopped him.

"Wait a minute," she whispered. "Look down there. It's like

the setting for a tragedy. All we need is a hound-dog baying."

"It's like the places you see sometimes in a dream," Nils said, and his low, matter-of-fact voice gave an instant reality to the night. It didn't look so strange then, the buildings huddled darkly together, the open field with the luminous fog floating across it, the Head rising in blurred majesty beyond.

They went through the gate and down the path, and as they passed the silent barn Joanna saw the yellow glow of lantern light down in the fish house on the shore.

The house was lighted too, in kitchen and sitting room, and in the instant before Nils lifted his hand to knock at the entry door, she heard the boys' voices. The sense of oppression she had felt by the gate fled instantly. They'd be raising the devil in there, and Helmi wouldn't know what to make of it. . . .

Nils knocked, and there was silence for an answer. No sound from within or without the house. She and Nils looked at each other. "Now what are they cooking up?" she said. "Be careful when we go in, we'll have a pan of water dropped on us, or something."

"Spring in their blood," said Nils. Joanna opened the door carefully and they went into the dark entry. Somebody crossed the kitchen floor then, and opened the door. She stepped over the threshold into the warmth and light, and looked into Stevie's face. Her eyes aglow, her lips framing a quip, she saw no answering twinkle in his face — only a sort of wry dismay. She met it with bewilderment, and a strange premonitory dryness in her throat. Behind her Nils said quietly,

"What's going on?"

She looked beyond Stevie then and saw Mark and Owen. She thought with a horrid sinking of her heart, *What have we walked into?*

Mark stood in the center of the kitchen, big in his red plaid shirt and corduroys, his black head lowered; he watched Owen from under his eyebrows and never shifted his gaze to Joanna or Nils. She could see a muscle tighten along the clean hard line of his jaw. His arms hung at his sides and the hands were fists. It was the sight of those clenched fists that staggered Joanna. Owen leaned against the door casing between kitchen and sitting room. As if the arrival of Nils and Joanna had given him the chance he'd been waiting for, he took out a cigarette, lighted a match with his thumbnail, and put it to the cigarette.

As if the flare of the match broke the spell, there was sudden life and movement in the low, lamplit room. Joanna was conscious of the clock ticking; light flashing from the shiny surface of the well-polished teakettle; spilled water on the floor by the sink, reflecting the lamp.

"Come in," Mark said. "And make yourself at home." He didn't take his eyes from Owen, who watched him idly through the cigarette smoke and didn't move. "You're just in time."

"For what?" Joanna tried to sound humorous.

"To see me give this goddam son of a bitch the lickin' of his life."

Behind Joanna Stevie moved. Nils said easily, "What's he done? Tied small buoys on long warps? That's a hell of a mess."

Mark looked around at him then, as if Nils' cool voice had penetrated to the hot core of his rage; a rage which flung out its vibrations into the room as a rock thrown overboard sends out ripples. It seemed to Joanna that she could feel those waves strike her. Mark's eyes were burning as if with fever, and all color had drained away from his skin.

"He's been after my wife," he said thickly. "The bastard. Sneakin' up to the house for a drink of water. Then he tried to take her over. She showed me the marks on her arms." His words came with difficulty, as if his throat were clogged. "I'm goin' to cut his heart out and hang it up for the crows."

Nils said, still unexcited, "If you're going to fight, go outside. You don't want to mess up Helmi's kitchen."

Mark's eyes wavered toward him. "Sure," he said huskily, "I'll take the bastard outside to lick him."

Nils said, "Come on, Joanna. This is no place for us."

She looked at him in amazement. Did he propose to turn his back as if he had seen and heard *nothing?* Her surprise made her voice crisp.

"I'm not going *yet,* Nils."

Owen laughed. It was a soft chuckle, and the insolent sound was like a match set to the dry tinder of Joanna's anger that he should bring this situation into being. She brushed by Nils as if he weren't there and faced Owen's mocking eyes.

"You've succeeded, haven't you? You couldn't come home and leave things as they were, you couldn't be happy till you'd made some trouble, somehow! And with your own brother!"

"At least I keep it in the family," Owen drawled.

She felt Nils' hand on her arm. She brushed it off as she had brushed by him a moment ago. "Everything was too peaceful for you," she accused Owen. "You came home to see us all working hard trying to build up the Island; you couldn't bear to see us getting along so well, so you had to stir things up." Her words echoed in her head; she remembered in the instant all the times Owen had made her so violently, sickly angry and ashamed. The memory gave her new fire. Her words were meant to cut.

"What do you suppose Helmi thinks of the Bennetts, when she can't be left alone in her own kitchen? I'd hate to know what her idea of Mark's family is right now."

"There wasn't anything for him to get upset about," Owen said, cocking an eyebrow at her. "I never bothered the kid enough for her to run and tell—"

"Why shouldn't she tell?" Joanna demanded. "He's her husband, and she doesn't have to put up with you just to keep peace in the family!" She saw by the stiffening in Owen's face that he was getting mad. "A fine thing for the Island," she said. "A fine thing for a Bennett to be laying his hands on his brother's wife. How does that sound?"

"You keep hollerin' at me," said Owen, "and the whole bay will know it, and tell you how it sounds. Anybody could hear you from here to Port George." He shifted his big shoulders lazily. "Anyway, why don't you mind your own business? This is between me and Mark."

"It's Bennett business," Joanna said calmly. "Just as much as it is Mark's."

Mark, at the sound of his name, looked around at them all swiftly; the savagery was gone from his face, leaving it bleak and tired. He shrugged his red plaid shoulders at nothing, and went to sit down by the table, dropping his head into his hands.

Beside Joanna Nils moved, but she wouldn't look at him. He would only tell her they should be going home. And she wasn't going to be taken out of the room by her husband like a meek and ordinary wife; she was going to stay here and take care of this situation. After all, it involved her, they were her brothers. And when they were so angry with each other they needed her. They weren't able to judge for themselves.

Nils spoke quietly to her. "Come on, Joanna. We'd better go."

She glanced at him briefly. "No. I'm going to straighten this mess out."

"Mark and Owen are old enough to take care of their affairs — they don't need you."

She hated the cool finality in his voice, especially when she knew without looking how Owen's eyebrow was tilting. But of course what happened between her brothers would never upset Nils. . . . He could go home if he wanted, but she was staying.

Mark was still sitting with his head in his hands, but Owen went over to the sink and drank some water. Over his shoulder he glanced at Nils and Joanna as he set the dipper back into the pail.

"Well," he remarked, "might as well be headin' home. Nothin' more to stick around here for."

There was no answer to that. Even Joanna was silent as he opened the door and went out. When he had gone, Joanna went over to Mark. His elbows on his knees, his chin in his hands, he stared at an invisible spot on the floor between his feet.

The lamp on the table fluttered slightly in the draft stirred by the door's closing. It picked out coal-like glints in Mark's rough head.

"Mark," Joanna said softly, "I'm sorry for Owen's actions. But I'll talk to him —"

"Talk, hell! Talk to Owen, what good did that ever do?"

"I don't believe he'll bother Helmi any more," she said.

"I don't think he will either, but it's not because it made me mad or because she's his brother's wife —" He lifted his head, his black eyes narrowing. "It's just because he knows he won't get anywhere with her." He stood up and put his hands in his pockets. "I don't want to see Owen on this end of the Island again. That's all."

Joanna had a sick feeling at the strange finality in his face, in the sudden quieting of his voice. A breach in the Bennett family. She had fought against things like this all her life, and at the moment she felt very tired. She had wanted the boys to be working for each other and the Island — not flying at each other's throats. . . .

"Helmi's outside," Nils said to Mark. "Maybe you should go —"

Joanna swirled. "I'll go," she said.

"Never mind, Jo," Mark said. "I think I know where to look. Much obliged, sis, for droppin' in this evening. Sorry you and Nils had to run into this mess."

"I'm glad we came," she said earnestly to her younger brother. "I'm glad I could be here to talk to you and Owen."

The corner of Mark's mouth lifted in a small, rueful grin. He opened the door and the smell of fog came in. He walked out, and in a moment he was beyond the yellow reach of the lamplight; they didn't even hear his feet on the grass. The kitchen was silent again, except for the teakettle and the clock.

Nils said, "Going home, Joanna?"

"I suppose so," she said reluctantly. He shut the door behind them and they stood for a moment on the doorstep, adjusting their senses to the night world outside. The moonlit fog was light and cool against Joanna's hot face. She listened for the sound of Mark's voice or Helmi's. There was only the long-drawn-out sigh of the water on the pebbled beach of Eastern End Cove, the wind rising, the foghorn out at the Rock—distant because of the wind—and the low, muted crying of the gulls.

They walked up toward the gate in silence, but halfway through, she stopped. "I *ought* to see Helmi before we go home, Nils," she said. "Maybe I could talk to her a little—"

Nils' hand on her elbow propelled her through the gate. "You've done your talking for tonight, Jo. Let Mark handle her. After all, he's married to the girl. You told Owen off—now you can take it easy."

She walked along with him willingly, conscious of a pleasant pride. "I did tell him, didn't I? And I got him out of the house before anything happened. I'm glad we walked into that kitchen when we did."

"I'm not," said Nils. She swung her head to look at him in amazement, but she could hardly see his face; they were walking in the dense shadow of the trees.

"If we hadn't come in, they'd have been trying to kill each other," she protested.

"After they'd bloodied each other's noses, they'd have stopped," Nils said quietly. "And that would have been the end of it. Now they've just put it off for a while."

Tired, her nerves overtense, she couldn't let that pass but must challenge it. "I suppose you think I did wrong to say anything."

"I think we should have gone right out again when we saw what was going on. It wasn't any of our business."

She stopped in the path, her hands clenched in the pockets of her jacket. Her voice came as levelly as his. "It was *my* business, Nils. I wasn't going to see my brothers beating each other up."

"It's not for a woman to try to separate two men, no matter if they're her brothers or strangers," he said. He began to walk on, but she reached out and caught hold of his arm.

"I suppose you think you could have handled it better," she said, a slight tremor in her words. It was hard to keep them so steady. " Do you know the Bennetts better than I do?"

"I know that Owen's been in line for a damn' good licking all his life, and Mark's as big as he is—Mark could do it." She was appalled by his calmness. Her brothers, fighting—it was a sickening thought. And for Nils to speak of it was to bring a chilling sensation to the pit of her stomach. *Nils,* of all people.

"All his life he's had folks walking around him on tiptoe, trying not to get him mad. He's never had a come-uppance. Oh, I know something sent him back here to the Island, but I mean a come-uppance from any of his own people. He should have got it tonight. But you walked in and took over, Jo. He got out of it again. And meanwhile Mark's still brooding. You didn't help him any."

She walked in silence for a little while, trying in all fairness to see his point. But all she could see was the scene in the kitchen, brother facing brother, and not in friendliness but in enmity. She still felt bruised from the impact of Mark's fury, she could still hear his voice, and it was louder than Nils' voice, so that his recent words faded out. Her mind could only reiterate that Owen and Mark mustn't fight—they must work, like herself, for the Island. That must come first with them as it must come first with her. It was their past and their future. It was themselves. She'd talk to them about it when she got them alone again.

She and Nils had reached the clearing by the Eastern End gate. The fog had blown over in damp white waves, and now, suddenly, the moon-washed sky arched over them, the Island lay sleeping on a pale and dreamlike sea, lit by the gleam of foam on the rocks. The Island slept, but it listened, too. . . .

She turned and faced Nils. "I don't care how you figure it," she said, "*I'm* not going to stand by and have the boys beating each other up. There are more important things for them to be doing."

"What things?" he said quietly.

"Things for the good of the Island."

He stared at her for a long moment, his hand on the gate, his eyes shadowed by his visor; yet she could feel their intentness. "The Island always comes first, doesn't it, Joanna?"

There was something in his voice that made her hesitate, but only for a second, and then she plunged on. "We're just getting the Island back on its feet again. We can't go off on tangents now. We can't let the boys—"

"*We?*" he said. He put his hands in his pockets with a curiously deliberate gesture, and did not take his eyes from her face. He watched her for a long moment before he spoke again, as if he were studying her in the moonlight. "Joanna, let me ask you something—something I've been wondering about for a long time."

"You can ask me anything, Nils," she said slowly. "You know that."

"Then tell me this. Just how much do you figure I'm worth in your scheme of things?"

She stared at him in blank surprise. The question wasn't fair, it came too swiftly. "Why, Nils!" she cried out. "You're worth *everything!* And look what you've done! Fixed up the wharf, fixed over the long fish house, and you're rebuilding the boatshop—"

She stopped, making a helpless gesture with her hands. "Nils, whatever made you ask that?"

His eyes swept across the moonlit stretch of sea and then came back to her. "That's what I thought you'd say, Joanna. Well—" The old gate creaked faintly as he swung it open. "It's a good thing to know just where I fit." He motioned her through the gate.

"Nils—" she began, hardly knowing what she wanted to say.

"Never mind, Joanna. I think I understand."

She walked wordlessly beside him through the Island's fields, with the sea on either side. It was a world hushed with sleep and white with moonlight. They passed Schoolhouse Cove and came to the corner where they turned between the old gateposts and started up the rise to the house. There was no sound except the soft rush of waves on the beach and their feet on the gravel of the road.

Joanna knew she was walking in beauty—the beauty of the night and the Island. But at the same time she walked in loneliness, a strange and sudden loneliness. She looked at Nils as he walked beside her; sometimes his elbow brushed her arm. But she had the odd sensation that if she reached out to take hold of him, he would not be there.

21

SEPTEMBER AND OCTOBER SEEMED TO BE the first months of a new year on the Island. That was the time of the fall spurt. In the summer the lobsters were always scarce; they crawled under the rocks to shed and breed, and though the men kept some of their traps out, it was what Nils called "playing at lobstering." Some of the men went handlining and made money in cod and an occasional big halibut. There was a good market for them in Vinalhaven, and it wasn't too far to run at the end of a day's good fishing. All of the men helped in the gardens after supper at night. Every family had a garden, even the newcomers, the Fennells, and the canning kept the women busy through the summer.

The canning started in July, with the first wild strawberries that seemed to grow wherever there was grass to shelter them. Sou'west Point was the richest ground, although it was a long walk, through the woods and over the rocks, to reach them; the Bennett meadow was full, so were Uncle Nate's fields, and the field at the Eastern End. Young Nora Fennell was ecstatic about the berries she found around her new home. For the month of July everybody feasted on wild strawberries, picked in drooping red clusters whose sweetness melted on the tongue and tasted of cold, clean fog, and summer rain, of concentrated sunshine flavored with bay and red clover and spruce, and born of the lambent blue sky of the Island summer.

They ate strawberries picked along the overgrown path through the orchard, they ate them crushed and sugared, and whole with cream; they ate them between tender crusts, and poured in their own bright juice over split and buttered hot biscuit. And the women cooked them down into jam that, eaten in winter, would hold the essence of summer in its wine-red richness.

The vegetables matured in the gardens, and those not eaten fresh were canned; beets, beet greens, swiss chard, beans — string and shelled — some tomatoes, though they were hard to raise on the Island. The potato blossoms danced in the light winds, in time with the buttercups and daisies and red clover that carpeted the fields, splashed with the blazing orange of devil's paint brush. The turnips and squash were meant to last through the winter and spring, to be eaten as fancy dictated with soups, roasts, corned fish and pork scraps.

The canning was the major thing in the summer, and it seemed an endless round. Between picking berries — raspberries and blackberries followed the strawberries — and working in the garden, and canning, Joanna was never idle; and she was always ready for sleep at night. Nils filled every spare moment too. He built over the boatshop, with some help from the others; but sometimes he was up before daylight and down at the harbor, working alone before anyone was up. When he went to bed at night he was ready to sleep, like Joanna, and the next day always came so quickly. . . .

The men had stopped selling their lobsters to one of the big concerns. Charles Bennett had written about a friend of his who was starting up a business and would pay even more for carred lobsters than the big companies. It was true. Richards was eager for all the lobsters he could get, and he paid five cents extra, to the others' three cents. Like the big companies he ran a lobster smack. It was small, and he was his own captain, but he came promptly every two weeks and collected the lobsters from Jud's car, so that now no one had to go ashore with the crates. Moreover, Richards, a laconic but obliging sort, took in the grocery orders and delivered the supplies on the next trip. Jud said it was like the old days, when he was a young sprout.

Joanna had written to Portland about the return of a postoffice to Bennett's Island. If she could get it, then the mailboat would have to run down to Bennett's and deliver mail and freight. The next step was a store. Oh, things were moving along.

The spring and summer had been richly peaceful for the Island. Brigport had kept its distance. Except for the mail and occasional freight, there was no need for the Bennett's people to go to the larger island. And if Tom Robey thought they would come to him again for bait, he was disappointed; whenever Owen went ashore in the *White Lady* — for she was back again — or Nils in the *Donna,* they brought out several barrels of bream. In September the *Marianne* had come out several times and seined herring. And Richards could always be depended upon to bring bait out on the smack.

It was a time when you could imagine almost any dream and hope coming true; and Joanna had enough dreams and hopes — and plans — to last her a lifetime.

On a late October morning — so incredibly warm and peaceful as to be an echo of midsummer — she stood on the stone front doorstep, picking an armful of the small white and lavender-rose chrysanthemums that grew under the front windows. Her mother had planted them there, years before. . . . Joanna looked out across the Island, warm as summer, yet tinted with autumn over the marsh and the fields, and the yellow-leaved birches and alders, the fire-red bushes at the edge of the woods, and the tiny scarlet vines creeping among the tall, tawny field grasses. The smell of the chrysanthemums was cool and spicy, blended with the sunny, aromatic odor of the earth beyond the shade of the house; bird-voices were loud in the windless, dreamy day. It seemed as if they always chattered and fluted and whistled with an extra throat-bursting energy in the fall, to make up for the silent winter to come.

She saw some black ducks fly up from Schoolhouse Cove, their flight criss-crossing the long, effortless arcs of the gulls. It was an instant of loveliness, or rather of the pure essence of beauty. It quickened her heart. Sometimes she had moments of indefinable anxiety, even of depression; sometimes she felt edgy and short-tempered, and that bothered her, because she had never been nervous. But these moments didn't last. And on days like this one, she felt energy fairly teeming through her.

She should soon hear about the postoffice, she thought. Perhaps today, since it was a boatday. . . . She stood on the shady doorstep and listened to the silence of the house behind her. Ellen had gone back to school, to the third grade, and Mrs. Robey. Stevie was taking Nils to Brigport, and would bring back the mail when he returned. The *Donna*'s engine was not working right, and Nils was going ashore to see what he could find for a new one.

She realized suddenly that she was looking forward to the next few days. It would be a change to sleep alone, to read as late as she wanted to, and then fall asleep with no sense of restraint. She told herself often that Nils asked nothing of her now because he was so tired; but sometimes when he came to bed she wondered if he had really fallen asleep so quickly, and she would be nearly engulfed by a wave of mingled compassion and guilt. *If he feels cheated,* she would think, *why doesn't he hate me?* She felt at those times that it would be easier if he looked at her with contempt; and then she would tell herself that they had agreed to make their marriage a partnership for work, and he had nothing for which to reproach her. If she couldn't look at him as she had looked at Alec—was it her fault?

And when it came to reproaches, she had her own resentments, if she cared to let them flourish. The reproofs he had given her; the way he had assumed control of the Island business and the way her brothers let him do it; the lobster car, where Jud now reigned. . . . If Nils ever felt cheated, didn't she feel cheated—though she never showed it—when she saw the business Jud was doing? Not only with the Bennett's men, but there was also a handful of men from Brigport who for reasons of their own didn't like Ralph Fowler. It was turning out just as she had planned—except that she wasn't running the car. Oh, she could have the postoffice—Nils approved of that. Once or twice she'd known a childish, furious impulse to throw up the idea, but such impulses never lasted. After all, the postoffice was for the good of the Island. More people would come to it when the mail ran regularly.

She thought of all those things as she stood on the doorstep, twirling a chrysanthemum in her fingers, its petals still dotted with dew. She looked past the schoolhouse at Tenpound between the Islands, and heard the *Aurora B.*'s high whistle as she entered Brigport harbor. In a little while now Nils would be gone, and for a few days she would relax.

"Why can't things be the way I want them?" she asked the ragged flower. She could not hide from herself the fact that sometimes she knew an almost intolerable tension, and a frightening sensation that life could not go on like this.

In the warm October silence, the drone of Caleb's hauling gear, down in Goose Cove, reminded her that when Stevie came back with the mail he'd want to go out to haul. No time for dreaming or anything else now. She went into the house, cool and empty this morning, and put the chrysanthemums into an old pitcher. She set it on the table, where she could sniff the cool, frosty scent whenever she went by.

Dry, seasoned spruce made a quick hot fire, and she had the water on for coffee while she cut up the cold potatoes and corned hake for the fish hash. Stevie would want a good dinner, and fish hash was the thing, with a whiff of onion in it, and the pork scraps left over with the fish and potatoes from the night before. She had apple pie for him too. And after he had gone out, she would be at no one's beck and call until it was time to get supper, and he and Owen came home.

The old, winged, sensation of freedom came back to her. She began to whistle as she fixed Stevie's dinner. When next she looked out the window, the sturdy little *Elaine* was coming into harbor.

While Stevie washed, she looked over the mail. There was a letter from her mother, and that was all for Joanna. But Nils had two besides the *Fishing Gazette* and the *Atlantic Fisherman*. She read the return addresses in the corners of the envelopes. Eric Sorensen, Nils' uncle in Camden; and P. S. Grant, in Limerock.

"Why, that's Pete Grant!' she said aloud, and Stevie lifted his face from the towel.

"Huh?"

"What's he writing to Nils about?" she demanded, frowning. She turned the letter over and looked at it on both sides.

"Maybe he wants to sell Nils something," Stevie said helpfully.

"Maybe he's heard you're trying to get the postoffice, and he figures you could use the store and wharf."

He sat down at his place, and Joanna laid the letter aside slowly, her brows still drawn. She put the dinner on the table for Stevie and herself, and then read their mother's letter aloud. It was Donna at her best, the even tempo of the words, the little touches of dry humor. Charles was doing well with his seining this fall. And he was doing well in other ways too; Mateel was expecting another baby. . . .

All the time she and Stevie were smiling over the letter, Joanna thought of Pete Grant's letter to Nils, and wondered. If it was private business, what on earth was it? And if it were Island business, why didn't Pete write to her about it? She wondered about the letter all through the meal, and Stevie, catching her glance as it shifted swiftly from the envelope, teased her.

"How are you going to hang on till Nils comes home and opens that? Now if it was from a woman you'd have something to really get all hawsed up about." He pushed back his chair. "Good dinner, Jo. Want me to bring in some lobsters tonight?"

"If you do we'll have some baked and stuffed for supper," she said. She got up and tucked Nils' magazines and letters behind the clock.

"Strong-minded, huh?" said Stevie. He grinned at her and went out. She was alone, her long lovely afternoon was about to begin. But its shining surface was dimmed. *Pete Grant's letter*. It must be Island business, she thought again. And if it should be, she was justified in opening it.

Just the sight of Pete's ungainly, hardly legible, handwriting evoked him before her as he'd looked striding down the wharf to the lobster car, a bluff, mustachioed giant of a man, who had been one of the first young men to work for Grandpa Bennett on the Island; he'd been a hired fisherman then, like Nils' grandfather, Gunnar, and Jud's father and the rest.

But Pete's enterprising Scots blood had put him into something else. One of the other young men who lived in the camps had wanted to buy some of his Saturday-night baked beans—Pete was the best cook of all the bachelor fishermen—and he saw the possibilities of a good business.

It *was* a good business, too; baked beans and brown bread once a week, then a sideline of doughnuts and pies. In no time he was prospering, and not merely as one of Grandpa Bennett's fishermen, who were obliged to sell their fish to the Captain at a minimum price and buy their supplies from him at a maximum one. By the time Pete had married and started a family he had a store all his own, and there was nothing Captain Bennett could do about it, since in a moment which he had always regretted afterwards he'd sold Pete a piece of land.

Grandpa Bennett's store had gone out of business eventually, when neither of his sons, Nate and Stephen—Joanna's father—had wanted to carry it on. But Pete Grant flourished, and in his thirty-five years of store-keeping and lobster-buying he had been a good friend to the Island. A sharp-tongued one, almost too blunt—but still he'd been one of the Islanders. Even when he bought one of the harbor points, and built his house on it, and sent his boys away to school and college—that was during the Golden Period for anyone who bought or sold lobsters—the older men never forgot that he was still the big, boisterous, canny youth who could bake beans as well as any woman, and had peddled them around the camps on a Saturday night. And Pete never forgot it, either.

He'd left Bennett's Island—one of the last to go—when it seemed as if there were no more lobsters left to buy and not enough trade coming into his store to count. But he still owned his point, his house and store and wharf, and the other buildings; and it was said that he still considered himself an Islander, though he was too old and lame now to come back.

So, smiling a little to herself at her memories of Pete, who had been such an important figure in her life ever since she could first remember, Joanna opened his letter. She sat by the table, with the fragrance of the chrysanthemum in her nostrils, and read what he had written to Nils.

It was only a note. She read it and understood it in something under five minutes. And when she had finished she sat very quietly in her chair, her fingers tightening gradually on the slip of paper. She couldn't tell whether she felt shock, or sickness, or panic, or a sheer primitive fury; perhaps it was a mixture of all of them. But for a moment she could not move. Then she read the letter again.

Dear Nils, (it began). You'll want to know this right off, so I'll be brief. Randolph Fowler has been up here to see me and wants to buy my point and shore front down on the Island. He is offering me a good price, and will pay cash. I don't mind saying I can use the money — Stella and me are both getting on, you know — but I thought I'd offer you folks first refusal. Fowler is a good business man and maybe he could do something for the Island, but I don't know how well he sets with you people, not being an Island man. Let me know right away. I don't mind telling you I'll accept any reasonable offer from Bennett's Island people. I'm still a Bennett's man. Fowler is offering me more than the place is worth. If you don't want it, he can have it.

Yours truly,
Pete Grant.

She stood up and went to the window, staring down across the meadow at the harbor. The October afternoon was at its loveliest. But she hardly saw it. She was thinking of Randolph Fowler. So, all the time he'd been handing out mail and nodding courteously to her through the postoffice window, he'd been planning this . . . actually to lay his hands on a piece of Bennett's Island. To be able to call a strip of its shoreline *Fowler property;* one of its most beautiful points, and the best place in the harbor for a wharf — why, he could control over half the harbor! She thought of his smooth, polite face and voice with an almost physical loathing.

Yet there had been one thing he hadn't planned on — that Pete Grant would notify her of the offer. Not herself, actually, but Nils. But that didn't matter, as long as they knew.

They must have the point, and without delay. She throttled down her sense of outrage — she mustn't let that interfere with her thinking, which must be clear and logical. One thing was certain; she could not wait two days for Nils. Anything could happen in two days. She couldn't bear to sit still and wait, and do nothing till he came.

The thing to do was to get the money somehow, and get it to-day; and it must come from the Island. The fall spurt had been going on for some six weeks now, everyone had been doing well, and nobody'd been spending much. They'd all have money in the house; for most of the fishermen let it mount far into the hundreds before they banked it — if, like Nils, they believed in banks. She knew that at this moment there were at least four hundred and fifty dollars in Nils' money box, and that Stevie and Owen each had a good sum. Mark would have plenty too. Why, right in the family there must be enough cash for what might be called a "reasonable offer"; no, not quite enough, she must make it a very good offer. After all, the wharf and buildings, though in bad repair, were fundamentally solid.

She looked down at the harbor again. In the bright flood of afternoon sunshine it was empty, except for the *Donna*. No one was in from hauling yet, and she was tormented by her impatience, till she remembered that Jud would be available. Jud, as lobster-buyer, was always around. And—as lobster-buyer—he had money put by.

She changed her housedress for a tweed skirt and yellow sweater, brushed her hair to a crow's-wing smoothness, took the letter and went out. She took the road toward the harbor, intending to try the lobster-car first; she hoped Jud wasn't still at home, dallying over his dinner, because she felt she could talk to him best without Marion around. She didn't want any possible obstacle to Jud's giving her three or four hundred dollars.

He wasn't out on the car, but on the beach, painting his skiff a vivid robin's-egg blue. His solid, pudgy figure was quite alone and at peace, except for a couple of young gulls arguing over a dead fish at the water's edge. Joanna, approaching him, felt suddenly as if the October sun were burning her face and drying her lips.

He heard her step and looked up, mopping his red face with his bandanna "Hi, Jo. Hot, ain't it? Weather-breeder."

"It's a beautiful day," she said. "So's your punt."

He looked pleased. "I think it's real pretty. Marion, she don't think much of it. Says it's too giddy for a man o' my years an' discretion."

"*Your* years!" Joanna laughed. "Jud, you're younger than I am this minute!"

"Lonesome for Nils?" he inquired sympathetically. "That must be love, huh? He ain't been gone but an hour or two." He shook his head. "By God, I stay out on the car all mornin', go home to dinner, and the old lady, she looks at me and says, "What you home so soon for?" Still shaking his head, he went back to his painting. "That's what it is when you git to my age!"

Joanna sat down on the side of a dory. "I've got a good reason to feel old." She held out the letter to him. "Read this."

He squinted at it. "Ain't got my specs, Jo. You read it. Ain't bad news, is it?"

"It depends on how you look at it," she told him, and read the letter aloud. When she had finished Jud sat back on his heels and looked at her.

"That son of a bitch!" he said softly. "Tryin' to cut our throats when our back is turned!"

Joanna's heart quickened. The letter was doing what she wanted it to do. Jud was at least three shades redder, verging on purple. She went on, speaking quietly.

"You know what he can do with Grant's place, don't you? He could put hired fishermen in the buildings to live, and under the law he'd have a right to. Ten men with a hundred pots apiece—that's an extra thousand to choke up these waters so you could hardly get a power boat through. . . . Of course," she added, "they'd be selling to Ralph, over at Brigport."

"I wouldn't buy the bastards' lobsters, anyway!" Jud said violently. He struggled to his feet. "And even five fishermen with a hundred pots would be five too many—'specially if they was Fowler's men!" He glared up and down the empty beach as if he saw them there already. "What are we gonna do, Jo?"

"We're going to buy the point outright," Joanna told him. "If I can get enough money together today, I'll get Stevie to take me ashore tomorrow morning, and the business will be done by noon. How about it?"

"You want money right now, Jo?" he asked uneasily. "How much do you want from me?"

"As much as you can give me." She forgot to be calm. She slid off the dory and faced him, taller than he, her intensity making her seem taller still. "Oh, Jud, can't you see how important it is? What's it worth to you to keep the Fowlers from getting their hands on any piece of this island?"

"Worth plenty, Jo," he said soberly. "Look—I'll be up to the house by'mby. I'll bring you up—well, how 'bout three hundred dollars? I got to save some to buy lobsters with, tomorrow."

"You won't be sorry about chipping in," she said. The sound of an engine grew in the sunlit hush; they looked up, watching Eastern Harbor Point, and saw the nose of Caleb's boat come in sight. She rounded the point, her wake throwing a creamy surge against the rocks, and headed for her mooring. "I'll talk to Caleb next," Joanna said. "I'll walk around to the house and be there when he gets in."

"Better give him a chance to eat his dinner first," Jud advised her.

"This can't even wait for dinner," she retorted. She went up over the pebbly slope to the road. A flock of grackles flew up from the edge of the marsh, shiny black bodies wheeling against a luminous sky.

22

THE NEXT MORNING SHE ATE BREAKFAST at sunrise with her two brothers. It was another lovely day. The sea lay mirror-calm in the coves and in the harbor, and the chatter of birds was loud and sweet, as the light began to filter through the woods.

Owen, coming in with the water pails, said, "Sure is a pretty day. But when this stretch ends, all hell will break loose."

Joanna laughed. "And all hell will break loose in Fowler's store when they find out we own Grant's point!" She went to the dresser for more bread, and patted her pocketbook affectionately when she passed it. "There it is — I never carried so much money in my life."

"You scraped the bottom of the barrel, all right. Gathered up everybody's hard-earned dollars," said Stevie. "Only hope Pete's ready to do business when we get in there."

"Of course he'll be ready." She rested her chin in her hands and looked dreamily out across the paling sea. Two gulls flew across a peach-flushed sky that was already turning to gold. "Isn't this a heavenly day?"

"Look," said Owen. "What if you run into Nils over there?"

"He'll be glad I've done this," she answered promptly.

"You sure?" Owen looked quizzical. "After all, you go around and make everybody fork over their savings — tell 'em it's practically a matter of life and death. . . . That's not exactly Nils' way of doing things."

She said angrily, "What else was I supposed to do? It was an emergency. I couldn't wait for him to come home! We've *got* to have that point!" She pushed back her chair and left the table. Owen's voice followed her to the mirror, where she stopped to adjust her blouse collar.

"Don't fly down my throat, darlin' mine. I was just wondering. . . . And what am I having to eat today?"

"Well, your dinner-box is all ready, and when you come in, there's cold boiled lobsters in the cellar way, and potatoes ready to fry, and some apple pie — I guess you'll make out." She had stopped being angry with him; she couldn't be angry on such a flawless pearl of a day, when she had this deep, solid knowledge that what she was doing was *right*. And she had done it by herself; she had talked Caleb and Jud and Matthew and her brothers into realizing the urgency of the situation. Forever afterward, whenever she looked at Grant's point, walked on the wharf or on the solid rocks of the shore, she would feel a special relationship with the timbers, or the granite boulders, because of her part in helping the Island to hold them fast.

Stevie, in his good blue serge trousers and clean white shirt, and yellow pullover, his new leather jacket under his arm, his brown cheeks ruddy from his recent shaving, was waiting for her. She caught up her tweed topcoat and her hat, and the precious handbag. She gave the kitchen a swift inspection. Everything was in its place, Owen knew where to find the lobsters and eggs and coffee, and anything else he'd need. Now she could go. And when she came back, well — she grinned at her two brothers.

"So long, Owen. Okay, Stevie? Let's go."

There was no one stirring as they walked down through the dew-wet marsh, their shadows falling before them. Only the birds seemed to be awake, the little birds, and the gulls weaving back and forth overhead. The cool, windless air touched their faces. They smiled at each other, and walked down the damp, stony beach without speaking, feeling no need for words. She helped him shove the punt off, and she took her place in the stern. The oars dipped in the glassy green water, and the wet blades shone, and shining drops of water ran off them and left tiny dimples where they fell. Always the sun was climbing, and outside the harbor, toward the mainland in the west, the sea already wore its morning blue, the soft bright blue Joanna had once seen in a stone called lapis lazuli.

But the mountains were misted in a lilac haze.

Stevie had some business of his own to do, so she went alone to see Pete and Stella Grant. It was early afternoon when she met him, as they had agreed, at the Limerock Public Landing. On such an unusually mild day, the Landing was busy with people who had come down to take out their little sailboats or sea sleds for a run around the harbor, and the afternoon boat from one of the large islands up the coast was discharging its passengers on the float. But when Joanna saw the intrepid little *Elaine* tied up between a visiting yacht and a sleek gray Coast Guard boat, she ran down the slip as if no crowd existed, and jumped down into the *Elaine*'s cockpit.

"I've got it, Stevie!" she said joyfully, her whole face alight. She unzipped her pocketbook and took out the long brown envelope that held the deed. "There it is! All registered, and everything." Regardless of an interested sailor aboard the Coast Guard boat, and a crew member on the yacht, Joanna and Stevie bent their heads over the deed.

"What's this mean—'Joanna Bennett et als'?" Stevie asked.

"That means 'and others,' " she said. "They do that instead of putting everybody's name down on the outside. But we're all inside." She unfolded the deed; never had a mere folded strip of paper meant so much to her as this one did. "See? Everybody's there. And we own the whole thing, outright." She hugged Stevie's arm, and laughed aloud. "You should have seen Pete's face when I brought out the money! Of course, they made me stay and eat with them, and then we went to see the lawyer—gosh, it doesn't seem *real*, Stevie."

"This deed is real enough." Stevie read it carefully. "Golly, I never knew he owned so far along the west side."

"Don't you remember the fight he had with George Bird once— George said he owned a strip in there between Pete and Barque Cove?" She read the deed with him. "Look—two days ago at this time I wasn't even thinking about Pete's property. And now we own it."

She put the deed back in her pocketbook, and began to stow

away her parcels in the bow of the *Elaine*. The Coast Guard sailor looked at her appreciatively, and it was hard for her to restrain a wink; she was bursting with happiness. She called to Stevie.

"Look, here's some candy, and I've got steak for supper tonight. Let's get started, Stevie. I can hardly wait to get home again."

Stevie didn't move from the engine box. "Hey, wait a couple minutes, can't ye? What's your pucker? I ran into your husband over at Ray's Machine Shop, and told him to come along home with us, if he was ready."

Joanna, for one blank moment, realized she had forgotten Nils. "Are we waiting for him?" she asked slowly.

"Sure. He's got a good engine too. He's leavin' it at Ray's to have the valves ground."

"That shouldn't take long," Joanna said. "He'll only have to come right back again."

"Oh, they've got a pile of work ahead. He'll have to wait a week, anyway." Stevie grinned. "He wanted to know what we came over for, but I told him that was your secret."

She sat down beside him on the engine box and pulled off her hat, welcoming the sun's warmth on her head. She moved her shoulders luxuriously. She ought to store up as much of this sunshine as she could, she thought comfortably. The scent of Stevie's cigarette blended with the breath of salt water, freshened by a faint breeze from the east.

"Airin' up," Stevie said. "He'd better get a move on."

"Did he seem interested in my secret?" she asked him. She too wished Nils would hurry; not because there might be a stiff breeze outside Owl's Head, for no boisterous winds held any awe for her. But she wanted to show him the deed, to tell him what she'd done— what they'd all done, all the Islanders. They'd done it together, and it welded them closer than anything else could ever do. It was all very well to say "We must work together." Just words. But it needed the threat of a common enemy, an instant defense of their own, to join them in one tight, hard-fighting cluster. Even Matthew Fennell, the newest member, had given his savings to her instantly when he knew how urgent it was for them to secure Grant's property at once.

"Well, you know how Nils is," Stevie was saying, and she had to think for a moment to remember what he meant. She laughed aloud.

"Oh, sure! The impassive type. But let's see how impassive he looks when he finds out!"

"Finds out what?" Nils' voice said above them. They looked up and saw him leaning on the rail along the edge of the dock. There were people passing to and fro behind him, high schoolers, sailors, the rest of the crowd to be found at Limerock's Public Landing on a mellow and tawny afternoon. But to Joanna, in the instant of recognition, they were a noisy backdrop for Nils alone, as he leaned on the rail and looked down at her. Only the autumn sky belonged, against which his head gleamed white-blond, and his skin looked warm and ruddy-brown; the gulls belonged too, riding far above him.

But because of the brilliance of the sky, and the sun in her eyes, his face was hard to see. It was like one of those dreams when you are companioned by people who are real enough, yet you can never quite make them out.

" Come on down!" she called to him. "I'm getting a crick in my neck!"

He ran down the slip to the float, down another very short slip, and ran across the small float to the *Elaine*. Now she could see him clearly, as he walked along the washboard and jumped down into the cockpit. He smiled at her and Stevie as if he liked them both very much. She saw what she hadn't noticed before—the deepening of the little short lines at either end of his mouth.

"What's going on?" he said.

Stevie shrugged. "Ask my sister. Get off the engine box, Beautiful. This critter's got a starter, but it only works on State days 'n' Sundays 'n' bonified nights."

Joanna moved up to the bow and picked up her topcoat. Nils helped her on with it. She had a sudden conviction at that moment that she didn't want to tell Nils about the sale while the *Elaine* was still at the wharf. She looked at him over her shoulder, smiling.

"Well, what goes on?" he asked.

"Wait till we get out of the harbor," she told him. "And I'll tell you all about it. But I know you'll like it. . . . How's the new engine?"

"Fine," he said absently. His touch on her shoulders was impersonal. "I was lucky. Fellow knows my father and Uncle Eric. He knew your father too." Nils took out his pipe and studied it for a moment. Then, as the *Elaine*'s engine began her sturdy chugging and backing, he went to join Stevie by the wheel.

The *Elaine* backed out between the yacht and the Coast Guard boat, her propeller churning the green water into a confusion of jade and ivory. The sailor, sprawled on the gray boat's deck, bare and brown to his waist and his dungarees, waved to Joanna, who waved back. He looked wistfully after the *Elaine,* as she headed for the mouth of the big harbor. Joanna waved again, her deep satisfaction in her two days' work making her feel friend to all the world, and turned her face to the bow. She felt the curious sensation of delight she always knew when she stood like this, the wind flowing against her face, sleeking her hair back from her forehead; the water rushing away from either side of the bow, the foaming wake behind them. The *Elaine* looked tiny, flying across the harbor, under the towering noses of the lumber schooners and coal lighters, slipping close to a destroyer that had come up the coast for her trial run. She lay at peace on the crinkling peacock water, a giant above the *Elaine.* Far up the sleek, sun-washed gray side of her Joanna saw the white caps of sailors who looked down at the infinitesimal *Elaine,* and waved. Joanna waved back; then she looked astern at Stevie and Nils, and saw the way Stevie's eyes were climbing up to the topmost point of the destroyer, and knew by his face what he was saying. He thought the ship was beautiful, and somehow he was telling Nils so, for she could read Nils' face too as he listened.

She turned away quickly, the brightness of the day tarnished by a breath. If there was a war, Stevie wouldn't care if fishermen were essential or not. He'd head for the place where they'd tell him the way to a ship like that.

They passed the house on the end of the long breakwater, and the breeze was already stiffening. Owl's Head was next. When she was a small girl, the keeper had owned a little white dog who used to run out on the steep slope to bark every time the *Aurora B.* entered or left Limerock harbor. You couldn't hear him bark, but you could see how he raced himself and how his mouth moved. Link always blew the whistle twice at the dog. Every child who ever rode on the mailboat in those faraway times knew that dog. From habit, Joanna looked for him now. Thinking of him, she forgot about the war, and her secret excitement came back to her.

As the boat passed Monroe's Island, Nils came to stand beside her, looking ahead for the long blue cloud of Brigport on the horizon. His pipe smelled even better than Stevie's cigarette. Little translucent green wavelets slapped at the *Elaine*'s bow, and Joanna tasted spray. She turned to Nils with a smile.

"This is going to be good!" she said.

"How good is your surprise? That's what I want to know."

She said, "Oh, you do, do you?" Laughing, she picked up her pocketbook from a coil of rope under the washboards, took out the deed, and handed it to him. He gave her a quick, questioning look, as he saw her name on the outside; then, unfolding the crisp paper, he began to read.

She watched his face with something approaching an agony of suspense. Why didn't he *show* anything? Must he always be the impassive Scandinavian, keeping his emotions locked behind an unreadable face? . . . Toward the end, he took his pipe out of his mouth; she watched to see if his fingers tightened on the bowl. But he might have been reading almost anything; in fact, he showed more interest in Ellen's spelling papers.

At last he was through. He folded the deed and put it back in its envelope and returned it to her

"How come?" he said. "What happened?"

She was still staring at him, her dark eyes intense. "Well? Don't you think it's pretty good?"

Quite unexpectedly he smiled, his whole face smiled, and he reached out and shook her shoulder gently. "Of course it's good! But you took the wind out of my sails. Now I want to know what happened."

Of course it's good, he'd said, and from Nils that was praise. She'd been foolish to expect him to make a lot of noise about it and practically dance a jig. After all, he wasn't a Bennett. She began eagerly to tell him about the letter.

"It was addressed to you, but I knew it concerned the both of us," she said confidently. "I knew you wouldn't care if I read it. You don't, do you?"

"Well, it's opened now, isn't it?" said Nils, and put his pipe back in his mouth.

"So," she went on briskly, "I thought I'd better do something about it. So I did. I went around and talked to everybody and they agreed."

"What are the terms? Pete make 'em easy?"

"But that's the good part of it, Nils! No payments to meet, nothing hanging over us—because it's all paid for. In one lump sum! Cash."

Nils' blond eyebrows drew together. He said quietly, "Where did you get twenty-five hundred dollars together in one afternoon?"

"Everybody chipped in," she said. She felt her shoulders tensing, her chin tightening. "You did, too. Out of the money box."

"You mean," Nils questioned her, "that you got twenty-five hundred dollars from the seven fishermen on Bennett's Island yesterday? That they just handed it over?"

"Yes, they handed it over, and they were glad to," she answered serenely, "when they found out that we needed to hurry. . . . And I knew you wouldn't keep back your savings, either."

He turned his head and looked out across the water toward the islands. They made a chain along the sea, from the Camden mountains, as if all the green islands in the chain were the tops of mountains that had sunk. Far out, Brigport lay on the horizon. Beyond it was Bennett's. Joanna watched Nils' profile. She was on the defensive now. No matter what he said, she knew she had done right.

"Pete would have taken a down payment," he said finally. "We could have paid the whole thing in the good seasons. . . ."

"Am I wrong—or isn't this a good season?"

"Sure, it's a good one. But Pete probably didn't expect you to take everybody's fall earnings and pay him in one fell swoop."

She said tensely, "The fall spurt's still going on. In the next six weeks you'll make as much again as you made in the last six weeks, the way lobsters are coming."

"You sure of that?" He turned and looked at her directly. "Are you positive there won't be a bad storm, say next week, that'll wipe us out, clip and clean? What do we do then?"

She fought desperately for a come-back. She'd never known his words to bite her so. They made her skin burn, she knew her cheeks were reddening and he would see the color in them.

"That would still mean Fowler had a chance of buying—"

"You think Pete would pull anything like that on us?" Nils said. "Then you don't know him."

"Well, anyway," she said stubbornly. "It's ours. Later on we can buy out the others and make it Bennett-Sorensen property."

"Did you have that in your mind when you made them open up their money boxes and shell out?" he asked her quietly. "You'd better make it just *Bennett* property, Joanna."

He left her and went astern to Stevie at the wheel. Alone, she stood in the bow and looked out toward the islands. Bennett's was there, the little world of red rock and fields and spruces that meant more to her than anything else in the world; with which she felt an even stronger kinship than with her daughter Ellen. When she used to read fairy tales, she wondered sometimes if she hadn't once been one of the straight young green spruces, and had been turned into a maiden; it had seemed to her that almost she could remember the feel of roots in the Island's soil, and the beating of the rain and snow and wind, and the sun making her grow.

She remembered that now, as she looked out across the sea, over the roughening, glistening folds of blue-green. And she felt lonelier than a spruce tree, lonelier than a gull; for they were what they were and nothing more was expected of them — but if you were a person, if you were Joanna Bennett, and you tried to be what you were, it was always wrong. At least as far as other people were concerned. It was lonely and it was hard to know that you were right, and that no one else believed it. She wondered by now if the other men — Matthew, Caleb, Jud, her brothers — were thinking about storms; were thinking there might have been another way of securing the property.

But I was right, she said fiercely to herself. *We have it now. Nobody can ever take it away from us.*

Spray washed suddenly over the side and its cold splatter felt like ice against her hot face. The *Elaine* bobbed a little, then plunged smoothly through another swell. There was more spray. The decked-in bow gleamed wetly in the sunshine, and the wind was sharp. She could have gone back where the men were, and sat on the engine box — boats rode easier amidships. And it wasn't a good idea to get soaked at the outset of the trip, she'd be cold by the time they reached the Island. But she would not go back and face Nils. Not yet. It would show in her face, the resentment that she felt.

There won't be any big storms this fall, her mind stated with passionate assurance. *No storms. This was all meant to be, so there won't be any storms.*

Now she could go back and sit on the engine box. Her self-assurance had returned, her spirit had lightened, almost like a gull soaring up to the zenith. She took a box of candy and a bag of oranges from her carry-all bag, and turning toward the men, confidence in the carriage of her head and shoulders; smiling, she held out the fruit and candy to them.

23

IN THE MORNING JOANNA WAS RESTLESS and excited. Her dreams had been charged with the thought of her triumph over Fowler. Though Nils slept beside her, in the deep entirety with which he always slept, it was to Joanna as if she were completely alone, she was so absorbed in what she had done. When she awoke for brief intervals during the night, she lay watching the paling twinkle of stars above the saw-toothed black wall of the woods, and listened to the surge on the shore, the wind around the house, and remembered again and again the moment in which the deed had been put into her hands. She would have to send it back to have it recorded, but not until she knew almost every word of it by heart! She had worked for that deed, and she had worked alone. Nils, lying unconscious beside her, had no part in it. She savored her proud confidence, and fell asleep again.

During the day she had not much to do in the house beyond the routine picking-up, and the walls seemed to stifle her. The wind was too brisk for the men to haul; just enough top-chop to make the buoys almost invisible, and hard to reach. But it was as bright as yesterday had been. It matched Joanna's mood, and she wanted to get out into it, with the wind blowing hard against her, and the strong, salt-scented sunshine on her skin. As soon as the men had gone down to the shore, to hunt out the source of a mysterious tinkle in the *Elaine*'s engine, she went out too. At first she considered going over to Uncle Nate's field to see if there were any cranberries left in the warm boggy spot beyond the ice pond. But she knew she would never be content to kneel quietly and pick berries when her energy was teeming down to her fingertips.

She thought of the deed, back there in the house. She was walking on the small, sheltered curve of Goose Cove beach then, watching the easy surge of rollers come in from the sea; they held a smooth glitter in the morning sunshine. But when she remembered the deed, she glanced up at the house. Everyone on the Island had a right to see that deed, and his name on it. She should carry it around from house to house this morning, let them read it from one end to the other. But the men would be out around the shore, with their hands in bait or tar or something. . . . She considered, watching a pair of blue-winged teal who rode unconcernedly on the swell at the mouth of the cove.

She had it then. There was something better than carrying the deed around. A party—tonight. She and Nils had never had everybody up to the house for an evening together, and if this wasn't the occasion for it, what was? She turned and went up the slope from the beach, leaping from boulder to gray boulder as she'd done when she was fifteen; she felt as happy and intent as fifteen had ever been.

But almost at the doorstep, her feet slowed to a stop. Mark and Helmi wouldn't come . . . or would they? If she went down to the Eastern End to ask them, perhaps they'd come, and then there'd be an end to the strangeness between Mark and Owen. Nils would see that she'd really been right, about keeping them from blows. The thought of Mark and Owen comrades again added to her happiness.

She veered away from the house, down across the October-painted meadow toward the woods. Nora Fennell should have the very first invitation.

All the women were pleased at the idea of a party, according to their various ways of showing pleasure. There was enough child in Nora yet to be thrilled at the thought. Gram snorted, and shook her head; she hadn't liked it when Matthew had handed out his savings without a question. But when the snortings and headshakings were done, she announced abruptly that she'd wear her best black silk, though she'd have to press it herself because Nora would probably scorch it. Marion Gray said at once she'd bake a big devil's food cake, and get Jud into a clean white shirt if she had to hog-tie him first. Vinnie bubbled almost as much as Nora had. Caleb was home when Joanna came in. He said somberly that they ought to get together oftener, with the bad weather coming. It would make the winter shorter, he said.

She saved the Eastern End for the last, but her confidence was intact. She found Helmi and Mark in the kitchen, Helmi sewing, Mark having a mug-up after a spell of work in his shop. They were glad to see her, and Mark wanted to know about the purchase; but when she told them about the party Mark gave her a dark look and shook his head. Helmi's needle slipped steadily along the hem of a curtain.

"Mark, it's a sort of special occasion," Joanna said quietly. "It's more important than any one of us."

"Listen, I did my part," Mark retorted. "I shelled out like the rest of 'em. And I don't feel like goin' in for any of the flagwaving and handshaking afterwards."

Joanna shrugged, grinned at him as if she weren't disappointed, and got up to go.

"A cup of coffee first, Joanna?" Helmi said unexpectedly.

She drank it, so that they wouldn't wonder afterwards if she'd been annoyed with Mark, but she didn't linger when she'd finished.

Nils and Stevie took the news as she'd expected, Stevie cheerfully, Nils with an agreeable nod.

"Hell," Owen said. "If I'd known this was in the wind, I'd have had you fellers bring me out a couple of quarts yesterday." They were all good-natured about having a party sprung on them so suddenly.

Her preparations didn't amount to much. The house was clean, though she gave the sitting room an extra dusting, and hunted up two new decks of cards and the cribbage board. She had checkers, and Chinese checkers. There was enough to amuse everybody. The only shadow across her afternoon was the fact that Mark and Helmi wouldn't be there. But this couldn't go on forever, she told herself.

Something would happen to bring them all together again. She refused to worry.

The refreshments were as simple as the cleaning. Nora and Vinnie had both offered to bring sandwiches; they had plenty of bread on hand, for the smack had been out only a few days before. They had no fear of using it all up in sandwiches, for they could always *make* bread. The men liked that better anyway. . . . Joanna would make a big white cake, to go with Marion's devil's food cake, and they would have coffee.

Beating up the cake, Joanna whistled as she had not whistled for a long time. They were through with Fowler; there was nothing more he could do to persecute them. He knew better than to start a lobster war, for the Bennett's Islanders could cut off Brigport traps as fast as their own were molested. She didn't let her mind dwell on what could have happened if Pete hadn't written to let them know of Fowler's offer.

We wouldn't have let them stay, she thought, beating the batter fiercely. *They'd never have got a trap set.* But it was foolish to cloud this day with fury now. No alien fishermen had come, the battle was won, and tonight she was giving a party.

The men cleaned up before supper. While the potatoes were cooking, and Owen and Stevie were upstairs in their room, she went into her room. Nils was putting on a blue necktie before the mirror over the tall chest that had been Joanna's father's. She stood behind him and met his eyes in the glass. They were even bluer than the tie.

"Do you mind having them all come up tonight?" she asked him.

"Did you think I minded?" He smiled at her in the mirror. "I think it's a good idea. Remember how they all used to get together in the old days, when we were kids? Before everybody had radios to keep 'em from going out to somebody's house?"

She nodded, but wouldn't be diverted. "I mean — the reason for a party," she insisted. "You didn't think much of it yesterday."

"That was yesterday," said Nils. "You sprung it on me — took me by surprise. You want to be careful how you startle the old man, Jo."

"There's more of Grampa Gunnar in you than I thought," she said, and was surprised to find a slight edge to her voice. Was there ever a time when she'd been able to guess what Nils was thinking? She hardly believed it. "He didn't like new ideas, either."

Nils turned and smiled directly at her, not at her reflection. "Jo," he said softly. "You sound a little sticky."

"Do you have to keep talking like your grandfather?" she demanded. "And can't you say, at least, that we've got the point, and nobody can take it away from us—and that it's all paid for?"

"I do admit that, Jo." He was serious now. "And I want it to work out right for us. But you'll have to grant that this is a bad place and a bad time of year to bank on a long spell of good weather, and a good lobstering season."

So he was back on that again. She stared at him for a moment longer, her face burning with her suppressed irritation; then she turned to leave the room. Nils' hand on her shoulder stopped her.

"You wanted to know what I thought, Jo—didn't you?"

"Yes," she said. "I think the potatoes are burning, Nils." He took his hand away, and she left him.

But her excitement came back after supper, as she brushed her hair and changed her dress. The dishes were done, the cake was iced, the kitchen was shiningly clean. From her room she could hear the muted tones of the radio in the sitting room. She knew how the lights of the house shone out across the dark meadow, and how the light in her room sent its steady ray down into Goose Cove; she pictured the house under the star-pricked autumn sky, set in its high place on the Island. She pictured the Island, lying on the sea, with its black and silent woods, its fields, its empty, listening houses. But in her own house and the others there were lights and warmth and voices; under each roof there was a warm and secure small world that knew no fear of the dark, windy spaces of sky and sea.

In the face of this thought, she had no room for petty irritation. From the other end of the house she heard opening doors, voices, laughter. She fastened her grandmother's gold-and-garnet heart at the neck of her wine-red dress, tucked a crisp tendril of black hair behind her ear, and was ready for her party to begin.

Gram Fennell, in her best black silk, was enthroned in the best easy chair in the sitting room, watching everything with her bright eagle's eyes. Somehow everyone had sorted out, so all the women were in the sitting room, and the men in the kitchen. Joanna heard the rumble of their conversations as a deep-toned background for hers and the other women's. She and Nora, Vinnie and Marion, were playing Chinese checkers. It was not an exciting sort of a party, but it was the kind the Islanders liked best, when they outgrew Postoffice and Spin the Cover. It was a pleasant, unhurried get-together. The men could talk at the shore, and the women visited back and forth, but this was different. There was no watching the clock because dinner had to be started, and nobody had to go out to haul in a few minutes, or put his bait aboard, or gas up. They'd met for the pure sake of sociability . . . and to read and enjoy the deed.

They had all studied it, and in turn Joanna had studied their faces. She was sure she saw no anxiety there, no doubt, no fear that they had done something too drastic in not asking for easy terms.

Yes, it was the right kind of a party, the women together, the men in the kitchen playing cribbage, as Jud and Stevie were, or pinochle, or just talking around the stove, as the others were doing. When she was a girl, she'd liked the other kind, when they'd sat before Uncle Nate's fireplace and sang to somebody's guitar, or played forfeits—nothing tame about their version of it. Couples were always being sent out on impossible errands, to bring something in from the barn, or a certain kind of rock from Schoolhouse Cove, or a bag of cucumbers from somebody's garden patch.

Then there'd been the dances. . . . She wondered how long it would be before the clubhouse would ring with laughter and singing again, and the floor shake under dancing feet. She remembered how the accordion used to sound. Nils' brother Sigurd had played for the dances; he was much bigger than Nils, and his hair was a yellow mane.

She started violently, and her checker rolled across the board. For surely that was an accordion! It started tentatively, and then gathered speed; the old hornpipe, "Stack of Barley," began to dance through the rooms.

Vinnie laughed aloud at her bewilderment. "That's Caleb's old squeezebox, Joanna. Didn't you know he brought it?"

"I didn't even know he had one!"

"Well, he don't play it much these days. But Jud knew about it and asked him to bring it along. You should've heard him back when Joey was a baby, and Caleb played at the dances." She cocked her head. "Listen to him!"

They all listened. Gram began to tap her foot. The tune changed, and out in the kitchen, Owen began to sing, his voice sure and strong and merry, even without bottled help.

Buffalo gal, ain't you comin' out tonight,
Comin' out tonight—comin' out tonight?
Buffalo gal, ain't you comin' out tonight,
To dance by the light of the moon?

Stevie and Jud picked it up, clear deep young voice and cracked elderly one. They sang it together to the end of the song and then Caleb began another. Joanna couldn't sit still, she must go to see how he looked. The gay music sounded so foreign to his gaunt, solemn self. He still looked solemn, playing "My Money Is All Spent and Gone," with Owen and Stevie roaring it like seamen in a bar on the waterfront, but there were twin glints in his eyes.

He finished with a flourish. Joanna saw Owen make a beeline for her. "Choose your partners for Lady of the Lake!" he shouted, and began to swing her in a wild whirl to the tune of "The Devil's Dream." A delighted, laughing Nora was clapping from the doorway. Vinnie and Marion were there, and a determined Gram was pushing her way between them.

Matthew Fennell went toward his young wife, smiling. She said excitedly above the tumult, " I don't know how to do it, but it looks like fun!" Stevie and Jud left their cribbage game and pushed the table back against the wall. Nils moved chairs out of the way. They began to pair off, Owen and Joanna, Matthew and Nora, Jud and Vinnie, Nils and Marion. Stevie led Gram to the rocker, and took up his position as caller.

The accordion seemed possessed of a life of its own. The familiar calls rang out above it. "First and every other couple cross over! Balance and swing the sides! Swing in the middle and go down the center!"

The teakettle danced on the stove and the cups jingled in the cupboard. The younger men danced without effort or lack of breath, keeping up the pace set by the music, which grew wilder and wilder. Incredible that Caleb Caldwell was making all this joyous noise, for them to skip through the figures, laughing, possessed by the exhilaration of the moment. Joanna found herself swinging with Nils, his arm was tight around her waist.

"Having fun, Nils?" she asked him, her eyes brilliant.

He laughed and let her go to her partner, Owen, who seemed to be having a good time without the couple of quarts he'd mentioned. His laughter was the heartiest in the kitchen, coming out from his great chest; he lifted the women off their feet when he swung them, and made them shriek, and he swung Nora Fennell just a little longer than anyone else. When he stopped she was so dizzy she clung to him, her eyes shut tight. And he kept his arm around her until Joanna caught his glance and held it. With an ironic lift of his eyebrow, and a wink, he pushed the girl toward her husband.

Joanna, still dancing, still laughing, thought with relief that everything was going fine, even if Mark and Helmi hadn't come. She'd been half-afraid for a moment that Owen—but she knew in her bones that it wasn't so. He wasn't going to bother with Nora Fennell.

When they finished dancing, she'd make the coffee. Oh, it really was a fine party. Everyone looked happy, even Gram. Perhaps it was the way Stevie bent over to speak to her, he was so very gallant and handsome. She was not snorting or shaking her head now. . . .

"Promenade the hall!" Stevie shouted, and the dance was over. Marion, red-faced and frankly panting, sat down hard in the nearest chair. Nora went to the water pails, drinking deeply from the shiny dipper instead of bothering with a glass from the cupboard. Vinnie, her amber eyes glowing, was miraculously not out of breath. She patted Caleb's shoulder and said, "I guess you'd kind of say he had hidden talents, wouldn't you?"

"I guess *so!*" said Joanna.

The kitchen table was covered with a brightly colored cloth, and in the center of it, on Grandma Bennett's best cake plate—the one with a beaded edge for ribbon to be run through—Joanna laid the deed. After all, it was in honor of the deed that they were gathered here together. Marion's devil's food cake and Joanna's white cake flanked it; sandwiches rose in mounds all around—lobster, egg, chicken salad. Vinnie had brought those, she had the only flock of chickens on the Island and had already canned some for winter. The coffee had reached the right perfection of dark golden-brown, and they were all hungry. There was nothing like dancing and singing and good fellowship to make people hungry, Joanna thought. But through the friendly talk, the laughter, the eating, her eyes went again and again to the deed.

We've beaten Fowler, she thought. *We're safe now.* Suddenly she was ravenously hungry. And she felt as though she would never be worried or afraid again.

24

JOANNA AWOKE IN THE MORNING to the sound of rain. She was alone in the pineapple-topped bed, and she lay comfortably under the quilts, listening to the sound of water running down the window panes. It was not light enough yet to see it. *A real, honest-to-goodness, drenching, rain,* she thought, and had to smile, remembering how everybody had called the good days weather-breeders. And this was all that had happened—a rain-storm. It had been a long time since they'd had a good rain. . . . The line storm hadn't hit them this year, and the leaves had clung for a long time to the birches and alders. Perhaps now the last of the yellow leaves would be washed away, and then it would look as if November was really coming to the Island.

She heard Owen's laughter in the kitchen, and knew she should get up; the men were all stirring and Nils had probably been up for hours. He always got up so early. But she was warm, and still drowsy, and her mind wandered lazily back to the party last night, and the day before yesterday. It had been such a perfect day, from the moment she and Stevie rowed out to the *Elaine* in the early morning until . . . when had it stopped being perfect? There were those things Nils had said, and for a little while they'd clouded her pleasure in everything, but not for long. Afterwards she knew she'd been right not to brood over what he'd said. For the storm he'd worried about was only a good heavy rain, after all, and when it cleared away, there'd be another week of fine hauling weather.

On this last thought she hopped out of bed and began to dress. Her clothes were cold against her warm skin, and she dressed hurriedly. She gave her hair a short but vigorous brushing and sped out through the chilly front hall and into the sitting room, where Nils had already kindled a fire in the round stove. She stopped to warm her hands at it, listening to the male voices in the kitchen.

"Looks like a day in the woods," Owen said. "Jesus, can I do with one, too! This hauling every day is kind of strenuous, when you haven't touched a damn' trap in six years."

"Think this'll amount to anything?" From his voice, Stevie was standing near the window.

"Just a hell of a lot of water," Owen said. "What's the glass say, Nils?"

"Cloudy," said Nils dryly. "More coffee?"

On that, Joanna came into the kitchen. She smiled at them all. "Morning, everybody." Her eyes came to rest on Nils' face. "Hello, Nils."

In mid-morning, there was an easterly breeze blowing the rain in a gusty spatter against the windows, and the gray water was choppy, ringing Green Ledge and Goose Cove Ledge with surf. But it was nothing out of the ordinary; there was hardly enough to notice. The men put on their oilskins and sou'westers and went down to the shore. Joanna watched them go down through the meadow, their oilskins a gleaming, sunny yellow against the drabness of the day.

The meadow looked dead and drenched this morning, against the somberness of the woods; sea and sky and blowing sheets of rain were gray. It was a dreary world. Joanna watched the men go between the gateposts, and then turned back gratefully to her colorful kitchen, still lamplit. Mrs. Robey probably hadn't sent Ellen to school this morning; she'd be up in her small room playing with the doll named Phoebe.

Joanna got the deed from her pocketbook and studied it again. She felt the way she'd felt when she was little and had something new and precious. Like her first wristwatch. She'd only worn it on special occasions, and between times, just the thought of owning it made her heart thump. She'd go and open the little box, and see it lying on its blue velvet. . . . It was almost better not to wear it; the joy of beholding it like this, when she hadn't seen it for several hours, was infinite.

So now she read the deed through very carefully, folded it, and put it away again. The very first minute that she could, she was going to walk over Grant's point again, just to enjoy this new feeling of possession.

The men came back to the house again, water streaming from their sou'wester brims, their faces stung red by the cold rain. "Well, we tied up the punts and dories," Nils said. "The tide's coming, and it'll be plenty high—full moon tonight."

"Everything all set now?" said Joanna. "If you're in for keeps, I'll give you a mug-up."

"I guess we can dig in for the rest of the day." Owen stretched luxuriously. "I see where I sleep this afternoon." Oilskins stowed away, boots off, they sat down to their coffee and doughnuts. There was a sense of leisure and comfort in the kitchen.

The house was warm and pleasant, bulwarked against the cold autumn rain. Owen and Stevie played rummy in the sitting room; Joanna cleaned up the kitchen and started dinner, while Nils worked in the shop. That was the difference between Nils and her brothers, she thought. Owen and Stevie took a rainy day as a holiday, but Nils could always find some work he'd saved for just such a time.

Suddenly Owen called out to her, "How far up is the tide?"

"Wait a minute, and I'll tell you." She opened the back door, sheltered from the wind by the barn, and looked down across Schoolhouse Cove. What she saw made her dread to turn and go back into the house to tell the boys, to tell Nils. And yet, they would see for themselves in a minute . . . She stood in the open doorway, the cold raw air chilling her, and looked down at the waves rolling up the beach. The tide had an hour to go, and already it was up to high water mark, and *beyond;* while she watched, a comber broke into spray against the remains of the sea wall. In an hour, where would the tide be?

She could look down at the harbor beach, too. It was more sheltered than Schoolhouse Cove, the water was not so rough as it came up the stones, but it was lapping at the camps on the brow of the beach.

She went back into the kitchen. "If you've got any loose stuff on the wharf down there," she said steadily, "you'd better move it."

They dressed again to go out, Owen cursing under his breath, Stevie looking philosophical. She tried to see if Nils looked worried. After all, there was nothing dangerous in an extreme high tide — it just meant the men had to run around making things fast. These gusts of wind would probably stop when the tide turned. She was certain they would stop. But she heard herself saying, casually, "Do you think this wind'll amount to anything?"

Nils, stripping his sou'wester under his chin, glanced at her remotely. "The glass is dropping."

"But —" she began, and then stopped. There was no sense in saying anything now. All she could do was *hope*. When the tide turned . . . why, the weather often changed when the tide turned. Did a complete-right-about-face.

"Probably in for a goddam good gale of wind," Owen grunted, and went out. At the same time he shut the door another strong gust hit the house, and the rain beat like hailstones against the seaward windows of the kitchen. Stevie grinned at her and followed Owen. Nils was the last to go, and there was nothing she could say to him. Because he had said there was likely to be a storm, and she had said there wouldn't be.

Please God, let the wind die out when the tide turns, she prayed fervently, and said aloud, "So long, Nils. Be careful."

"The marsh'll be flooded," he said. "First time since we were kids. Remember how they used to come and get us at the schoolhouse in a dory?"

She laughed. "You'll probably have to row home in one this time. As far as the gateposts anyway." She went with him to the door and watched him go down through the field. Yes, the wind *had* strengthened; she saw how he had to brace himself against the gusts that wanted to drive him forward. She knew how those gusts could turn into a steady, roaring gale; a gale that could churn up the sea, drag the pots and fling them against the ledges, but it mustn't happen now. *It mustn't.* She shut the door and went across the kitchen to the stove, warming her hands automatically.

In a little while she couldn't stand to stay in the house and listen to the wind shrieking around the corners. Besides, she couldn't tell what was happening down at the harbor. She got into her rainy weather clothes: her knee-length rubber boots, trench coat, and sou'wester. But when she went out, she knew she couldn't walk down through the marsh. For the tide had come over the sea wall, flooding the marsh, and from the harbor the tide had covered the beach and was coming up the road. When the two sheets of water met, the Island would be divided. Joanna had seen it happen before, with this same coincidence of a full moon and a strong wind. She had seen waves roll in over the sea wall and slosh around the schoolhouse steps.

She walked from the house to the edge of the bank overlooking Schoolhouse Cove, fighting the wind that swept down on her in an unbroken assault. The rain lashed at her face like needles, rattled on her sou'wester. Below her the cove was broken gray and white water, breakers rising at its mouth and rolling with a deep, increasing thunder toward the shore. The cove's points were buried in foam. The beach was white with it. She waited for a moment longer, to watch a gull flying close to the water. They always seemed to be so happy and excited about storms; she knew it was because the bottom was churned up and they found things on the surface that they liked to eat. She wondered if that lone gull could see any pot buoys out there, and then she tried not to think of how the traps could be dragged along the bottom and smashed to kindling on the rocks.

She couldn't go to the harbor by the road, for now the sea was racing across the marsh, streaked with foam; racing to meet the harbor. She went down across the meadow to the alder swamp behind the house where Gunnar Sorensen, Nils' grandfather, had lived; came out past his barn and went down to the harbor from there.

In the pouring rain and the rising tide, water flowing around their boot tops, the men worked, carrying everything that could be carried; traps that had been stacked on the newly repaired wharf by the boatshop; buoys; planks. She saw some loose planks floating. When the tide brought them close enough, someone caught them and dragged them in. They were working hard, for the unbridled sweep of the wind blowing straight across the marsh from Schoolhouse Cove was strong enough to knock them down if it caught them off balance. She saw Jud stumble and go down on his hands and knees in the icy water and Caleb pull him up again.

The lobster car had been made more secure with extra lines to the wharf, but the wharf was almost flooded now. Dories and punts that had been tied above the usual high water line had been dragged up to the marsh; now they had to be moved again. Nils and Owen brought a dory over towards the higher ground near the Arey house, and they saw Joanna standing there, in the shelter of the porch. Owen waved, and Nils nodded. Then they went back again.

The noise of the sea and of the wind seemed to be growing with every instant. Even with her sou'wester over her ears Joanna could hear the din of it. She was thankful that the boats were safe at their moorings; an easterly couldn't hurt them. Only the traps . . . She felt cold and miserable, but she couldn't go back to the house.

Quite suddenly the old pinky, that had been heeled over in the marsh ever since Joanna could remember, began to sail. Owen's first powerboat, not much bigger than a good-sized dory, danced along beside her. They sailed halfway across the marsh before they came to rest, the pinky on a small rocky hillock that rose above the fast-flowing sheet of water, the little power-boat in the middle of the road. The men let them go as they pleased. They had more needful things to do.

Turning her head, Joanna could look out the other way, past Jud Gray's old fish house, at Pete Grant's wharf. . . . Only it wasn't Pete's wharf any more, she reminded herself. If the tide kept coming it would flood that wharf too, she thought, and then she saw something else, something which floated placidly about the harbor, dangerously near the moorings. It was Pete Grant's old lobster car, which for so many years had been hauled up on his little stretch of rocky beach, beyond Jud's and the Sorensens' fish houses.

Nils was wading across the road from the old wharf to the long fish house. No sense to call to him; he couldn't hear with the rain pounding at him and the wind tearing at him. She ran forward along the road until the water was rising coldly around her ankles, and he saw her and came toward her.

"You'd better stay out of this, Joanna," he said. "Get along up to the house where it's warm." A faint smile touched his mouth. "And make some more coffee. We'll be through with this job pretty soon. Nothing to do then but wait."

She knew what he meant. Wait to see how the traps were. How

many were wiped out beyond repair. She said quickly, "The old car is afloat. Out there."

He went back along the road with her as far as the Areys' front steps, and looked where she pointed. Owen would have said, "Jesus Christ!" But Nils wiped the rain from his face and said, "Looks like we'll have to take care of that." He started back to the beach; then turned toward her for a moment. "Thanks for keeping an eye out, Jo."

She watched him wade into the water and stop Matthew Fennell, who was carrying the last load of buoys into the long fish house. Then he called to Mark, who was nearby. They came over and got one of the dories. It was queer to see them row out over the top of the old wharf. As they rounded the corner by the boatshop and disappeared, Owen came wading across from the camps.

"Where the hell are they going?" he asked.

"The old car's afloat. It's going to be bumping against Matthew's boat in a minute," she told him.

"Jesus. Always something," grunted Owen, fumbling inside his oil jacket for a cigarette. "I suppose this little mess'll make matchwood out of my new pots. . . . Well, we got everything that's movable lugged out of harm's way for the time being. . . ."

The dory came in sight again. Rowing close to the shore, Nils and Mark handling the two pairs of oars, they were in the lee and they made good time. Then they turned and sent the dory flying over the steel-gray water toward Matthew's boat. The car had almost reached it. Joanna and Owen watched while Matthew made a line fast to the car and the dory headed for the little strip of beach beyond the fish houses. When it disappeared again Owen blew out a long puff of smoke. "Hell, they managed that all right. Guess I'll go home and dry out."

"I'll go with you,' Joanna said.

"Thought you came down to walk home with your old man," Owen remarked, grinning broadly at her.

"I'm cold," Joanna said briefly. "Come on."

The wind didn't die out when the tide turned. To Joanna it was the longest day she had ever known. The men sat up until the tide rose again, and went down to the shore in the wet and howling blackness; Joanna waited in the kitchen, shivering in spite of the brisk fire in the stove. She was so tired that she ached, yet she knew she couldn't sleep.

But when they trooped up again, and hung their wet oilskins in the woodshed, and kicked off their boots, they told her the wind was beginning to die out.

She went to bed when Nils did. He fell asleep almost at once, but she lay tense in the darkness, unable to relax, listening to the gusts hit the house. Yes, they were farther apart now, there was more of a lull between them. But how long would there be a heavy sea, to keep the men from going out to their pots? Oh, it wasn't fair, for this to happen to her. Supposing, tomorrow, someone said, "What'll I do for trap stuff? I've no money in my pocket."

But we had to have the point, she argued fiercely, lying there in the darkness. *Before Fowler could get his hands on it* . . . And then the words would come back to her, irrevocably. *Down payment* . . . *Pay in the good seasons* . . . *Lease.*

At last she fell asleep.

The next day the sun shone, there was no wind, and the sea was blue; but it was a wild sea that roared and tumbled along the Island's rocky shores without cessation. As far as the eye could see the water glittered under the sun like boiling metal, and there was no escaping from its monotonous muted thunder. Schoolhouse Cove was cupped out, where the long and powerful undertow had sucked gravel from the beach. The harbor shore had a deep gully splitting it in two from the water's edge to the marsh, and water ran down through the gully all day long like a mountain brook, brown rain water to mingle with the clear green salt water.

But in the night the seas flattened out, and by the next morning the men could get out to their traps. Joanna saw them go, one at a time, and dreaded what they would find. Nils went out as if he were on his way to an ordinary day's hauling. Another man might have been sarcastic; in a way she wished Nils would be a little less amiable. If he would only say, "I told you so," it would give her an excuse to give way to her edginess.

She did an immense washing that morning. Vinnie Caldwell came up for a few minutes, to discuss, round-eyed, the unusually high tides, and to bring a young rooster from her flock. Nora Fennell, with

Bosun at her heels, ran up through the woods to stay a few breathless moments and then race back again before Gram missed her. For the rest of the time Joanna was alone.

With her sheets swaying mildly in the sunshine, the men's work shirts and woolen socks all hung out, she had dinner to get. If Stevie had lost a great many traps he would still be good natured, and Nils wouldn't say much about his losses. But Owen would be in one of his black moods. . . . "Oh, for heaven's sake!" she said aloud, "anybody would think you blew up this storm by yourself!"

It made her laugh, but she couldn't help feeling guilty. It was Nils' fault. He had put the idea into her head. Maybe sometime she'd do something that would be exactly right, and he wouldn't be able to find even the smallest fault with it.

The young rooster was tender and small, and she stewed it, hoping the boys would like it. She didn't have much appetite, herself. Onions, squash, cranberry sauce she'd made last fall from Island berries — it would be quite a dinner for them, if they weren't too discouraged to eat it.

Stevie came home first. She didn't have to beat around the bush with Stevie. She asked him at once how his traps were.

"Oh, so-so," Stevie said, putting his thick gloves to dry on the stove shelf. "I brought in a load. Couldn't find some of 'em." He washed at the sink, and combed his hair, smelled appreciatively of the chicken. "Serves me right for setting so many to the east'ard."

He looked rueful, but good-tempered. And hungry. Joanna gave him a piece of Swedish coffee bread to stay his stomach, and a cup of steaming coffee, and he went into the sitting room to turn on the radio for the news.

She looked up from setting the table to see Owen and Nils coming along the road through the marsh. The tide had not come so far this noon, and though the water covered the beach to the edge of the marsh ground, the road was clear. The men came by the old pinky, resting rakishly on its hillock, and passed the little powerboat; she saw them stop to look at it. Probably Owen was talking about the old days, when he'd lobstered from that small craft, and made unbelievable money for a boy in his teens. She watched his big, arrogant figure as he stood in the road, hands shoved deep in his pockets, head back. Nils stood by him, a smaller man, head bent thoughtfully.

Then they started along again, toward the house. When they came in, she knew by the way that Owen slammed the door and began to pull off his outdoor clothes, without speaking, that there was no need for her to ask him about his traps. His dark face and drawn black brows, his sullen lower lip, were answer enough.

Nils said, "Hi, Joanna. Dinner smells good." But he looked absent-minded. As he was tidying up at the sink, Stevie came out from the sitting room, carrying his empty coffee cup.

"How'd you guys make out?" he asked cheerfully.

"Oh, go to hell!" Owen growled. Stevie grinned. "How about it, Nils? You got anything left?"

"Not much," said Nils. "Nobody's got much. It looks as if we'll be spending the next few weeks building new pots and patching old ones." He stood by the window looking out to sea; in the clear brilliant light from the sky and water his eyes looked tired. They seemed deeper-set than usual. And the little lines at either end of his mouth were deeper too.

"I went up alongside Caleb down by Pudd'n Island," he went on. "Jud was with him. Caleb's string was shacked, and he hasn't got any more trap stuff than the rest of us. Needs laths and hoops, and marlin for trapheads. Matthew Fennell didn't lose many, and he'd brought some extra stuff with him. As for the rest of us—"

Owen, one foot on the stove hearth, his big shoulders hunched, said roughly, "The rest of you gave me your spare trap stuff. That's why you're short."

"Sold it to you," Nils corrected him. "You've paid for it. For God's sake, Owen, stop looking like a black crow. You're in the same boat with the rest of us, and no more."

His words were sharp, for Nils; but Owen grinned, and went over to the sink to take his turn at washing up. "Sounds like Gunnar was around," he said. "The old man's on the prod."

Joanna glanced covertly at Nils. She saw him rub his hand across his forehead; and she remembered with a stabbing clarity when she had seen him do that before. Back in the old days, when he'd lived with his tyrannical grandfather—old Gunnar—he had done it sometimes. It meant that his temper and nerves were at a pitch that in a Bennett would have meant an explosion. But Nils always held on, long past the stage where anyone else would have given in. *Anyone human,* Joanna thought now, and, startled by her spitefulness, realized that her own nervous system was humming.

Somebody would have to say something, and it might as well be herself. She moistened her dry lips carefully, and then heard her voice come out, clear and strong.

"Why doesn't somebody say," she inquired, "what you're probably all thinking? That you haven't any money laid by to get all the new trap stuff you need, because I took it away from you."

Nils said nothing. Owen's face was buried in a towel. But Stevie said quickly, "My God, sis, nobody's blaming you because there was a gale of wind on the full moon! And we got the Point, that's one sure thing."

She looked at Owen's back and then at Nils as she answered. "Maybe you'd rather have the trap stuff than the Point. How do I know?"

Owen emerged from the towel. "Hell, we can always get credit, can't we? What's a lobster-buyer for? Richards'll supply us."

She'd forgotten all about Richards. He'd get them all the things they needed—laths, bows, funny-eyes, marlin. And they could pay him right back again, within a few weeks. It was miraculous, the lightening she felt. She cried out before she thought, "Oh, Nils, I'd forgotten about that!"

He rubbed his forehead and looked around the room at her and the boys as if his eyes ached. "I thought of it," he said evenly. "I spoke to Jud. He asked me to swing into Brigport and call up Richards."

"When's he sending the stuff out?" Owen asked. He was watching himself in the mirror carefully, as he tried to comb down his damp, springy black hair.

"He isn't," said Nils. "No credit."

Stevie's jaw dropped. Owen swung around from the mirror, his black eyes ablaze. "What's he mean—no credit? The son of a bitch!"

"Take it easy," said Nils. "It's not his fault. He's got a hell of a job to keep going, with the big companies trying to squeeze the little fellows out of existence. He's been all over the place trying to get trap stuff for his fishermen, and he hasn't got any credit himself. He needs cash and plenty of it. The big concerns get first pick." He added, smiling a little, "Ralph Fowler's fishermen don't have to worry, I guess."

"I'm still glad I don't sell to that bastard," Owen said. He sat down and stared morosely at the floor.

"You and me, too," said Stevie. "I'd still rather come in and meet Jud instead of that down-east chowderhead, even if Jud's company is so small you can't hardly see it. . . . Well, Cap'n Sorensen, what do we do next?"

"I don't know," said Nils. "Unless we eat dinner." For the first time he looked directly at Joanna, and smiled. "Smells good. When do we get a look at it?"

She hurried to get the food on, the chicken in its golden gravy, the wine-red cranberry sauce, pale onions and deep orange squash, potatoes mashed and beaten. Yes, it was a feast; but the smell of it nauseated her. She would have given almost anything to get out of the house and stay out, to walk until she was exhausted, and then come home and go to bed, and *sleep*. It was the only way she could think of to escape the way she felt. For now she must recognize the truth; there was no evading it, no justifying herself.

Pete *would* have taken a down payment; and with money to pay for what they needed, the fishermen could have bought their trap stuff almost anywhere. There was no shortage of it. There was only a shortage of credit. . . .

She made herself serve the men, who were hungry in spite of their discouragement. After all, they'd been on the water all morning.

Stevie and Owen began to eat at once, without talking. Joanna looked at her plate. She would have to eat everything on it and pretend she enjoyed it. She'd be damned if she'd act guilty. . . . She didn't know when she became aware that Nils was not eating. She looked across at him and saw that his arms were folded on the edge of the table and that he was gazing past her, toward the window behind her, as if she didn't exist. There was such a remoteness in his eyes that she couldn't help asking,

"What's the matter, Nils? What are you seeing?"

He answered without looking at her, "When I was talking to Jud and Caleb this morning, between Pudd'n Island and Eastern End Cove, I could look up between the Islands and see the *Janet F.* hauling along between the sou'western end of Brigport and the Spar buoy."

"You mean they found enough left to haul?" grunted Owen.

Nils went on as if he hadn't heard. "Well, Jud told me he didn't like to do business by telephone—made him nervous, he said—so I went to Brigport and called up Richards. When I came out of the harbor, I went out around Tenpound. I saw the *Janet F.* down by the Hogshead." He hesitated for a moment, his eyes still distant, as if he were seeing the scene. Joanna was conscious of a tightening through her body, as she wondered what was coming next.

"Randy was in the store this morning; Winslow was out alone. I could see the boat was drifting, so I watched her for a while, to see if Winslow's head poked up—I thought he was down on his knees fooling with the engine." He rubbed his forehead again. His voice was very quiet in the room.

"I didn't see anybody, and she was so damn' close to the Hogshead by then that I swung around and went down there, to see if he needed help. She was empty."

Stevie put down his fork. "Empty?" he repeated.

"Jesus," said Owen. "You mean he'd gone overboard?"

"Somewhere between the Islands, or between the southern end of Brigport and the Hogshead."

"Maybe it had just happened, before you saw the boat," Joanna said slowly.

"Could be—they had a few traps down that way, too." Nils pushed back from the table. "I'm not very hungry, I guess. I thought I was . . . I towed the boat in. Everybody was around. Randolph came down to the wharf. He looked sick."

"Almost makes me sorry for the poor bastard," Owen muttered.

"I'm sorrier for Mrs. Fowler," Joanna said. "Poor thing. She isn't much more than a wraith now, living with the Fowlers all these years. This might kill her."

"Losing Winslow?" said Stevie unexpectedly. "I don't think so. Randy, maybe. He's a good-natured cuss. But not Winslow." He helped himself to more chicken, more of everything. "Excuse me for being so cold-hearted, folks. But I'm hungry."

"Gruesome Gil," said Owen, grinning. "Sure, stow it away, kid. Come on back and eat, Nils. You can't do anything about it, and you need your food. Gives you strength, man."

Yes, you need your strength, Joanna thought. *We all do.* She felt as cold as if a winter wind had blown through the warm, sunlit kitchen.

She sat very still in her chair, holding herself tightly together; she could not have relaxed, she thought, to save her life. A nightmare breath was blowing feathers of dread along her backbone. *This is a foreboding,* a voice said clearly in her brain.

25

IN THE AFTERNOON STEVIE AND OWEN went out. Stevie went down to the Eastern End to see how Mark had fared in his day's hauling. Owen headed for the shore, to help Jud fix the lobster car, which had been somewhat battered by the constant pounding against the wharf during the height of the gale.

Joanna cleaned up the dishes and brought in her washing. She was surprised when Nils followed her out to the clotheslines, in the sheltered place behind the house and overlooking Goose Cove. It was as warm as early fall there this afternoon; the sun had shone there almost all day, and the clothes, drying so close to the sea, smelled delicious. Nils took down the sheets and folded them, and put them in the basket while Joanna took down the shirts and socks and underwear.

"Thank you, Nils," she said gravely, as the last towel was folded and laid on top of the pile.

"You're welcome. I'll carry the basket in for you."

"All right," she said. She couldn't help a certain stiffness in her tone. She wished he had gone out with her brothers. His presence around the house irked her this afternoon—not because she disliked him, she reminded herself hastily. But he'd been so right about the storm. Sometimes she wished he'd be wrong, for once.

He didn't pick up the basket right away. Instead he stood looking down the slope, where the wild roses bloomed so pinkly in June, at the soft blue and gray and lavender tints of Goose Cove beach; and at the Cove beyond, the hardly murmuring water on the stretch of wet pebbles, the purple and green shallows around the rockweed-maned boulders. Joanna followed Nils' eyes. When he lifted his head and gazed at the woods across the cove, the tall spar growth and the young emerald-green trees so vivid among their elders, she stood beside him and gazed too, down to where Schooner Head stood out in bold relief against the dreaminess of sea and sky.

"Let's talk a minute before we go in," he said. Joanna sat down willingly enough on a neat stack of four-foot spruce logs. It was always easier to talk outside . . . whatever it was Nils wanted to talk about. He sat down beside her and took out his pipe.

"I've decided what to do about the gear," he said. "I'm going ashore on the mailboat and go along the coast till I find somebody who'll give us trap-stuff on credit."

"How do you know where to go?" she asked.

"There must be plenty of places that we don't know about." He filled his pipe without spilling a grain of tobacco. She wished vaguely that he would spill something, make a mistake in his calculations, once in a while. . . . "If we have to make our own bows and funny-eyes, we can," he went on. "But there must be someone with a sawmill somewhere that would trust Bennett's Islanders for laths and sills." She saw his mouth twitch. "The name ought to be good for something."

"Well, I hope you can find what you want," she said, and stood up. His contemplative blue glance followed her; it seemed to measure her, and suddenly she was stung by it. "I suppose you're thinking," she remarked with a forced nonchalance, "that if it wasn't for me, you wouldn't have to make the trip."

His eyes narrowed, but only for a second. "Joanna," he said gently, "I'd almost think you had a guilty conscience, the way you put words into my mouth."

"*Guilty conscience.!*" She whirled around to face him squarely, her chin set hard. "Is that what you think? Well, I've no guilty conscience, Nils, but what I ought to have is an inferiority complex! And I *would* have, if I was fool enough! Everything I do is wrong, everything I say is pure foolishness — I'm of no consequence whatever!"

She stopped, aghast at her recklessness; but still, there was relief in it. Nils stood up, and shook his head at her.

"No, Joanna. You're important enough. You're Joanna Bennett, and nobody must forget it. *I'm* the person of no consequence around here."

"What do you mean by that?"

"I'm just Joanna's husband," said Nils. "She runs things. I do what she can't do with her own two hands. The hired man that gets treated like one of the family. I mean, *almost*."

She had never known Nils' words could ever cut like this, coming so quietly from his mouth. She stared at him with widening eyes, throat drying with the heat of her amazed indignation.

"How dare you talk like that, Nils? When you've stopped me from doing all the things I've wanted to do, and criticized anything I *did* happen to do—"

"I could keep you off the lobster car, because you needed my money," said Nils. "But that's all. Think back, Jo. Think back and see if you needed me for anything else. You could have got one of the boys to tarpaper the long fish house, and you could have hired a carpenter to rebuild the wharf. But I did it all right, and it kept me busy, didn't it, Joanna?"

"Nils, you—" She stopped helplessly. She felt torn apart with anger.

"You think nobody cares about the Island but you, nobody knows what the Island needs but you." He sounded almost kind, now. "And you were thinking about just one thing when you married me, Joanna. How you could use me for the good of the Island."

"How long have you been thinking these things, Nils?" she asked him, her voice a dry whisper.

"For a long time. I didn't like thinking about them, but I got used to them. Anybody gets used to things . . . like knowing you didn't really need me, or even want me. I'm not blaming you, Joanna, because you didn't know those things. I didn't either, for a long while." He looked away from her, out at the shimmering cove and the silent wall of woods, and that remoteness came to his face again. The brilliant afternoon sunshine carved deep-angled planes in his face.

"Nils, you're lying," she told him fiercely. "You're my oldest friend—you've always been." She fought desperately for her self-control; she would not look into the depths, she would not give in. What if she were to be humble now, and say, *I know. I've been wrong.* That was what he wanted. But she couldn't do it. She was Joanna Bennett, and how could she submit to anyone?

To admit, ever, that she was wrong was to be lost. So she stared at him with fire in her cheeks and in her eyes, knowing this for a duel in which she must not be conquered, and repeated, "You've always been my oldest friend!"

She saw his contempt at her stubbornness. But it was better for him to think she was stupid than to think he had smashed her armor.

"I was your friend till I came too close," he said. "Till I got a foolish idea in my head that I was your husband. But I never was your husband, Joanna."

So he had chalked *that* up against her too. Well, she could be as poised as he was. "Whatever else you want to say about me, Nils," she told him evenly, "you can't say I ever refused you."

For the first time color deepened on his cheekbones and his eyes searched her face and her strong, slim throat. "You never refused me. But you never wanted me, either. You did your duty, that's all. It was just another chore to you."

"Well, at least you can give me credit for not neglecting my work," she said, and knew that had touched him. She turned around and went toward the house.

She walked through the empty rooms to their bedroom and stood listening. After a little space of silence she heard the back door open, and the sound of the clothesbasket being put down. She waited, her body aching with its tautness, the sound of her blood beating loudly in her ears. If he came to apologize, what could she do? She had a crazy, panicky impulse to climb out the window and run for the woods, but she stifled it. He would come and apologize for the hateful things he had said, he was so much in love with her he couldn't help but make that gesture. She was in his bones, where she'd been since she was fifteen. And she would meet him with her back straight and proud, her head lifted.

She heard the back door close again. A thick and absolute silence settled over the house. She remembered, then, a little and

treacherous thought she'd had once; that she was always listening to
a door shutting, and then—nothing.

26

THERE WAS SUPPER TO GET, and then the evening to come after. To
Joanna the time stretched out to an eternity. It was not too hard to
keep up appearances, because Nils had never been demonstrative
when anyone else was around. It seemed no strain for him to be as
polite and friendly as ever. Joanna envied his ease, and resented it.
Yet the boys didn't notice any change in her, though she was on the
alert for a quizzical glance from Owen or a puzzled one from Stevie.
I must be doing as well as Nils, she thought, and wondered how she
could, when the inner Joanna was holding herself so tightly and coldly
aloof from everyone. Especially from Nils.

Even the night passed by, somehow. Joanna had thought she
couldn't sleep; yet she found herself waking at daybreak, just as Nils
went quietly from the room.

This was the day he was to go ashore. He had told the boys
last night of his decision, and they'd offered to go over his string while
he was gone, bring in the shattered pots, and re-bait and set the good
ones back in line.

Joanna went through the motions of starting him off. A substantial breakfast; a small bag packed with toothbrush, shaving things,
clean shirts and socks in case he had to stay more than a few days.
He intended to bring back his new engine, too. *He'll be all right when
he comes back,* Joanna told herself. *He'll be sorry he said those things.* Perhaps when he had a chance to think, away from her, he'd understand
her better. Funny to think that Nils didn't really know her, after all
these years. But she didn't know him very well, either; it had been

a stranger who confronted her out there behind the house yesterday.

Owen was going to take him to Brigport to board the mailboat. Joanna walked down to the shore with them. It was November weather today, clear and cold, with a bite in the wind that blew down from the northwest, turning the sea to a dark brilliant blue, driving big billowy clouds across the sky. Joanna listened to the idle conversation of the two men. Walking down to the shore was another way of keeping up appearances; she wondered if Nils would kiss her.

He didn't. He helped Owen push down the punt, and stepped aboard. Owen pushed off with the oars and there was a widening strip of water between the beach and the punt. "Good-bye," Nils said to her. "Take care of yourself."

"When will you be back?" she called after him, but by that time the punt was going out by the corner of the wharf, and Jud, puttering around on his lobster car, hailed it; if Nils answered Joanna, she didn't hear.

The gulls were screaming overhead this morning, swinging in circles with the wind, and the sea was washing noisily at the rocky shore of the harbor. She stood on the beach a few minutes longer, watching Nils and Owen board the *White Lady* and cast off the mooring. Then she turned and went back to the house, walking up the road where the tide had been a few days before, passing the boats lying crazily up there in the marsh; she walked quickly, as if the wind at her back were pushing her along.

The next day was Saturday. Ellen was home again — Caleb brought her and Joey in the early morning. It was a dull, quiet day; voices carried far under the low ceiling of cloud, and on the horizon Matinicus Rock stood up very large and clear, and to the west of Brigport the mainland showed a long dark gray line on the horizon. It hardly ever showed like that. The land was looming. Brigport looked near enough to call across to; and Tenpound, with the sheep on it, was mountainous between the islands.

Ellen spent her day out-of-doors. She went down to the Eastern End in the morning and called on Helmi. In the afternoon she visited Nora Fennell. Stevie and Owen were busy all day, and Joanna was alone. When her work was done, she read; or listened to the silence all around her. It was a restful silence, as full of peace as the silvery quiet of the water in the harbor and the coves. Even the gulls were still. It was not a day to torment your senses, to keep calling them to see and smell and hear, like those brilliant days full of color and flashing sunshine and noise.

I need peace, Joanna thought, lying back in her chair by the sitting room stove. She closed her eyes, and immediately saw Nils, as he'd looked that afternoon, rubbing his hand across his forehead, watching her as he spoke. She tried to drive Nils away by thinking of Goose Cove as it looked now. Silvery water, quiet by the rocks, quiet in the shadow of woods untouched by the faintest breath of wind. . . . She tried to imagine herself a gull, drifting across the cove, dreaming on the surface of the water that mirrored his white breast. . . .

Now she *was* drifting.

The step in the kitchen brought her wide awake, sitting up, her heartbeat quickening.

"Is that you, Ellen?" she called. There was no answer.

She got up and went to the kitchen door. Randy Fowler stood by the stove in a plaid mackinaw, heavy trousers, and rubber boots, his cap and woolen gloves in his hand. He grinned at her.

"Hi, Joanna," he said softly.

"What are you doing here?" she asked, and then checked her harsh tone, remembering Winslow.

"Hope you don't mind my droppin' in," he said. "Had to. It's hell over home, Jo. Everybody takin' on about Win, and everything."

"I'm sorry about Winslow. How is your mother?"

"Oh, she's doin' better than anybody expected." He looked around the room. "I know you prob'ly think I got a hell of a nerve, comin' in, but I'm goin' right out again."

He was very subdued, for Randy. Maybe he had a girl now; perhaps he'd come to apologize for being a nuisance. In all fairness, she shouldn't turn him out too quickly.

"Sit down for a minute, and get warmed up before you go," she said.

"Gosh, Jo. Thanks," he said gratefully. He settled down in the rocker beside the stove. "Well, how's things? Storm hurt you fellers much? Over home we lost plenty of pots."

"Well, we lost some here," she admitted.

"Yep. I was in the store when Nils called up about gettin' some trap-stuff. You can hear everythin' right through that booth," he added candidly. "Saw him goin' off on the mailboat yesterday. Does he figger on gettin' enough for everybody?"

"He'll do all right." If she sat down, it would seem too cordial. She leaned against the dresser and studied him as he opened a fresh package of cigarettes. He was a nice-looking boy, well-built in spite of his slenderness. She wondered what he would have been like if his father were a different sort of man; and what Randy would be twenty years from now.

He turned his head and looked up at her suddenly. "Jo, Nils is gonna have himself a damn' hard time tryin' to get trap-stuff. The big companies have it all sewed up. I know. Look at my Uncle Ralph—he buys for the Leavitt company. He's got enough laths and sills and marlin—everything—come out on the mailboat yesterday to fit a hundred fishermen each with a brand new string."

Joanna shrugged. "That's nice. It must make your uncle feel good."

"Well, I wasn't sayin' it to show off, Jo." The match flame reflected in his eyes as he looked at her. Then he blew it out and tossed it onto the stove, and got up. She folded her arms and watched him come toward her; she saw the telltale flush in his thin cheeks, and knew with a cold dismay that he hadn't got himself a girl. . . .

"Are you warm enough to go out again now, Randy?" she asked.

He stopped moving. "Not yet, Jo. I just wanted to tell you somethin', that's all."

"Make it quick, Randy. I've got work to do."

He came nearer, so near she could smell the woolly scent of his mackinaw and see the yellow specks that gave his eyes their odd sunlit effect. He was looking at her queerly; his glance kept going again and again to her mouth.

"*I* can get Uncle Ralph to give the Bennett's Island fishermen credit for everything they need," he said. His eyes narrowed into mirthful, sparkling lines. "I know somethin' about the old rooster that Aunt Josie don't know. And he likes to keep on the good side of me."

"Nils is taking care of the trap-stuff," she said patiently. If he meant what she thought he meant, it was best to be stupid, though in the back of her mind she was thinking, *His brother drowned two days ago, and he's over here making propositions to me!* It was so fantastic she felt unreal.

"Sure, but maybe he can't manage like he thinks he can," Randy reminded her softly. "And you don't know how long before he'll be back. I can fix it all up for you, when I go back home. Providin'—"

Joanna turned her head and saw Owen coming up through the meadow. In this day when everything loomed, Owen loomed too; he was like a giant, approaching the house with long, easy strides. She turned back to Randy who said, "Providin' you treat me decent, Jo."

"Do you want to leave the house under your own power, Randy, or have Owen throw you out?" she asked him pleasantly.

He stared at her so hard, so unbelievingly, that the pupils in his eyes dilated against the yellow-specked brown, his nostrils and the space around his mouth whitened sharply. Whatever pleasant dream of power he'd been living in, he'd come out of it with a rude swiftness. For a moment he was speechless. Then he grated the words out at her thickly. "Goddam you, Joanna—"

Before her folded arms and steady, even indifferent, glance, he turned and went across the kitchen, catching his boot toe on a chair leg, finally reaching the door. The kitchen door crashed behind him and then the back door. Without moving she reviewed the incident. At another time she would have been angrier, she supposed; but to-day she was too tired to be angry. She laughed with sheer astonishment at the idiotic strategy the boy had cooked up.

She was in that mood of amusement and amazement when she felt like telling someone about Randy. She heard Owen's voice sing out a greeting.

"Hey, Randy! What's your hurry?"

Randy's answer was indistinct. Looking out, she saw him going down the slope. She went over to the stove to push the teakettle forward for coffee, and wondered what Owen would say if she told him about Randy's proposition. Perhaps his laughter would warm her; she hadn't laughed hard—achingly, tearfully, *hard*—in months.

But when Owen came in, she decided not to tell him. He looked out of sorts; that came from an afternoon of patching pots. He kicked his boots into their place in the entry and came to glare morosely into the woodbox.

"Almost empty," he muttered, and went to the woodshed. She heard him banging around out there, heard a crash, and his voice, "Oh, bitch-bastard!" When Owen was mad he was always kicking things over, she thought drearily. *Oh, we're a fine family. A Fowler wanting to make love to me, and my brother cursing his head off at a stick of wood when he feels like cursing me.*

She made coffee and brought out some of the filled cookies that Owen liked. He came in with a load of wood, let it fall into the wood-box with a series of crashes, and washed at the sink, unmindful of the soapy water that dripped to the floor. He said nothing at all until he had put sugar and cream in his coffee and demolished a cookie in two bites. Then he looked across the table at his sister.

"Why didn't you go with Nils yesterday?" he said.

She looked up, startled, from the cup of coffee which she didn't really want. "Why . . . I couldn't. The weekend, Ellen coming home—"

"God in Heaven, if Stevie and I couldn't look after that kid be-tween us," he said violently, "we're a couple of numbheads. You could have gone. Nils doesn't know how long it'll take him to get that stuff— you helped push us into this fix, the least you could've done was to go along with him and keep him company in the evenings."

She got up from the table. "Owen, has anybody asked for your opinion?"

"I don't notice that you wait to be asked for yours—you give it free and often enough." He added, brutally, "If it was Alec goin' away, you could've fixed it to go with him—couldn't you?"

"If I didn't know better, I'd think you'd been drinking," she said coldly, and walked out of the kitchen, through the sitting room to her own room, and shut the door behind her. Owen had noticed, after all. She felt suddenly as if she had no shelter anywhere; for even when she locked the door, her thoughts flocked after her, and some of them she didn't want to own.

27

THE WEEKEND WAS FULL OF WIND and fog and a raw cold that penetrated into the houses through the very walls. Everybody stayed close by the fire and the radio. Joanna cooked for the boys and for Ellen, fixed Ellen's clothes for the next week at school, and in her spare time read avidly; she was going through her grandmother's Dickens series, and the familiar stories helped to keep her from being too restless. She hated this restlessness, but it had come, and she would have to find some way to drive it off again. Perhaps, she thought, she should start making a quilt, or do some sewing for herself and Ellen, or—then the few minutes with Nils out behind the house would come back to her, and Owen sitting at the kitchen table, scowling at her, trying to shame her in a half-dozen brutal words.

The next boatday was Tuesday, and a crisp, light breeze blew from the west. Joanna awoke believing that Nils would be on the *Aurora* today, with the trap-stuff and his new engine. Perhaps they could be friends again.

Mark had gone to get the mail. Coming back, he put in at the harbor and brought her mail up to the house. Nils hadn't come, he said. But there had been plenty of trap-stuff sent out on the *Aurora B.* and he'd brought it over and stowed it in the new boatshop, until they could divide it up, according to whose traps had got it the worst. . . . He stayed to talk a few minutes longer, and then went back down to the harbor and his boat again. He was going home to dinner, he said, and then get out to haul the traps he had left. Lobsters were a damned good price. It had hopped ten cents after the storm and was still going up.

She knew he wanted to get out of the house before Owen came

in. That nagged at her like an old lameness. But not for long. There was a letter from Nils for her. It was no more than a note, short and to the point without being too curt. He didn't know when he'd be back. He was going to help Uncle Eric on his new boat. If she wanted to get in touch with him, she could reach him at his uncle's house, in Camden.

She tucked the note behind the clock with the rest of the mail and went about her work. Sometimes she thought there would never be an end to peeling potatoes for men's dinners. . . . While she peeled, she thought of Nils' note. Probably his engine wasn't ready yet, and she didn't doubt but what Eric would welcome Nils' help. Eric's son-in-law lived near-by, but he was shiftless and untidy. At least he'd always been that way when he lived on the Island. Helping Eric would fill in the time for Nils until his engine was ready and he could come back to his own work.

It had been such a quiet note, and it had sounded so much the way Nils always sounded, that for a few minutes its actual meaning didn't get through to her. And then, all at once, she thought: *He's still angry with me. That's really why he's staying away from the Island and his own work.*

On those last few days he must have found it hard to be civil to her. And he wasn't a Bennett; he couldn't take it out in noise and swearing, and a fight to raise the roof. No, he would stay away until he could bear the sight of her again; and it made her cold to think of the extent his feeling must have reached.

She put the potatoes on to cook. There was nothing to do but wait for him to come home again. Perhaps they needed a change from each other. She'd write him a letter next boatday, telling him the trap-stuff had arrived safely — if next boatday didn't see him arrive on the *Aurora*. He couldn't stay away from the Island long, she thought confidently. And meanwhile he could get over his sulk in Uncle Eric's barn, working on the boat. . . . She was Bennett enough to believe that anyone who didn't take out his general displeasure and discontent in noise was sulking. She was glad Nils didn't do it very often.

When it was time for the boys to come home for dinner, she remembered the note tucked behind the clock, and burned it. Stevie came home first, and looked around expectantly.

"Where's Nils? He come today?"

She shook her head. "No. His engine isn't ready yet. But he sent out plenty of trap-stuff. . . . Did you get a good haul?"

"Averaged two to a trap. That's not bad, at fifty cents." He flipped several bills across the table at her. "There's my board money, and some extra. How about sending off to Monkey Ward for another one of those plaid shirts for me?"

"Sure thing, Stevie," she said absently. She took the money into the sitting room and put it in the desk. While she was there Owen came in. He was whistling loudly, which meant he was in a good mood.

"Hi, son," he saluted Stevie. "Nils home yet?"

"Nope. Engine not ready. How'd you do today?"

"Finest kind," said Owen expansively. "Engine, huh? Hell, he's more likely having himself a fling!"

"Who, *Nils?*" said Stevie, and laughed.

The clatter of the washbasin and the splashing of water meant that Owen was at the sink. He spoke again, through the towel. "You can't tell about those Swedes, boy. Those fellows like Nils. I've met plenty of 'em, and once they kick over the traces they stay kicked."

"Who—the Swedes?" said Stevie. Joanna, standing in the next room, knew by his tone that he was laughing at Owen. Stevie wouldn't think anything of Nils' staying, no matter what Owen said; but she was wishing, fervently, that Owen would mind his own business. She almost wished that he hadn't come home to the Island at all.

Then she crushed the thought, as she'd crush a spider, and went out into the kitchen to put dinner on the table.

In the afternoon she went out. There was the whole of the western end woods to rove in, but not today. Her mind was restless as well as her body. . . . She walked down to the Whitcomb place hoping Nora would be at home.

Bosun met Joanna at the gate that opened into the woods, his small round body frantic with joy; he raced in wide circles around her over the dead brown grass as she walked toward the house. He was at the top of the steps before her, panting, his brown eyes sparkling under the black bang, tongue hanging.

"You're a love," Joanna said, dropping to her knees to hug the firm little body hard against her. That was what she wanted—a dog. She ought to have a dog.

Nora heard her voice and came to the door. She looked harassed and her cheeks were red. But she smiled when she saw Joanna, and her wide mouth was meant for smiling.

"Gosh, I'm glad to see you!" she said fervently. "Come on in—no, you stay out, Bosun, or you'll be in trouble again." She scratched the floppy black ears hastily, and then led the way into the house.

She was in the midst of ironing, the kitchen was hot with the brisk fire and the steamy smell of damp, just-ironed, clothes. "Sit down," she invited. "Anywhere. I'm darned glad you came, but do you mind if I keep on ironing?"

"No, go ahead. Maybe it won't seem so much of a job if you've got someone to talk to."

Nora looked grateful. She had an apron tied on over her dark blue slacks and white blouse, and had caught her chestnut-glossy hair back at the nape of her neck with a ribbon. She sighed heavily. "I've been at this forever, it seems like," she said, picking up a flatiron and testing it with a wet finger. "I'm not very good at ironing. You see, all the time Matthew was lobstering on shares for Clyde Sparrow, he lived down on Sparrow Island, and he wouldn't let me stay with him—it wasn't fit for a woman, for an old one like Gram, anyway. So—"

The iron was too hot, she looked ruefully at a brown mark on the pillowcase. "Oh, damn! Excuse me, please. . . So we had a flat in Limerock, and Gram puttered around and kept house, and I worked in the supermarket."

Joanna said softly, "Where is Gram—I mean Mrs. Fennell?"

"She's just this minute gone up to lie down, after she saw that I got Matthew's shirts right," said Nora, without malice. "Now I s'pose Bosun will start barking at a gull or something. But if I bring him in he gets acting up and racing around." She wiped a wisp of hair away from her damp forehead. "Gram wants me to have kids right off, but I bet they'd make her just as nervous as Bosun does . . . poor little feller."

"Why don't you sit down for a minute," Joanna suggested, "and let me iron for a while?"

Nora looked shocked. "Oh, I *couldn't*!" Then, with a sudden shininess in her eyes, and a rapid blinking of her lashes, she muttered, "You'd just get started and Gram would come down."

Joanna wanted to laugh, and at the same time, to comfort the girl as she'd comfort Ellen. "I'll iron the pillow cases, and you keep an eye out, and the minute you hear her we'll change places."

Nora giggled. She folded into the rocking chair like a schoolgirl, all legs, rolled her eyes skyward, and sighed blissfully. "Oh, glorious! You're wonderful, Joanna. Did anybody ever tell you?"

Oh, yes, a lot of people think I'm wonderful, Joanna thought dryly. She began to iron pillowcases with swift efficiency, while Nora watched and chattered softly.

"I love this place, don't you? I'd like to be out tearing around in the open air this afternoon, like Bosun, instead of working. . . . Only Monday's washday, and Tuesday you iron, and if you don't, the sky will fall or there'll be a tidal wave or something. . . ." She stiffened suddenly, the sparkle dying away. "Oh, golly, she's coming downstairs!" she hissed, and leaped toward the ironing board like a young gazelle.

When Gram appeared in the doorway Nora was hanging the last of the pillowcases on the rack, and Joanna sat in the rocking chair. She stood up quickly. "Hello, Mrs. Fennell, how are you today?"

"I'm all right." The old lady marched into the kitchen and examined the clothes on the rack with her sunken but brilliant eyes. Nora watched her nervously, but Gram merely said, "Mmm," and went to sit down in the rocker Joanna had just vacated.

"And how are you today, young woman?" she asked. "And how's that man of yours?" A smile tugged at her grim old lips. "He ain't been in for a long time—I miss him."

"He's gone to the mainland, Mrs. Fennell."

"And you let him go *alone*? A handsome one like him, with all the women there are who've got their eye out for just such a one, quiet and polite and hardworking?" Gram shook her head vigorously. "I never let my Jeffrey go 'way from home alone, even when it meant leaving the hired girl with the children." She chuckled. "Never left my Jeffrey alone with the hired girl, either."

Joanna caught at a straw and said, "Jeffrey's a nice name. I have a cousin Jeffrey."

"And you got a good husband, my girl. You'd ought to take better care of him."

Nora said breathlessly, "Gram, would you like a cup of tea?"

"Tea?" said Gram fiercely. "What do I want with tea? Just had my dinner, didn't I? You leaving us, Joanna Sorensen?"

Joanna smiled at her. "Yes, I'm making the rounds this afternoon. Fifteen minutes in each place. You know—like Emily Post." She winked at Nora, and let herself out. Bosun met her with a wild *woof* of hysterical pleasure, and as she shut the door she heard the old lady begin again.

"Nora, that dog's a pure nuisance. Listen to him now—anybody'd think he was ugly—"

Joanna shut the door quickly, and went down the steps, with Bosun dancing around her. He escorted her along the path to the front gate, opening on the lane. She slipped out, keeping him back with her foot. The gate safely latched, she looked over it at his eager black face and glowing eyes. "If it gets too tough for you up there," she told him, "you can come and live with me . . . and my handsome husband."

She went down by the clubhouse, boarded-up and lonesome among the spruces with only Gunnar Sorensen's overgrown fields to look at. There'd be a time when the clubhouse was open again, with Saturday night dances and monthly suppers; perhaps by next summer they could manage something, start off with a supper for the Seacoast Mission. That would bring out a crowd from Brigport. . . . Brigport reminded her of Fowler.

She broke off a green, scented twig from a young spruce branch and pulled it to bits as she walked along. Grant's point was safe, and forever. So what did one storm matter?

She turned in at the clamshell walk that led to Marion Gray's back door. Not only Marion was there, but Vinnie, and they received her gladly.

"Another pair of hands," Marion said briskly. "Sit down to the kitchen table there, Jo, and help cut out quilt blocks. There's the pattern, and here's a pair of scissors."

Joanna cut and snipped with concentration, until she realized Vinnie's amber eyes were on her profile. She looked up, surprised, and Vinnie said candidly, "I was just sayin' to Marion before you come in—you must be at loose ends today, with Nils gone so long."

"Oh, I know he'll be back as soon as he can get here," Joanna answered. *As soon as he gets over being mad with me,* she thought.

"You know," said Vinnie, nodding her head wisely, "sometimes I think it's good for husbands to get away once in a while. Then the wives can have a chance to do things, like readin' in bed as long as they want to."

"Land o' love, I should say so!" agreed Marion. "I'd of tunked Jud over the head plenty of times if he'd been around under my feet too much. . . . And that's more truth than po'try. That man can make me the maddest—" She took a long breath, and then her eyes began to twinkle behind her glasses. "But that's not sayin' I'd want to live with any other man but Jud. He knows my ways and I know his, and that's that." She settled comfortably into her chair—as comfortably as she'd settled into her marriage, Joanna thought, remembering Marion and Jud from her childhood when they were just Tim's and Pete's mother and father, but comical and nice just the same.

"Caleb's good, too," said Vinnie, "but he's such a silent soul."

"That reminds me," said Marion, "speakin' of husbands bein' away—Jud was sayin' just at dinner he hoped Nils wouldn't stay long, because there was somethin' he wanted to talk to him about."

"What was it?" Joanna asked.

"I can't remember. So I guess it wasn't very important. How about some coffee? I made a frosted spice cake this morning, too." She pushed back her chair and got up.

"Over across they're rationin' sugar," said Vinnie. "You s'pose they'll ration food here if we have a war? Caleb says it's the only fair way. Only I hope—" Her words trailed off, and she shuddered.

"I guess everybody feels the same about war," Joanna said hastily. She watched Marion's chunky figure working around the stove. "Marion, can't you remember anything about it?"

"About what? Oh, what Jud said? Blessed be, it was jest some little thing! I never bother with the men's business. Jud says for me to keep my nose to home, so I do!" Laughing, she began to take the cups from the cupboard.

When the cake and coffee were finished, and she had cut out a dozen more quilt blocks, Joanna left. She didn't want to wait for Vinnie; she wanted to walk alone through the empty village in the last cold light that fell across the harbor and shone redly on the rock walls of Eastern Harbor Point. And she wanted to see Jud. Whatever he meant to ask Nils, perhaps she could give him the answer.

As she reached the boatshop and the old wharf—which was almost a new wharf now—she saw him coming up over the side of the wharf from the car, through with his work for the day. Mark's boat was just tying up at her winter mooring, out beyond the *Donna.*

"Hi, fair one!" Jud saluted her. "Don't you look handsome tonight! Too handsome for a sorrowin' gal whose husband is afar!"

Does everybody have to mention that? she thought with a grating of anger. But she grinned back at Jud. "No time for sorrowing, Jud. I have to look out for my husband's affairs, and that keeps me busy."

"What kind of affairs?" said Jud.

"Strictly business," Joanna retorted. "Look, Jud, Marion told me there was something you wanted to talk to Nils about. Now I don't know how soon he'll be back—he's helping Eric with his boat while waiting for the engine. So why don't you tell me what you want to know, and maybe I—"

Jud shook his head. "Nope! T'ain't nothin' but won't keep, Joanna, so don't you bother your pretty head about it! It's too much to expect a woman to do her own work and her husband's too, so you take it easy and don't worry!" He nodded his head hard at her, grinned again, and was stumping off. "Now I'm goin' home and raise a little hell teasin' Vinnie and the old lady!"

Joanna remembered to smile and say "So long," and then she turned toward the beach, passing the gully-hole that hadn't yet been filled in by the sea.

But her feet walked of their own accord and knowledge, because her brain was busy with something else. Jud had deliberately told her to mind her own business; that was what it had amounted to. He'd laughed, and he'd patted her arm, but all the time he'd been telling her she had no right to ask questions, that what he and Nils talked about was no concern of hers. *No concern of hers*—and it was about the Island! Of course it was about the Island—Jud and Nils had no other common ground but the Island and their life there. But she, Joanna, was to—what was it Marion had said? *To keep her nose to home.*

She walked faster. Jud, that stubby, round, ribald little man, daring to tell *her* what not to think about! She knew the truth of course. Jud was old-fashioned, he wanted all women to be like Marion, absorbed in cooking and children and grandchildren and cleaning house and making quilts; he wanted to be Lord and Master, to keep his wife in ignorance of the world, so that he could enlighten her and see her hanging on his words whenever he spoke. And he still saw Joanna as the little kid in pigtails and overalls who hung around the beach waiting for a chance to row somebody's punt.

I shouldn't blame Jud, she thought, *because he's ignorant.*

She had to slow down on the slope, she had been walking so fast. A pearly-lavender light tinted the sky above Schoolhouse Cove and in the east; the little wisps of cloud were purple, edged with rose, and the cove lay in comparative peace, sheltered from the wind. In the west, a tawny glow beyond the trees marked the sunset. The air was cold, but exquisitely clear, and scented with the clean breath of the Island.

Involuntarily Joanna sighed, and with that long sigh some small measure of peace came to her. She began to walk again, toward the house.

28

TIME MOVED. IT WENT SLOWLY, but it moved. Nils didn't come on the next boatday, Friday, but Joanna wrote him a note, to tell him the trap-stuff had been divided up, and everybody was working very hard at patching old pots and building new ones; they were getting out to haul, too, and making a good dollar from the handful of traps that were still good. Owen and Stevie took turns hauling his string and bringing her the money. She was putting it back in the money box.

Late Friday afternoon Mark brought Joey and Ellen from Brigport, and another weekend began.

"Week after next is Thanksgiving week!" Ellen chanted, arriving in the kitchen with the impermanent air of a song sparrow lighting on a wild pear bush.

"You don't say so," Joanna said, busy at the dresser with supper. "Come on in, Mark."

"Can't stay—just thought I'd see the kid up from the shore, it was pretty dark." Mark stood briefly in the entry and then went out again; it was because Owen was in the sitting room.

Ellen took off her things and hung them on their hook. She looked around the kitchen, she walked softly to the door of the sitting room and looked in at Owen and Stevie. Then she came back to Joanna. "Didn't Nils come home?" she asked. "I thought sure he'd come today."

"He can't come till his engine's ready," Joanna said quickly. "Will you set the table, Ellen? You're just in time."

Sighing, Ellen put on her clean, ruffled apron and began to lay the knives and forks on the bright-flowered cloth under the lamp. "Golly, looks as if they'll never get it done!" she said. "But it ought to be fixed by *Thanksgiving*, don't you think so, Mother?"

"You miss him, don't you, Ellen?" Joanna didn't look at her daughter as she spoke.

"Don't you miss him, too? And I wanted him to see my spelling papers." Ellen put the plates around; her small face was sober and intent. "Nils never says much. But he leaves an awful big place when he's gone."

It was like a conspiracy, Joanna thought. You'd almost believe nobody ever went to the mainland and stayed a week or so, the way they all talked about Nils. She was getting sick of it; the big spoon mixing the griddlecake batter slipped and clattered against the side of the bowl, and it was all she could do not to throw the spoon as far as it would go. *I'm too nervous*, she thought. *I ought to do something . . . have a change . . .*

"Cranberry sauce on the table, Ellen," she said aloud. "Maple syrup—here, I'll get it down for you." She spoke, she made the familiar motions, but her mind went on its independent way. It was always trotting along by itself, lately, like a dog out for a walk alone, getting into all sorts of odd corners — some of them not very satisfactory. . . . If Nils stayed away another week everybody would think it was queer; they'd know it couldn't take that long to get the valves ground. . . . The pup out by itself discovered with a thrill of pleasure a new scent. . . . She'd write to him by the next boat and tell him that if he was about ready to come home she'd go over on the *Aurora B.* and make the trip back with him. She could do some shopping for Christmas, and see a movie. The change would be good for her. And she'd be making a gesture that Nils must recognize.

All at once she felt calm and assured again. The independent dog trotted home, obedient to the leash. Joanna poured creamy batter on the griddle and smiled, sparkling-eyed, into Ellen's lifted, questioning face.

"Hungry, dear?"

"Y-yes. . . . Nils likes griddlecakes too."

This time Joanna didn't feel like throwing the spoon. Her smile deepened. She flipped the cakes gently, already golden brown on one side, and said, "We'll have them again, as soon as he comes home. And it won't be long, Ellen."

Life became, all at once, a routine. Joanna hadn't noticed it before. The week was divided into neat little sections. Tuesdays and Fridays were boatdays; also, on Friday, Ellen came home — if the weather permitted — and went back late Sunday afternoon or early Monday morning. You lived from one event to the next. With winter coming, so that you couldn't spend every possible daytime hour outdoors, and with the strangeness of Nils' absence, these days stood out as sharply as though they'd been marked on the calendar with black pencil.

Sending Ellen off with Stevie early on the cold bright Monday morning, the awareness of Tuesday haunted Joanna. On Tuesday, if the *Aurora B.* didn't break down or a gale blow up, Nils might be home, and then everybody would stop asking her what was keeping him over there on the mainland. But he might not come at all, and that was why she had given Ellen the letter to mail when she walked past the store on her way to Mrs. Robey's.

"Did you tell Nils I had a lot of papers to show him?" Ellen asked.

"Of course I told him that, and then I told him I might go over next weekend and come home with him." She kissed Ellen's upturned face, framed in the blue hood. "Be sure and have some more good spelling papers to show him."

"Oh, I will!" said Ellen joyfully. To her, it was as good as done; Nils would be home for Thanksgiving, and that was final. She went out of the house happily, running ahead of Stevie to see if Joey was ready to go with them.

Stevie waited for a moment after she was gone. Owen had already started out to haul. "Jo," he said hesitantly. "You sure Nils is coming home, then?"

"If I have to escort him home in person—" she began gaily.

"Well, it'll be swell to see him. I miss the guy." He smiled at her, and put on his heavy plaid cap and went out. For a moment the memory of his smile stayed with Joanna. Stevie had such a nice smile, gentle and easy, like Stevie himself. He was tender-hearted, he'd always been quick to pity—*Pity*. Was it that, in his smile? Almost as if he thought it was no use for her to look for Nils, or write to him. . . .

She shook her head violently, to clear it. It was another sign of nerves, when she began imagining things, reading pity into Stevie's voice and smile, giving even the slightest attention to the idea that Nils wouldn't respond to her note. Of course he would answer, by the very next boat, and tell her to come; and that would end all the chatter. At least it would shut Owen up. And as for pity—well, Stevie knew better than that. She'd never needed pity yet, and this certainly was no occasion for it.

With the housework done, her time was her own. The boys had a long hauling day ahead of them, taking care of their own gear and Nils' too, and they wouldn't be home for dinner. She ought to make some Thanksgiving and Christmas plans; if she went to Limerock next weekend she should have a list. . . . She sat down with paper and pencil, and managed to get her ideas into rough order.

In the afternoon she dressed in heavy slacks, warm sweater and trench coat, tied a kerchief under her chin, and went out for a walk. The day was one of those which seem powdered with diamond dust. Everything sparkled; in the places where the sun had just reached the melting frost glittered, and the choppy sea splintered the sunglare into dancing bits of light. Down at the harbor, the boats were beginning to return from hauling. Caleb's boat was just leaving the car as she walked out to the end of the wharf.

Jud's "Office" these cold days was in the end of the boatshop, where he had built so many boats for the Island. Now the long shed was used for storage, except for the corner where Jud had his little pot-bellied stove, his desk where he kept his books, his window where he could look over the harbor and see the boats coming in.

Now he came puffing up the ladder from the car and grinned at Joanna, his round face looking rounder still in a deerstalker cap, earlaps, and a scarf. "Hi, Joanny. Now don't you laugh at my outfit. Marion, she makes me wear this sissy muffler so's I won't get a kink in my neck and groan all night. . . . Come on in and set awhile."

She followed him into the shed and sat down on a box, stretching her feet toward the stove. Jud fussed around with his books, writing down his last purchase with a forlorn stub of a pencil.

"I'll make you a present of a good pencil, Jud," Joanna said idly.

"Hell, this one'll work till it's gone," Jud assured her. "Spit on the lead and she writes just as black as when she was new. . . . If that Caleb had all the traps he started out with this fall, he'd be a rich man, b'God."

"What are lobsters now?"

"Gone up to fifty. Fellers could make good money out of half a dozen pots right now." Jud whistled under his breath and looked out the window. "Time for Toby Merrill to be comin' along. Merrills don't have no use for the Fowlers, neither do the Bradfords. Always come here, since I started buyin'."

He did a little dance-step and Joanna smiled. "You like this job, don't you, Jud?"

"Best one I ever had. I'm too old to climb around buildin' boats, and I never did care much for haulin' pots in the winter. But this is fine. Kind of a sociable business, too. . . . Here comes Rich Bradford."

He hurried out, and Joanna followed him. As she stood on the wharf watching the Brigport boat cut across the dancing chop in the harbor and head for the car, she remembered how she'd always loved to be around the wharf when the boats came in. She was small, then, and someone was always sending her home. She'd promised herself that when she grew up she'd stay at the wharf as long as she wanted to. . . . And here she was. No one was sending her home.

The boat slid gently alongside the car and was made fast; the Brigport man, oilskins over his heavy clothes, nodded at Joanna and lifted his lobster tubs over the side to the float. Jud put them on the scales, one tub at a time, and grinned at Bradford. "You're doin' all right, son."

"I guessed about three hundred pounds," Bradford said.

"You guessed just about right." Jud weighed back the empty tubs and nodded. "Little less. Two hundred and ninety-five pounds. That make you feel bad, son?"

"Not very," the other man said dryly. Jud wrote out his slip and gave it to him, then reached into his pocket for the money. It was a familiar proceeding. When she was ten, Joanna had watched Pete Grant produce similar rolls of bills—no wonder she'd thought him the richest man in the world, till she had grown up and realized the ins and outs of lobstering.

"One hundred and fifty-three dollars," Jud declaimed solemnly, laying the last bill across Bradford's calloused palm. "And forty cents." He counted out the change meticulously, and then beamed as Bradford tucked the money away in his billfold.

"Thanks, Jud."

"Don't thank me, thank God for this weather . . . and salt that money away, son—hard days a-comin'."

The Brigport man's lean Yankee face split in a grin. Joanna went back into the boatshop, and put another stick of wood in the stove. She stood there warming her hands, figuring in her mind, wondering if Jud's arithmetic was as faulty as it seemed. Two hundred and ninety-five pounds at fifty cents a pound. . . Jud had done something wrong somewhere, and had apparently cheated himself out of three dollars or more.

The Brigport boat's engine roared as it backed out from the wharf and swung around. Then Jud was coming in, stamping his feet, clapping his hands together. "Wow! Them lobsters are mighty frigid critters to handle on a day like this! You poked up the fire, Joanna? Good girl!" He went to his desk and picked up the stub of pencil again.

"Rich Bradford," he spelled aloud. "Two hundred and ninety-five pounds. Paid out one hundred 'n'—"

"Jud," Joanna said swiftly behind him. "Jud, don't think I'm interfering, or anything, but are you sure you figured that out right? Aren't you cheating yourself?"

"Nope," said Jud briskly. "See, I give them Brigport fellers two cents over the price, for comin' here." He went on writing. Joanna stood behind him, still holding her hands out automatically toward the stove, and looking at his broad back, bent over the desk. *So you pay Brigport two cents over the price you pay here,* she thought. *I suppose they need it, and we don't.*

She made some excuse and got out of the boatshop quickly. Jud had often annoyed her in all the years she had known him; but she had never felt like this before. For a little while she had been at peace, sitting there by the old stove, looking out at the harbor. Now all her suppressed tensions and angers fought their way to the surface and concentrated on Jud.

She wondered when he had begun to add the extra two cents. Probably he'd decided he could make it up when Richards' smack came around to collect the lobsters. She kicked at a stone in the path. It wasn't fair for Jud to be paying the Brigport men two cents extra. If he was going to make presents, the Bennett's Island fishermen deserved a share. After all, it was really the Bennett's Island men who were bringing Jud his living. If he had to depend on Brigport fishermen for his money, he wouldn't stay in business long. . . . It was time the other men on Bennett's Island knew about that two cents, and she intended to let them know.

Owen and Stevie came in late in the afternoon, looking pleased with themselves, and immensely hungry, in spite of the big dinner boxes she'd fixed for them. She had a substantial mug-up ready.

Owen was in one of his best moods. He'd put some more traps out, and they were fishing well. "Hello, darlin' mine," he greeted her. "Let me rub my whiskers over your cheek, sweetheart, and don't look so black."

"Anybody'd look black at the thought of you huggin 'em," Stevie said. He winked at Joanna. "Don't mind him. He's got money in his pocket and no girl. Hell of a mess."

"I'm going to town and find one," said Owen, and crashed his fist down on the table to make the dishes jump.

Joanna had intended to talk to them as soon as they'd finished the hot coffee and thick lobster sandwiches. But the warmth of the kitchen, and the comfort of food in their stomachs after the long day on the water, had them yawning helplessly. Watching Stevie's drowsy eyelids as he kicked off his boots, and the languid way Owen tossed a half-finished cigarette into the stove, Joanna knew they were in no mood for a discussion of Jud and his methods.

She let them go without protest, Stevie up to his room, Owen to sprawl on the sitting room couch, where he would fall instantly and heavily asleep.

After supper, the boys brought two balls of green marlin from the shed, and prepared to knit trapheads in the kitchen. Joanna was making baitbags from a ball of fifteen-thread. This knitting was necessary business, for there were always traps to be replaced.

The fire burned steadily in the stove, radiating the aromatic warmth and a certain personality that only a wood fire can give to a room. Owen worked at the window where Nils always worked, looking toward the sea, the bracket lamp on the wall shedding a clear, soft light on the green twine and the flat wooden needle. The head was started from a loop of twine hooked over a nail in the window sill, and as it grew, he had to move his low chair constantly backward—until the finished head went to join the others behind the stove. One day soon, those heads, laced tautly into the traps in the proper fashion, held open by the hoop called the funny-eye, would make a funnel of mesh through which the lobster would seek the bait. And the bait—salted herring in these winter months—would dangle lusciously from the top of the trap, in one of the bait-bags that Joanna was making.

Each man had his own pattern for his trapheads; when he told it aloud, it sounded like some mystic incantation.

"Take up twenty, knit down ten; widen twice on the fourth row; drop off to three, and knit down ten." That was a big head. In a four-headed trap, a man used two big heads and two little ones.

There was never an end to the knitting. You had to do it, no matter what cataclysm came into your life. It was like eating and sleeping. . . . And so they were knitting, Owen at his window, Stevie at one of the harbor windows, Joanna at the other. They were quiet, all three. For her brothers it was a contented quietness, Joanna knew. She could glance sidewise at Stevie's peaceful, serious face, and she could hear Owen whistling under his breath, across the room.

But for herself, she could stand only so much of it. She found herself pulling the knots tight with much more of a yank than was necessary; and when she dropped a needle while she was filling it, she felt like snapping it in two. She finished the bag she was working on, took it from the hook in the sill, and threw it into the cardboard carton with the others.

At the dresser, she took a drink of water and let the dipper clatter back into the pail. It had the right effect. It startled Owen and Stevie out of their day-dreaming. Seeing their heads turned toward her, and the identical twitch of their black eyebrows, she had a silly impulse to put out her tongue at them, and wiggle her hands like a donkey's ears.

Instead, she spoke quietly. "How do you like the idea of Jud paying Brigport two cents extra on the pound? Two cents more than he pays you?"

Stevie was lighting a cigarette; above it his dark eyes glanced up at her in a quick question. Owen pushed back his chair and stretched his long legs.

"Two cents extra? Sure, why not?. . . Don't be so narrow with your cigarettes, Steve."

Astonished, she watched Stevie toss the pack across the room to Owen; she was astonished by their lack of indignation, when she had been smoldering all day.

"But it's not fair!" she burst out. "Why should they get a higher price? I don't like it!"

"Oh, for Christ's sake," Owen said impatiently. "Dry up, Jo. What's it to you?"

"Jud talked it over with us a hell of a while ago, Jo," Stevie explained. "It's just a little come-on to bring those fellers over here. About pays for their extra gas, that's all."

"You mean, everybody knew it, all the time? *Everybody?*" She was slightly bewildered. "But I never heard anything about it!"

"All the men knew it," Owen said sardonically. "Didn't figure it was any of your business, so we didn't inform you." He stood up, grinning at her, and she felt like slapping the grin from his face.

"How about Nils?" she demanded. "Did he know? Or did you talk it over after he'd gone?"

"You think he wouldn't like it?" inquired Owen. "Well, it was his idea, sweetheart. Takes money out of Ralph Fowler's pocket. And the extra two cents'll keep 'em from makin' up with Ralph in a hurry." He yawned in her face. "If Nils didn't tell you anything about it, after we talked it over, maybe it was because he figured the way I do — that it's men's business, and not yours."

"I don't like your tone, Owen."

He stretched, and seemed twice as big in the low-ceilinged room. "Sorry, my love. . . . Guess I'll go in and turn on the radio."

"You might wait and finish what you've started." She spoke serenely. It wasn't the way she felt inside, but she knew how disastrous it would be to let her voice get away from her.

Owen's eyebrow tilted. "I didn't know I'd started anything, Mrs. Sorensen. Just reminded you we could do a few things around here without your help." He lifted his hand. "No, wait a minute before you blast my ears off. Sure, you're smart and you're a go-getter. But you're still a woman, Jo, and none of us takes much to petticoat government. So why don't you start mindin' your own business? Everybody'd appreciate it, includin' Nils, I'd almost think."

She watched him walk out. In the sitting room the radio blared, insolently loud. She remembered a time when she would have called him back and matched his insults with her own, "blasted his ears off," to use his own phrase. But today she let him go, hating his arrogant certainty, and fighting an agonizing impulse to burst into tears.

Stevie sat back in his chair, one ankle resting on the other knee, and looked thoughtfully at his moccasin. "That boy," he said softly, "is in a hard position. For him . . . So think nothin' of it, Jo."

"He didn't have any call to jump down my throat." Her voice wobbled, and she swallowed hard to steady it. "I could *kill* him."

"Think nothin' of it, Jo," Stevie repeated. He smiled at her, and got up. "I'll go in and fix that radio. Want any special program?"

"No, wait a minute, Stevie." It would take courage to ask him; but Stevie would tell her the truth, without sarcasm. "Stevie, you heard him. He said if I'd mind my own business, everybody'd appreciate it. . . . What did he mean by that?"

"That's just some more of his —"

"I want to know, Stevie," she insisted. "Do people think that about me? That I don't mind my own business?"

Stevie said, "Look, Jo. Owen's got the itch again. For a woman or a quart. Both, if he could have 'em. So you just let everything he says go in one ear and out the other." He winked at her and went into the sitting room.

She was alone in the kitchen. She let out a long breath, and with that breath all the stiffening went out of her spine. She sat down wearily, and shut her eyes.

29

ON FRIDAY JOANNA WOKE VERY EARLY. Today was the day when she was going ashore. She'd seen Mark the afternoon before, and he wasn't going to haul, but would go over to meet the boat and bring home the Island mail; and she was to go with him, pick up Nils' answer to her last note, and then go aboard the mailboat. She had no doubt of Nils' answer. It would tell her to come ahead. . . . *If he can't meet me at the wharf in Limerock,* she planned, lying awake in the windless gray dawn, *I'll go up to Camden, where he is.*

Nils would be glad to get home, she was sure of it. He would be finished with his sulking by now, ready to resume life on an even keel. Everything would assume its proper proportions. . . . She remembered, involuntarily, his words on that last bright afternoon. That she didn't want or need him. But if she went all the way to Camden —

She got up and began to dress. She had found, lately, that it was not a good idea to think far ahead. One thing at a time. Like breakfast, and leaving lists for the boys for their meals, so they wouldn't eat everything up at once, and writing out a note for Ellen.

Early as it was, the boys had already gone to haul when she came out into the kitchen. She was relieved. No need then of being distantly civil to Owen, of fighting for her poise when she saw his eyebrow go up and knew he was waiting with diabolic delight for her to lose her temper and fly at him. Yes, he'd like a real John Rogers brawl. But she wasn't going to give it to him, even if she had to stop speaking to him entirely.

It was a soft gray day outside; it smelled like spring, and the sea lay against the shores like smoke-colored watered silk. There was no sound of wind or water. *Another weather-breeder,* she thought; but it didn't matter as long as the rain and wind held off till she reached Limerock.

She ate breakfast, tidied the house, made out her lists and wrote Ellen's note; packed her small dressing case, and dressed in her good dark suit, with an immaculate and snowy blouse, whiter than a gull's breast. Finished, she stood in front of the mirror in the kitchen and looked at her reflection. There was a little line vertically between her peaked black brows: it felt as if it had been there always. She lifted her firm round chin slightly, and smiled at herself in the glass. The little line disappeared.

Shortly after nine she saw Mark and Helmi coming along the road past Schoolhouse Cove. She gathered up her winter coat and dressing case, and went down to meet them. No need to lock the house. No one ever locked houses on Bennett's Island.

The *Aurora B.* had just come in, when they reached Brigport Harbor, and was tied up at Ralph Fowler's lobster car. The tide was down, too low for the big boat to go in alongside the wharf.

"No need of you going aboard till she's ready to sail, Jo," Mark said. "I'll take you two girls in to Cap'n Merrill's float while I get the mail."

Helmi, standing beside Joanna, smiled at her. "Nils will be glad to see you."

"I hope so!" Joanna laughed. She felt confident, her color glowed. "Owen says I should've been over there long ago. According to him, I probably haven't got a husband by now."

"Owen has strange ideas," said Helmi. It was her only reference to Owen since the night he had kissed her. "Nils is good. A one-woman man, too. And you're the woman, Joanna."

They waited beside Cap'n Merrill's float while Mark went up to the store for the mail. The sunless harbor was quiet. It always was that way at low tide. Hardly anyone appeared; they were all in the store.

Helmi, lost in her customary air of remoteness, watched the gulls walking gingerly over the rockweed under Cap'n Merrill's wharf. After her remark about Nils — the one personal remark Joanna had ever heard her make — she seemed to have nothing more to say. Perhaps some day Joanna would get to know her well enough to find out what she thought about other things.

In a little while Mark came back down the wharf and slip to the float, whistling. He dumped an armful of mail into Helmi's lap. "There you are. Pick out your own, girls. . . . No sense you going aboard yet, Jo, Link's got to take some lobsters on." He went up the slip again. "I'll be here in the boatshop if you want me."

Helmi's mouth moved in a faint smile. "Here you are, Joanna. From your husband." She handed the envelope to Joanna, who said, "I don't really need to read it. It'll just say, 'Come ahead'—"

She tore the end off the envelope and began to read.

"Dear Joanna," Nils had written in his firm, methodical hand. "I still don't know when I'm coming back. I'm telling you this so you won't make the trip for nothing. Of course if you want to come to Limerock anyway, that's your business. I only wanted to tell you that I wouldn't be going back with you. . . . The boat is coming along well. Everybody is fine here. Tell Ellen not to eat too much dinner on Thanksgiving day."

There was nothing else. Only his name, simple and strongly written. *Nils.*

She thought vaguely, *He wouldn't write "Yours" or "Sincerely," because then he would be lying.* He had left her. He had left her and the Island both, and he was not coming back.

After a little while the world broke in on her again, piece by piece. The lonesome fluting of a solitary gull standing on a rock; the sound of the hoisting gear on the *Aurora B.*, getting the lobster crates aboard. Mark's laughter from the open door of Cap'n Merrill's boatshop. The gentle motion of the boat as the tide pulled at it. And Helmi, sitting motionless on the washboards, her raised profile pure and far-away.

It gave her time to recover her poise. After a moment she managed a creditable chuckle.

"Now Owen will be sure he's right!" she said, and Helmi turned her fair head toward her.

"Why?"

"Nils says I'm not to come." She smiled confidently into her sister-in-law's unquestioning eyes. "Something about the boat his uncle's building. He can't leave it yet."

"That's too bad! And you're all ready to go, too," said Helmi. "Why don't you go, anyway? He'd be glad to see you."

Joanna shook her head. "There's likely to be another storm over the weekend; I might not get back Tuesday. And there's not much room up at Eric's. Besides—" she shrugged, and laughed. "If Nils tells me to stay at home, I'm supposed to mind."

Helmi smiled, and Joanna felt relieved. That was over with, anyway. Now to convince Mark there was nothing wrong, and then—hardest of all—to face Owen. The thought of it set her teeth on edge. *If he twits me*, she thought, *I'll not answer. I'll get out of the room.*

She heard Mark's whistling again, and took a long breath. By the time he reached the float and came aboard the boat, she had assumed a mock-forlorn expression. "Take me home again, Mark," she said. "My husband doesn't want me."

She was back in the house again long before Owen and Stevie were due in from hauling, and had torn up and burned the list, and the note; and Nils' letter. And now that she was alone, she faced the incredible fact that Nils hadn't responded to her offer. She had been so certain he would want her to come that the shock of his refusal was nearly physical. Her heart seemed to be pounding, her body was alive with beating pulses. And she was cold. She sent the fire roaring up the chimney and stood over the stove, rubbing her hands.

Nils has left me, she said to herself. Then she said it aloud—and how ghastly clear it was in the empty house—made it cold fact at last, and then panic was upon her, the panic of pride. How long could she keep the truth to herself? Mark and Helmi hadn't questioned her today. But what about the brothers who lived in this very house with her? How long could she stave off their knowledge? And then the Island's knowledge. . . . When Thanksgiving came and went without him; when his gear went neglected, or left to the others to tend; what then? Everybody would know at last that Nils had gone; and they would realize how terribly wrong something had been, when a man like Nils would walk away, without a backward look, from his work and his home.

Then they would watch her. And wonder. And conjecture, with sidewise glances and lifted eyebrows. . . . Hovering over the stove, trying to warm hands that would not warm, already she felt naked and terrified. Eyes, everywhere eyes; the neighbors', her brothers', Ellen's.

I will have to tell her tonight, she thought. *Tell her that Nils won't be here for Thanksgiving. . . . And after that, I'll have to tell her he won't be home for Christmas.*

And after a while, Ellen would look at her without asking about him, but the question would be in her crystal-clear, unswerving eyes. *Why?*

They will all ask Why, thought Joanna, *and they'll never be done watching me.* Suddenly she was warm, too warm; she felt suffocated. She moved away from the stove and flung open the back door. The soft air, heavy with rain, touched her face. She heard an engine down in the harbor, loud in the stillness, and recognized Owen's *White Lady.*

She felt trapped and harried, like a gull tied down to earth by a string, circled by enemies whichever way it turned, wanting to fly up and up, wanting to escape so much that its heart seemed bursting; but there was no way of cutting the string, and the circle was closing in. . . . This was what Nils had done to her, she cried out wildly inside herself. If he had wanted to repay her for what he said she'd done to him, this was it.

30

BRIGHTLY AND PITILESSLY COLD, December began. The wind blew almost without stopping. It was too rough to go out and haul. All day and all night the sea stormed against the Island and boiled into the rocky coves; for miles around the Island every ledge was a cauldron of white water, spray blowing off the combers like smoke.

Thanksgiving was over and done with, and Ellen had gone back to Brigport again. It had been a strange Thanksgiving; Joanna had given her thanks when the day was safely past. To the boys, she'd been rueful about poor Nils, whose family loyalty was keeping him over on the mainland when he'd rather be home. She was thankful that the pose had carried so well, she was thankful that Owen had held his tongue.

She was taking a certain pride in herself these days; in keeping her head up and a smile on her lips, in laughing a good deal—though sometimes she had to catch and hold on to her laughter, so it wouldn't be too hilarious. Sometimes it tried to get away from her. Deep in her brain she knew she should be making plans, but so often her head was aching, when she went to bed at night, that she allowed herself to think of only one thing at a time.

There was Christmas to get through—Christmas with Ellen, who would wonder why Nils wasn't there. And after that, she promised herself, there was time enough to plan. *After that;* sometimes she had a premonition that those two words were all that stood between her and a black abyss of confusion. And because she had always known exactly what she was going to do, and how, and when, the thought was terrifying. Rather, it *could* be terrifying, if she dwelt on it.

Every morning that first week in December the vapor curled up from the sea, a shimmering, moving blanket of freezing mist, and every morning the men looked at the weather and knew they couldn't go out to haul that day. You had weeks like this often through the winter. But never, to Joanna, had one seemed so long.

One bitter morning when she felt she couldn't bear another day in the house—with Stevie hanging over the radio and Owen taking up most of the kitchen—she bundled up and went out. No matter if she were frost bitten, she wouldn't stay in. If she had to climb over Owen's feet once more on her way to the stove, she would be tempted to throw the teakettle at him. Inwardly she was trembling with nervousness, and that made her angry with herself.

The cold, bright air burned her throat when she breathed, and cut her face; it struck through her mittens, and her heavy shoes and woolen socks. The ground rang under her feet, hard as iron. And the sea glittered too much for her to look at it.

Except for the smoke from the chimneys, plumes of grayed purple against the sky, the Island might have returned to its deserted state. She saw no one as she walked down to the harbor and around the shore towards Grant's point. She had a share in the point now, she reflected ironically—she might as well walk on it, though she doubted she'd feel any thrill of accomplishment or ownership. That pleasure had been very efficiently taken away from her. . . .

She walked through the long covered shed and came out on the wharf. There was always enough water here for a boat the size of the *Aurora B.;* Link had never had to tie up out in the harbor and row his passengers ashore in a dory because of a lack of water, even at the low-dreen tides.

She gazed along the length of the wharf, noting the rotted planks, the gaping squares where planks were missing. She became absorbed in the problem of repairs, and gave herself to it gratefully. If new planks were laid, the wharf could be used by the men to pile traps on for drying out, instead of their dragging them up the beach and stacking them on the top of the bank. It would save them time and labor to use the wharf. There was no reason why the men couldn't fix the wharf in a few days, in a few forenoons or afternoons when it was warm enough to work outdoors, but too windy to haul.

She went back to the solid ground by the store. She felt excited; this was what she needed, something to take an interest in, something to plan out. She hesitated, wondering whom to approach first, and then received her answer. Caleb Caldwell was out in the harbor, pounding ice off the bow of his boat. Caleb was one who would help her.

She hurried back around the shore to the beach, feeling warm and alive. Even her fingers and toes had stopped stinging. She was almost happy. On the empty beach she waited for Caleb to row ashore, tapping her feet to keep the blood moving in them. It was a glorious morning after all. She was glad she'd come out. She looked up at a single gull flying overhead, and waved a red-mittened hand at it.

Caleb's punt came in sight beyond the lobster car, and she ran down to the water's edge to help pull it in.

"Well!" Caleb looked down into her glowing face. "Seems like you ain't much scared of the weather."

"Not me!" she answered. She waited for him to make the punt fast, and then walked up to the road with him. "Look, Caleb, I know you're in a hurry to get home and warm up, so I'll talk fast. How about fixing up the big wharf? We've got planks left over from the other work."

Caleb stopped in the shelter of one of the old camps to light his pipe. His deep-set eyes shifted somberly from the pipe bowl to her eager face; there was a deliberation in his glance, as there was in all his movements, and in his slow voice.

"Well, Joanna, it's like this. You see, Nils had sort of a good idea about fixin' the wharf, and there's more to it than layin' a few planks."

"Well, why haven't you fellows got around to do something about it then?"

"Well, you'd ought to understand how we feel about goin' ahead with it while Nils ain't here. Jud can't climb around much, and Matthew and me, we never worked on a wharf."

She leaned against the camp wall, trying not to show the sickening disappointment she felt.

His long humorous mouth twitched. "I s'pose that makes us out to be a couple of proper numbheads, but there it is. Maybe your brothers could do it the way Nils said. I dunno."

"I see," said Joanna. "Well, if that's the way you feel about it, Caleb—"

"Nils is the one to be takin' care of that wharf-business," Caleb said. He grinned at her. "You ought to be proud of him, Joanna. . . . Prob'ly are, though, ain't ye?"

She smiled back at him. "Go along home and get warm, Caleb. . . . So long!" She stood with her back against the ancient shingles of the camp and watched him go along the board walk, a tall gaunt man in heavy clothes and oilskins, leaning against the wind.

It was she who had spoken for him when he wanted to come to the Island to live, she had overridden Nils' caution about strangers, she had made the house ready for his wife; but it was not for her that he would work, but for Nils.

She did not know how long she stood there, the two shabby camps keeping off the wind, and the faint warmth of the sun reaching through her clothes. The marsh lay frozen and dead before her, a light sifting of snow glittering among the hummocks; the spruce trees looked rusty-black. There was nothing moving now, not even a gull. She shut her eyes, trying to feel the sun on her lids. Instead she felt the hot, warning moisture of tears gathering, and she opened her eyes quickly. Something flashed past her face and hit the beach rocks at her feet. A shingle blown from the roof of one of the camps.

Slowly, as if she ached in every muscle or were very tired, she straightened up, and began to walk up the frozen road toward the Bennett meadow.

The camps haunted her for the rest of the week. They'd been built before her father was born, for Grandpa Bennett's hired fishermen. There'd been some others that had been torn down or burned down, but these two had remained, standing small and sturdy and independent at the edge of the marsh, on the brow of the beach. Sometimes a high tide—at the full moon—washed around them, but it could never move them. She could remember them from the time when she stood hardly as high as the anchor, with the silvery-green pigweed against the weathered shingles in summer, and the snow drifting against their lee sides in winter.

She remembered the swallows lining up on the ridgepoles, and old Nathan Farr splitting his evening firewood outside his door, and Johnny Fernandez sitting on his heels against the wall, at sunset, with his cat Teresa bending her lean head under his hand. She remembered herself on the beach in dungarees, waiting at Nils' peapod for him to come and take her hauling; and the old men, Johnny and Nathan, mending nets outside the camps and trying to tease her. . . . As if anyone could tease her about Nils, who was like a sixth brother, only better than a brother because he was nicer to her. . . .

She didn't want the camps to fall down; she didn't want any more shingles to blow off. And there would be more and more wind.

The sea was too rough for Ellen and Joey to come home this weekend, too rough to go for the mail on Friday. So there was nothing to break up the week. By Sunday she knew she was sick of the boys being in the house; sick even of Stevie, who had never annoyed her in any way before.

There were no boiled lobsters in the cellar-way, and Richards' smack hadn't been able to come out and bring groceries and fresh meat. Sunday dinner was creamed salt fish, baked potatoes, and mashed squash; she made a pie from a jar of blueberries she'd put up last summer.

Owen brought his magazine to the table. Stevie was lost in his own thoughts. So they ate dinner in silence. But when she served the pie and coffee, Owen laid aside his magazine in anticipation.

"Blueberry, huh? Hey, you're not so bad after all, sis! Been lookin' a mite ugly lately, but I'll forgive you, since you went and made me a blueberry pie."

"Thanks," she said laconically. She sat down at her own place, empty of pie, and began to stir her coffee. She had forced herself to eat dinner when every morsel scraped her throat. But she couldn't force down pie.

Owen picked up his fork and glanced at her quizzically. "None for you, kid? Don't you like pie?"

"Leave her alone, she's watching her figure," said Stevie. "You know how girls are."

Owen shrugged. "Never knew Jo to go off her feed for anything." He took his first mouthful of pie, and dropped his fork, to stare at Joanna with his brown face wry and puckered.

"What the hell's the matter with you, Jo? You slippin'?" He pushed his plate away from him and took a mouthful of coffee. "I've heard about these women that can't remember how to do things right when the old man's away, but I never thought you'd be one of 'em, Jo."

There was a glint in his black eyes and a twitch to his mouth that said he was teasing. But she was in no mood to take it. He pushed back his chair, its legs scraping the floor, and the rasping sound was more than Joanna could stand.

"What's the matter with the pie?" she demanded ominously.

Stevie answered her, his voice mild. "I guess you forgot to sweeten the blueberries, Jo." He lifted the top crust and sprinkled sugar over the filling.

"Nossir, I never thought Jo'd be one to make a mistake like that," said Owen. "Jesus, were *they* sour!"

So he was going to keep it up, was he? She felt the familiar burning in her cheeks, as if the room were too hot. "Maybe I *did* forget something, for once! And maybe it *is* bad enough to swear about! But at least I make an effort to do something extra around here, and that's more than you do!"

"Oh, for God's sake, Jo—you mad? What are you jumpin' down my throat for?" He looked at her in disgust. "What's wrong with me now?"

"Nothing. Nothing at all, except to sit around in my way." *I won't shout at him,* Joanna promised herself. *I won't shout or swear. . . .* "For a solid week you've done nothing, with all the stuff outside waiting to be done. But *you* can't do it—" sarcasm crept heavily into her voice and gave it a cutting edge. There was nothing worse to infuriate Owen, and she knew it. "*You* can't do it—Owen Bennett, of Bennett's Island—unless Nils is here to team you around! You and Stevie and Mark are the Bennetts, but Nils has to show you what to do, because you can't see it with your own eyes!"

"Do what, for instance?" Owen challenged her.

"You could fix up those camps before they fall to pieces! We've got nails and shingles and hammers—why don't you get to work?"

Owen scraped a match viciously across the stove. "The goddam things can rot into the ground before I'd touch 'em," he said. He looked at her from narrowed black eyes. "Listen, Jo, you tryin' to get rid of me? Because you're makin' a damn good job of it . . . same way you got rid of Nils! You don't want brothers, or a husband either— all you want is a hired man to keep the woodbox full."

She was standing up now, holding on to the back of her chair. She spoke slowly and carefully from a tightening throat. "You want to be careful, Owen. You talk too much."

"So do you," said Owen. "You always did. That's what's the matter with you." He walked out of the room. She stood rigidly still, looking down at the table; at the cooling coffee, the dark blueberry juice running out on the white pieplates. She heard Owen go through the sitting room and upstairs to his own room. Then, one at a time, her fingers unclamped, her knuckles stopped showing whitely through the brown flesh.

"Jo, listen," Stevie said. She had forgotten him entirely, and there he was, watching her with concerned eyes. "Jo, you don't want to let Owen get under your skin like that. And I'm sorry about the camps. Fact is, I never even see 'em half the time—"

She didn't answer; she was studying his face carefully. He got up and came around the table to her, and she turned to him. "Never mind the camps, Stevie," she said. "I guess they don't matter much . . . if they *do* fall down."

Stevie took hold of her elbow. "Jo, you look tired. Why don't you go lie down, and I'll clear up here?"

Suddenly her head cleared, and she could push Owen's crude statements away and see out past them, and realize with a rush of shame that Stevie was worried about her. About *her*. What had he seen on her face—what had she showed that wasn't meant to be seen? Panic wanted to assail her, but she held it off.

"Oh, gosh, Stevie!" She laughed up at him. "I did let him bother me, didn't I? But I think I bothered him a little too. Anyway, he's gone to his room to sulk, but I'll be damned if I'll go and sulk!" She began to clear the table, with a brisk clatter of dishes. "You go back in the other room and get your Sunday programs."

"I'll wipe the dishes for you," he offered, but she took him by the shoulders and turned him toward the sitting room door.

"I like the galley to myself, Cap'n. Go on."

Stevie went. She was safely alone again, she could let the aching smile slip from her face. *I can't live in the same house with Owen any longer,* she thought. *Maybe he'll go away now.* . . . Immediately she was horrified by the knowledge that she wanted one of her brothers to get out—to go anywhere, even to leave the Island, as long as he left her alone.

Stevie had the radio on again. He kept it turned down low, and lay on the couch near it, his hands behind his head, his eyes fixed on the ceiling. She hated the sound of the radio today, but she hadn't the heart to make Stevie turn it off. When she had finished the dishes, she went into her own room; with two doors shut between her and the sitting room, she could hear nothing.

She took off her shoes and lay down on the bed, pulling the Rose-of-Sharon quilt over her. She could look across at the woods; and as she lay there, trying to make each tense muscle relax, she remembered another time when she had lain in the pineapple-topped bed and looked over at the woods. Only instead of this harsh, cold, December light, there had been a soft snowfall at daybreak, and she had watched the gently dropping veil that made no sound, knowing that her baby would be born that day.

In January Ellen would be nine. She wanted a birthday party. . . . Joanna closed her eyes and wished she could drop off to sleep, and not wake up until dusk. . . . Because this had been Nils' bed too, he came into her mind again and again. She tried to imagine him in Uncle Eric's house, talking patiently with his uncle's wife, answering Eric's questions about the Island. He wouldn't find it hard. He wouldn't be tormented, as she was tormented; for he had simply made up his mind, and that was the way things were to be. He had put her and the Island behind him.

Once he had put the Island aside, after he had been such an integral part of it for so long, it wouldn't matter to him that the Island needed him. And that it *did* need him, Joanna was forced to recognize. The fact stared her in the face at every turn. Once she had worried about Nils' moderate ways, thinking he was of the same stamp as her father, from whom the Islanders had accepted all that he could give them, and had offered nothing in return. Money, advice, his unfailing friendship—they'd taken it as freely and unconsciously as they took water from the well, or wild strawberries from the field. And how very few among them had thought to *offer*, without prompting, their labor for an hour or so?

But she had proof that it was different with Nils. As she lay alone on the bed, watching the sunlight shift along the wall of the woods, she began to feel a reluctant admiration for him. It was clouded with her own hurt, for she was always being hurt these days; sometimes it seemed as if the Island itself were turning its face from her, who loved it so passionately. And Nils, who didn't love it half so deeply, could do for it what she ached to do, and couldn't.

She didn't know when she fell asleep. But at last the ceaseless, shifting cloud patterns above the spruces had their way, and they were the last things she remembered before there was nothingness.

It was Stevie who woke her up. She struggled back to awareness in the shadowy room to see him standing in the doorway, saying her name in a hushed tone.

"Jo . . . you awake?"

She sat up, her heart beating hard. "What's the matter?"

"I've been waitin' for you to wake up," he said. His voice sounded curiously tense, for Stevie. "Finally I thought I'd come and get you."

She slid out of bed, leaving the warmth under the quilt. "But what *is* it, Stevie? What's wrong?"

"Those damn' Japs are bombin' Hawaii," Stevie said. "Pearl Harbor." His words caught oddly in his throat. "Sinkin' our ships. They started this mornin'. . . ."

She followed him out into the sitting room. The radio was going; Owen sat beside it, his elbows on his knees, his profile somber and iron-hard in a shaft of late sunshine.

"But there's a peace conference in Washington," she protested. "They couldn't bomb us, when they're talking peace!"

"Peace conference, hell," growled Owen, and turned back to the radio and the voice that came from it, bringing treachery and bloody, choking death into the sitting room to blot out the empty fields and the unmoving spruces. The bulletin was agonizingly brief; its very curtness was worse than long details which would at least have given one something to go on. The report ended, and swing music blared into the room, frantically, as if the players were infected with this terrible shock that Joanna felt now; that burned in Owen's eyes as he snapped off the radio, and flattened Stevie's voice when he spoke.

"I'm goin' to enlist. Go in Tuesday on the mailboat. The Navy'll take me." He went over to the window and looked out toward the sea. Owen stayed where he was, his head bent forward, his eyes on the floor. Joanna looked swiftly from him to Stevie's back; she could sense the way Stevie's muscles had pulled themselves tightly together under his plaid shirt and corduroys. She went to stand near him, and saw a slight twitching in one flat brown cheek.

The sea stretched away from the flatly shelving tawny rocks out toward the lighthouse on the horizon, its bright surface dimmed by clouds blowing past the sun. As Joanna watched, the dulling shadows moved swiftly across the face of the water; and then a fresh gust of wind followed, sending a diamond shimmer over the sea.

And somewhere, in waters that sparkled as brilliantly, though under a warm sun instead of a wintry one, American boys like Stevie had fought and died, and were fighting and dying still. And some had had no chance to fight. . . . She looked at her brother now, knowing what had set his jaw like stone and what must be passing through his mind as he looked out across the sea he'd always called his "own special piece of ocean." And now, suddenly, he didn't belong only to the Island, nor the Island to him; the whole United States was his, and he owned vaster stretches of sea than he'd ever dreamed of crossing.

So he would go. . . . She remembered the destroyer in Limerock Harbor, and Stevie's lifted, intent face as they went by it.

"Maybe they'll send me down there right away," Stevie said, in this new drawn-out-taut voice. In the room behind him and Joanna, Owen got up from his chair.

"I'll be goin' to Portland with you, Steve," he said.

31

THEY DIDN'T WAIT FOR TUESDAY and the *Aurora B.*, after all. They left the very next morning, in the *White Lady*, heading for Pruitt's Harbor, where they would spend the night with their brothers Charles and Philip, and their mother. The next day they would go to Portland. They expected to be back before the end of the week, to get their traps up and put their boats on the beach.

There was not much to do, as far as Joanna was concerned. She was alone in the house day and night now. It was the first time she had ever been alone, except for a few months after Alec died, and then she was not really alone, for she had been always conscious of the baby, as yet unborn.

Now she had so much to think about, so many new prospects to try to understand and assimilate, that she was scarcely conscious of her solitude. Marion and Vinnie came up, and Nora Fennell. It seemed as if they must get together and talk out the horror and amazement and dread that they felt.

Like everyone else, she kept the radio going until she thought she could bear no more, and then, after a time of silence, she would go back to it. She listened to the declaration of war — on the same day the boys left to enlist. She heard the warnings for the air-raid scare on the next day, and knew a thrill of pure animal terror when she heard an airplane engine, coming near; but it was one of the big Coast Guard flying boats that would be doing patrol duty now, every day. Standing out on the windswept point behind the house, her hair blowing back from her lifted face and the incisive edge of the December air cutting through her coat, she watched the plane go over. It flashed silver against the sunwashed blue. She made herself imagine, deliberately, what she would feel to see an enemy symbol on its wings.

She wasn't frightened or panicky. After the first stunning disbelief had passed, and she realized, like everybody else, that one nation *could* betray another nation's faith in its good intentions, she was angry; and with such a sheer hate as she felt, there was no room for fear. She only hoped that her mother wasn't too nervous, and that Ellen, going to school, wasn't too frightened by the wild tales that children liked to tell each other. Over the weekend she could talk to her, and try to give her some idea of what this war was all about.

The thought passed through her mind that Nils would have been able to explain to Ellen. He would be talking things over with Uncle Eric now, or he'd be down at his father's, trying to make it clear to his grandmother, who had cried so when the Germans invaded Norway, because she'd grown up in Sweden close to Norway's border and loved it almost as much as she loved her own country. She would be crying again now, the heartbroken tears of an old, confused woman, and it would be Nils who comforted her, speaking to her in Swedish, the language of her heart.

But perhaps he wouldn't be able to comfort her, Joanna thought. For Nils had always been Anna's delight, and if she asked him if he would go, and he answered *yes* —

On this thought Joanna got up from her chair and began to walk through the empty rooms. It seemed to her that her feet echoed almost as they had done when the house had been empty for so many years, and had smelled of loneliness.

Nils might be enlisting now, like the boys. They might run into each other on the way to Portland. He wouldn't think to write to her about his plans, either. She was out of his life. . . . He had left her. . . . She folded her arms tightly across her breast and watched the cold shadows lengthen and darken across the faintly whitened meadow. It was a stormy sunset tonight, dull red, blocked out by a foreboding bank of dark purple cloud. She could imagine that purple cloud sweeping on, covering the Island in its cold mist, and those who lived on the Island caught in it as if it were a whirlpool, spinning in chaos.

She knew then she must get away from the house and away from the radio. Nightmares were bad enough; nightmares in daylight were too much.

She dressed warmly and went down to the Eastern End while the wintery red light still poured over the Island. Everything looked unnatural, the water, the beach stones, the dead grass in the fields, the spruces. The Island seemed unprotected, spread out under too much sky; and Joanna felt small and impotent, walking along the road in a world where nothing else moved. Not even a gull.

When she entered the woods, the gloom seemed almost friendly, at least it shut out the sunset light. The sound of the sea on the rocks below the path was a familiar voice. At least that would stay the same, no matter what happened to everything else.

The light had faded to a dim afterglow by the time she came out on the slope above Mark's place, the sea had darkened. Already the lamps were lit in the house, but as she walked down the path toward the buildings she heard the ringing impact of an axe. Mark was splitting wood out by the barn. In the clear colorless light that precedes dusk, he saw her and called to her.

"Hi, Jo. How goes it?"

"All right." She stood watching him, her hands deep in her coat pockets. He leaned his axe against the barn door and took out his cigarettes.

"Heard anything?" he asked. She knew he meant the boys, and shook her head. "No. Too soon. Besides, they'll be back before long." In the flare from the match Mark's face showed, withdrawn and somber. He looked old tonight, she thought.

"I ought to go," he said. "I've been thinkin' that ever since Sunday. But I don't know what to do about Helmi."

"What does Helmi say?" Joanna asked.

Mark shrugged. "You know Helmi. She never says anything, and I can't tell what she thinks." He began to gather up the wood he'd just split; Joanna helped him, and they went toward the house, their arms full. "Owen and Stevie don't have to plan for a wife," he said. "Christ, I don't know what to do, Jo! I don't feel like sittin' snug out here while some other poor bastard does my fightin' for me. . . . But Helmi won't go back to her family, and she hasn't got anybody else but me."

"She's got the Bennetts," Joanna murmured.

"Yeah—but—" They had almost reached the door. Mark stopped and looked at her over his armful of wood. "I might's well tell you, Jo. I'm worried about her for another reason too. No, it's not a baby, though I wish to Jesus it was." His voice sounded bewildered. "I don't know *what* it is . . . that would make a woman cry in her sleep."

Until now, Joanna hadn't been cold. But now she was chilled to the bone, the wind had a freezing breath. She shifted her load of wood and tried to see Mark's face in the deepening shadows.

"How long has she been doing that?"

"Just since Sunday. Seems like the war's preyin' on her mind or something." He was groping for words and staring at the lamplit kitchen windows; following his gaze, Joanna saw Helmi through the thin, crisp curtains. She was sitting by the table, reading; and the bright sheen of her hair was like a second lamp in the room. Without shifting his eyes from her Mark went on. "The first time I woke her up. I thought it was a nightmare. . . . In the morning I asked her about it and she said it wasn't so . . . said she never cried, any time. She was so—upset, I never said anything more about it."

Poor Mark! Joanna thought helplessly. She heard herself asking, "Does she cry every night?"

"Every night. I don't wake her up now." His voice dropped low, still groping, and Joanna knew only his desperation had driven him to tell her about this. "Now I—put my arm around her and snuggle her up to me . . . and she puts her arms . . ." Joanna could hardly hear him now—"around my neck and holds on hard, and keeps on crying, as if her heart would break. And all the time she's still asleep. That's what makes it so—so damn' hard."

He turned away from the window. "Jo, how am I going to walk out on her, even if it's my duty?"

"I don't know, Mark." She would have to tell him something, even though her own mind and spirit were so tired this new business made them ache and grow numb. "A lot of women are upset right now. Probably Mother is. Vinnie's scared to death; she'd like to grab Joey under one arm and Caleb under the other and go inland as far as Kansas, she's so terrified of submarines. That's what she feels, but what she thinks is—she's got to keep her chin up for Joey and Caleb, and make out that she believes Caleb when he says the Germans can't bomb us and no submarines'll come in as far as Matinicus Rock."

The arm-load of wood was getting unbelievably heavy. "Vinnie has nightmares, probably. From trying hard not to show anything. Marion's worried about her boys having to go, but she tries not to show it. So I imagine she doesn't sleep too well, either." She added, smiling faintly, "I woke up crying myself, last night, Mark. God only knows how much I've cried that I don't know about."

"Nils ought to come home," he said gruffly. "Eric's got a son-in-law who could help him. . . . You oughtn't be alone up there, Jo."

"Nils will come home when he can make it." She didn't see the sense of telling him she'd slept badly before December seventh; already he seemed to feel better to think Helmi wasn't the only one who cried nights. . . . Already he'd forgotten Nils.

"Then you think Helmi'll get over those spells?" he asked.

"As soon as she gets things straightened around in her mind, yes," said Joanna practically. "Let's go in, Mark. This armful of wood is getting to weigh a ton."

When they came in, Helmi got up and walked slowly toward them. "Hello, Joanna," she said in her low voice. "You were nice to come all the way down here."

There was nothing about this tall, unhurried girl to suggest crying in the night; nothing about her lucid green gaze to speak of nightmares, except, possibly, the new, faint, hollowing around her eyes.

There were a few more days before the boys came back from Portland. They were dreary days, spitting snow; night began early. But surprisingly they did not drag. Now it was Helmi and Mark Joanna thought about in the intervals when she was not thinking about the latest accounts of the Pearl Harbor bombing, and the news from the Philippines, and the islands that lay beyond. Everything was mixed up together in an odd chaotic fashion. . . . She thought of Nils too, remembering him every time she went out to the woodshed to bring in the wood he had cut at odd moments during the summer and fall, and brought out of the woods on a sled after the first good snowfall. He was before her as he had looked when she'd gone up to the cutting on the hill above Marshall Cove, taking coffee to him; the sun pouring down on his blond head and stripped, sweat-glistening, shoulders, the glint of sunlight on the swinging axe, the muscles, made powerful by years of hauling pots, moving smoothly under his skin. She could remember so many little details, the mist of perspiration on the fine blond hairs on his upper lip and on his eyebrows, and the surprising cool blue of his eyes; the way he sat on a stump drinking coffee, and laughing when a hornet scared her away from a raspberry thicket.

He was Nils then, she thought, meaning that he was the Nils he had always been, her friend who was better than a brother.

Then something would recall Mark and Helmi to her again. There was a strange foreign thing nagging at her when she thought of Helmi, and for a long time she couldn't isolate it from her other feelings. Then, one gunmetal morning toward the end of the week, she knew it for what it was.

Envy. She, Joanna Bennett, who had never wanted to be anyone else but Joanna Bennett, or have anything that another person had, envied Helmi. For she remembered too well how it had been to love a man with all her soul and body. If this war had come when she and Alec had been a year married, she would have cried in her sleep too, and clung to him as Helmi clung to Mark. . . . She would not have guessed, when Mark first brought Helmi home, what passion there was in the girl, what a capacity for loving. But now she knew, and now she envied.

Whatever agony Helmi was enduring, it was a token of life. And anything, even agony, would be better than this state where you felt neither dead nor alive. You didn't even want to cry, when here was all the solitude in the world to cry in, and no one to hear you. No one.

An hour later the boys came. She didn't know it, until she saw the *White Lady's* jigger mast swaying against the leaden sky; the boat was hidden by the boatshop, all but the masthead flying its tiny bright red flag. They would be coming up to the mooring, and they had made the harbor just in time. An evil wind from the northeast was raising its voice around the house, and the snow was flying faster and thicker. Already Brigport was blotted out; in another hour the Island would be indistinct, and the sea wiped out, except for the thunder of it.

She came out of her apathy and put more wood on the fire, set the teakettle over the blaze, and began to get a meal ready. Until this moment their enlistment hadn't seemed actual. But in another week, perhaps, they would be gone. *All over the country,* she thought, *women are realizing the same thing.*

They were a long time getting to the house. When she saw them coming through the gate the percolator was bubbling, the scent of bacon was racy in her nostrils, and the eggs were frying, slowly and delicately as her mother had taught her, in the big iron spider. She turned away from the window and set the table. Her hands were cold, and the plates clattered more than usual.

Finally she heard them at the back doorstep, and then they were coming in, making a good deal of noise in the entry. She heard Owen swearing, and Stevie shushing him; then Stevie himself came into the kitchen, with his cap on the back of his head, his dark eyes shining with his smile; he had a new white scarf tucked into his leather jacket, and against it his skin was as brown as a gypsy's, but a warm, ruddy brown.

He took her by the shoulders and kissed her, the smell of the cold still around him, snowflakes melting on his jacket; while he still held her, he whispered quickly against her ear.

"Take it easy, Jo. Owen's in a bad way. They took me and turned him down."

Owen was kicking off his boots in the entry; it sounded as if he were throwing them against the door. She said swiftly, "Why? Why didn't they take him?"

"Heart goes too fast, or something. . . . Tell you later. He's drunk as a coot, and ugly." He released her shoulders as Owen came into the room.

From the entry door he contemplated her and Stevie, his head lowered so that he looked up from under his brows. He steadied himself with a hand against the door casing. The fingers were gripping hard; the knuckles were white.

"Dinner ready?" he growled.

"As soon as you get washed up it'll be ready," Joanna promised him cheerfully. Inwardly she felt sick. Only once or twice had she ever seen Owen as drunk as he was at this moment. And this was not a joyous spree. That was what made it worse.

She hurried to get the eggs and bacon on the table, and poured the coffee. Stevie washed, and urged Owen toward the sink.

"Hurry up, Cap'n. You want to eat cold eggs?"

"To hell with the eggs!" Owen muttered. He went to the sink and stood looking down at the wash basin, rubbing his hand over his square, unshaven chin, swaying slightly. Joanna couldn't bear to look at him; there was a gaunt desolation about him that made her set her teeth hard and become very busy around the table.

Stevie had refilled the basin for him, and Owen stared down at the surface of the water, his black eyes fixed. "Ought to drown myself," he said indistinctly. "No damn' good. A Bennett, too. . . . Not good enough for the Navy. Owen Bennett, fisherman. . . . Stay where you are, you goddam bastard. Right on your own hunk of Island. Because you're not good enough to fight for it." He gripped the edge of the sink. "Why don't you jump overboard, Owen Bennett?"

Joanna reached out and touched Stevie's shoulder, without realizing she did it. She felt as though she could not stand another moment of this. Stevie winked at her, and pushed back his chair.

"Well, you can't drown yourself in that basin, by God!" he said easily. "You'd better wash yourself in it, and have your dinner. It's bacon and eggs. Finest kind."

Owen, still holding tight to the edge of the sink, turned his head and looked at the table. "Eggs?" he said thickly. "*Eggs!*" The brown of his face became greenish. He looked horribly sick. "Oh, my God!" he said, and plunged toward the door.

Stevie sighed. "Keep my dinner warm," he directed Joanna, and followed Owen without hurrying.

She put the food into the oven, and poured out a cup of coffee for herself. Her own stomach shrank, quivering, from food. She was annoyed that she should be so upset; in the old days she would have taken it in her stride. But somehow everything was different now — so different that it frightened her. Once, to see Owen so drunk, no matter what the reason, would have disgusted her; she would have despised both him and his weakness. Today she felt a pity for him that made her ache. It was too much, having to worry about Mark and Helmi, and feeling pity for Owen. No one ever worried about her, or pitied her—not that she wanted it! She must never let herself get so weak as to want pity.

She spoke briskly to Stevie when he came in again. "Where is Owen?"

"I bedded him down in the shop." Stevie washed again and sat down to his re-warmed dinner.

"He should be in his own room," Joanna said.

"Nope. He's sick as a horse, and the shop's easier to clean up than a bedroom." Stevie looked tired. "Poor cuss. When they turned him down it just about knocked the tar out of him. Then I didn't know if I could get him back home again. He set out just as tight as he could go to join the Merchant Marine."

Joanna sat down opposite him and rested her chin in her hands. "But what's the *matter* with him, Stevie? Owen's always been so healthy."

"At first I was kind of worried," Stevie admitted candidly. "I thought maybe—well, you know what could happen to a guy who's been raising hell for five or six years. Sometimes he isn't as careful as he ought to be."

Joanna felt a cold emptiness where her stomach should have been. Stevie took a mouthful of food and went on. "So I asked around, and finally got a chance to speak to the doctor and ask him . . . said my brother wouldn't tell me, and was it anything we ought to take care of. He was a nice fellow, gray-haired, gold braid. . . . He told me it wasn't anything too bad. Owen's pulse just sort of gallops when he gets excited."

"What do we do about it?" Joanna said. "Will it get worse?"

"It shouldn't, the doctor said. But he says Owen's high-strung, and living wild didn't do him any good. Then that pneumonia . . ." Stevie shook his head. "Anyway, he's going to be damn' hard to live with for a while. I'm sorry for you, Jo."

She returned his affectionate smile, her mouth steady. "When do you have to go?"

"They've given me a week to get my traps in and haul up my boat. Then I have another going-over in Boston, but there won't be any hitch about that. Doc said I was tops in everything."

"I'm glad of that, Stevie. . . . I'll miss having you to talk to, though." It was the nearest thing to an admission of weakness that she could make.

"Golly, Nils'll be back before I'm gone, probably. . . . Any dessert, Jo?"

"Devil's food cake." She set it before him with a ceremonious flourish. "Cut your own, as big as you want it. I'll get you more coffee." She went over to the stove and paused, her hand on the handle of the coffeepot. She looked back at Stevie, who was cutting the cake with the same happy absorption with which he'd painted his toy boats, when he was six. He still had those long black eyelashes that he'd tried to cut off with the scissors once—and they'd only grown thicker.

In a week Stevie would be going to war, and she would be alone with Owen. Unless Nils came back, as Stevie said. But Stevie didn't know that Nils had left her; that she was a woman without a husband. When he found it out, as of course he must, he would be away from home, perhaps in foreign waters, and someone's letter would tell him. And perhaps, out of them all, Stevie would be the one who wouldn't blame her.

32

IN THE LATE AFTERNOON of the day before Stevie was to leave, he borrowed the *White Lady* and went to Brigport for Ellen. It meant she would lose one day of school before the weekend really began, but Stevie was set on having her home, and Joanna consented. It would be a dull enough leave-taking for him anyway, with Owen either drunk or sullenly furious, and Mark, who would ordinarily be in and out of the house, staying away because of the unfinished situation between him and Owen.

Ellen walked up from the harbor alone; Stevie had stopped to talk to Jud.

"Hello, darling," Joanna said. She gave Ellen a swift, hard hug and a kiss, cherishing the feel of the slim, strong little body in her arms.

"Hello, Mother." Ellen hugged her back. But there was an anxious, strained quality about her smile. Joanna helped her off with the heavy ski suit, which Ellen usually took off alone, and made no comment on the child's lack of sparkle. She established her at the table with a cup of hot cocoa.

"That'll hold you till supper time, I should think," she said and went on peeling apples for a pandowdy. If Ellen wanted to talk, she would talk; no sense to question her about anything, even her spelling paper, until she wanted to answer. It could be almost anything that had bothered her. A touch of seasickness — it was a bright, windy day, the water was choppy, and the *White Lady* bucked and plunged sometimes like a wild horse between Brigport and Bennett's. The little *Elaine* was steadier, but she was on the beach now, for the duration.

Or it could be Stevie's going that saddened her. No one knew what thoughts moved in endless procession through a child's head;

and what fears and terrors of the war lay under Ellen's yellow crown, Joanna could only imagine, and not hope to find out.

Or—and the thought made Joanna's hand heavy and slow with the knife—she'd set her heart on seeing Nils. Joanna felt a surge of resentment against him; for what was she to say to Ellen about him? She glanced at her daughter now; Ellen was gazing remotely into space, her cocoa untouched, her mouth pale and tight-lipped in her small face.

There was a clatter at the door of the shed, and Owen came in. He'd been working out in the barn; working and drinking—the lobster smack had come that day, and Richards had brought him some liquor he'd ordered. Joanna stared across the kitchen at him, in pity blended with exasperation. He *would* have to come in now. . . . But he didn't see her. He was looking at Ellen, who gazed back at him somberly.

"Hello, Owen," she said. Owen didn't answer. He looked at her scowlingly, almost as if he were trying to see past some obstacle; then, without a word to her or Joanna, he walked across the kitchen and into the sitting room. They heard his slow, heavy step on the stairs. At the top, he stumbled.

Life came into Ellen's face. "Mother, Owen's sick!" she cried out. "He didn't see me very good, and he walks funny."

"He'll be all right after he's slept a while," Joanna said.

"Poor Owen," Ellen sighed. She began to drink her cocoa.

The sun slid into the sea, leaving a trail of red and gold on the sky behind the black saw-toothed spruces; the meadow became a pool of shadow that grew deeper by the moment. The evening star shone out from the wash of pure turquoise that spread above the fading sunset, and it was time to light the lamps in the house, and draw the shades.

Joanna and Stevie and Ellen ate supper together; Owen didn't come down again, and Joanna was relieved. Stevie's last evening might be dull, but at least it could be pleasant—as pleasant as she could make it.

After supper, while Joanna washed the dishes and Ellen wiped them, Stevie smoked and talked. He was in a cheerfully expectant mood; he was the only one of them who didn't have something on his mind, Joanna thought. Even Ellen was deeply intent on her own affairs; she wiped the dishes in silence, her face shadowed.

But it was Ellen who, pulling back the shades to look out at the stars which clustered so thickly over the Island tonight, saw the flashlight moving up the path to the house. "Company coming," she announced. "We better hurry with the dishes." A faint sparkle came back into her face.

"Caleb and Vinnie, probably. Or Jud and Marion." Joanna stacked the dishes away. Ellen hurried through the last of the silver. "I'd better start a fire in the sitting room," Stevie said lazily, and went into the other room.

Whoever owned the flashlight didn't knock at the outside door, but came straight through the entry into the kitchen. It was Mark and Helmi.

"Thought we'd walk up for a little visit," Mark explained quickly, as Joanna overcame her first swift astonishment. It was the first time Mark had been inside the kitchen since the trouble he'd had with Owen; and the first time he and Helmi had come to the house to call.

Joanna moved forward, holding out her hands for Helmi's things. "Well, I'm glad you came up! This is wonderful." Helmi, smiling, pulled off her kerchief; her silvery-blonde hair made Ellen's look dark in contrast. She spoke directly to the child.

"You here, Ellen? This is nice." Her voice was warm and honest. Stevie had come out of the sitting room by then, he and Mark were talking; but Joanna hadn't missed Mark's narrowed, keen glance around the room.

"Owen's asleep," she said smoothly.

"He's sick," added Ellen. Mark looked down at her, his dark face somber. But only for a moment.

"Okay. I see," he said, and went to sit down and stretch his legs out to the fire. Joanna turned to Helmi.

"Let's go into the sitting room and leave the men to their own company." She caught sight of Ellen beyond Helmi's elbow, and glanced at the clock. "You're up late, Ellen. I tell you what. You go in with Helmi and keep her company while I put your lamp in your room and light the stove."

The cool silence of the upper floors she met gratefully. There was no way of heating this part of the house, except by the small portable oil stoves; but tonight she didn't find it too cold. And it was so bless-edly quiet. . . . She was glad Mark and Helmi had come up, she told herself; but she knew how desperately tired she would be at the end of the evening. If only Helmi would carry along the conversation some-times . . .

Carrying Ellen's lamp, she tiptoed past Owen's closed door, and then halted for a moment to listen for his heavy breathing. When she heard it, she was reassured. He wasn't waking up, then. . . . She walked down the hall in a circle of yellow light; the lamp in her hand bathed her in radiance, and yet found odd hollows and shadows in her face.

In Ellen's little room, which had once been hers, she lighted the small round oil heater, and turned back the bedclothes; she laid Ellen's flannel pajamas over the back of a squat red-painted chair, near enough to be warmed by the stove, not close enough for danger. The teddy bear which Stephen Bennett had given to his granddaughter on her second birthday was already tucked under his share of the covers; he looked at Joanna with his shiny, wistful, shoebutton eyes as she went by the foot of the small bed and stopped by the window.

The ceiling slanted, and one had to kneel to be able to see, really, from the window. Joanna knelt now, and looked out at the Island in the winter night. The stars looked back at her, a thick and glitter-ing throng. A feeling of nostalgia came over her, almost too strong to bear. It made her lean her head forward until her brow was against the cold pane. *Do I really want to go back?* she thought. *Do I really want it to be as if nothing had happened?* Alec and Ellen would have to be wiped out then; and Nils, as he had been in the last year. If she could go back, she would have Nils as she'd had him once, when they had been comrades with never an instant of doubt between them.

But how could she wish Alec had never come to Bennett's Island, or that she did not have Ellen? . . . She rose from her knees, and turning, met the pathetic gaze of the teddy bear.

When she went downstairs again, Ellen was kneeling on the floor in front of the sitting room stove, her small face uplifted and rapt. Helmi was leaning forward in her chair, speaking in a low voice. There were more color and laughter in her voice than Joanna had ever heard before.

She sat down near the door and listened. Helmi was telling Ellen a story; it was about herself, when she was a little girl. Strange to think of Helmi as a child. It seemed as if there were never a time when she was not tall and birch-slender, and curiously remote from those around her, even from her husband.

Except, Joanna remembered involuntarily, when she cried in her sleep, and turned to Mark, sobbing, to put her arms around his neck. . . .

The story was finished. Helmi leaned her fair head against the back of her chair and said, "That's all, Ellen."

Ellen drew a long breath. "Tell me some more."

"No," said Helmi. "Not tonight. It's your bedtime now."

Ellen got to her feet, and came to Joanna. Her blue-gray eyes looked dark and big.

"Did you hear it, Mother? Wasn't it a good story?"

"The best in a long time, dear." She put her arm around Ellen and held her close to her side for a moment. "Now say goodnight to Helmi and go up to bed. I'll come in a few minutes."

Ellen took her grave departure of both Helmi, and her uncles, in the kitchen. Joanna heard her going up the stairs, walking carefully, quietly.

"Ellen has something on her mind tonight," Helmi said. "That was why I told her the story. But whatever it was, it came back to her after the story was finished."

"I think it's something to do with Stevie," Joanna answered. "I'll see if I can find out, when I go up." She took her knitting bag and moved nearer to Helmi and the stove. Now the evening was about to begin; already her leg muscles were crawling with nervousness, and the palms of her hands were sweaty. From now to bedtime looked as long as a year.

When she went upstairs again, Ellen was already in bed, her clothes folded neatly on the short red chair, Teddy snuggled in the crook of her arm. Her eyes looked enormous, and her cheeks were pale. *She could be coming down with something,* Joanna thought doubtfully. She laid her hand on Ellen's forehead, but it was moist and cool.

She sat down on the edge of the bed and smiled at her daughter. "Did you know Stevie is going to send you a picture of him, in his uniform, for your own? To have up here in your room?"

"Is he?" said Ellen politely.

This would get them nowhere. Joanna asked directly, "Is something wrong, Ellen?"

Ellen turned her head uneasily on the pillow, and looked down at the teddy bear's head. "No, Mother . . ."

"Bad spelling papers? I used to have them too, Ellen."

She waited. Again that small, courteous voice. "No, Mother . . . Is Stevie going early in the morning?"

So it was Stevie after all. Joanna felt a pleasant loosening of tension in her chest. She'd been half-afraid Ellen was going to ask her if Nils would be home for Christmas. . . . She must figure out an answer to the question, and have it ready. But for tonight, anyway, she was safe. She leaned over and kissed Ellen.

"He's going on the mailboat, so you'll be up in time to see him. Won't you be glad to have a picture of him, Ellen?"

"Yes, Mother," said Ellen. Joanna turned off the oil heater; then, on an impulse, she went back and kissed Ellen again. This time Ellen's arms came up around her neck in a fierce, tight hug. "Mother—"

At the same instant Joanna heard Owen's door open, down the hall. The sound rang in her brain like an alarm bell. She laid Ellen back on the bed, careful to speak easily, "There's Owen. He may want something—I'd better go see."

Ellen said nothing. Her big eyes remained on her mother's face as Joanna fixed the covers with a hasty automatic gesture. "Goodnight, dear." Joanna took the lamp from the chest of drawers and went out of the room, closing the door behind her.

Owen stood at the head of the stairs, one hand on the newel post, his black head bent. He was listening. . . . Joanna went toward him with the lamp, moistening her lips. She'd get him back in his room before he realized Mark was down there, or Helmi—he was in the mood to be ugly—

She spoke casually. "Owen, go back and take it easy, and I'll bring you up some coffee."

"The hell with you," said Owen, just as casually. "If I want coffee I'll go downstairs and get it."

He started down the stairs, and there was nothing for her to do but follow him. He went slowly, his hand on the banister. Joanna, watching his leisurely descent in the light from the lamp, stared at the back of his head and knew with a sick certainty what awaited at the foot of the stairs.

If there's trouble, her mind said evenly, *I'll pitch this lamp into the midst of it and walk out of the house.*

He went into the sitting room, where Helmi looked up at him from a magazine, calmly. Joanna held her breath; but Owen merely glanced at Helmi, and continued to the kitchen.

In the doorway Joanna stopped. She remembered the lighted lamp in her hand and blew it out; she was still behind Owen, but over his plaid shoulder she watched Mark and saw the instant immobility of his features. He was still sprawled comfortably before the stove, his feet on the oven hearth; but she had the impression that he had tightened in every cord and muscle.

Don't say anything, Mark! she begged him wordlessly, and by some miracle, not even the expression of his face changed. It was a long moment, while Owen stood motionless by the table, and Mark regarded him. Then Owen walked toward the woodshed door.

When it had shut behind him, Joanna realized that the hand holding Ellen's lamp was trembling. She put the lamp on the shelf, and took a drink of water to moisten her dry throat. Behind her she heard someone's thumbnail scratch a match into flame. Stevie said normally, "Here, have one, Mark."

When she turned around, both boys were lighting cigarettes, and from the sitting room came the sound of a magazine leaf turning gently. It was as if Owen had not appeared at all. . . . But there was a noise of hammering in the barn.

"He building pots at this time of night?" Mark said.

"The other night he got up at midnight and went to work out there," said Stevie.

"Sounds like one of those Nils tricks," Mark observed dryly. "What's the matter with him?"

Stevie shrugged. "I told you he was taking it hard, because the Navy turned him down."

"I didn't know it was *that* hard." Mark looked at the door into the shed through a cloud of cigarette smoke, his dark eyes thoughtful.

"It's been pretty awful," Joanna said. "I've never been so sorry for anyone in my life. It was a terrible shock to him." She felt like talking, now that the moment of dreadful strain was past. "He just can't get used to the idea that a Bennett couldn't pass the physical."

"Whatever is wrong with him, it won't kill him, will it?"

"No," Stevie answered. "But it's just as hard on him as if they'd told him he had only six months to live." He studied the burning tip of his cigarette, his dark face somber. "Poor devil. Any of the rest of us could take it better than Owen."

"I couldn't take it," said Mark abruptly, and stood up. There was almost a savagery in his face. "When I — *if* I go, and they turn me down, I'll pull the damn' place apart around their ears." He lifted the stovelid with a clatter, and threw his cigarette into the fire. Without another word he turned and went toward the shed door.

The latch clicked behind him, and Stevie and Joanna looked at each other. Joanna leaned weakly against the dresser; Stevie lifted an eloquent eyebrow. "I'll wait five minutes. Then if Mark doesn't come flying head first through that door, I'll go out and join the friendly congregation."

He winked, and Joanna managed to wink back at him. She went into the sitting room. Helmi greeted her tranquilly. "Well?"

"Everything's fine," said Joanna, and hoped with all her heart that it was so. If only Mark and Owen could be friends again, so she need not have that on her mind any longer. . . . It would be nice if they could make comrades of each other, as Mark and Stevie had done. Owen would get over his disappointment quicker, and perhaps Mark wouldn't miss Stevie so much. . . . *I didn't know Mark could be so sympathetic,* she thought.

Then she remembered what he'd said; his barely perceptible hesitation, and correction. "When I — *if* I go. . . ." Mark wanted to go; he wanted badly to go, she had seen it in his face. She looked across at Mark's wife, sitting so quietly, her head bent over her magazine so that Joanna couldn't see her face. He hair fell forward past her cheeks, fine and silky, shimmering in the lamplight.

I wonder if she'll let him go, Joanna thought, and realized that she intended to find out.

She heard the shed door closing, and knew Stevie had gone out to join the others in the barn. Her eyes moved swiftly around the sitting room, a new sparkle in them, looking for an excuse to take her and Helmi outdoors. It was easier to talk in the dark, under the stars; easier to say things you would never say in daylight or lamplight.

33

THE EXCUSE WAS A BOOK she wanted to return to Nora Fennell. Helmi agreed to go with her; they put on their coats and mittens, and went out. Directly the door shut behind them, they were alone in the winter night. The pure dry cold burned in their throats when they breathed, and the stars blazed with a dartling white fire.

Joanna had brought along a flashlight, but after a few moments they didn't need it. The slantwise path that sloped gently across the meadow toward the woods was well-defined under their feet, and metal-hard with frost. . . . They didn't speak at first. To Joanna, if she had not always been so conscious of the sea, they might have been on some clear, wide, inland space, the night was so still.

What had been the house was now merely a house-shaped blackness on the rise, stamping out the stars with its roof and chimneys; it was printed with tawny rectangles of lamplight, but they didn't give the house substance. The woods towards which Joanna and Helmi walked made a towering wall of more blackness, notched sharply against the sky. It appeared such a solid wall it seemed impossible to think of walking through it; and yet, here was where the meadow ended and the woods began, and already Joanna and Helmi were walking under the tall old spruces.

Now you saw the stars through shaggy boughs, or perched crazily on the tops like Christmas-tree ornaments. Christmas was too near, Joanna thought with a little shiver of dread. . . . Aloud she said, "I read a creepy story once about a man who had a crazy spell whenever he found himself in a certain combination of a cold night, stars, and pine trees. For a long time whenever I walked through here I was thankful these were all spruces."

"Do you think you'd have a crazy spell, too?" asked Helmi.

"Well, I figured you never can tell what's in your background. Maybe one of my ancestors thought he was a wolf too, and handed on the memory. That's what the story was about."

"Was the man a Finn?"

Joanna laughed. "His ancestors were Vikings."

"I only asked," explained Helmi indifferently, "because some people think Finns have crazy spells." They had reached the apple orchard; there was a faint glow of starlight among the small, gnarled trees, and at the far end of the orchard the cemetery gateposts glimmered. Helmi stopped. "Did you ever feel scared to go near the cemetery at night?"

Joanna stopped too. The silence had that peculiar hushed quality she'd noticed about Island silences. A waiting stillness, in which her voice sounded clear. "No. I was never nervous about the cemetery. Not even after—"

"Not even after your first husband died?" said Helmi.

"Not even then," said Joanna. *So you believe in being direct, my girl,* she thought, without anger at Helmi's bluntness, but rather with relief. *That will make it easier for me.*

She placed her back comfortably against the nearest apple tree's trunk. She could see Helmi quite clearly now in the starlight. They'd come without kerchiefs, and Helmi's hair had a pale sheen.

"I've been thinking about Alec lately," she said slowly. "You see, when I'd been married to him a year—as long as you've been married to Mark—I was about your age. And I've been wondering how I'd have felt if a war had come along then. Whether I'd have been very patriotic about sending him off."

"You probably would have been very brave," Helmi murmured.

"Oh, I don't know." Joanna leaned her head back against the rough trunk, and looked for Andromeda through the bare, twisted boughs. A flock of memories were whirling through her head, like a flock of blackbirds, and Alec was stronger before her than he had been for a long time. Those winter nights when sleep itself had been the essence of delight because she shared it with Alec. . . . She said, half to herself, "I might have been brave enough in the daytime. But I don't know about the nights. I was—crazy about him, Helmi. So I know what it is to be so wrapped up in a man you can be perfectly happy just looking at the back of his neck, or one of his eyebrows."

Helmi was looking up at the sky too. "Nils has a good neck to look at," she said in an impersonal tone. "Nice eyebrows, too."

Joanna's fingers curled inside her mittens. She didn't want Nils brought into the conversation, least of all in that remote way of Helmi's that was so hard to fathom. Nils had nothing at all to do with this.

"Oh, *Nils.*" She made her manner light. "Nils and I are old compared to you, Helmi. We're in our thirties. We're — well, settled down. But you and Mark — "

"Mark," said Helmi quietly, "could go and enlist tomorrow, if he wants to. That's what you're trying to find out, isn't it?"

No need to fumble now. Joanna straightened up. "He'd go, too — if he wasn't worried about you."

"Why should he worry about me?"

"Because — " Joanna hesitated. She sensed that Helmi was like herself in one particular — she would resent her husband's discussing her with any other person. She groped for something to say, and then Helmi said it.

"Joanna," she asked slowly, "did he say I cried in the night?"

"He only told me because he was so upset, Helmi. It frightened him. I know he wouldn't have mentioned it if he — "

Helmi drove her hands deep into her pockets in a fierce gesture. There was a sort of suppressed fury in her voice. "He didn't have to be worried. It was only once. That Sunday night, after the news came."

Joanna said gently, and with pity: "When he told me, it had been every night for almost a week, Helmi."

She hated having to say it. The girl was so jealous of her privacy, so locked within herself, this must be terrible for her. But say it she must. . . . "That's why he was scared. You can't really blame him, Helmi. He's afraid you can't get along without him . . . after the way you held on to him — you're the only one who can tell him it's all right."

There was no immediate answer. It seemed like a long time, the waiting. The cold began to creep through the soles of her shoes. It nipped her ears, too. *I shouldn't have told her all he said,* she thought. But it would clear away the strain between them. She was confident of that.

"He said—I held on to him in my sleep?" It was a blind voice, feeling its way.

"Yes," said Joanna.

Helmi turned sharply, and began to run, up through the orchard, her feet ringing on the frozen ground. It was so sudden that at first Joanna couldn't move. Then she ran after her, and caught up with her at the cemetery gate. "Helmi, it's nothing to take on about," she said.

It was as silent and swift as the way snow begins to fall, the way Helmi cried. She didn't put her hands to her face, she merely turned her head away from Joanna. "And I thought it was a dream," she said harshly. "All this time I thought it was a dream, and that I could keep on dreaming it after Mark went."

"You thought it was a dream that Mark held you, and you held him?" Joanna's head felt thick with bewilderment.

"Not Mark!" the girl said fiercely. "I don't want Mark! I didn't ever want him! I wanted—" She caught her breath in a gasp that was like a sound of pain.

Joanna felt the coldness of shock settle over her. Her numbness made it possible for her to speak so evenly. "You wanted—"

"Stevie," said Helmi. "The first time he came in the library. It was always Stevie . . . but it was Mark who liked me and talked to me . . . and said all the things I wanted Stevie to say. Only Stevie wouldn't have said them like that."

"Then why did you marry Mark?" asked Joanna.

"They were coming out here and I knew I wouldn't see Stevie again." As quickly and easily as the tears had come, her words came out; and Joanna realized, in that moment, that all Helmi's poise and quiet manner had not been the stillness of repose, but the instinctive freezing of a wild spirit which hopes to be unseen, and knows that any move, however slight, will show its hiding place.

"I know now how crazy I was, Joanna. I'm crazy now to tell you this. But you know half of it already. . . . You remember the night when Owen kissed me, and I ran out? That was a foolish thing to do, but I couldn't help it. Do you know," she said wonderingly, "that Stevie kissed me once? After the wedding. Then I used to think how it would be if he kissed me as if—as Mark does. The night Owen kissed me, I couldn't bear it. Because I thought at that moment: *What if this was Stevie?*"

Joanna leaned against the cemetery gatepost. She was, for once, hopelessly mute. Helmi was wiping her tears away with her mitten, and her voice was natural again.

"Do you think I'm a bad woman, Joanna?"

"No," said Joanna truthfully. "And I can see how you love Stevie so much. But you know you've done something wrong, don't you? I pity Mark. Where does he come in?"

"He thinks I'm a good wife," Helmi said. "It makes him happy—even though he's worried—to think I can't live without him." She moved around until she could face Joanna squarely. "Are you going to hate me for this? I couldn't help loving Stevie. And he didn't know, and I couldn't make him know, and when I knew he was going away I thought I would die if I didn't see him again. So when Mark asked me to marry him . . ." The desperation began to creep back again. "Then when we came here, I wanted to die. Those first few weeks . . . to be Mark's wife, always pretending, and to see Stevie all day long, and not be able to touch him, and the way he looked at me, so sweet and friendly, like a brother. I knew then what a terrible thing I'd done. So I made up my mind that when he was through working every day down at the Eastern End, it would be all over. I would be a good wife and not think of him again."

Her voice held an ironical little smile. "I was doing all right until the Japs bombed Pearl Harbor. And he came down that night to say he was going to enlist. . . . So now you know all about me, Joanna."

"Not all," said Joanna. "I don't know what you're going to do next. What do you *want* to do? Tell Mark and Stevie?"

"No," said Helmi instantly. "I never intended to tell them. Stevie would be embarrassed. He would feel awful, as if I'd made a fool of him." She spoke tenderly. "He's so innocent, Joanna. He sees me as his sister. Imagine what he'd think if I told him all this. . . . And there's no sense in hurting Mark."

"Then what are you going to do?"

"Nothing." Helmi shrugged. "Go back to the house. Be a good wife."

Joanna gave way to an impulse and put her arm around the girl's rigid shoulders. "Helmi, I'm sorry. Believe me. It's hell to love anybody like that, and never be able to tell him."

"Every time I see you with Nils, it's a double hell for me," Helmi answered with a quiet bitterness. "Because you can tell him you love him whenever you please, and you can see it in his eyes, what he thinks of you. When you tell him, you get an answer. Joanna, a woman like you is the richest woman in the world."

"*No.*" Joanna's lips formed the word, but she caught herself before she said it aloud. Helmi, after stabbing herself, must turn and stab her. Only she didn't know what she was doing. . . .

All Joanna could think of was to move. She began to walk down through the orchard, keeping her arm around Helmi's shoulders. She was so cold she thought she would never be warm again.

"How can you keep apart so long?" Helmi asked her, wonderingly. "How can he let his uncle's boat keep him away from you? Joanna, I would go in tomorrow and go up to Camden, and walk into that boatshop and say, 'I love you, Nils.' Like that." Her voice was shaking. "Just to remind me that I could say it whenever I wanted to."

"Helmi, don't talk like that, or you'll be crying again, before we get back to the house. . . . And I don't think we'll go to Nora's tonight."

"I'm through talking," said Helmi. "And I will never hurt Mark. I promise you that."

They walked under the great spruces with the stars perched on the ends of the boughs, and found the slanting path across the meadow. Their feet made a swift, crisp sound on the frozen earth. They didn't stop or speak until they were just below the house, so near that it began to look like a house instead of a long dark blot against the sky; they could see a faint starshine on the white clapboards, and hear one of the boys laughing in the kitchen, where lamplight streamed down the slope and touched their faces.

"You know, Joanna," Helmi said diffidently, "it's a little easier now. Because I could say it aloud, I think. Now I have more courage."

"I'm glad," Joanna said, and that was all, because her throat was beginning to ache, the familiar tight throbbing that came from wanting suddenly to cry. But she reached for Helmi's cold hand and held it tight in her own the rest of the way to the house.

*   *   *

Stevie didn't want them all to go to Brigport with him to meet the mailboat. Owen would take him over in the *White Lady*, since Mark had to go early to haul. The good-byes were said in the kitchen, while outside the house a raw, brilliant day was boisterous with wind and sea, alive with color and a piercing cold. Mark and Helmi had come up, Ellen hadn't developed measles or chicken pox during the night, Owen was shaved and reasonably sober, and not too savage.

There was a moment when Mark and Helmi came in, when Joanna's eyes met Helmi's, but did not linger. There must be no trace or mention of last night—even though Joanna had slept in restless, dream-beset snatches after she'd gone to bed.

Everybody had a final cup of coffee with Stevie, and then it was time to go. Owen shrugged into his jacket, and tossed Stevie's to him. "Come on, Steve. Don't drag it out. You'll probably get stationed in Portsmouth and be home every two weeks."

"Oh, that would be nice!" said Ellen. Stevie lifted his niece off the floor to hug her hard. "Don't forget my picture," she reminded him.

"You bet I won't," Stevie promised. He put on his jacket and zipped it up, looked around for his cap and gloves. Joanna held them out to him, and found herself caught tightly in his arms. "Behave yourself now, kid," he said. "And if Nils wants to sign up, tell him to just mention my name. I'll probably be Chief Petty Officer in another month."

Laughing, his thin dark face vivid with excitement, he kissed her soundly. Then, releasing her, he went to Helmi. "Here's my other sister," he said, and before she could save herself he had her in his arms.

She held her head down, she put her hands against his chest to push. "Oh, kiss the guy!" said Mark impatiently. "He's in a hurry."

The pain began again in Joanna's throat when she saw Stevie's brown fingers take Helmi's chin and tilt her head up so that her shining hair fell back from her lifted face. Her own muscles ached as Helmi's must have ached in that torturous effort to stand there, to keep from putting her arms around Stevie's neck and clinging to him as she had dreamed of doing.

It was only an instant—too quick an instant for Helmi's face to stop being a mask. Then Stevie kissed her with a brisk, unromantic, brotherly kiss, and let her go.

She said, "Best of luck, Stevie. And when Mark goes, can he mention your name, too?"

"You bet. Just say, 'Hey, Steve Bennett sent me,' and they'll give him the works."

At last he was gone, still smiling. The first one to go, but not the last. . . . Joanna watched from the window, as the three brothers went down to the harbor. When at last she turned back to the room, Helmi was tying her kerchief under her chin.

"Don't hurry," Joanna said.

Helmi shook her head. "I want to do some housecleaning," she explained gravely.

Ellen said wistfully, "Can't you tell me another story about when you were little, before you go?"

It was Joanna who answered her. "Helmi hasn't time today, dear."

"After today," said Helmi, "I will have plenty of time." She smiled at Ellen quickly, and went out.

34

ELLEN LAPSED INTO HER THOUGHTFUL MOOD as soon as the excitement died down; and Joanna, watching the child wander through the rooms like a disconsolate little ghost, felt chilled and sad herself. But she didn't show it, nor did she hector Ellen with questions. Besides, there was no need to ask. She had asked her last night, and been satisfied that Ellen hated to have Stevie go away.

She left Ellen by herself in the sitting room, kneeling in a chair pulled up to the harbor-side windows; elbows on the sill, chin in her hands, Ellen gazed steadily down across the meadow to the shore, where the *Elaine* rested in her cradle. In mid-harbor the *Donna* lay restlessly at her mooring, her masts bobbing against the sky.

Joanna fixed two of Ellen's favorite dishes for dinner. Neither one, and more particularly the creamed toast brightened with slices of hard-cooked egg, filled her with enthusiasm; but this concoction, with chocolate custard for dessert, never failed to cause an ecstatic excitement in Ellen. She had it rarely, because it was not a meal to serve when the men were home. Sometimes food worked miracles; perhaps by the time Ellen leaned back, pink-cheeked and replete, from her first custard, she would already be over the worst part of missing Stevie, and would be looking forward to receiving his first letter, and his picture.

Joanna set the table with a bright cloth and napkins, and the flowered dishes the other women in the sardine factory had given her when she married Nils. Ellen loved those dishes. Joanna used them seldom. Though she had been touched by the gesture, she didn't like to think back too often to the five years when she'd worked in the sardine factory at Pruitt's Harbor, making a living for herself and Ellen; she'd begrudged every moment of those years, for they had kept her away from the Island. Then Nils had come home; and because of that, she had come home too. . . .

Nils made it possible for me to come back, she thought, as she laid the plates for her and Ellen. *Now I'm here and he's gone.* The sound of it was wrong. But it was like the storm that blew up after they'd bought Grant's point; she'd had that foolish sense of guilt, and there was no need of it. There was no need of guilt now. She called Ellen to dinner, her voice crisper than she meant it to be.

Ellen didn't answer, and Joanna went to the doorway of the sitting room. Ellen still knelt like a small statue in the chair. She didn't turn her head toward her mother.

"What are you looking at, dear?" Joanna asked her finally.

"I was watching for Owen," Ellen said.

"He won't be home for dinner, Ellen. It's just you and I today. Owen was going to haul as soon as the mailboat left."

Ellen looked over her shoulder at Joanna. Her narrow-boned face seemed smaller and paler than ever, and Joanna wanted all at once to sit down and rock her and sing to her, as she'd done when Ellen was a baby. But Ellen was almost nine now; and besides, she had her own young dignity.

"If somebody was on the mailboat to come over here, Owen would bring them, wouldn't he?"

"I suppose so," said Joanna. "But then Owen would have been back long ago. Come to dinner, Ellen. It's special."

Ellen got out of the chair slowly, rubbing her cramped and reddened knees. "I thought maybe Nils would come today," she said. She walked by Joanna into the kitchen; and Joanna, looking after the slight straight figure with the blonde braids, had the bewildering and painful sensation that Ellen was more Nils' daughter than hers.

Ellen put her apron on over her brief pleated skirt and white blouse, washed her hands, and slid into her chair. "That's nice," she said politely, as Joanna set her steaming plate before her. "But I don't feel like eating any dinner, Mother."

"But you always like this, darling!" Joanna said. "Is your throat sore? Do you feel sick?" Then, before the sheer despair in Ellen's colorless face, her heart quailed. "Ellen, what is it?"

"I'm not going back to Brigport," Ellen said, "till Nils comes home . . . and maybe not then."

Joanna sat down in the low rocker. "Come here, Ellen," she said. The child came to her, her young composure broken. Her lips were beginning to quiver. Joanna pulled her gently into her lap and began to rock, slowly. "Now tell me, Ellen," she commanded, keeping her voice easy and sure of itself, though inside she was trembling.

She knew too well why Ellen didn't want to go back. It didn't take gossip long to reach the schoolyard. Something had been said about Nils' staying away so long; some cruel jibe flung at Ellen — God alone knew what those older children could say and do. Joanna had been a little girl once herself; she had come home just as bewildered and afraid, trying hard to tell what bothered her, yet sensing that there was something shameful and bad about the remark that had been made, the word written out in the sandy schoolyard and erased quickly as the teacher approached.

I'll teach Ellen myself before I'll let her go back, she promised herself in a wild fury. *They shan't tell her those things,; they shan't touch her.* . . . A new idea sickened and chilled her. "Ellen, has anyone slapped you, or — tried to hurt you?"

"No, nobody touched me," Ellen said. "Only I wish Nils would come. He'd go over there and tell all those kids —" She stopped.

"Tell them what?" Joanna urged.

"That he never killed Winslow Fowler and then threw him overboard!" It was out, in a weeping rush, and Ellen's face was burrowing into Joanna's neck, her tears were soaking Joanna's collar. She held to her mother with a wild, frantic strength, and Joanna hugged her close. She didn't try to soothe her. Ellen would have to cry it out, the shock and anxiety she'd been carrying by herself for so long. It had been a tremendous burden for such a small person.

Over Ellen's head and the sound of her crying, Joanna's mind raced back to the day when Nils had told her and the boys at dinner about finding the *Janet F.* She saw him towing the empty boat back to Brigport; the men standing awkwardly silent on the wharf as Randolph Fowler came down to look into the empty cockpit and then at Nils, and realized his son was really gone.

Ellen was quieter now, but Joanna's arms tightened around her. So this was what Fowler had done, when he could think of nothing else. He'd talked, he'd cast suspicion with a word; her mind said it, shuddering—the word was *murder*.

But how could anyone on Brigport believe it? It was so impossible that for a moment she felt almost like laughing at the absurdity of it. And then, with an intolerable sensation of dread, she knew that people did believe such things—even of men like Nils.

She wondered with a morbid fascination when the idea had come into Randolph's mind that Nils had killed Winslow; or perhaps he didn't really believe it, perhaps he had seen a new weapon to use against the people of Bennett's Island. That was worse, for then he wasn't a man—he was a devil, if he could use his boy's death like this.

Joanna looked around at her familiar kitchen, at the food growing cold on the table, the teakettle steaming, the pendulum swinging in the clock on the shelf; now they had all grown strange under the shadow of a new thing, a new word. Brigport was whispering the word; it hadn't yet become loud enough for the other islands to hear. But if it had reached the schoolyard, how long would it be before the whisper became a cry? A cry that would go the whole ragged stretch of the Maine coast—Nils Sorensen had killed a man and thrown him overboard.

Her arms were so tight around Ellen now that the child stirred against her. "Don't, Mother! You're hurting me!"

"I'm sorry, dear," she said, and loosened her arms. Hurting! That
was it—there had been too much hurting, too much pain, too much
holding in against the people who caused it. Ellen slid off her lap and
stood looking at her. "Mother, what did they want to say that about
Nils for?"

Joanna tried to appear calm. "I think somebody was just trying
to make you mad. You know how some people like to tease."

"But that's an awful thing to say—"

"I know it is. But don't think about it any more. Sit up and have
some dinner."

Having laid her burden upon Joanna's heart, the child was
relieved, and now she sat up to the table, eating with the enjoyment
that only children can know. But Joanna couldn't eat; she made herself a cup of coffee and drank it black.

"Aren't you hungry, Mother?" Ellen asked her.

"I think I've got a little pain, dear," Joanna told her lightly.
"Maybe I've been eating too much these days."

"Perhaps you ought to take some medicine." Ellen wrinkled her
forehead and looked anxious.

"I think if I just go without my dinner, I'll feel fine," Joanna said
reassuringly. "So you go ahead and eat, dear, and I'll tidy up the sitting room."

She had to get away from the child. She felt so futile and helpless when she sat still; here, at least, she could do something with
her two hands, if it was only beating the cushions into fluffiness, or
taking the braided rugs out on the front doorstep and shaking them
into the raw, bright day until her arms ached.

It was while she stood there, the stinging cold striking through
her clothes to her skin, that she saw Caleb's boat come into the harbor. He was home from hauling, then. As soon as he had his dinner,
he'd go to Brigport and get Joey—

Joey. Joey would know just what was being said, and in more
detail. At least it seemed impossible that he wouldn't know in a school
of some fifteen children.

She went back into the house, its warmth replacing the chill on
her flesh. She would go down and talk to Joey as soon as she knew
he was home. But, after she talked to Joey—what then?

*   *   *

She didn't have to go down to the harbor to find Joey. In midafternoon she saw Caleb and his young son coming up the road. Ellen saw them too.

"Joey must have got out of school early today," she said wonderingly. "And what's he coming up here for?"

"I don't know," said Joanna, but she did know, and she sought frantically for an excuse to get Ellen out of the house. Now that the child's mind was free again, after a fashion, she didn't want her to hear the review of the whole sordid business. *Murder*. She couldn't get the word out of her head. And Caleb was bringing Joey up to tell her what he'd heard. Caleb thought she ought to know. . . . They were halfway up through the meadow now, man and boy swinging along with a curious likeness to one another in their gait.

She put her arm around Ellen and heard herself speaking; the Mother, unhurried, unalarmed. "I think Caleb wants to talk to me about Stevie's traps, he probably wants to buy them. Joey must have come along for the walk." She looked candidly into her daughter's face. "You haven't been out today. How about doing an errand for me?"

"All right." Only a very small sigh came with the words. "I don't think Joey would play dominoes with me, anyway. He prob'ly thinks he's too big."

"That's the way with boys. Now you get into your ski suit and hustle down to Marion's and ask her if Mother can please borrow the—" inspiration came to her—"the last four issues of *Good Housekeeping*." It was a shame to bother Marion, but she had to keep Ellen out for half an hour, anyway. . . .

She glanced out the window. Joey and his father had almost reached the house.

"Hurry, darling, so you'll be back before dark," she said, and Ellen obediently hurried. She was going out when Caleb and Joey came in.

Caleb's lantern-jawed face was set. He nodded briefly to Ellen as she slipped past him, and pushed Joey into the kitchen before him with a big hand on his shoulder. It was a protective hand, and Joanna could see why. For Joey looked at her uncomfortably; one of his eyes was blackened and nearly closed in his pale face.

"Hello, Joey," she said briskly. "Hello, Caleb. Won't you sit down?"

"Guess we better," said Caleb. He added abruptly, "Guess you've heard somethin' already, so you know why we're here, don't you?" "I've heard—from Ellen." Her eyes met his calmly. "I wanted to see Joey, and find out what else had been said." "You can see his eye. . . . Set down, Joey. Don't look so scared." His mouth twitched. "He tells me the other feller looks pretty awful. Lost one of his front teeth."

"Good for you, Joey," Joanna applauded him. It was surprisingly easy to smile at the boy and see the strained look begin to leave his face. You had to keep up appearances before children; they must think you were serene and unbothered, that gossip was nothing, it left you untouched. . . . She hoped that was how she looked. It would not be easy to fool Caleb, though. She felt as though his cavernous eyes saw all the tiny twitches she felt in her skin, and could see past her skin and hair and guess at the turmoil in her brain.

She sat down and looked at Joey. "Tell me when they started and what they said," she commanded. "I just want to get it straight, Joey. Ellen was muddled. You know how little girls are."

Joey wet his dry lips, and a faint color came into his cheeks. "Yes'm. . . . It started this week, at recess one day. One of the boys— Willy Pierce it was—he was talkin' about Winslow, and then he said it was funny about Nils bringin' the boat in.'Cause one day on the wharf Nils told Winslow he better shut up, or he'd tend to him." Another gulp. "Willy Pierce's father heard them fightin'."

"I remember that, Joey," she said easily. "It wasn't a fight. Winslow was—fresh, that's all. Nils told him to be careful." She looked over at Caleb's lined, attentive face. "You remember the time they interfered when Mark and Nils were putting the oil on. Jonas Pierce was standing there."

Caleb nodded. Joey went on, as if he was eager to get the story out. "He never said Nils—did anything to Winslow. Just said it was funny. It was somebody else said it, right afterward. Then we had to go into school. I was mad, and I was goin' to find those guys on the way home, but I couldn't. So next day—" his voice gathered color and momentum—"Next day I told 'em they shouldn't say things like that, or they'd get into trouble. And Bart Robey said, 'Well, how come Nils went away the next day after he brought the boat in, and never come back yet?' "

Joey had to stop for a breath. Again Joanna looked at Caleb.
"So—" she prompted the boy.

"So that's when I got my black eye," said Joey. "Bart Robey said
a lot of stuff about Swedes bein' sneaks and never fightin' in the
open—" he blushed and gazed at Joanna helplessly.

"Never mind, Joey. I want to know all they said. Don't hold anything back."

"Well, he said his old man knows Swedes pretty well, and that's
what *he* said—that Nils prob'ly'd been plannin' it ever since that day
on the wharf. So I hit him. He busted me in the eye, but I knocked
out his tooth, and he spit blood all over the place—"

"You can leave that part out, son," Caleb said. "What happened
next?"

"After that the kids talked about it all the time at recess . . . all
of 'em. That's how Ellen heard it. One of the girls—she's an awful
pain in the—I mean she's a pest, Peggy Bradford, she made up a
kind of a song."

Inside Joanna was cringing. Outwardly she spoke without hesitation. "What was it like, Joey?"

"Aw, you know how they kind of sing-song." He contorted his
face and chanted in a crude, nasal, caricature:

> Ellen's fa-ther killed a man
> And threw him in the o-ce-an!

He began again, but Caleb said, "That'll do, son. She don't have to
hear any more. You can run along home now."

Joanna heard herself saying in a bright voice, "Joey, help yourself to some cookies. In that blue jar on the dresser."

Joey said earnestly, "She was a girl and I couldn't smack her,
but I told her a story and scared her foolish. I said there was a man
buried in the cellar of her house, and some night he'd come up in
her room, all drippin' blood, and—"

"You go on home, Joey," said Caleb.

"Yessir." Joey put a whole cookie in his mouth and went out.

"I hope Peggy has bad dreams for a month," said Joanna, and
began to laugh. But her laughter sounded so queer, and Caleb looked
at her so oddly that she stifled the sound. She got up and walked

around the kitchen. Caleb took out his pipe and began to fill it.

"I brought Joey up because you ought to know what's goin' on," he said. "I don't know jest what anybody does in a case like this, but . . ." he put a match to his pipe. "Nils ought to be home pretty soon, hadn't he? It's nearly Christmas."

She came to a stop before him. "Caleb, it's just possible a lot of people would believe that story, isn't it?"

"A lot of people are believin' it already, seems to me." He shot her a quick glance from under his shaggy eyebrows. "When the kids start talkin' it over in the schoolyard, it looks like some folks are acceptin' it for gospel."

"Nils wouldn't hurt anybody," she said, trying not to sound desperate. "You can tell it by looking at him."

Caleb shook his head. "You can't tell nothin' about a man by lookin' at him. I know Nils, you know him. But there's a pile of people who'd follow the line of reasonin' Joey told about—he's a Swede, and he's quiet, so it means he's got one hell of a temper that could turn him into a killer if the circumstances was just right. Like meetin' Winslow alone, down between Pudd'n Island and Tenpound." He stopped, and puffed hard at his pipe.

"Anybody who knows Nils would know better than to think he'd kill a man." She put her hands into her slacks pockets; they felt cold and weakly shaky, as if she'd been carrying a load in them that strained the muscles of her wrists. And there was a tiny hammering in the calves of her legs. She tried to tighten them. "But this story—if it gets around—can blacken Nils' name all along the coast. And his family's too. It isn't fair! Nils has always abided by the law, he's been kind and good—"

Caleb was getting up, with a leisurely unfolding of long legs. He picked up his cap and mittens. "Well, Joanna, take it easy now," he said.

She smiled at him. "Thanks for coming up, Caleb. And tell Joey not to get any more black eyes on account of—well, tell him to take it easy too."

Caleb nodded and went out. She remained standing in the middle of the kitchen, letting her breath out in a long sighing sound. *Now I can think,* she said to herself, but even as she said it, she knew she couldn't think as she wanted to—logically, reasonably, making plans.

There was nothing to work on. She couldn't build a strategy against gossip that was worse than any other gossip she'd ever encountered. For it said *murder*, and by now the word had the power to make her physically ill. Qualms of nausea began to surge over her like rolling billows of fog, and with each one the perspiration stood on her forehead and in her palms, and she could feel it, cold against her backbone.

She walked unsteadily into the sitting room. The fire needed prodding, but the thought of leaning over the woodbox weakened her. She lay down on the couch and stared at the ceiling overhead.

She was beset by a panic that seemed to drain the blood from her heart. For she was an island woman, she had lived among these outermost islands all her life, but for those few years away from it. She knew how the smallest slight could be magnified, the faintest suspicion grow to enormous proportions in this life where there was so much unbroken solitude. A man hauling his traps, alone for six or eight hours between sea and sky, had all that time to conjecture on the unexplained word, the unusual circumstance. At night he spoke to his wife about it, and told her what someone had suggested or hinted down at the shore; in turn she told him what a neighbor had implied, or had even spoken in bold and definite terms. . . . To Joanna, it was like the grass-fires when they used to burn off the fields, in the old days. The little flames ran swiftly along the ground, so swiftly that the men had to watch them every second, and be ready to turn them away from the ground they shouldn't touch.

Only you couldn't turn this back. Not talk of murder. She saw, against the ceiling, the flames of a grass fire that had once licked at Uncle Nate's barn. They had saved the barn, but it had been a dangerously narrow escape. . . . She was shivering so hard that her teeth were chattering; the tighter she clenched them, the harder they chattered. She could not lie still, or she would go crazy.

She was out in the kitchen again, dizzily stoking the stove. No, they didn't take people out and hang them, up here on the solid, sensible coast of Maine. It was only in the South they did that. Not up here. The lobstermen she had known all her life didn't throng together in a sinister crowd and go to a man's home and drag him out. . . .

"I *am* crazy," she said aloud. "But dear God, why doesn't Owen come home?"

She swung around to the window, and narrowed her eyes against the late afternoon sunglare across the harbor. The *White Lady* was at her mooring.

Ellen hadn't come back yet when Owen banged the back door loudly behind him. Joanna blessed Marion for keeping her down there. If only she'd stay away for a little while longer —

"Got any coffee?" Owen was demanding loudly. Then he came closer to her, where she stood by the stove. "Christ, what's the matter with you, Jo? You look as if somebody'd tied you up in knots! You sick?"

"No, I'm not sick," she said. She looked back at him steadily; her eyes felt as if they took up most of her face.

"You're damn' white. Speak up — what's the matter?" He sounded furious, because he was worried.

"Owen, they're saying at Brigport that Nils killed Winslow, and threw his body overboard, and then went away because of it."

Now it was out, blunt, cold truth, and Owen glared at her in amazement. *"Nils!* By God! . . . You sure?"

"Ellen told me — and Joey. Ellen was sick about it." She smiled faintly. "Joey got into a fight and had his eye blacked."

His face changed and quieted. "The kids would have it before half the grown folks knew it."

"Knew it!,' she exclaimed. "You sound is if you thought it was *so.* That he *did* do it!"

His great hands took her by the shoulders and forced her into a chair. "Sit down and take it easy, Jo. I'm not saying that. I know better. I'm just figuring that anybody who passes that lousy goddam fairy tale around believes it's true."

"But they can't believe it. Not of Nils."

"Yes, they can too." Owen stalked back and forth before her, his jaw set. "Because any time there's ever been a murder off this coast, it's been the same thing. They don't sneak up and shoot a man in his camp, or bat him over the head. They do it so nobody ever *knows* it's a murder. . . . Like — what about the kid over in Port George who fell overboard? Sure, just an accident; but he'd been warned to keep his hands off the other guys' traps, hadn't he?" He stared hard at the floor, his black brows heavy, his lower lip thrust out. "His father found him—what was left of him—three months later, in the rockweed one day. That was the bitchly thing. . . ." He lifted his head and looked at Joanna. "See why they talk? Because they know what *they'd* do if they wanted to get rid of a guy."

With a fierce gesture he pushed the teakettle forward on the stove. "I want some grub, dammit! You been broodin' about this all day, Jo? You better snap out of it. There's nothing you can do about it."

"Isn't there?" She stood up, feeling a little stronger. The weakening nausea that had attacked her was gone. "That's what you think, Owen. Maybe you figure I'll stay here and do nothing, and let Nils find out for himself, after the story's gone so far there'll be no stamping it out! And he's the only one who can stop it, if he does it now."

"Jo, let me tell you this for your own good," Owen said. His voice was no longer roaring, but strangely gentle, as if it were on tiptoe. "Maybe it'll save you from getting your fingers mashed. . . . Jo, maybe you're foolin' yourself, and maybe you know it, deep down, but Nils won't thank you for rushin' over there after him. What they say about him out here doesn't mean a good goddam to him. Because he's *through.*"

"Are you sure of your facts, Owen Bennett?" She felt her spine pulling out and stiffening, it held her straight and tall like a steel rod. She didn't take her eyes from her brother's face.

"Nothing else would keep Nils Sorensen away from his boat and his traps this long." Owen shrugged. "His engine was probably ready long ago. If he'd wanted to come home—he'd be here now. . . . Jo, I'm sorry as hell you two couldn't work it out, but that's the way it looks to me, and I almost think you'd better tend to your knitting and forget all the chew on Brigport."

She couldn't shout. She spoke just above a whisper, in a passion of rage. "And I almost think you'd better keep your tongue to yourself, Owen Bennett. . . . Are you going to take me to the mainland tomorrow?"

Owen said sadly to the teakettle, "It's a damn' shame some women never think a man means it when he says he's through."

She laid her hand on his arm, and with a strength beyond herself pulled him around to face her. "*Are—you—going—to—take—me—ashore—tomorrow?*"

The sardonic twinkle came to life in his eyes. He opened his mouth; then looked rather intently into her face. "Damned if you don't mean it, Jo," he said softly, and shrugged. "Oh, what the hell? Sure, I'll take you in."

35

IN THE MORNING OWEN TOOK ELLEN down to the Eastern End, while Joanna tidied the house and got herself ready for the trip to Limerock. She was finished before Owen came back, and could not endure waiting in the house; she went out to the back doorstep to see if he was coming. The day had begun with a clear wash of topaz light and a faint, singing breeze, which touched Joanna gently as she stood watching for Owen to come through the gate from the Eastern End woods, far across the dark blue loop of Schoolhouse Cove.

Even in winter the Island sustained its beauty; even without the songbirds and the early-morning iluting of the gulls over the house, and the wild flowers that spangled the meadows with color. The rocks remained the same, and the shape of the woods, a rough slope here, a straight and solitary spruce there, black and stark as an ink drawing against the winter sky and the far horizon.

Standing there now, not noticing the cold, Joanna realized with a small guilty pain that she had not looked much at the Island lately. She'd been too preoccupied with herself, too rushed, too confused. But this morning she could look at it; in fact it clamored for her attention. The sun climbed higher and higher, the tide was flowing into Schoolhouse Cove, a surge of white broke on the great russet rocks and on the silvery lavender of the beach. The tall, sharp-edged grass around the seawall was flattened down and dead now; like the evening primroses and the beach peas, the morning glories that hung their pink bells from the marsh grasses, and the speedwell that was so tiny you were likely to miss it. . . . They were all dead, but only until spring. And meanwhile the Island lived. The never-static tide was its pulse.

All this Joanna knew, just as she knew that she would never forget this instant of perception. It was as if the Island had called out to her. She felt alive with an aching awareness; she had ached a good deal lately, but not with this sense of life.

It's because I'm going to do something at last, she thought. *I'm through with wringing my hands and wondering what to do next. I know what to do.*

She saw Owen coming then. He had said he would be ready to leave as soon as he came back, so she got her dressing case from the kitchen, locked the back door behind her, and went down through the meadow to meet him where the road turned toward the harbor.

He swung past the seawall, his rubber boots ringing on the frozen gravel, his cap on the back of his head. He was whistling as he came up to her.

"Is it all right?" she asked him instantly. "What did Helmi say?"

"She said sure, she'd be glad to look out for Ellen." They fell into step together.

"Is that all?" Joanna said. "Did she ask any questions?"

"Nope, but Mark did. Wanted to know why you were tearin' off in such a hell of a hurry. I told him I didn't know." He grinned at her. "So probably Mark thinks you're crazy as a coot."

"That's all right," said Joanna. As long as they didn't know, it was all right. She shrank from telling Helmi about Nils and the Brigport story, for already Helmi had too much on her mind. Perhaps Ellen would keep her from brooding. That was what Joanna had hoped, when she sent Ellen down to the Eastern End. Helmi was sincerely fond of the child, and would try to entertain her; that would help her over these first black days of Stevie's absence. . . .

There was no one in sight when they came to the beach. Caleb and Matthew had gone to haul, and Jud hadn't come down to the car yet. At least she wouldn't have to answer any friendly questions. She didn't want to speak to anyone; only to Nils, when she would tell him he must come home.

"Hey, Jo." Owen came over the beach toward her. "There's a good breeze outside. You sure you want to go?"

"The *White Lady* can take it, can't she?"

"Yep." Owen shoved his cap back farther. "But it's not exactly the kind of a sea I'd take women and children on."

"I'm not women and children. I'm one woman and no sissy." The thought of delay set her muscles to quivering again. "Come on, Owen."

He shrugged. "Okay. Let's go."

The harbor wasn't glassy-smooth when they rowed out to the mooring, but it wasn't choppy. The day was cold enough, without the cutting glitter of the day before. The sun danced across the riffling water, and the *White Lady*, dressed in her winter sprayhood, bounced on her mooring chain, her wet white sides shining.

Joanna felt the old exhilaration warming her. They were on their way, and it would be a good way, too. Owen and his breezes! Had he forgotten what sort of sailor she was? She was conscious of her growing excitement through the familiar routine of warming up the engine, taking up the mooring—the ringing clatter of the chain was as sweet as birdsong to her; and then the moment when the *White Lady* swung around and headed for the harbor mouth, the skiff painter snapped out taut behind them. They were on their way.

Crossing between the harbor mouth and the southern end of Brigport, they met the pleasant top-chop that made no difference to the *White Lady*. She sped across it, and her engine-beat made a song about the white water flung out from her bow, the frothing sea in her wake, the cold blue brilliance of the sky.

Owen stood with one hand on the wheel, the other in his pocket, watching past the edge of the sprayhood. Joanna stood behind him, loving the flow of the wind against her face. Not for her, to sit tamely on the engine box in the shelter of the sprayhood. . . . The dark-wooded end of Brigport grew steadily larger—there was surf break-ing on the bold, rocky point flung out into the sea, and Joanna braced herself for the swell. But it wasn't bad. She stepped past Owen into the complete shelter of the sprayhood to tie her kerchief tighter and fasten her coat at the neck. With all her heart she was glad she was on her way to the mainland. She'd been right to insist on coming.

The *White Lady* rose under her feet, and kept on rising. It was a slow and deliberate sensation. Joanna waited for the fast down-ward smack that made a choppy sea exciting; it didn't come. This was no chop, this lifting of the *White Lady*'s bow until her stern was flush with the bubbling wake, until it seemed as if the water must boil over into the cockpit; this was a heavy sea, and when the boat plunged down on the other side—

She saw Owen's hand dart out to the engine box, and the swift turning of the flywheel was instantly checked. The *White Lady* slid down a shining hill of water, and Joanna, looking astern, saw the sea rushing on, and the punt flung high on its crest. Owen touched the throttle and the low murmur of the motor quickened to a loud throbbing again. He looked out by the sprayhood, and then ducked his head back quickly, but his face glistened with salt water. "Jesus, did I get wet!"

"Where are these seas coming from?"

"We're off the Black Ledges. It's always nasty here when there's any wind. And I told you there was a good breeze, didn't I?" He was on watch again, and then she felt the bow rising once more; she stepped quickly astern into the open part of the cockpit, and looked past Owen. It seemed as if the whole thirty-four-foot length of the *White Lady* stood on end; as if anyone watching from Brigport would see her entire washboards from stem to stern outlined against the great roaring sea that rose up under her. Joanna knew nothing in that instant but a horrible awe. Her mouth formed an O through which she drew her breath.

Owen reached down to move the throttle again. The power inside that box could drive the *Lady's* nose down under the next comber, down and down. But even shutting off the power couldn't keep the boat from its sickening leap into the trough. An enormous wing of white water rose on either side of the bow and curved outward in a sweep of crystal. Water poured over the cuddy roof, seeped in between the washboards and the sprayhood, ran down the washboards to the stern, fast rivulets shining in the sun.

The engine throbbed louder again. Joanna moved up beside Owen, who watched keenly past the sprayhood to where his boat's high bow tossed against the horizon. His eyes were slitted against the wind and the spray. Already the salt had left white lines on his dark skin, and the black hair over his forehead was wet.

Joanna peered by the edge of the sprayhood and saw a wild, flashing, twinkling expanse of blue-green ocean, and the thin and faraway line of islands on either side gave no protection from the strong, sweeping wind. The racing gusts feathered the rolling wave-crests into seething foam. Joanna looked out upon the vista of restless water, that was tormented and angered by the lash of the cold, stinging wind; the *White Lady* seemed like a mere cockleshell, frail and innocent; but she met each wave steadily, rising over it, or plunging through it. She moved slowly but surely upon the invisible line that the compass needle drew upon the sea.

"Will it be like this all the way?" she shouted at Owen.

He shrugged. "If the wind keeps risin', it'll be worse." He didn't take his eyes from the sea. "Hold on—here comes another bastard!"

She caught at him as the boat leaped and heeled. When it was over she realized she'd shut her eyes tight. She'd never done that before. She called to Owen. "Everything's falling down in the cabin. I'd better go pick things up."

He looked at her with a grin. "Not much sense in doing that; they'll only get thrown around again. But if you want to lie down, go ahead."

The *White Lady* began to climb another sea. Down in the cuddy, Joanna lost her balance and staggered into a corner, just as the sea broke over the deck. It sounded as if it were about to crash in upon her head. She made a faint attempt to pick up the things strewn about the cabin, but the boat rolled and pitched so that she had to sit down. She was conscious, then, of her weakness; a dreadful weakness, as if her strength were oozing out through every pore. Her skin felt clammy and numb. This nerveless sensation was new to her, at least as far as the sea was concerned; she had never before wanted to throw herself into a heap on the locker, shut eyes and ears and cling—if she had the strength to cling—until the worst was past.

Only—what if it didn't pass? They'd hardly begun the trip. They had a good two hours yet to go. *I can't stand any more of it,* her brain cried out, and with that she recognized her trouble. She was terri-fied. She, Joanna Bennett, who had never in her thirty-one years been afraid when she was aboard a boat.

Moreover, this utter weariness was centering in her stomach. Every roll and leap of the boat made it worse; she was beginning to sweat. If something happened to the *White Lady* now—if her nose went under or her round bottom rolled her over too far—Joanna would be utterly unable to help herself. She felt a shuddering relief at the thought of surrendering to her misery; she couldn't be both seasick and terrified at once.

She lay flat on the hard locker and closed her eyes. It was no wonder she was seasick for the first time in her life. She made excuses for herself, remembering how strained and tired she'd felt for so long, how for the last month her stomach had been so easily upset. Just then, a new wave of horrible nausea went over her, and swamped her pride completely. She didn't try to think of any more excuses.

She must have dozed at last, for when she became aware of the cuddy again, and the thin sunlight slanting through the salt-dimmed ports, the *White Lady* was thrumming along at a self-possessed rate. She might have been back in her home harbor. Joanna got up from the locker, tightening her lips when her cramped muscles and aching spine asserted themselves. She took her compact from her bag and looked at herself. She was pale, but not greenishly so, and her hair was mussed. The shadows around her eyes had been there for a long time. . . . She combed her hair back from her face and powdered her nose, and went out under the sprayhood to the wheel.

Owen was sitting on the washboards, smoking. "Hi," he said laconically. "You been asleep?"

"It just crept up on me," she explained. The sharp, clear air, almost windless now, was as refreshing as cold well water. She looked out past the sprayhood and saw the Camden mountains against the sky. They rolled down to the sea, the nearer, lower ones patched with fawn-color and brown, the farther, higher ones grape-blue with forests and snow-crested slopes. Over them all, the huge white clouds sailed from the west, and their shadows moved across the rolling lands below.

The *White Lady* was almost into Limerock Harbor.

She wanted to go alone to find Nils. She had a right to go alone, she believed. But Owen overrode her, and there was nothing for her to say, because she didn't know where Nils' uncle lived, and Owen did. Besides, he had dropped his work to take her on what he thought was a wild-goose chase. She couldn't argue with him now. And she felt too tired to talk; the trip had exhausted her. She ached from lying so long on the locker and there was a hot throbbing behind her eyes.

They walked along Limerock's narrow Main Street toward the bus stop. The day had turned mild, and the sidewalks were crowded. Ordinarily people were of enormous interest to Joanna, but today she walked through them as if she were completely alone, following one of the deserted trails on the barren end of the Island.

"Hey, wait a minute!" Owen said, and she stopped. They stood on a windy corner with some half-dozen others. At another time she would have catalogued each one of them in the five minutes before the bus came. Today her thoughts were turned inward. . . . Nils would go home with her when he realized the necessity of it. . . .

The bus lumbered on toward Camden. There was a sickening odor of exhaust, but it seemed to bother no one but herself. She looked around at the others, wondering how they could stand it. Probably they were used to it. . . . She remembered, with a little twitching of her lips, how the disreputable bus that ran between Limerock and Pruitt's Harbor was minus a door, so you had plenty of air in all sorts of weathers, including blizzards.

She sat back in her seat, trying to release the tightness in her shoulders and neck, making her fingers loosen on her bag. She and Owen sat behind the driver, and in his mirror she could see herself. She didn't look too bad; it was probably her hat brim and the bad light in the bus that made her so pale. But at that she had better color than most of the mainlanders in the other seats. She was lucky, being a brown-skinned Bennett to begin with. No one would ever think she'd been so nearly seasick, and so weakened with fright out there in the boat. And she would never admit it.

They had to walk from the bus stop to Eric Sorensen's place, away from the town and down a narrow dirt road through spruce and birch. The frozen ruts were hard to walk on, and there was sparse warmth in the thin sunshine. Owen smoked one cigarette after another, and the smoke was very blue in the still, biting air.

"Jesus, I'm hungry," he said. "But you wouldn't let a man stop to get some dinner, would ye? Had to grab that bus as if there wasn't another one for a year."

"You didn't have to come with me," she answered, her eyes on the next twist of the road. "You could have stayed, and had twenty meals if you wanted."

"And how were you to get here? I've been to Eric's, and you

haven't. You'd never find the place by yourself. They'd find you a month later, roamin' around the woods like a blind cod in a school of herring."

She didn't answer. She was too near the end of her journey. She was beset by her desire to reach Nils; she knew that once she had seen him, and told him to come home where he belonged, and put an end to this vicious Brigport story, she could relax. When she tried to think how long it had been since she had lain down to sleep, or sat down to read or eat, without this tremor in her stomach, this involuntary clenching of her muscles, she couldn't remember.

They came around the next bend in the road, the spruces thinned, and Owen said, "There it is."

The bay opened up before them, such a calm sparkle of blue in the winter afternoon that the *White Lady*'s trip might have been a dream, except that she, Joanna, was here; she stood on the hard rutty road, and looked at the white farmhouse on the rise from the shore. *There it is,* Owen had said, calmly lighting another cigarette. It was just a farmhouse to him, but to her it meant Nils.

Her eyes flew swiftly to the huge barn that loomed beyond the house, dwarfing it. That would be where Eric and Nils were building the boat. She found herself straining for the sound of hammers; it would carry far in this hushed, crystalline atmosphere.

"For Christ's sake, you intend to stand here all day?" demanded Owen, and started up the winter-brown slope to the house. "Maybe Mrs. Eric's got something to eat up there."

She followed him without speaking. She had a premonition that no one would be at home; but suddenly, when they were halfway to the house, there was movement. It was as if at a given signal everything *began.* She knew it was only that she had noticed nothing until now, nothing but the barn. Now she saw the smoke rising from the chimney, and the big mongrel shepherd dog lying on the doorstep. He saw them too, and came toward them, barking; the ell door was flung open, and Eric Sorensen's wife, Karin, stood in the open doorway.

"Peter!" she shrieked, and clapped her hands. At the same instant she recognized Joanna and Owen and shrieked again, this time in joyous welcome.

"Well, I *never!* Of all people! *Peter!* Friends, Peter . . . be good now!" She came out on the doorstep to greet them, fatter than she'd ever been on Bennett's Island; but her little blue eyes were jolly, and there was not a thread of gray in her yellow hair. "Peter, you be good —"

"Peter's good," said Joanna. The dog went from her to Owen, and she glanced around the dooryard quickly. The dog's barking might bring Nils out of the barn to see what was wrong; but what if he wasn't in the barn? What if he was away this afternoon?

Mrs. Eric was hustling them into her kitchen, talking all the while. "I'll make you some coffee—I made fresh coffee ring this morning! Now give me your things." She giggled as Owen chucked her under her chin—or chins. "You'll have to excuse the kitchen, it looks like it's ready to ride out, I know—"

"The kitchen looks fine," said Owen, who towered head and shoulders above this little Swedish dumpling of a woman. "Almost as good as you do, Karin. Did you say coffee? And how about a couple of eggs?" he added without shame.

"Eggs, and bacon too, you can have!" Tittering and rosy, Karin turned back to Joanna, who stood by the stove warming her hands. "You poor darling, are you cold? Sit down now, and I'll open the oven door—I'll put more wood on—"

Joanna moved back from the stove. It was odd; her hands were cold, but already it seemed as if the kitchen were hot enough to stifle her.

Owen was settled in the most comfortable chair in the room, exchanging light banter with Karin, who'd always liked him, ever since the long-ago Bennett's Island days. Joanna pulled off her hat and ran her hands through her hair to loosen it from her aching head.

"Karin, is Nils around?" she asked simply. "I'd like to speak to him."

"Why, child, he's right out in the barn this minute! And all alone, too. Eric's gone to town." She flung open the shed door. Owen said, "I'd like to get a look at that boat."

"Now that can wait," returned Karin, with a portentous wink for Joanna. "You sit here quiet while I fix your bacon and eggs. . . . You go along, child. The coffee'll be ready when you want it."

"Thanks," Joanna said briefly. The door shut behind her; the shed stretched before her. It was the longest shed she had ever walked through. At the other end of it she saw the door into the barn. . . . She stood quietly for a moment, between the long bulwark of stacked and split firewood on one side of her, and the oilskins hanging on the other wall. Karin's voice in the kitchen was small and far-off; from the barn ahead there was no sound, and outside there was the un-moving hush of the afternoon, as if the essence of all expectant si-lence had run like rainwater into this clearing between the woods and the sea. And in the middle of it Joanna stood; she felt herself its pulse.

It was hard to believe that somewhere also in this well of silence Nils existed. But he was there in the barn; there was no reason for his aunt to lie. In a few moments now they would be talking as they had always talked, calmly, without lifted voices, and she would ex-plain to him why he must come home. He would understand. He knew how to be reasonable. She would tell him about Stevie's going away, she would admit freely that she needed him there on the Island, that no one wanted to work without him; and she would tell him about this filthy, impossible story the children had brought home. Even now it was growing larger, and more people were listening—and believing; the longer Nils stayed away, the more easily they'd be convinced they knew the truth.

She opened the door into the barn, reassuring herself that Nils would go back with her. She would insist upon it.

She saw the boat first. There was no escaping it. It towered above her and seemed to fill the barn; it looked much bigger than it really was. The fine, tenuous lines of winter sunshine from the windows softened the raw yellow timbers and planks to warm gold, coppery-toned in the shadows; she was a golden boat, rising out of the warm, quiet gloom around her.

For a moment Joanna gazed at the boat. Then, shutting the door noiselessly behind her, she looked around for Nils. . . . A workbench had been built against the wall, reaching from the shed door to the end of the barn and the big doors through which the boat would move on her journey down the slope to the sea. Nils stood at the farther end, fitting a small shiny blade into a block plane. So quietly had Joanna come that he didn't yet realize she was there. She had in-tended to speak to him evenly and decisively, but now that the mo-ment had come, she only stood there, watching him.

His hands held the plane over the bench, his pipe was in his mouth, he looked as he had always looked; absorbed, intent, and very clean.

She couldn't just stand here, indefinitely. She must speak to him. . . . But curiously, it was difficult to say his name and walk toward him, as if she'd seen him only yesterday. She felt all at once as if he had been gone for a lifetime.

It was then that he turned away from the bench, and saw her.

He was incredibly still. *As if I was dead,* she thought. *As if he thought he'd never see me again.* The pulses were loud in her ears, and she found she was still holding the doorknob with a fierce grip.

"Joanna!" said Nils softly. "Is it you, Joanna?"

The astonishment didn't leave his face; it was almost a dazed astonishment, and it was reflected in his voice. He didn't move, except to take the pipe from his mouth. Joanna had a frightening sensation that if she spoke to him from where she stood, he wouldn't be able to hear her. She must walk toward him. But she felt a reluctance to let go of the doorknob. If she did, the barn floor would rise and fall under her feet as the *White Lady* had done. . . .

She took a step toward him, and he said nothing at all; he only stood watching her, his pipe in his hand, and she could see him better now; her eyes were used to the dimness. The dazed look, as if he'd been startled from a dream, was gone.

"I'd just been thinking about you," he said. "But how — why did you come over here, Joanna? What's happened?"

She opened her mouth to answer, but she felt again that sensation of her strength oozing from every pore, and with it the trembling she couldn't stop — she'd always been able to control it, but now it was growing wilder and wilder. Her eyes felt too big again; but they saw only Nils standing at the far end of the workbench, waiting for her, his hair a blurry bright spot in the thickening shadows; only Nils, strong and clean and calm. . . .

She put out her hand and felt the cool, firm, scarred wood of the bench as she walked. It helped her, too; it helped the watery feeling in her legs. Nils didn't take his eyes from her face, and she sensed, rather than saw, his disquiet and unbelief. *I can't look as queer as that,* she thought in some vague corner of her mind. *That mirror on the bus* . . .

At last she reached him. Her journey was over; she could tell him to come home, and then she could go somewhere and sleep, and get over being so tired. . . . Nils' hands came out to touch her shoulders, they gripped her with their strength, their warmth went through her coat to her skin and into her blood.

"Joanna, what in God's name has happened to you?" he asked harshly. "Are you sick? Is that why you're here?"

She was past answering. The touch of his hands had done that. She could not have spoken then to save her life. She looked at him for one long, drowning moment and then the last of her strength was gone. She felt her arms go around his neck, and the quick, tumultuous springing of her tears. There was no holding them back, and she was beyond thinking of her pride.

"Joanna, what *is* it?" she heard Nils say, and then, blessedly, his arms came around her and held her so tightly and strongly that they hurt her and her breath came hard; but she would not have relinquished one snatch of the pain. When she trembled, his arms tightened even more. He had never known her to tremble or to cry, but she couldn't stop either.

After a while he didn't try to speak to her, and the only sound in the barn was that of her sobbing. Joanna Bennett, sobbing like this! It was an incredible thing and she knew it; but the knowledge didn't quiet her. It was journey's end in more ways than one. For she was safe now; she was secure. She forgot shame and resentment and frustration in realizing that one certainty.

She didn't know how long it was that she cried out her weakness and defeat in Nils' arms. But finally she felt herself growing quiet. Her head lay passive against his shoulder, her face against his neck. The fresh scent of his skin and the smell of his clean shirt had been in her nostrils as she cried. . . . The stillness descended around her again, like a shadowy cloak. She realized that it was growing cold in the barn. The cold was aromatic with the new wood of the boat.

She felt Nils' face move against her hair. "Tell me now, Joanna," he said gently. His voice sounded oddly shaken. Not like Nils' voice at all, except in its gentleness. He tried to hold her away from him, to look at her, but she felt an intolerable pain at the thought of letting go of him. It was a new and foreign sensation, but she didn't question it.

"Don't make me let go of you, Nils," she said in a choked voice.

Again that blessed tightening of his arms, so that she felt weightless and almost light, almost like a child carried in the strong, unfaltering arms of an adult. "All right, Jo. Only for God's sake tell me what's wrong."

Her helpless confusion eddied around her. "Oh, Nils, I can't. . . . When I try to straighten it out, I—" She began to cry again and it frightened her. "Everything's wrong . . . the Island's going away from me, and nobody will do anything, and Winslow—" She lifted her head then, to stare through her running tears at his face.

"Nils, aren't you ever coming home again?"

"I didn't say I wouldn't be home."

"Because if you don't want to go back to the Island," she said with infinite care, "I'm never going back either. I don't care where you go. Only don't ever leave me behind again, Nils!"

"You don't mean that, Joanna," he said, so near she could feel his breath on her cheek. "You wouldn't give up the Island for anybody."

"I do mean it," she answered with a curious serenity, and knew that she was telling the truth. "Nils, wherever you are, that's my Island. I never knew it until now."

He said swiftly, "You're beside yourself, Joanna. You're sick with crying so hard, you've let yourself go to pieces, and I never thought you'd do that. . . . Come in the house now and let Aunt Karin put you to bed. You need rest."

He moved, but her hands held him. "Nils, don't send me away from you!" Her voice shook with panic. "Oh, my dearest, don't send me away!"

For a long moment he didn't answer her; she felt the rigid poise of him and a new and frightening thought set her head to swimming in blackness. He didn't want her. It was true then, that he'd put her behind him; he'd held her in his arms, and let her soak his shirt with her tears, out of kindness and pity, nothing else. . . . She couldn't square her shoulders and lift her chin. She was defeated.

"Joanna, listen. You said—" His words came slowly, as if he framed them with difficulty. "You said *dearest*. Are you going to tell me you mean that, too?"

"I mean it, Nils." From what depths her words came, she didn't know. But she knew that she was not lying when she said, "You *are* dear to me, Nils. You're my dearest."

"Oh, Joanna," he said on a long, tormented breath. *"Joanna. . . ."* He pulled her close to him again, this time it was not as if she were a heart-broken child. In the dimness she turned toward him, unseeing, yet sure. As sure as the blind, instinctive seeking of her mouth for his.

36

SOMEBODY OPENED THE SHED DOOR and stood gazing into the shadows of the barn. By the tilt of his head and the set of his shoulders, silhouetted against the clearer light of the shed, it was Owen. He stood without moving, looking up at the boat; it was no longer a golden boat, for the sun had dropped below the level of the hayloft windows. It was a ghost boat, a shadowy glimmer rising above him.

Joanna and Nils, standing close together at the far end of the workbench, didn't move; but in an instant he saw them and hailed them.

"You fellers got your business all talked over? Nils, she read the Riot Act to you yet?" He laughed. "I thought I'd take a look at the boat—"

"You can see it better in the morning," said Nils pleasantly.

"My God, man, sounds like you're kicking me out. Oh, hell, don't ever say I can't take a hint!" Still laughing, he shut the door noisily and they could hear him whistling as he went back to the kitchen. They didn't move until the faint sweet thread of sound had died away completely.

Nils kissed Joanna again, gently now, on her temple and on her cheek. She stood peacefully within the barrier of his arms; it seemed as if all her life and all her world had condensed to the radius of this small circle. Yet it was not small. It was as big and as boundless as space. And wherever she moved, she would never leave that circle again. She knew it for an irrevocable fact; and she knew the strangeness of it. The remembrance of nights when she had felt trapped and dismayed by Nils' nearness seemed a chaotic dream. This was like the awakening to a sun-washed morning, and the glimmer of endless, benevolent ocean and of unbroken sky arching from horizon to horizon; it was like the first opening of eyes still clouded by the dream, yet glimpsing through the mist the familiar and safe and beloved. And because of the horror of the dream, even the familiar would take on a new lustre. It was as if a whole new world had been given to her.

Nils sighed. "Aunt Karin'll be bringing the coffee out here next," he said. "I suppose we'd better go in. . . . Hungry, Joanna?"

"I don't know. . . . I guess so. Nils, I was almost seasick coming over today. And I was scared." She remembered as she spoke that no one was to know; but suddenly it was imperative that Nils know. She even took pleasure in telling him, and in feeling his hand stroke her hair, hearing him murmur, "Poor kid."

"I thought we'd never make it. I thought we might drown," Joanna said. "And for the first time in my life, I hated the sea."

"It was because you were tired," Nils said quietly. "It probably wouldn't happen like that again." They walked slowly toward the shed door. She was tired, but it was a good sort of tiredness, as if she could fall asleep without effort and without dreams; and Nils' arm was like iron around her waist.

Now she was content to sit in the comfortable rocker by the stove, drinking strong coffee and saying nothing. Karin rattled dishes in the pantry, singing to herself in Swedish while she mixed up a special cake for a company dessert. Eric Sorensen had returned from his errand in the town. He was a square-built, solid man with reflective pale blue eyes and a calm good humor; though it was said he had a touch of his father's temper. But he had none of Gunnar's cruelty, or Nils would never have stayed with him for so long.

Watching Nils as he talked with Owen and his uncle, Joanna's mind moved in dreamy circles, not touching for long at one spot. But it hesitated on Gunnar's name. Nils had really hated his grandfather, she knew. He'd had a barren childhood and youth in Gunnar

Sorensen's house; no woman had ever held him when he was small, or spoke to him with little love-names as he grew up, for his grand- mother had been too much afraid of her husband. . . .

Joanna's mind stopped its wandering. She gazed at Nils over the rim of the coffee cup. The lamp had just been lit, and as he leaned across the table to point out to Owen something on the boat-plans, his face was clear to her. It had an extraordinary clarity; and it seemed to print itself with the same brilliance on her brain. There was *something* — something she'd just been thinking . . . if she could go back and pick up the thread, she would find out something about Nils that he had never told her. If only she could recapture it — that instant of almost-perception.

It was gone. But perhaps it would come back. She looked at Nils' face again, and in that moment he glanced across at her. Not a line of his face changed, but there was a quick, subtle lighting of his eyes. As surely as if he had touched her, a warmth ran through her that didn't come from the coffee. Then, for the first time that afternoon, she remembered that on Brigport they were accusing Nils of murder. She fought to keep this new and comforting safety, and shut away the other thought; it had no place in the circle. At the same time she knew she must *not* shut it away, Nils had a right to know and to prepare himself.

The rest of the afternoon slipped by and it was time for supper. Baked beans, brown bread, home-made white bread, pickled herring and onions, cole slaw, and a hot and spicy upside-down cake; it was a lordly supper, over which Karin presided, red with heat and ex- citement and pride. Joanna was hungry, but her stomach wouldn't let her eat. It had been under a strain too long. And she was in- tensely aware of her wish to be alone with Nils; her eyes went to him again and again across the table, holding fast to him as she wished her hands might do. And while the hard-headed logical portion of her brain warned that the others might notice and tease — Owen especially — this new abandoned manifestation of Joanna did as it pleased. No, it did as it *must*. Not even with Alec had she felt this compulsion. It seemed as if Nils was her strength.

"Joanna, you're not eating!" Karin accused her. Joanna looked back at her in instant, flushed concern. Nils pushed back his chair.

"Leave her alone, Aunt Karin. I think she's coming down with a cold, and I'm going to put her to bed." He spoke across the table to Joanna, "Come on, Jo."

She stood up at once, conscious of Owen's wildly astonished eyebrow, and the way his black eyes shot from her to Nils, and back again. Karin got up too.

"I'll take her to the spare room if she wants to lie down, poor child. You go right on eating, Nils—"

Nils smiled at her. "Sit down, Aunt Karin. Eat your supper."

"Sit down, Karin," said Eric without looking up from his plate, and she obeyed, looking flustered and nervous until Owen reached over and patted her plump wrist.

"Can I hold hands with the woman who makes such damn' good brown bread?" he asked, and Joanna and Nils left the room to the crescendo of Karin's delighted laughter.

Upstairs in the spare room Nils set the lamp on the stand beside the bed. His aunt had been up and kindled a fire in the airtight stove, and now it mulled along comfortably. The covers had been turned back on the big walnut bed, and one of Karin's best quilts had been laid across the foot.

Joanna looked at the bed and sighed. "It looks wonderful, Nils."

Nils pulled down the shades and instantly the room became a snug and impenetrable fortress. It seemed as if even Brigport couldn't enter here. Yet she shuddered, in spite of herself, and Nils saw it. He came to her quickly and took her by the elbows. "I said I was going to put you to bed, and that's what I'm going to do."

"My bag is downstairs with my things in it—"

"Never mind that. I'll get you something to sleep in." He let go of her and went out. *I could be taking off my shoes,* she thought mistily, and didn't move. It was much easier to sit still and wait for Nils. . . . Wait for Nils. . . . How long had she been waiting for him? She couldn't count all the days now. *But I didn't really know what I was waiting for,* she said in wonder.

Nils was back again, holding up a tentlike nightdress. "Aunt Karin's. I helped myself out of the bureau drawer."

"Why, Nils!" she said, and they both laughed as if they'd made a very funny joke. Joanna was still a little shaky from her laughter when Nils went down on one knee before her to untie her oxfords. She felt his light, sure touch on her foot; she looked at his bent fair head, and the wetness in her eyes was not from laughter after all. She widened them and blinked fiercely; and then, as if she had no control over it whatsoever, her hand went out to his hair.

He was about to slip her shoe from her foot. But he paused and looked up at her, and she saw it in his eyes, the thing she had once seen, the thing Helmi had mentioned. When he took her hand and held it against his lips, it was more than she could endure.

"Nils, I'm not fit, I'm not good enough!" she cried, and put her hands over her face in a passion of weeping. "Why should you take my shoes off for me? Why should you do anything for me?"

"Because you're my wife," Nils said, and added in such a low voice that she barely caught it, "and my dear."

He took off her other shoe then, and helped her with her clothes; she was as quiescent as a child. She could not remember having felt like this since she was very small, and even then she'd been fiercely independent—unless she'd been on an adventure that had turned out wrong, or had been spanked. . . . Aunt Karin's nightdress enveloped her and Nils held back the bedclothes while she crept in between the sheets; then he went to the commode and brought back a wet washcloth to sponge off her face, hot with windburn and a touch of fever. She found herself leaning her head against his shoulder, watching him with absorbed eyes.

"I never thought you could be like this, Nils," she said at last.

"You didn't give me a chance," he told her gently. She would have been stung, once; now she took his head and pulled it down to hers.

"Why didn't you beat me, Nils?"

"You'd have hated me then, and never got over it." He laid her back against the pillows, and stood looking at her. "You know," he said, "I used to think of the way your mouth is, and the way your eyelashes curl. I thought I remembered them right. But—" He bent and kissed her swiftly. "I didn't remember your mouth right at all."

"If you remembered it always talking, that was right," she said bitterly. He dropped to his knees beside the bed and put his arms around her. The cool blue of his eyes darkened; and was no longer cool.

"Don't," he said. "Joanna, don't." He kissed her again, this time not swiftly.

After a few moments a little smile touched her mouth, and she looked at him from under her lashes, her long eyes darkly brilliant. "Aren't you hungry?" she asked him softly. "Don't you want to go down and finish your supper?"

He got up from his knees and turned the lamp low. She watched him, her eyes widening. She held her breath, expecting to see him go to the door. Instead he came around the bed, put another chunk of birch in the stove, and lay down beside her.

"We've got too much to say to each other," he said, "for me to think about beans."

She opened her eyes with bewilderment; where was this room, with the lamp burning low beside the bed, and the great walnut head-board towering over her; the religious pictures, with their Swedish titles, on either side of the mirror? And the arm that lay across her — against whose side was she so firmly held? Not Alec's, surely — Alec was dead. . . . She came to full awareness then, turned her head and saw Nils' sleeping face.

She lay watching him, trying to remember when it was she had dropped off to sleep. He hadn't stayed awake for long after, she was sure. How clean and good he looked, she thought. Not remote, now; his face was still locked and faraway, as it would always be when he was asleep, and many times when he was awake. But some of its strangeness was gone, it was a face that she knew.

The last thing of which she remembered speaking had been Ste-vie's enlistment. She'd told him everything, up to Stevie's departure. She'd told him how they all spoke of him, and would do nothing un-til he came. She'd thought it would hurt to admit that; but it hadn't hurt. Once she'd begun to tell him the things that had stung her, and bruised her, in fact, the whole long story of the weeks he'd been away, she had felt an exquisite sense of relief. If they were to start again, Nils must know her as she was, stripped bare of all the small, mean resentments and the idiotic pride.

She had told him almost everything that had happened; but not about the talk of murder. It had come to her tongue, to be thrust back. Tonight wasn't the time for it.

Nils had talked too. Not much, but what he hadn't said she'd guessed; by the way he'd knelt to take off her shoes — because she was his wife; by the way something quivered in his cheek when she called him *dear*. And she had known then what he had meant when he'd tried to talk to her on those nights at home, saying he wanted to work for her and give her his strength. In return he had craved her tenderness, the woman-tenderness he never had.

He was lying outside the covers, and the fire was almost out. She lifted his arm with infinite caution and slipped free of it, laying it down again along the coverlet. She unfolded the thick quilt from the foot of the bed and laid it over him. Tall in the full white gown, her cheeks flushed from sleep, she stood looking down at him in the dim lamp-glow.

Unbidden, her mind slipped back and for a sudden shocking moment she was in another bedroom, looking down at another sleeping face—Alec's; a narrow, lean-boned, Scottish face, with a bold nose and a wide humorous mouth that often smiled in sleep. She had watched him as she watched Nils now, but with a slow, corroding dread that made a pain in her breast. That was what Nils had wanted to save her; and when he'd tried to tell her she'd struck out at him, and cut him into silence.

She tucked the quilt more closely around his shoulders, went back to the other side of the bed. She blew out the lamp and lay down beside him, lifting his arm again to put it across her body. The darkness spread around her, but she didn't hate it tonight. She would go to sleep again, and not think of her mistakes—they were of yesterday, and had no part in tomorrow and all the tomorrows to come.

37

SHE DIDN'T KNOW WHEN NILS LEFT HER; but when she awoke the room was luminous with the silvery light from the blizzard that whirled past the windows, and the fire had been built in the stove. She lay listening to the snow against the panes, and the small, soft hissing the fire made. Distantly in the house she heard the radio, and knew Karin and Eric were listening to the Sunday morning church services from Tremont Temple in Boston. It was late; she could hardly remember the last time when she had slept so late.

She felt no compulsion to get up and dress and hurry downstairs. Instead, she watched contentedly the rush of the storm, or studied with deep interest the pictures on the walls. *Cupid Awake* and *Cupid Asleep* she'd seen before, and that wretchedly lonesome wolf standing on the hill above the town. She'd always felt sorry for him but that was unreasonable; he probably liked the way he lived.

She wasn't familiar with the picture of the beautiful youth in satin and ruffles, trying to kiss the maiden while her father absentmindedly clipped roses. She was contemplating the view dreamily from half-closed eyes when Nils came in with a tray. At the sight of him in the doorway she was no longer dreamy. When she had last seen him he was asleep, and withdrawn from her. Now as they looked at each other across the room, she felt the force of his new consciousness of her, mingled with her new recognition of him.

She sat up in bed. "Hello, Nils. Why don't you dress like him?" She pointed to the boy in satin. "You'd be real purty."

"A damn' good outfit to go hauling in," Nils said. "Ought to wear well. I could catch some herring in all that lace."

He put the tray down on the stand beside the bed. Then he went out into the hall again, and came in with her dressing case. "Your comb in here?" he asked. "I thought you'd want to tidy up before you ate."

"Can't I just taste my coffee before I comb my hair?" She looked with pleasure at the tray: coffee, black and steaming, in a yellow cup; hot muffins wrapped in a napkin; butter, and Karin's currant jelly; an orange, the rind scored and turned back in four creamy-pale petals. "It's like a picture in a magazine, Nils. Did Karin fix it?"

"*I* fixed it," said Nils, busy with opening her case. He found her comb and handed it across to her, and then met her bemused eyes. "What's the matter, Joanna?"

She laughed, a faint red running up under the clear translucent brown of her skin. "Nothing . . . only the tray. It's so — well, it's not the way most men are. On Bennett's Island, anyway."

He went over to fix the stove. Over his shoulder he smiled at her. "On Sunday morning my father always fixed my mother's breakfast. Kristi and I used to trot along behind him with the milk and sugar." He took a piece of birch from the woodbox and turned it over in his hands. "That's about the earliest thing I can remember. Kristi never could remember it at all — she couldn't even remember my mother."

"What did your mother used to say when you all came in, Nils?"

He turned around and looked directly at her then, and spoke as though he had always kept the words fresh and green in his mind. "To my father she would say, 'Good morning, Karl, my darling.' She always looked at him first, you see," he explained without resentment. "Then she would take Kristi into bed with her, because she was the baby, and then she'd thank me for carrying the milk."

"But what did she *say?*" Joanna insisted.

"She used to say, 'Thank you, dear. Come here where I can kiss you.' " His blond eyebrows drew together in a little frown. "Your coffee's getting cold, Jo."

She began to butter her muffin in silence. Nils put the wood in the stove and came over to sit on the edge of the bed. "Why did you ask all that, Jo?"

She smiled at him over her cup. "Just trying to think how you looked when you were four, and all about it. I can't remember you, because I was only two. But you must have been darling, Nils. So serious, in your little blue sailor suit for Sunday best, and with your yellow hair combed just so."

Nils said dryly, "I was always still in my nightgown."

"Then you were even sweeter," said Joanna, and leaned toward him. "A kiss with my breakfast, Nils? For Sunday best?"

His lips touched hers lightly, and then held fast; his hands came out and took her by the shoulders. She couldn't have squirmed free if she'd wanted to. When he let her go they smiled at each other unsteadily.

Nils sat back and took out his cigarettes. "Owen handed me out quite a line this morning," he said. "About not coming down to supper again."

She glanced up at him anxiously. "He didn't get under your skin, did he? You know how Owen likes to plague."

"Finish your breakfast, Jo. Nothing can get under my skin now. . . . How about some fresh coffee?" He reached for her cup, but she put her hand on his wrist.

"Nils, there's something I want to tell you before I eat another mouthful, or before you step out of this room again."

She spoke quietly enough, and his answering tone matched hers. "What is it?"

"There's a story going the rounds on Brigport, Nils. It's about you." It was in the room with them now, the ugliness and the threat that she'd tried to keep away from her and Nils in the hours just passed. It was as if suddenly the blizzard had broken through the glass, and even the glowing stove had no power against its bone-piercing cold. Yet her voice didn't falter, nor did her eyes shift away from his.

"They say that you killed Winslow and threw his body overboard — that day you brought the boat in."

"Who says it?"

"I don't know. Ellen and Joey brought it home from school. Joey got into a fight over it, and Ellen—" her child's small, strained face came before her as she spoke the name. "Ellen says she won't go back there. They tormented her, Nils."

She saw the shifting and tightening of muscles and bone in his face, the almost imperceptible hardening of mouth and eyes. Still he said nothing. Smoke streamed up in a thin ribbon from the cigarette between his two fingers. Joanna's own fingers were cold.

"If you don't want to bother with it, we don't have to, Nils," she said. "We don't even have to go back to the Island, if you don't want to go."

"We'll go back," Nils said. He reached again for her coffee cup and she didn't stop him. "We'll go back as soon as the weather clears. This needs a little tending to, I think."

He went out of the room with her cup and she stared at the door closing behind him, and listened to the sound of his feet going down the stairs. She thought of what he'd said, "This needs a little tending to, I think." Yes, he'd tend to the malicious story the way he took care of everything. . . . As she waited for his return she felt a new stab of shame. The assurance in his bearing was heart-warming to her now; it could have been thus through the past months, if she had not been so blind, so foolishly selfish.

She'd lived through a great many hours recently which were to be remembered always, some of them for penance. *This* hour she would keep close to her until she died. . . .

38

THE BLIZZARD HAD STOPPED BY MIDNIGHT, and at sun-up the next day the snowplow came in from the main road, and turned around in Eric's meadow accompanied by a deafening grinding of gears and Peter's delirious barking. He had seen the snowplows every winter for eight years, but he still wasn't convinced that they wouldn't continue straight up the hill and plow up his favorite doorstep, to say nothing of the people he owned.

Nils and Owen went down to the meadow with their rubber boots pulled up to their hips, and their shadows blue on the snow, and found out from the operator that the Limerock bus would be running as usual. Then the snowplow went back to the highway along the road it had just cleared. Peter chased it, almost sure that he had it in a proper state of terrified retreat, but determined to make certain. Then he came swaggering back to the house, to receive a piece of Joanna's doughnut for his valor.

She and Nils and Owen left that morning, walking along the hardpacked snow through the spruce woods to the highway. The trees were powdered with the glittering dust; the same sparkling stuff flew up from their feet, and blew like spangled smoke from the tops of drifts. The world had an aching brilliance; the sky's aquamarine hurt the eye, and the tree shadows thrown across the snow were sharp blue on dazzling white, each one perfect in itself.

"Regular Christmas weather," Owen said. His breath came out like smoke from a chimney.

"I made a list this morning," Joanna said. "Somehow I hadn't got around to Christmas. . . . It crept up on me, I guess. I'll have to do everything at once, before we go back."

"You'll have the whole day for it then. This wind won't die down till tonight sometime." Owen fell back to light a cigarette and Joanna and Nils walked on; it was too cold to loiter.

"How about a doll for Ellen?" Nils asked her in a low voice. "She'll have a good Christmas — she won't miss Stevie like the rest of us, and she doesn't know about the Philippines."

"Of course she'll have a doll." She reached out her mittened hand to his. "What'll you and Owen do while I go shopping?"

'I don't know what Owen'll do, but I've got a few ideas about it." He looked at her steadily, and then, flushing very slightly, he said, "You mind if I go along with you? I can help carry the stuff."

Their hands dropped apart as they heard Owen's feet behind them; but all the way to the bus stop, and even after they'd clambered aboard, her fingers remembered the firm pressure of his.

Owen waved them a nonchalant farewell when they got off the bus, and strolled off in the windy sunshine, looking very handsome; he towered over most of the people he passed, and the women turned to look at him. Nils and Joanna didn't see him again that day.

They stayed at a Limerock rooming house that night. They pondered the idea of going down to Pruitt's Harbor, but decided against it. The bus—the one which lacked a door—went on a spasmodic schedule, and if the next day should be clear and calm, Owen would be ready to go as soon as it was light enough to see. Besides, Joanna found to her shame that she was tired by mid-afternoon. She was worried, too, that her stamina played her false. It was Nils who reassured her.

"You've had a lot on your mind," he told her. "You can't expect to start dancing jigs the first thing. You get rested up, and lose those circles under your eyes, and then we'll come over and make a real visit with your mother, and Charles, and the rest of 'em. Now you'd better go to bed."

She obeyed him, loving his matter-of-fact way of calming her, and the way he changed to tenderness when he tucked her in, and kissed her. She felt neither foolish nor ashamed; she was happy, and no longer lonely. If only Nils felt the same. . . . He went out to buy her a magazine and some candy, and she lay in the drab, impersonal room looking peacefully at his suitcase beside hers, and praying, somewhere in the innermost chambers of her soul, that she could make him happy always.

When he came back he gave her the bundles to open while he hung up his outdoor clothes. Magazines, candy, grapes, a bottle of vitamin capsules. She held them up to him, smiling, as he came into range of the lamp.

"Do I really need 'em, Nils? I never had to take medicine in my life!"

He didn't answer at once, he was looking beyond her into the shadows of the room, his face set; it was the way he'd looked when she had told him about the Brigport story, about Joey and Ellen.

"What is it, Nils?" she asked him swiftly. She put out her hand to take his, and made him sit down beside her.

"Rich Bradford and his wife are staying here tonight," he said. "I met Rich in the hall downstairs."

She waited, her eyes feeling hot, her heart beating hard.

"Rich walked by me without speaking. Turned his head away."

"Oh, Nils, he couldn't have known you. He always liked you!"

He said angrily, "Didn't know me—with this hair? I had my cap off, and he met me right by the light. He knew me, Joanna." Then he moved his hand in hers, and tightened it around her fingers. "I thought it could wait until after Christmas," he said simply. "But now I know it can't wait."

At noon the next day the *White Lady* sailed into her home harbor. The wind had dropped, and the sun shone across the blue bay and the whitened islands that rimmed it, the gulls circled against the sky, and their voices were needle-sharp in the silence after the engine was cut off.

It had been a quiet trip out, except for the very start, when Owen had pounded on Nils' and Joanna's door at the first edge of dawn and announced through the panels that he was going home now, by God. He was in a bad mood, and stayed in it, until the *Lady* was halfway home. Then, with the Mussel Ridges far behind and Vinalhaven growing smaller, and the first glimpse of Bennett's Island coming out beyond the end of Brigport, Owen began to brighten. Perhaps the flat pint bottle in the empty bait tub under the washboards had something to do with it.

The harbor was empty of powerboats when they came into it, except for the *Donna*. The skiffs bounced gently at the moorings, orange and buff and white and green; Jud's robin's-egg-blue masterpiece was tied up alongside the lobster car. All the men had gone to haul, and the fact that no smoke rose from the boatshop's chimney meant that Jud had gone home for his dinner. No one would be in before mid-afternoon.

To Joanna it seemed right and fitting that there should be no one on hand to take a line or call greetings to Nils as the *White Lady* came alongside the wharf. It meant that she and Nils could walk up to the house alone—Owen would take the boat out to the mooring. She could reach for his hand if she wanted to, and know he wouldn't hold back from her. And they could walk alone into the house, and it would be as it should have been on that long-ago September evening.

Of course, Owen would be coming in afterward, but if the whole world trooped into their kitchen, what difference could it make to them, when they could glance across the room at each other and in an instant reaffirm the truth?

When they actually started up the frozen road, with its snow-filled ruts, they had too many bundles to hold hands. But they could look at each other, there was no limit to that. The Island never held the snow; the high places of the Bennett meadow were bare, but down by the gateposts there were drifts and Nils tramped a way through them for Joanna. She caught up with him, exhilarated by the bright, winy cold, laughing for nothing but excited happiness. For this little while, when they might have been the only two persons on their Island, there were no spectres, no shadows; only themselves in a world of pure white and blue, with snow-dust glittering on their eyelashes and the sun dancing in their eyes.

From the crest of the meadow the Bennett house looked down on them benignly, waiting for them to take possession again.

Nils had the fire built by the time Owen came with the rest of the load, and while Owen pulled off his gloves to warm his hands, Nils took the water pails and went down to the well. Joanna, still in her outdoor clothes, was unpacking the groceries. By the time the kitchen was warm, dinner would be almost ready. It was wonderful to feel so hungry; it was wonderful to be home again, seeing the thin rectangles of sunlight slanting across the creamy boards, catching the glint of sea and curl of white on the tawny ledges when she passed the seaward windows. . . . And from the harbor windows she saw Nils, breaking the ice in the well with the well-pole. . . . She paused, watching him, and forgot that Owen was in the room until he spoke.

"God Almighty, Jo, how in hell did you get around him?" he asked with a lazy curiosity. "Got him in line again, didn't ye? I didn't think you could do it."

"Well, that gives you something to wonder about," she countered easily. Only a week ago, any reference to Nils and herself would have thrown her into a fury. She marveled at the difference; she had turned to her brother, smiling. She knew that nothing he could ever say, in good temper or bad, could really touch the private, secret world she and Nils had now found for themselves.

With dinner over, and Owen gone upstairs for a nap—Joanna guessed that he'd not been to bed at all the night before—she and Nils decided to walk down to the Eastern End to get Ellen. But when they came out of the house, Nils hesitated, and looked down the meadow toward the smoky-lavender cloud the bare alder swamp made. His grandfather's house lay beyond the alders.

"Come down to the old house with me first," he suggested. "I promised Gramma I'd look it over, and now is as good a time as any."

"A little longer won't make any difference to Ellen," Joanna said. "She'll be so darned relieved and happy to see you, because of Christmas and this other thing. . . . Does your grandmother get homesick for the house, Nils?"

"No, but sometimes she thinks about the flowers she had and feels bad for them. They used to be a comfort to her, I guess."

They cut down across the meadow, tramping a path through the pocket of snow at its foot, and came into the alder swamp. It was sheltered here, and held the sun, and there was a constant drip of melting snow and the loudly busy chatter of chickadees. They flashed across the path before Joanna and Nils, holding undisputed possession of the alder swamp until the juncoes and sparrows came back, and then the ubiquitous warblers.

They came out onto the Sorensen place and skirted the big barn and the woodhouse. Nils had the key to the back door of the sunparlor; and so they entered the house where Nils had grown up. Joanna hadn't been in it since she was a young girl. That meant she had never been in it when it was empty. Always Grandma Sorensen had been working around in the long sunparlor, where the family had eaten in warm weather, where she and Kristi had washed and ironed; or she had been making bread in the kitchen, tending the chowder that simmered in the black iron pot, singing hymns in her sweet, tremulous old voice. And Joanna had never been there when the fact of Gunnar Sorensen's imminent entrance hadn't hung over the house like a pall.

Joanna looked back over the years as she followed Nils through the empty house, listening to their echoing footsteps, wondering what he thought as he stopped to look at a picture on the wall, or his grandmother's small collection of ornaments on the what-not. These sunny windows in the dining room had always been full of plants; this was Anna's chair, this was Gunnar's. He used to sit here of an evening and rock, and read the Bible aloud by lamplight while his grandsons Sigurd and Nils and their sister Kristi knit trapheads out in the sunparlor. There were windows on that side of the dining room too, so he could see all three blond heads, and know that they were listening respectfully. Or at least not slacking their work. Little David, the youngest — their mother had died when he was born — would be in bed by that time. He was subject to nightmares and would cry out, but Gunnar wouldn't allow his wife Anna or Kristi to go to him. The nightmares had a reason, he said; when David became a good boy, the devil would stop tormenting him. It was Nils who had figured out the arrangement—"to save space," he told his grandfather— whereby David slept with him.

Nils was going upstairs now. Joanna followed him silently. This was no time to speak to him. She contented herself with her own thoughts, trying not to dwell on the memory of the time Gunnar had come in late from a seining trip and found that Nils hadn't white-washed the henhouse as he'd been told. It didn't matter that his small, trembling wife told him Nils hadn't had time to do the henhouse, because he'd split up some extra firewood for her cooking; he had come upstairs in his heavy rubber boots, spangled with herring scales—they'd sparkled on his beard too, Nils had told Joanna once—and dragged the sleeping boy out of bed, kicking him awake, and set him to white-washing the henhouse then, at one in the morning.

Here was the bed in which Gunnar and Anna had slept, in which Gunnar had died; he had simply stayed asleep one morning. *He always hated me,* Joanna thought, looking at the bare mattress and pillows in the big bed. *There should be something fighting against me in this room, trying to drive me out.* Then she remembered that he hadn't hated her always. Once, just once, a little while before he died, he had spoken to her humbly.

"If Nils had married you, I would have been glad. . . . You are a good woman. Nils is right about you all the time, and I am wrong."

And here we are, thought Joanna now. The pale sunlight lay across the bedroom floors and Nils was walking through the other rooms. She heard his deliberate feet, and went quickly to find him.

He had stopped in a small room under the eaves, with a slanting ceiling like her own room at home. "This was mine," he said. It was the first thing he had said since they came into the house.

She looked at the narrow bed under the small window. It was at the front of the house, and in the old days Anna's seven-sisters rose bush had climbed up to this window. . . . She realized that Nils was watching her quietly.

"What are you thinking?" he asked.

"I was seeing you," she said. "Lying in bed with your arm under your head, the way you do, on a summer night, with the breeze blowing up from the harbor and coming in through the roses. . . ." She wanted to touch him, break through the shell of loneliness that had seemed to enclose him when he entered the house. "I know you weren't reading, because Gunnar wouldn't let you read in bed. So you were thinking."

"No limit to that, anyway," he said dryly. "Know what I'm thinking now?"

"Tell me." She moved closer to him, and put her hand in his with a now-familiar gesture.

"Well, I used to swear that if I ever got out of this house, I'd never come back into it. And after I did get out of it, I had the funny feeling that if I only stepped inside the door, all those old things would rush at me and drive me out again. But it's funny." He shook his head. "Instead, I've been thinking about the way we've all turned out. Grampa could bully us, and plague us, and hang us up by the thumbs, and insult us about our mother until we wanted to kill him. But in the end he couldn't really hurt us. . . . And he *did* teach us how to work."

He sat down on the bed and pulled Joanna down beside him. "Sigurd's skipper on his own sardine boat, down East. He's married, and has a hell of a good time out of life. Kristi's married, and happy with a family of kids to spoil. And she married the man she wanted, too. Grampa couldn't stop that."

"He tried hard enough," murmured Joanna.

"Then my father put David through high school after Grampa died, and Dave put himself through the University of Maine, so he's the family pride and joy."

"What about Nils?" Joanna asked him softly.

"Nils?" He turned his head and looked down at her. "Oh, he did himself proud, too." He put his arm around her and pulled her close to him with a suddenness that made her gasp and laugh.

"He married a wild woman that needed taming," she said. He cut off the last word with his mouth on hers, and she felt a quicksilver sweetness run through her body. The back of his neck was strong under her palm; while their mouths held in an intensity of hunger too long denied.

When he lifted his head, it was as if she came back by a long and enchanted way to the bare room under the eaves. She burrowed her head against his shoulder and let her fingers explore the back of his head, under his ears, to the hard corner of his jaw and thence to his chin.

"End of the line," she said with regret, and sat up. "Back to work, Nils."

"What do you mean, work?" asked Nils. She found she couldn't move away from the arms that held her against his chest. She knew by the way he smiled at her what he was thinking.

"Nils, not here!"

"Why not? Nobody knows we're here—"

"Because—oh, Nils—" Laughter bubbled out suddenly. "The ghost of your grandfather."

Nils' arms were tightening. "Nothing for him to hang around here for. Everybody works too hard. He'll be down East prodding Sig. . . ." The laughter went out of his face. "You're so beautiful, Joanna," he said simply. "Don't fight me."

When they came downstairs the sun had moved away from the dining room window. Nils led the way down the narrow, twisting stair; at the foot he waited for Joanna, and kissed her. "You know," she said slowly, "sometimes when I was all excited about something and you took your pipe out of your mouth and told me why my idea wouldn't work, you made me think of my father—and I felt like a little girl again, getting stepped on. I think that was why I tossed my head so much, Nils."

"Do you feel like a little girl now?"

"This," said Joanna, "is no way for a little girl to feel. . . . What did I do to bother you, Nils, besides teaming you around like your grandfather, and always trying to run things?"

"That's about it," said Nils candidly. "Except—well, you were so damned independent. You had some good ideas for the Island, and I was proud of you. But . . . You want the straight truth, Joanna?"

She lifted her chin and smiled at him. "Yes, darling."

"I felt as though I didn't have anything of my own, Joanna. Not even my wife. I was living with Joanna Bennett and her brothers in the Bennett homestead. That was what it amounted to. The night Mark counted me in as a Bennett, well—that hit me, Jo." His mouth quirked. "Sounds foolish, but that's the way it was."

"What about now, Nils?" she asked him carefully. She could feel the tightening along her spine and in her jaw. "How is it now?"

"It's different," he answered, and went to kiss her, but she turned her head away. His fingers caught her chin like a vise, and then in one deep breath drawn and released, she fought the impulse that had threatened her for a moment, and won.

"It may be different, but it's still not right," she said. "Nils, would you like us to live down here?"

His answer was simple and unadorned. "Yes." He didn't insult her intelligence by adding explanations and she was grateful. He knew what a step it would be for her, how much store she had set by the homestead; what it had meant for her to be in her mother's place in the Bennett house.

Her eyes didn't shift away from his for a second. "All right, Nils," she said. "It's up to you to choose where we'd live, anyway." She knew by the set of his mouth and the way the lines came in his forehead that he thought he had asked too much of her. He should not think that; he should know his right and claim it.

"And besides," she added demurely, "it wouldn't do for a lot of little blond Sorensens to be running around the Bennett house. They ought to grow up in a Sorensen house."

That did it. The hard lines broke into tenderness, as she went into his arms and heard his voice whispering against her hair.

39

THEY WENT OUTDOORS AND AROUND to the front of the house. "The seven-sisters bush is still alive," Joanna said. "And I'll plant holly-hocks all around the house, Nils."

"Delphinium, too," said Nils.

She smiled at him. "Of course, delphinium."

They walked past Eric Sorensen's house, and the Arey house, and took the road that led to the beach. They could see the smoke puffing up from the chimney of the boatshop, and they could hear the whining throb of an engine in reverse; someone was backing away from the car. The smoke, and the engine's sound, took away the Island's emptiness. Joanna and Nils were no longer the only two persons on it.

When they came by the end of the boatshop, they had a full view of the wharf. The tide was going, and the car was out of sight, but Jud was toiling over the top of the ladder, and Caleb's boat was moving slowly toward her mooring, Joey poised tautly upon the bow with the gaff in his hand, ready to hook the buoy. His slender figure was outlined distinctly against the warm red rocks that made a sheer rise from the water to the top of Eastern Harbor Point. At its base, the thick rockweed uncovered by the tide had a dark wet gloss in the sun.

"Bright kid, Joey," Nils remarked. Joanna said excitedly, "Isn't that Ellen coming up the ladder behind Jud?"

It was Ellen indeed. Jud reached down a hand to her and they could hear his wheezy chuckle as she refused help and landed nimbly on the wharf. Helmi followed. She turned to reach down for the package which Mark held up to her, and then he came over the top of the ladder. Joanna had a glimpse of his stormy face under the plaid cap before Ellen caught sight of her and cried out.

"Mother!" She ran over the wharf, her brownie hood slipping back from her radiant face. "You're here! We've been for the mail and you ought to see all the Christmas packages—"

Everything stopped at once, her clear high young voice, her eager rush. She had seen Nils. Then joy came, incandescent, and the headlong rush.

"*Nils!* Oh, Nils!" His arms opened to catch the flying little figure and her arms went tight around his neck. She talked in little snatches, punctuated by a child's breathless, throat-catching laughter. "I never thought—and you've been gone so *long*. . . . It seems like forever, Nils!"

They shimmered before Joanna's eyes, a shifting blur of bright blue, and the soft brown of Nils' jacket, his wheat-colored hair as his cap fell off in the violence of Ellen's hug. Her throat tightened at the recognition of the love these two bore for each other. . . . *It makes us a real family,* she thought inadequately, and winked back the wetness as she turned to greet Helmi.

Helmi seemed thinner and fine-drawn, but she was smiling. "Why did you come back so soon, Joanna? I'll miss Ellen."

"Helmi, she wasn't too much of a bother to you, was she?"

"I liked having her. It gave me something to do."

Mark bore down on Nils. Yes, he *was* stormy. "Jesus Christ, about time you got home!" he said violently. Jud, behind him, wheezed.

"Purty way of greetin' your brother-in-law, I must say! Whyn't you just shoot the poor son of a bitch and be done with it?"

"It may come to shootin' before we're done," Mark said, looking ominous. "Way they're chewin' over on Brigport."

Nils clapped Mark's shoulder. "Come on up to the house, Mark." He reached around Mark to shake hands with Jud, whose eyes were more watery than usual and who kept sniffing as if he had a cold.

"Buildin' boats, were ye? Whyn't you tell that uncle of yours that boat belongs in these waters, none of this fishin' in the bay with her! . . . It's good to see you back, son."

Matthew Fennell's boat swerved boldly around the harbor point, with a home-coming air about her, and came with an arrow straightness toward the car. Jud hurried back across the wharf, muttering. "Last man in, as usual. Works hard, that boy. Don't wonder he stays out all day, with that old woman waitin' at home for him. . . . Even if his wife is a nice girl. . . ."

Caleb was just beaching his punt, and Nils called down to him and Joey. Caleb's answer came, deep and unhurried. The boy's smile was dazzling, as Ellen's had been. That moment told Joanna more clearly than anything else what Joey had fought for, at school; Nils was his hero, almost his god.

It was surely not possible that she'd ever been jealous of Nils, and not proud. . . . They walked up to the house, the two men behind her and Helmi, and Ellen everywhere at once. Mark was talking vehemently in a restrained voice; it was always an effort for him to suppress either pleasure or rage, so he seemed to be talking between clenched teeth.

"What happened at Brigport?" Joanna asked Helmi.

"Captain Merrill told him something." Helmi gave her a side-wise look.

"Go ahead, Helmi. I heard about this before I went ashore."

Helmi didn't look surprised. "I was wondering about that, to-day. But I didn't tell Mark what I thought. . . . Captain Merrill called us into his boatshop when we landed on his wharf this afternoon. He said it had come to him—he wouldn't tell us who said it."

"Naturally," said Joanna. "But he wanted us over here to know what was going on. Cap'n Merrill's always been a good friend to us."

"He seems good," answered Helmi. She and Joanna had reached the path through the drifts by the old gateposts. They looked back at the men, Mark so black-browed and emphatic, Nils fair and reflective. Ellen skipped between them.

"Ellen hasn't been very gay, I knew she had something on her mind," said Helmi. "Look at her now."

"Nils is home, and he can fix everything. Ellen's sure of it."

The translucent green of Helmi's eyes darkened to a cold, grayed color, like a suddenly clouded sea. "It's—*abominable* for them to say such things about Nils! Joanna, how can you be so calm? You look perfectly peaceful."

"I wasn't peaceful when I left here, Helmi," Joanna said. "But I'm like Ellen—I'm not scared when Nils is here." She knelt suddenly and scooped up a double handful of snow. "Isn't this wonderful for snowballs?" she demanded, and was glad to see the faint smile that lighted Helmi's face.

"Throw it at me, Mother!" Ellen shouted. "I bet you can't hit me!"

She ran toward them on feet that seemed hardly to touch the ground.

Owen had got up from his nap when they reached the house. He had shaved and put on a new and brilliant plaid shirt. When he saw them coming he had made the usual afternoon coffee, and rummaged through the cupboards for one of the dark fruitcakes Karin Soren-sen had given to Joanna. In addition to the mug-up, he had what was left of his pint, and offered it magnanimously to Mark, who re-fused.

"Never touch the stuff, huh?" said Owen interestedly. "My, my, how times change."

"Don't try to start anything," Mark warned him. "We've got more to think about than what a comic feller you are. So sit down."

"Okay, Aphrodite." Owen patted his bottle and put it carefully in a remote corner of the cupboard. "What's happened? You just discover the Germans invaded Brigport?" He sprawled in his chair and grinned around at the others. "Now that'd be something. Link hands the mail over to the Limerock postoffice and says 'Funny thing happened out at Brigport this mornin'. Store must have changed hands again. German feller came down to the wharf to get the mailbags.' "

Nils laughed, and Mark relaxed a little. "Randolph Fowler's doing about as good as the Germans, the way he's spreading his propaganda around."

. "So you've got hold of that, have ye?" said Owen.

Nils went to the stove and came back with the coffee pot. "Who wants more coffee? Helmi, Joanna? . . . You're pretty sure it's Randolph behind this, Mark?"

"Who else would it be that would start such a story about you?" Joanna asked passionately, and then subsided. She had done all she could, said all she was going to say. It was for the men to take over now. And they'd not have the chance to say that she was talking too much again. She sipped her coffee and motioned Ellen not to take another piece of fruitcake, and watched the scene around her. The kitchen was warm with the pale gold wash of late afternoon sunshine, and the mulling fire. Helmi sat near her, finished with her coffee, her hands folded in her lap. Owen was beyond Helmi, his long legs thrust out before him, his bare ankles brown and gypsyish between the cuffs of his corduroys and his moccasins; the rich darkness of his skin and the Indian-blackness of his hair, the vigor of his face and changing expressions, made a startling contrast to Helmi's immobility and pallor. Across from him, Mark folded his arms on the table's edge and talked to Nils. His resemblance to Owen was shockingly vivid; yet the differences were vivid, too. Mark had a glow of freshness and youth, his cheekbones were tinged with coppery red, his voice resounded in the kitchen as Owen's had resounded years ago, when he'd been afire for action. But Owen at thirty-three was too tired to be afire about anything, now.

"Of course it's Fowler!" Mark was saying. "Look, this is the way the son of a bitch's figurin' it out. They whisper around, and finally they're sayin' it out loud, slicin' you in strips, soakin' you in pickle, and layin' you out on the flakes to dry. You can't take it after a while, so you leave and take your family with you. Then everybody else goes. Bennett's is wild again."

He spread out his hands, shrugged, and sat back in his chair. "What makes you think he's sure everybody else would go too?" Nils asked. He sat at the other end of the table, beyond Helmi and Mark and Owen. To Joanna, he dominated them. She told herself she thought that only because she had so recently ceased to pit herself against him. She was accepting him now as he was, with no sense of conflict. But reasoning didn't change the fact that he *did* dominate the others. And she was fiercely glad that her brothers turned to him as they did, without question or criticism. *It wasn't that way with Alec,* she thought, and then drove that sly, small memory away.

"Jud's set here," Nils went on. "Caleb likes it. So does Matthew. You're Bennetts, it's your home-place and you know the ropes. So why should Randolph figure it would make any difference to the rest of you, what I do?"

"He figures it the way I would," Owen drawled. "You hold this place together, Nils. Bennetts or no Bennetts."

Joanna agreed silently. Yes, it was Nils who held them all together. And the boys were telling the truth when they said that was what Randolph Fowler was counting on. It was strange to be thinking all this, with calmness lapping around her like the sea lapping on the beach in Schoolhouse Cove on a windless summer day. Thinking that Randolph couldn't hurt the Island; thinking that Nils would take care of everything. . . .

Mark said violently, "What I want to know is, are we goin' to fiddle-faddle around and act like we don't know it's goin' on, or are we going to *do* something?"

Owen scratched a match with his thumbnail. "What do you want to do, Wild Bill Hickok? Take your trusty .45 and clean up the joint over there?"

"There's a meeting tomorrow," Helmi's voice slipped quietly into the little space of silence after Owen spoke. "I read it on the board outside the store, while Mark was getting the mail. Everybody is to come together in the schoolhouse at two o'clock. It's to form a shore patrol to look out for submarines."

"That's it," said Nils. "I'll be there."

Mark followed swiftly. "I'll be there too, by God."

"I suppose I'll be on deck too," said Owen, and let the two front legs of his chair come down with a crash. "Any more coffee?"

The course was charted, as simply and undramatically as that. There was fresh coffee all around and the men began to discuss the winter lobstering, and the new engine Nils had brought out in the *White Lady* that morning. Joanna talked to Ellen, and told Helmi about the Christmas decorations in Limerock, the things she'd seen in the stores. But all the time she could feel a pulse beating in her throat — she hoped her blouse collar hid it. *Tomorrow, tomorrow, tomorrow,* it said. It was a fine and triumphant beat, like a tiny drum.

The three men went out again soon, down to the shore to bait up while the sunshine still lasted. Helmi stayed a few minutes longer and then left. She had a long walk across the wintery fields and then through the darkening woods, and at the end of it the houses were small and windswept and alone; one of them altogether empty, the other where she lived with Mark and dreamed of Stevie —

But she would fight her way through, Joanna thought, watching the tall, slender figure grow steadily smaller on the road beyond Schoolhouse Cove. She was willing to bet that Helmi would not go down under the strain; she had promised she would never hurt Mark, and she never would.

Ellen sang softly to herself in the next room. The sun dropped down behind the belt of woods at the foot of the meadow, and it would grow dark quickly. It would be time to light the lamps, and draw the shades, and set the table. Time for Nils to come home again.

After supper there were callers; Caleb and Jud and Matthew, filing in through the entry, pulling off their caps, refusing to sit down until they had stated what they had come to say. For some reason they had chosen Matthew Fennell to say it, though he was the youngest and shyest, and also the newest Islander. But there was a blunt and earnest sincerity about his words.

"Mark told us what you're plannin' on doin'," he said. His cheeks were redder than usual, but his tongue didn't stumble. "We want you to know we're with you. I mean, we'll be there too."

"He means, we'll show 'em they ain't dealin' with no pale-faced —"

Jud stopped abruptly, looked mortified, and then grinned. "Oh, hell, Nils, you know what he means."

"He ought to," said Caleb, "by the time you get through showin' off your plain and fancy vocabulary." He put out his rough, bony hand to Nils and looked at him from under heavy grizzled brows. "I don't know yet what we can do, Nils, but we'll be there."

"Thanks, Caleb," Nils held out his own hand. "Thanks, Jud . . . Matthew." He said nothing more about it, and Joanna knew they expected nothing more. He'd taken their offer for what it was — the sign of their loyalty — and that was what they wanted. Not speeches, or long words.

Men understand each other, she thought. *They don't need anyone — me or anyone else — to explain them to each other.*

They were sitting down now, their somber faces relaxing into smiles; they were reaching for pipes and cigarettes and matches. She spoke to them all, and went into the sitting room, where Ellen played with her paper dolls. She had darning to do — there was always darning — and Christmas gifts to wrap, and a letter to write to Stevie, telling him Nils had come home.

40

THE *White Lady* WENT OUT OF THE HARBOR with Matthew's boat following behind her. It was a gray and gold day, with the sun a pale, wide circle of light behind the thick veil of dove-colored cloud that meant snow. The sea was almost smooth between Bennett's and Brigport, silvery-gray; in the boiling wake of the *White Lady* each frothy crest held a glint of the sun's diffused gold.

Nils, Mark, Owen, Joanna, and Helmi were aboard the *White Lady;* Matthew, Caleb and Jud in Matthew's boat. And Joey. He'd been allowed to come at the last minute. Joanna had taken Ellen down to the Caldwells' to stay for the afternoon, and had discovered Joey standing at the sitting room window, looking across the harbor with a stern expression. Caleb was in the kitchen, pulling on his boots.

"Aren't you going over to Brigport, Joey?" she asked the boy.

He shrugged. "No place for kids, my father says."

"But you're the one who got the black eye," Joanna said. She went out into the kitchen and spoke to Caleb.

"Joey has a right to be in this, Caleb. He's as much of an Island man as any of you. After all, he was fighting for Nils before the rest of us knew what was going on."

"Well . . ." said Caleb. He reached for his cap. "I s'pose so. Get your things on, son."

Outside the harbor Owen slowed the *White Lady* down so that Matthew could come abreast of her, and the two boats moved side by side down Long Cove toward Tenpound. Joanna watched the Island slipping by. In the pale, chill light, with its winter colorings upon it, it was not beautiful, she supposed, but it was home, and more than home; if she were on the other side of the world, and were suddenly transported, blindfolded, across the miles and set down on the Island, her feet would know it before her head did. They would know the feel of Island soil, and of Island rocks with the sea beating against them.

She looked at Nils and Mark and Owen, clustered around the wheel, talking and smoking; at Helmi, standing beside her, her face turned to the wind, and she wanted to tell them what she was thinking, but she could not. . . . All over the world now, people like themselves were fighting, some of them dying, to hold on to the bits of land their feet knew as home. It was a fight that always went on, and sometimes the small, unimportant people won, and sometimes they didn't. But the battle never finished, because there would never be an end to the men who tried to take home away.

At the end of Long Cove the woods came almost down to the shore; spruce woods, black with winter, trees that had been little emerald-green saplings when her father and Uncle Nate were boys and played Indians among them with their bows and arrows. The little stretch of grass-ground between the fringe of the woods and the harshly carved shoreline was a sallow brown now; who would ever think that by July it would be brilliant with blue flag, and spattered with daisies like the Milky Way?

How would I feel now, Joanna asked herself relentlessly, *if I thought Fowler could drive us away, so we wouldn't see the blue flag again?*

She thought of the Philippines then; there was no escaping it, you heard it whenever you turned on the radio, and wherever the men talked. American boys like Stevie, and the Filipinos themselves, were fighting and dying and losing. . . . The Poles, the Dutch, the Belgians, the French — and how long had it been going on for the Chinese? Pain twisted in her breast like a knife. She looked at Nils, standing by the wheel; he was listening to Mark and Owen, and there was a little smile on his lips. She wanted to go to him and put her arms around him, and feel his arms around her, and be comforted.

The boats rounded the point of Tenpound and met a slight swell, they rose and fell on its billowing sweep with a smooth rhythm. The sun was reflected on the glossy water in small yellow circles. Surf broke unhurriedly on the back shores of Tenpound and slid back to the sea again, over slopes of red rock; shags and seagulls took off as the boats came near, the shags with their furiously awkward struggles for altitude, the gulls with their pure and effortless launching into the wind.

In the diffused, unshadowed light there was an unbroken view to the east, save for Pirate Island crouched on the horizon, long and very flat. Gray sea, gray sky, and it reached all the way to Spain. . . . Beside Joanna, Helmi stirred.

"I think a shore patrol is a good thing," she said in her cool, distinct voice. "I'd be willing to take my turn walking around the shore for two hours every day. . . . Sometimes when Mark is out hauling, I go up on the Head and look out to sea, and wonder what I would do if I saw a periscope."

Joanna, already tense, felt herself tightening even more. "Vinnie gets all wrought up about it, but you make it sound worse by being so calm, Helmi. What *would* you do if you saw a submarine?"

"The other night I thought I heard one. I woke up and heard heavy engines." She smiled faintly. "I was reading that they come up at night to charge their batteries. So of course I was sure."

"What did you do?"

"I woke up Mark and said, 'There's a submarine out between

the Head and Pirate Island.' And he said, 'What the hell can I do about it?' and went to sleep again."

"Why didn't you kick him?" demanded Joanna

"I didn't have to. In a minute he sat up in bed and said, 'Did you say a *submarine?*' He jumped out of bed and went for his shotgun. By then the engines had stopped." Her smile deepened. "In the morning there was a Coast Guard picket boat lying in the Cove. That was what we'd heard."

Joanna sat down on the washboards, and let her breath out again. "All the same . . ." She looked toward the east. "They *could* come in this way — only I've got faith in the boys in the tower at Matinicus Rock, and the patrol planes. In the whole Coast Guard, in fact."

"But have you ever thought the Army might order everybody to leave the Islands?" said Helmi. "If the submarine trouble became too bad?"

Joanna lifted her chin. "If the Army orders us out, that's one thing. But I don't care if the submarines surface in Goose Cove! They can't scare me away! I'll be like Mark and keep my shotgun loaded." Her tenseness dissolved into laughter. "Listen to us, Helmi. Trying to scare ourselves to death."

She sobered all at once, and looked ahead at Brigport; they had almost reached the mouth of the Gut that led into Brigport Harbor, and the boat was rolling in the swell. "We'll be there pretty soon, Helmi. We've got an even chance with Fowler. That's one thing the others haven't got."

"What others?" said Helmi, but Joanna, watching the narrow, rocky gates of the Gut grow near, didn't answer her.

The Gut widened out and the two boats from Bennett's Island were running the length of Brigport Harbor, past the high wharves and weatherbeaten fish houses on the point; among the moorings, leaving the boats rolling drunkenly in first one wake and then the next, sending the seagulls up from the ledges in a flurry of beating white and gray wings. Owen didn't check the speed of the *White Lady,* but let her roar her way toward the big stone wharf at the end, and in the cloud-heavy air the echoes flung themselves back and forth between the shores, a hammering, throbbing, thunder that sounded loud enough to bring most of the Brigporters down to the wharf. The wakes threw water to both sides, to surge and break against the rocks. The whole gray silence and tranquillity of the harbor was shattered.

It was odd, after such a noisy entrance, to see no one on the big wharf. The fish houses were shut up; no smoke drifted down from the chimney of Cap'n Merrill's boatshop, or from the store. There was an uncanny sense of emptiness about the place, when the engines were shut off and the only sound was the dying whisper and hiss of the water against the spilings.

They tied up beside Cap'n Merrill's float and went up the slip to the wharf. It was strange, how much noise the feet of nine people can make upon a wharf, even when those people are suddenly imbued with the silence of a place or a day. This was a hushed day, and a hushed and preoccupied village. Joanna had to remind herself forcibly that the islanders were meeting simply to form a patrol system, that they didn't actually know what was about to take place; the stillness was so marked. If it had been a normally bright, windy, December day instead of a weather-breeder. . . . She looked behind her and saw how intent and unnaturally clear Jud's and Caleb's faces were, and Matthew's earnest, more youthful one. Joey caught her glance. He still looked strained and stern, the traces of his black eye vivid on the pointed pale face between the big ear-laps.

She felt like winking at him, but she was afraid he would object to her marring the solemnity of the moment. Beside her Helmi walked along, her hands in the deep pockets of her raincoat. Ahead of her Mark and Owen flanked Nils. Her brothers had talked all the way across in the *White Lady,* she had seen their savage gestures and their white grins, and guessed at what they had said. Now they, like the others, were quiet.

The ground sloped sharply upward from the shore, and the spruces grew on the slope, keeping their scanty foothold among the rough gray granite outcroppings. The men took the path from Cap'n Merrill's boatshop past his house, and reached the road that led up through the middle of Brigport. The sound of rubber boots on the frozen road was the only break in the quiet. It drowned out the girls' footsteps, and it sounded like many men.

It's all of Bennett's Island, Joanna thought, and the words kindled a fiery pride in her that drove out the day's raw chill. She would have liked to have been walking beside Nils, but Mark and Owen had pre-empted him. But later on, when it was all over, she would have Nils to herself. . . .

It had always seemed a long walk up to the schoolhouse, but today they came to the last gate almost before they knew it; they had left the road that twisted between silent spruce woods, looking like a deep-country road instead of an island one, and were on the high part of the island, where they could look out and see horizon beyond Pirate Island, and could almost see over the head of Bennett's. They could look southward and westward too, and see the faint shimmer of gold that was the sun's mark on the gray sea as the veil of cloud thinned for an instant.

The land had been so thoroughly cleared here that it looked barren. The schoolhouse sat alone beside the long straight road, and the little boxlike building behind it stood out in ludicrous clarity. There was smoke streaming vigorously from the schoolhouse chimney, and a handful of children playing on the swings, apparently brought along by their parents. They froze into stillness like startled wild animals as they watched the Bennett's Islanders walk across the yard to the steps.

"Hello, kids," Nils said. He halted on the top step.

Coming up behind him, Joanna heard a timid, "Hi, Joey."

There was an aloof silence from Joey. It made Joanna's mouth twitch. Nils, his hand already on the knob, turned to look down at her. His eyes reached out for her in a way that made her heart jump.

"How's your courage?" he said softly.

"Finest kind! How's yours?"

"When he gets through keelhauling those bastards," said Mark between his teeth, "nobody'll give two hoots in hell for 'em."

"Amen," came Caleb's deep voice. Nils smiled at Joanna and opened the door.

They filed quietly into the dark entry. Beyond the closed door that led into the schoolroom, someone was talking; it was Cap'n Merrill, who'd apparently been appointed chairman of the meeting. There was an occasional throat-clearing, or a cough. A baby piped up and was quickly hushed. Outside in the schoolyard the children had resumed their play.

In the moment of waiting in the dimness, Joanna reached for

Nils' hand and gripped it hard. Jud muttered uneasily. "Why don't we get on with it?"

"Yeah, what are we waiting for?" said Owen in a normal voice. Nils' fingers crushed Joanna's for a second and let them go. At the same time the door opened into the schoolroom. Beyond her brothers' heads and shoulders Joanna had an impression of much light from the big windows, of the acrid smell of the fire, of a startled murmur, of Cap'n Merrill standing up by the teacher's desk; then she had followed Nils into the room.

Cap'n Merrill's hair and mustache were very white against his ruddy face. It seemed a shade ruddier than usual. He glanced sharply at Mark, and then his voice, made rich and penetrating with years of giving orders from the quarter-deck, rolled out in welcome.

"Well, it looks like Bennett's is int'rested in makin' up a patrol, and they've all come over to see how we're goin' to do it! Come in, come in, all of ye — glad to have ye aboard! Set down now, and make yourselves comfortable." Ralph Fowler, sitting near the front, spoke under his breath, and the Cap'n frowned at him.

"Seems to me *I* was elected chairman o' this little assemblage, Ralph." He raised his voice. "Don't think any of you'll find it hard to set in these school seats, unless maybe it's Jud there. . . . Hello, there, Cap'n Joey! Thought you wouldn't be makin' port here till after New Year's." He sat down at the desk.

Joanna looked at Nils. There was a moment when they all looked at Nils, who stood among them tranquilly, his cap in his hand. He reached his other hand up to unzip his leather jacket, and then he walked down the aisle between the desks to the teacher's platform. Everybody in the room was watching him; the women who had come with their husbands whispered to each other, and to Joanna it was a furtive, uneasy, whispering. Had *they* carried the story of murder? The seats creaked as the men shifted in them. She saw faces she had known all her life. A few smiled and nodded at her group. *They didn't talk,* she thought. *But it looks as if most of the others did.*

Nils had almost reached the platform now. Randolph Fowler sat on a bench at one side of the room, his dark, smooth-featured face impassive. His wife wasn't there, though Ralph's wife sat with her husband. Randy sat beside his father, staring fixedly across the room and through the opposite windows.

Nils stepped up on the low platform and spoke to Cap'n Merrill. The uneasy whispering gave way to an uneasy hush, as if all ears were straining to hear. Cap'n Merrill's forehead creased into deep furrows. He looked dubiously at his gavel. Nils, his hands flat on the desk, leaned toward the older man again. There was no knowing what he said, but there was a quiet emphasis in the way his lips moved, and came together hard on the last word.

Earl Robey was finding the room too warm. His pimpled forehead was wetly shiny. Rich Bradford, who had refused to speak to Nils in Limerock, looked, granite-faced, at the blackboard, where the words of "Good King Wenceslas" had been written. And Cap'n Merrill stood up; the gavel came down with a sharp crack that made everyone start.

"The meetin' will come to order. . . . Will you folks at the back be seated, please." He waited while the Bennett's Islanders found places. Jud tried to squeeze behind a desk, but couldn't. Red-faced and sweating, and tip-toeing with a whale-sized daintiness, he sat down on the same bench that held Randolph Fowler and Randy.

Cap'n Merrill went on. "Looks like we've got some business to be discussed before anything else . . . seems like it's more urgent. At least that's what Nils tells me, and I'm inclined to agree with him. So without fubbin' around any longer, I'll turn the meetin' over to Nils Sorensen."

Randolph Fowler stood up. "Mr. Chairman, *nothing* is more important than the submarine menace. I came here to discuss the war effort, and if you're passing that up, I refuse to waste any more of my valuable time."

"Randolph, you better sit down again," said the Cap'n without expression. "Stop talkin' like one of them executives, and listen. . . . Unless your boy Winslow don't matter to you any more, now he's dead."

There was an audible hiss of indrawn breath. A woman said loudly, "Well, I never!" Randolph sat down again. Randy was lighting a cigarette. Joanna saw with astonishment that the hand which held the match was shaking. There were hollows like dirty smudges under his eyes.

She looked no longer, for Cap'n Merrill had left the teacher's desk, and it was Nils who stood there now, looking out over the room.

Her hands closed tightly on each other in her lap, and they were sweating. *Go ahead, darling,* she told him silently.

"I'm not going to take up any more of your time than I can help," Nils said. His voice was quiet and unimpressive, after Cap'n Merrill's. And it reached out into a silence that fairly ached in its intensity. "The sooner we get this matter cleared up, the sooner you can get on with your business. . . . I guess most of you know what I'm talking about. But if anybody *doesn't* know, I'll tell you."

He looked around the room. His eyes held a chill, darkening blue. "You all know that I brought the *Janet F.* in, the day Winslow Fowler disappeared. The next day I went away on business. Somewhere, between then and now, I've been accused of killing Winslow Fowler and throwing him overboard. Nobody came and told *me* about it. But they told me through my little girl. She was little enough not to hit back," he added gently.

Mrs. Whit Robey, halfway along the aisle, cried out, "If anybody teased that child, I wish I'd known it! I'd have tended to 'em, Nils!"

For a moment Nils' smile warmed his eyes. "I know that, Mrs. Robey." He lifted his head, the smile was gone. "I'm not going into a lot of long-winded explanations. Every one of you here knows—or ought to know—that the story's made up out of whole cloth."

"If that's all it is, what are you over here makin' a stink about it for?" demanded Randy Fowler. He was on his feet, staring at Nils. There were assenting murmurs, rising like the sound of a wave. Randolph Fowler pulled his son down beside him.

"If it was any other story, I wouldn't be here," said Nils. "But this is the kind of yarn that a man doesn't turn his back on, if he's got a family, and a name that's clean." His voice grew colder, more incisive. It would be cutting deep, Joanna thought—very deep in some places. If only she weren't at the back of the room, near the door; all she could see were the backs of their heads. . . .

"If a seagull drops something on my deck," Nils said, "I don't expect him to come back and clean it up. He's a wild bird, and he doesn't know any better. But if a man smears my deck with gurry, he'll clean it up if I have to take him by the back of the neck to make him do it. So I'm here to find out who started this story. . . . Anybody want to give me an idea, to start with?"

There was an indignant hush in the schoolroom. The clock ticked noisily and impudently on the wall behind Nils' head. "If nobody can think of anything," he said, "I'll start with Rich Bradford. I could start with almost anybody, I suppose, but I'll take you, Rich. I know you've heard the yarn, because you didn't feel like speaking to me in Limerock a couple of nights ago."

A slow flush was deepening in Rich's bony face. He seemed undecided whether to get up or remain sitting. He decided to keep still, and stared back at Nils stolidly, as expressionless as a granite boulder.

"Rich, you want to tell me where you got the story that I killed Winslow Fowler?" Nils asked. "That's all I want of you."

After a moment Rich cleared his throat. He said abruptly, "What right have you to come in and take over this meetin'? You broke in, that's what you did. And I refuse to answer any of your damn'-fool questions."

Randy said audibly, "Then why don't we throw the son-of-a-bitch of a squarehead out?" The women looked shocked, and someone said, "Hush your noise."

Joanna, looking at Randy, felt a remote pity for him. He looked like a badly wrecked imitation of the boy who had once come so cockily into her kitchen. She'd heard that he'd been drinking hard lately, and was wild and uncertain of temper; he had taken his brother's death hard, it seemed. She imagined what memories must crowd in on him when he went out to haul alone in the *Janet F.* He and Winslow had always gone together. With his warm, affectionate nature, he'd probably loved his brother in spite of Winslow's sullen ways. It was too bad Randolph didn't have some of that warmth. . . . She could forgive Randy his jerky outburst against Nils, she could not forgive Randolph his iron composure as he sat there beside his son.

There was some confusion in the room, and Nils waited imperturbably until it had died down. "I know you all feel like Rich. You think I'm coming where I'm not wanted. Well, I know I'm not wanted. I know a lot of you feel pretty uncomfortable when you see me standing up here. And I promise you that I'll go—when I've found out what I came here to find out.

"Are you going to tell me, Rich? You going to tell me where you heard the story that made you decide you didn't see me, when we met the other night?"

Rich folded his arms and settled back firmly in his chair. His wife said shrilly, "He prob'ly never saw you! Can he help it if you're one o' them kind that goes around imaginin' insults? I knew your grandfather, Nils Sorensen, and you're just as much of a trouble-maker as he was!"

"You keep quiet, Virgie," Rich told her audibly. "Don't talk to him. We don't have to talk to him, nor listen neither. He don't belong in this meetin'."

There was a murmur of assent. Nils said with sober politeness, "You don't want to talk to me? Nobody wants to talk to me?" His voice changed, grew low, and yet held a chilling certainty. "This is your chance. You'll talk now—or you'll talk in court."

The silence in the room was the most profane and hating silence that Joanna had ever heard. For she *could* hear it. It pounded all around her, a sea of consternation and fearful doubt. They had intended sitting back like Rich, utterly secure in their refusal to notice Nils; and he had jolted them out of their security.

Rich stirred. "I never saw you in Limerock, Nils." He sounded sullen. "I don't even know what night you was talkin' about."

"You saw me all right, Rich," said Nils. "And it was your daughter who teased mine with the story in the schoolyard. She must have heard it at home. I want to know who passed the story on to you."

Bradford didn't answer. The hush was as thick and oppressive as fog.

"Who told it to you, Rich?" Nils prompted.

"I don't know," said Bradford. "I still don't know what you're chewin' about." He stood up, pulling his wife up by the elbow. "I'm leavin'."

A couple of others stood up too. "We don't have to stay and listen to this foolishness," a woman said. Joanna was dismayed. This was something nobody had planned on—that they'd walk out like this. Why, nothing could be proved then, and they'd think they'd made a fool of Nils. She looked around swiftly at her brothers. There must be *something*—

There was. Mark had come quietly to his feet, and was standing by the door. Owen got up without hurry, with a leisurely stretch of his big body, and joined Mark. They looked as immovable as the Black Ledges. She saw Rich Bradford hesitate in the aisle. His wife's eyes were furtive and worried. It was she who sat down again. Rich, blushing almost purple, sat down too. There was a muttering, a rebellious creaking of chairs, as the others settled back.

Nils hadn't moved. Now he said easily, "Well, Rich, if you can't give me any information, I wonder if you thought up that little yarn by yourself. Might be you've passed it on to quite a few, the more you thought about it. . . . You know about the slander laws, Rich? You know about lawyers' letters, and damages for defamation of character? Things like that can carve a pretty big hunk out of a man's bank account, Rich."

He was looking at Rich. But he was speaking to them all, and Joanna knew beyond a doubt that his words were reaching their goal. There were enough strong men in the schoolhouse to pull Mark and Owen away from the door if they wanted to; but even stronger was the impulse to find out just how much Nils knew about them.

A fist fight in the schoolhouse now, with the children outside, and the women looking on and screaming, wasn't going to clear anybody; who knew what information Nils possessed, and could still use against them, even if they tried to give him his come-uppance? They might down Mark and Owen, and black Nils' eyes. But he would still be an unknown quantity.

Joanna realized with pride how skillfully Nils was playing his cards. *Court action:* those words could scare even the most resolute of them, if he had anything on his conscience. And they weren't forgetting that Nils was Gunnar Sorensen's grandson. Gunnar had always been a great one to shake his fist under your nose and threaten you with law, and he never used the word unless he was sure of his rights. That was why no one on Brigport or Bennett's had bothered Gunnar very often in his eighty years.

"I just want to find out," Nils said mildly to Rich, "where this story *started.* I'd appreciate your help."

Bradford's face was glistening over the flush. He gave one quick furtive look around the room, and then said, "It was Ralph Fowler told me. Only I wasn't the only one he told, by God! He told Theron Pierce and Sam Robey at the same time, out on the lobster car!"

"What did he say?" Nils asked, as if Ralph weren't sitting just below him. "Did he hint at it, or did he come right out and say it? Careful now, Rich."

Joanna, looking at the back of Rich's head, thought she could almost see it grow rigid with concentration. "He come right out and said it!" he exploded at last. "I remember that, because Theron, he says he's not surprised, they was a damn' wild crew down on Bennett's. Somebody fired a shot at him while he was haulin' down there once."

There was a rumble and mutter at this, and Joanna glanced at Owen. He was grinning without shame, and he winked at her.

"All right, Rich," Nils said. "Thanks. You've been a great help. Well, Ralph—"

Ralph was a cruder version of his brother Randolph. By the tilt of his head, he was staring back at Nils without alarm.

"Well, Nils!" he countered, and chuckled. "You think you're goin' to scare me like you did Rich? Why, son, you couldn't scare me. You ain't hardly dry behind the ears yet!"

There was an eager ripple of laughter. Ralph was going to make a fool of Nils for them, there was nothing to be uneasy about now. But Nils wasn't annoyed.

"Did you tell Rich the story?"

"Sure, I said it," Ralph admitted easily. " 'Course, I wouldn't have thought of it if somebody hadn't put the idea in my head. I'm an open-minded feller, I don't usually go around lookin' for things like murder." He gave the word a bold emphasis, and someone in the room made a little sound of protest. From where she sat, Joanna could see the nerve jumping in Randy's thin cheek. His hands fidgeted.

"But I was sort of prejudiced in this case, I guess," Ralph went on. "The boy bein' my nephew and all. And then, when I was aboard ship years ago there was a Swedish feller you put me in mind of, Nils. He was a nice quiet feller without much to say, and neat as a pin, too. He knifed the third mate one night and threw him overboard. We wouldn't have known, except—" He pretended to pull himself away from his reminiscences with a start. His smooth voice was insufferable, to Joanna at least. How could Nils stand there so quietly, without striking that complacent face? "Well, you ain't interested in that stuff. But knowin' you'd had words with Winslow more than once—"

"Just once," Nils corrected him dryly. "All right, Ralph. You say you didn't think it up by yourself. Somebody gave you the idea. Who was it?"

Ralph was still heavily bland. "I couldn't say right offhand, my boy. And you can't scare me with your slander laws. You're likely to start somethin' you can't finish, unless you shut up and go home like a sensible man."

Nils didn't seem to hear him. He turned to Mrs. Fowler, a thin, graying woman with drooping shoulders. He spoke to her softly. "Are *you* scared of the slander laws, Mrs. Fowler?"

Joanna felt astonishment and pride in the same breath. Who but Nils would have remembered so swiftly, and used as a weapon, something which had been forgotten for years? It was dim in her own mind . . . something about Ralph Fowler's wife when she was a young woman, telling a story about a Brigport girl who'd had an operation. She'd got into dreadful trouble with the girl's parents.

And now she was speaking in a fluttery, terrified voice. "I talked to Ralph about it, yes." She wasn't bothering to defy Nils. "But all I said was, It *could* be . . . if circumstances was jest right. But I never said you'd really done it, it was jest because I kept mullin' over what she said to me that mornin', till I had to speak to Ralph about it."

Her head swung around like a frightened bird's; Joanna had a glimpse of staring eyes above ashen, sagging cheeks, and felt a brief pity for the woman. She herself knew how Nils' unhurried but inescapable presence could burn and freeze at the same time, like a piece of ice you hold in your hands, and cannot let go. But her pity was short-lived. They had had no pity for Nils when they called him a murderer.

"Who told you about it in the morning?" said Nils.

"Bella Merrill," she said on a gasp, and all eyes moved to George Merrill and his wife. George was a distant cousin of Cap'n Merrill's, and since there'd never been any great amity between his branch of the clan and the Captain's immediate group, Joanna didn't feel sorry for the Captain now; except to think that it must be hard for him to hear his family name disgraced.

George was in his thirties, a sandy-haired, thick-set man who now sat looking at Nils with open-mouthed amazement. He had never been considered very bright. Bella moved closer to him, her fleshy, rouged face tight with worried resentment; her eyes, small anyway, squinted to shut Nils out.

"You want to tell us about this, Bella?" said Nils pleasantly.

Bella's winter coat was one of the best in the winter catalogue. She pulled it close around her shoulders. "You think you're pretty smart, Nils Sorensen, comin' over here and tryin' to set us all by the ears!" The words tumbled out, thickly. "But what does all this get you? You *still* could've killed Winslow—you still could've done it, just the way we've all been sayin'—"

George looked at her in alarm. The murmurs were rising again, but Joanna noticed in satisfaction that most of the women seemed annoyed with Bella. She wasn't very popular on Brigport—with the women, anyway.

Nils cut smoothly through the confusion. "Bella, remember what I said about slander. This is no time for name-calling. Just tell me where you got hold of the story. If we keep this up long enough, we'll get to the place where it started, and that's all I'm interested in."

Not a pair of eyes moved away from Bella. Her own eyes were suddenly panicky. Behind the rouge and the powder she became a brilliant purplish red. She was a woman looking for a way of escape, but there was none.

"I don't have to answer you!" she blurted out. "If there was a half a man here, you wouldn't be allowed to come in and insult us like this! I'm gettin' out of here!"

"Would it be easier to tell me in court, Bella?" Nils asked.

She stared at him. Her mouth went slack and shaking. "It was Tom Robey," she brought out at last.

The story was easy to guess. Joana heard it in the stillness around her, and saw it in George's face. She saw it in the glances of the women, at once curious and disdainful; in the way the men shifted their feet, and moistened their mouths, and grinned. There was an uneasy creaking and straining from the corner where the Robey boys sat, and Tom's wife.

Nils didn't waste any time. "Anything to tell me, Tom?"

Tom was on his feet, massive of shoulder, black-browed, his big fists swinging at his sides. He was six-feet-four of seething rage; it was a question whom he wanted to strangle first, Bella Merrill or Nils. "You're damn' right I got somethin' to tell ye! Who are you to come over here and make trouble, and dig in your nose where it's got no right to be?"

Nils smiled. "Who do I have to be? Take it easy, Tom. Too bad you can't go seining all winter and then you'd stay out of trouble. . . . Who told you that maybe I killed Winslow, Tom?"

"Roger Stone," said Tom abruptly. He stamped to the back of the schoolroom, brushed by Joanna's seat, and went out, slamming the doors behind him. Mark and Owen didn't try to stop him. He wasn't necessary any longer. They sat down again.

Roger Stone. Joanna felt a sharp stab of dismay. He'd been one of the Brigport men her father had liked, one of the old-timers, the ground-keepers. She knew Nils had been set back too. She could tell by the way his voice chilled.

"Roger Stone," he said. Stone got to his feet, a neat, elderly man with a pleasant, keen face. At the moment it was an anxious face.

"Nils, I'm sorry," he said. "And I'm ashamed of Brigport today. But I want ye to know it wan't everybody that talked against ye. I'm no gossip-monger, and I never was. But I can't honestly tell ye that Tom was lyin', because he did hear me say somethin' about it. Only I never *told* him. He was listenin' in on a talk I was havin' with somebody else." He spoke earnestly, without taking his eyes from Nils' face. "It was Whit Robey I was talking' to, and it was a long time ago. Not long after you brought in the *Janet F.* that day. Whit ain't here today, on account of his rheumatism bein' so bad, but Mrs. Whit's here, and if Whit told her about it, she can tell you just what it was we talked about."

"Roger's never talked against you, Nils," Mrs. Whit spoke up. "He's right about that. At least I never heard of him doin' it."

A movement at the side of the room, down beyond Jud, attracted Joanna. Randy was getting up from the bench and moving quietly toward the rear. His father glanced at him, made no move to stop him, and looked back at Roger Stone and Nils. He seemed perfectly at ease. But the gray light from the windows caught the wet sheen on Randy's face, and the shadows under his eyes stood out like stains against his putty-tinged pallor. He looked sick. The change in him, since she had last seen him, shocked Joanna. This must be ghastly for him, to sit through such a session.

She watched him reach the back of the room. Now he was turning behind Mark and Helmi, he would pass behind her in a moment and reach the door. No one else noticed him. They were too much absorbed in Nils and Roger and Mrs. Whit Robey.

"Whit came right home and told me," she was stating in very downright terms, "that somebody'd been droppin' hints in people's ears — all the ears they could find, I guess, so the story would be sure to get a good start. And Roger, he'd heard this stuff, and he was madder'n a wet hen at such foolishness. And seein' that he and my Whit've been chums all their life, he told Whit just what he'd heard. And that Tom Robey was standin' around with his ears flapped forward, like a jackass, listenin' for all he was worth."

"That's how it was, Nils," Roger Stone said. Nils nodded, and looked past him at the back of the room where Randy was. It was only the briefest of glances, and Joanna couldn't explain why she slipped out of the narrow seat and went to stand in front of the door. She reached it just before Randy did. Mark and Owen and Helmi were still intent on the scene by the teacher's desk. Only she had caught that barely perceptible signal from Nils.

Randy stared at her — his eyes held no sunlit specks now, only a desperate hurry — and reached for the knob. She put her hand over it. Roger Stone was talking again, and no one turned toward the back of the room.

"What's the matter, Randy?" Her lips formed the words. "Are you sick?"

"For Christ's sake, let me out of here," he whispered.

"He'd been around my shop, talkin' to me," Stone was saying. "He asked me if I didn't think it was queer, all those things fittin' together like that. I told him he'd ought to be careful, he might start a lot of trouble." He added regretfully, "I guess that was jest what he *did.*"

"You said it was one of the young fry, Roger," Nils said patiently. "Who was it?"

Randy was strong and he was driven by desperation, but Joanna held furiously to the doorknob.

"It was Randy Fowler," said Roger Stone simply, and sat down.

"Goddam you, Jo!" Randy said aloud, and that brought Owen up out of his chair. He caught Randy's hand as it clawed at Joanna's shoulder.

"What in hell goes on here?" he demanded. Mark was up by then. Most of the rest were standing up too, staring, talking, and wondering aloud. The meeting seemed to have gone to pieces until Nils remembered the gavel and used it.

"Just a few minutes more, everybody," he said, and his quietness reached the others. They sat down again, reluctantly. Randy stood with a curious inertness between Mark and Owen. All the frantic drive had gone out of him. *Why wasn't he willing to brazen this out?* Joanna thought. *He's laughed off other things — why not this?* She leaned against the wall, aware of a shakiness in her knees, and of the hard pounding of her heart. She watched Nils, drawing steadiness from him. Nils could always meet everything.

They had come to the center of the web, in a minute now they would reach Randolph Fowler, who still sat so quietly on his bench. He wasn't going to like it; his very stillness had a deadly quality. What was he thinking as he sat there, waiting?

"Randy," Nils said to Randolph's son. "Just tell me who put all the details together for you, and then you can go. That's all I want to know."

Randy stared back at him without answering. He looked small between Owen and Mark. And trapped.

"Was it your father?" Nils asked him gently.

"To hell with him!" said Randy violently. "He never had anything to do with it! He ain't never mentioned Win since that day — you'd think I never had a brother!" Color blazed up into the yellowish cheeks. "All he thinks about is how you fellows snicked Grant's point over there right out from under his nose! But *I'm* the one who figgered out how you could've killed Win — or how to make people start thinkin' it, anyway!" There was a sort of ghastly bragging in his words.

"But you was right, Randy!" Earl Robey called out. "How do we know that he didn't do it? He could've, just like you said!"

"He didn't, because I know what happened to Win," said Randy.

"What are you saying, Randy?" Randolph Fowler got up, and he was impassive no longer. "What are you talking about?"

The water ran down Randy's face like rain — or tears. "I'm tryin' to say I found him! Are you all numbheads? I found him!" His voice cracked ludicrously. "It was a couple of weeks ago, and I could've gone around and told everybody, and stopped the talk — only I'd be damned if I would!" He wiped his hand across his forehead and Owen said, "Hey, take it easy, kid." He tried to push Randy down into a seat, but Randy backed away from him and stood against the door, his eyes wild, his face working.

"There wasn't much left of him," he said. "I let him go again—I didn't want to touch him. But there was enough so I could tell what happened to him."

His father had pushed his way through the crowd until he was facing him. "Son, are you crazy?" he said huskily. "Why didn't you tell me this before? Are you sure you—found him?"

"Sure?" Randy's voice scaled upward again. "Goddam it, I'm the one who's been havin' the nightmares, ain't I? I'm the one who's been goin' to bed drunk, so I wouldn't dream—but I always do! And I see him the way he looked, comin' out of the water. . . ." He pulled his voice down with an effort. He stared at the ring of intent faces. "It was funny how it happened. I mean, me shiftin' my pots around and settin' one where I knew Win used to have one that always fished damn' good. And then when I went to haul it, it was fouled up. I had a hell of a time with it . . . till I found out why. Win's trap was still there. I—I—" he wet his lips. "I got the two of 'em up together. And Win—he was all fouled up in the warps. Both of 'em." He looked as if he could hardly get the words out, as if the whole thing were before him again. "Mine had got wrapped around him since I set it. But his—that was what killed him. He was caught in a ridin' turn. It must've pulled him overboard."

He shut his eyes and leaned against the door. No one moved.

After a moment Cap'n Merrill cleared his throat. "We'd ought to get this clear, Randy . . . Randolph. We've all had narrow squeaks from ridin' turns. The trap pullin' one way, and the boat goin' another. If a feller can't reach his knife to cut himself free, when the warp gets around his wrist or his ankle, he hasn't got a chance."

"But the boat was driftin' when Nils found it," Jonas Pierce said. "And it wan't too far from where he said he saw Win haulin'. That don't sound right. Engine should've been goin'."

It was Randy who answered him, in a dreary voice. "Tank was empty when he brought her in. Win always forgot to put in his extra can of gas till she was on her last breath."

Randolph stepped forward and took his son by the arm. No one stood in Randy's way this time as he went out. There was a little space of silence after they had gone, and then confusion began. Nils was hidden from Joanna in the midst of the crowd. A few skulked on the edges; Rich Bradford, apparently wondering what stand to take, Ralph Fowler, scratching his head. Bella Merrill hurried out, George behind her. But for the rest, they surrounded Nils with their outstretched hands, their exclamations.

Joanna sat down again, answered Jud's radiant grin, winked at Joey at last, and then wondered how soon they could all go home again. She knew she should feel triumphant, but she felt worn and exhausted, instead She was shaken by Randy's behavior, she knew too well what was behind it. She had laughed at him, and convinced herself he would get over it. . . . It would be a long time before she could forget the horror stamped on his face in the last fifteen minutes.

Mrs. Whit Robey leaned over her and patted her cheek. The motherly gesture brought quick tears to Joanna's eyes. "Dear, it's been terrible for you, but it's all over now," the old lady murmured. "And I want you to know that it wasn't all of Brigport who talked about Nils . . . just a few, but I wish Nils could've got after 'em all this afternoon and made 'em squirm! And that Bradford young'un—if I'd known she was tormentin' Ellen—" she tightened her mouth, patted Joanna's cheek again, and moved away.

Others came and spoke to her. She thanked them, she was touched by their gestures, she knew she would never hate and distrust Brigport again, for these were the true people of Brigport whom her father and grandfather had known and respected.

But she wanted to go home with Nils! Would they ever let him go? She heard Owen's laughter ring out, and Mark's, and saw the quiet delight in Helmi's face as she stood at one side. Each thing was good to hear and see, but it was Nils she wanted.

At last they began to break up, and Nils came through the crowd, straight toward her, and held out his hand. He was not smiling; but his eyes reached out for her in the way she loved, and she was not ashamed for the rest to see how she put her hand in his.

"Let's go home now," he said simply.

41

NILS STEERED THE *White Lady,* going home, and Joanna stood beside him. She could hear Owen's and Mark's voices behind her, their occasional hoots of laughter, their joyous swearing. She knew Helmi was looking out to the horizon with her distant gaze, thinking about— what? *I wish Stevie had been with us today,* Joanna thought, and then looked down at the wheel. Her hand was there, and Nils' hand lay over it. She stopped thinking about Stevie then. . . .

The *White Lady* pitched, going by Tenpound; there was a heavier sea on, for the wind had risen. But it was a good wind, a clearing wind. It wasn't going to snow, after all, and the sky was brightening. The sun had come through the veil of cloud at last. As they came out by Tenpound, the *White Lady* leaped as eagerly as a porpoise, and then settled down to run steadily and sweetly for the harbor. The first real sunshine of the day streamed down upon her wet decks, and was warm on Joanna's face.

"I keep thinking about Randy," Nils said, just loud enough for her to hear above the engine. "What got into him? I've always been decent to him. . . . I used to think the kid liked me."

"He did," said Joanna. There was one more thing to tell Nils— the one thing she'd left out because she thought it didn't count. Today she had found out that it *did* matter. Nils had a right to know; he had been the one to take the blows Randy had meant for her.

"He did like you, in one way, Nils," she said. "In another way, I guess he hated you, because you were my husband."

Nils turned his head and looked down at her. "You know what that sounds like, Jo?"

"That's what it's supposed to sound like, Nils," she said calmly.

"Randy had a crush on me, and mentioned it several times. Remember the time he stayed all night because he fell overboard?"

"Yes. What about it?" Nils watched past the edge of the sprayhood.

"The next day he wouldn't go home, until I'd been pretty nasty to him. I thought that was the end of it. But he came back again while you were gone — to Eric's — and I said I'd have Owen throw him out. That time he was awfully mad. But I never thought he'd do anything like this."

"Well, he's done it, and it's all over now . . . poor cuss. I was sorry for him today. Joanna." Nils looked at her again, his eyes intent. "Why didn't you tell me about it, the first time he bothered you?"

She felt foolishly embarrassed. She was even blushing. Her answer was going to sound so silly — now. "I thought I could handle it. I didn't want to bother you with it."

"And you're the one who said Helmi was right to tell Mark Owen kissed her." Nils shook his head and looked sternly ahead. "You're the one who said it was a husband's right to know, so he could protect his wife." His mouth twitched suddenly. But Joanna didn't want to laugh.

"I'm sorry, Nils," she said simply. "I've made a lot of mistakes, and I guess Randy was one of the worst."

"Don't you think I've been looking over my mistakes, too?" said Nils. And then he added something which she couldn't hear. But she saw the expression in his eyes when he looked at her, and the way he moved his lips. They said, *My dearest.*

The *White Lady* rounded Eastern Harbor Point and flew across the harbor as if she knew her way, Matthew Fennell's boat close behind. She was home again; they were all home again. It was as if the Island reached out its arms to gather them against its breast, all its children.

The Island was safe now. Nothing could hurt it. It was a fortress which no siege could take, no wars disturb. Stevie had gone, as Island men had always gone to war, and others would go before it was finished. But they would come back to their rocks and their harbor, and the boats secure at their moorings. There would always be someone, even when Joanna and Nils had been dead for a hundred years.

The sun touched the weather-beaten fish houses, and threw a rose light across the rocks, brightened the dead marsh grass to bronze. The Island smiled.

About the Author

Elisabeth Ogilvie lives for the better part of each year on Gay's Island, Maine. There she enjoys long walks among the rocks and woods of the island, reveling in air and space and sky. The remainder of the year is spent across Pleasant Point Gut, at her nearby mainland home, where plumbing, a telephone, and other amenities await. Her interests include the Nature Conservancy, Foster Parents Plan, reading ("a necessity of life!"), and music of just about any kind.

Miss Ogilvie's latest book is a historical romance, the second of a planned trilogy. Despite some thirty-six books for children and adults produced over the past forty years, though, the author is still caught up in the spell woven by Bennett's Island and its inhabitants and is presently at work on a fifth installment (the fourth, An Answer in the Tide, *was published in 1978) in the continuing story of Joanna Bennett.*

To order the other two volumes of Elisabeth Ogilvie's Tide trilogy, or any of our other fine New England books, write for our free catalog.

Down East Books
P.O. Box 679
Camden, Maine 04843